ROB

Blood Magick

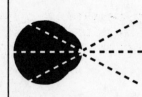

This Large Print Book carries the
Seal of Approval of N.A.V.H.

GALE
CENGAGE Learning®

Copyright © 2014 by Nora Roberts.
The Cousins O'Dwyer Trilogy #3.
Thorndike Press, a part of Gale, Cengage Learning.

Thorndike Press® Large Print Core.
The text of this Large Print edition is unabridged.
Other aspects of the book may vary from the original edition.
Set in 16 pt. Plantin.

LIBRARY OF CONGRESS CATALOGING-IN-PUBLICATION DATA

Roberts, Nora.
  Blood magick / Nora Roberts. — Large print edition.
    pages cm. — (Cousins O'Dwyer trilogy ; 3) (Thorndike Press large print core.)
  ISBN 978-1-4104-7116-1 (hardcover) — ISBN 1-4104-7116-0 (hardcover)
  1. Businesswomen—Fiction. 2. Witches—Fiction. 3. Magic—Fiction.
4. Ireland—Fiction. 5. Domestic fiction. I. Title.
PS3568.O243B5465 2014b
813'.54—dc23   2014035416

Published in 2014 by arrangement with The Berkley Publishing Group, a member of Penguin Group (USA) LLC, a Penguin Random House Company

Printed in the United States of America
1 2 3 4 5 6 7 18 17 16 15 14

BLOOD MAGICK

NORA ROBERTS

THORNDIKE PRESS

A part of Gale, Cengage Learning

GALE
CENGAGE Learning·

Farmington Hills, Mich • San Francisco • New York • Waterville, Maine
Meriden, Conn • Mason, Ohio • Chicago

For Kat,
one of the brightest lights in my life

How far away the stars seem,
and how far is our first kiss,
and, ah, how old is my heart.
— WILLIAM BUTLER YEATS

It will have blood; they say,
blood will have blood.
— WILLIAM SHAKESPEARE

1

On a bright day as summer faded, Brannaugh gathered herbs, flowers, foliage, all for salves and potions and teas. They came to her, neighbors, travelers, for their hopes and healings. They came to her, the Dark Witch, as once they'd come to her mother, with aches in body, in heart, in spirit, and paid with coin or service or trade.

So she and her brother, her sister, had built their lives in Clare, so far from their home in Mayo. Far from the cabin in the woods where they had lived, where their mother had died.

So she had built her life, more contented, more joyful than she'd believed possible since that terrible day their mother had given them all but the dregs of her own power, had sent them away to be safe as she sacrificed herself.

All grief, Brannaugh thought now, all duty

and fear as she'd done what was asked of her, as she'd led her younger brother and little sister away from home.

They'd left love, childhood, and all innocence behind.

Long years. The first few spent, as their mother had bid, with their cousin and her man — safe, tended, welcomed. But the time had come, as time does, to leave that nest, to embrace who and what they were, and would ever be.

The Dark Witches three.

Their duty, their purpose above all else? To destroy Cabhan, the dark sorcerer, the murderer of their father, Daithi the brave, of their mother, Sorcha. Cabhan, who had somehow survived the spell the dying Sorcha had cast.

But on such a bright day in summer's end, it all seemed so far away — the terrors of that last winter, the blood and death of that last spring.

Here, in the home she'd made, the air smelled of the rosemary in her basket, of the roses planted by her husband on the birth of their first child. The clouds puffed white as lambs across the blue meadow of the sky, and the woods, the little fields they'd cleared, as green as emeralds.

Her son, not yet three years, sat in a patch

of sun and banged on the little drum his father had made him. He sang and hooted and beat with such joyous innocence her eyes burned from the love.

Her daughter, barely a year, slept clutching her favored rag doll while guarded by Kathel, their faithful hound.

And another son stirred and kicked in her womb.

From where she stood she could see the clearing, and the little cabin she, Eamon, and Teagan had built near to eight years before. Children, she thought now. They'd been but children who could not embrace childhood.

They lived there still, close. Eamon the loyal, so strong and true. Teagan, so kind and fair. So happy now, Brannaugh thought, and Teagan so in love with the man she'd married in the spring.

All so peaceful, she thought, despite Brin's banging and hooting. The cabin, the trees, the green hills with their dots of sheep, the gardens, the bright blue sky.

And it would have to end. It would have to end soon.

The time was coming — she felt it as sure as she felt the babe's kicks in her womb. The bright days would give way to the dark. The peace would end in blood and battle.

She touched the amulet with its symbol of a hound. The protection her mother had conjured with blood magicks. Soon, she thought, all too soon now, she would need that protection again.

She pressed a hand to the small of her back as it ached a bit, and saw her man riding toward home.

Eoghan, so handsome, so hers. Eyes as green as the hills, hair a raven's wing that curled to his shoulders. He rode tall and straight and easy on the sturdy chestnut mare, his voice lifted — as often it was — in song.

By the gods, he made her smile, he made her heart lift like a bird on the wing. She, who had been so sure there could be no love for her, no family but her blood, no life but her purpose, had fallen deeper than oceans for Eoghan of Clare.

Brin leaped up, began to run as fast as his little legs could manage, all the while calling.

"Da, Da, Da!"

Eoghan leaned down, scooped the boy up in the saddle. The laugh, the man's, the boy's mixed, flew toward her. Her eyes stung yet again. In that moment, she would have given all of her power, every drop given her, to spare them what was to come.

The baby she'd named for her mother whimpered, and Kathel stirred his old bones to let out a soft woof.

"I hear her." Brannaugh set down her basket, moved over to lift her waking daughter, snuggled her in with kisses as Eoghan rode up beside her.

"Look here, would you, what I found on the road. Some little lost gypsy."

"Ah well, I suppose we should keep him. It may be he'll clean up fine, then we can sell him at the market."

"He might fetch us a good price." Eoghan kissed the top of his giggling son's head. "Off you go, lad."

"Ride, Da!" Brin turned his head, beseeched with big dark eyes. "Please! Ride!"

"A quick one, then I want me tea." He winked at Brannaugh before setting off in a gallop that had the boy shouting with delight.

Brannaugh picked up her basket, shifted young Sorcha on her hip. "Come, old friend," she said to Kathel. "It's time for your tonic."

She moved to the pretty cottage Eoghan with his clever hands and strong back had built. Inside, she stirred the fire, settled her daughter, started the tea.

Stroking Kathel, she doused him with the

tonic she'd conjured to keep him healthy and clear-eyed. Her guide, her heart, she thought, she could stretch his life a few years more. And would know when the time came to let him go.

But not yet, no, not yet.

She set out honey cakes, some jam, and had the tea ready when Eoghan and Brin came in, hand in hand.

"Well now, this is fine."

He scrubbed Brin's head, leaned down to kiss Brannaugh, lingered over it as he always did.

"You're home early," she began, then her mother's eye caught her son reaching for a cake. "Wash those hands first, my boy, then you'll sit like a gentleman for your tea."

"They're not dirty, Ma." He held them out.

Brannaugh just lifted her eyebrows at the grubby little hands. "Wash. The both of you."

"There's no arguing with women," Eoghan told Brin. "It's a lesson you'll learn. I finished the shed for the widow O'Brian. It's God's truth her boy is useless as teats on a billy goat, and wandered off to his own devices. The job went quicker without him."

He spoke of his work as he helped his son dry his hands, spoke of work to come as he

14

swung his daughter up, set her to squealing with delight.

"You're the joy in this house," she murmured. "You're the light of it."

He gave her a quiet look, set the baby down again. "You're the heart of it. Sit down, off your feet awhile. Have your tea."

He waited. Oh, she knew him for the most patient of men. Or the most stubborn, for one was often the same as the other, at least wrapped inside the like of her Eoghan.

So when the chores were finished, and supper done, when the children tucked up for the night, he took her hand.

"Will you walk out with me, lovely Brannaugh? For it's a fine night."

How often, she wondered, had he said those words to her when he wooed her — when she tried flicking him away like a gnat in the air?

Now, she simply got her shawl — a favorite Teagan had made her — wrapped it around her shoulders. She glanced at Kathel lying by the fire.

Watch the babes for me, she told him, and let Eoghan draw her out into the cool, damp night.

"Rain's coming," she said. "Before morning."

"Then we're lucky, aren't we, to have the

night." He laid a hand over her belly. "All's well?"

"It is. He's a busy little man, always on the move. Much like his father."

"We're well set, Brannaugh. We could pay for a bit of help."

She slanted him a look. "Do you have complaints about the state of the house, the children, the food on the table?"

"I don't have a one, not for a single thing. I watched my mother work herself to bones." As he spoke he rubbed the small of her back, as if he knew of the small, nagging ache there. "I wouldn't have it of you, *aghra*."

"I'm well, I promise you."

"Why are you sad?"

"I'm not." A lie, she realized, and she never lied to him. "A little. Carrying babies makes a woman a bit daft from time to time, as you should know. Didn't I weep buckets when carrying Brin when you brought in the cradle you'd made? Wept as if the world was ending."

"From joy. This isn't joy."

"There is joy. Only today I stood here, looking at our children, feeling the next move in me, thinking of you, and of the life we have. Such joy, Eoghan. How many times did I say no to you when you asked

16

me to be yours?"

"Once was too many."

She laughed, though the tears rose up in her throat. "But you would ask again, and again. You wooed me with song and story, with wildflowers. Still, I told you I would be no man's wife."

"None but mine."

"None but yours."

She breathed in the night, the scent of the gardens, the forest, the hills. She breathed in what had become home, knowing she would leave it for the home of childhood, and for destiny.

"You knew what I was, what I am. And still, you wanted me — not the power, but me."

Knowing that meant all the world to her, and knowing it had opened the heart she'd determined to keep locked.

"And when I could no longer stop myself from loving you, I told you all there is, all of it, refusing you again. But you asked again. Do you remember what you said to me?"

"I'll say it to you again." He turned to her, took her hands as he had on the day years before. "You're mine, and I am yours. All that you are, I'll take. All that I am, I'll give. I'll be with you, Brannaugh, Dark Witch of Mayo, through fire and flood, through joy and grief, through battle and through peace. Look in my heart, for you have that power. Look in me, and know love."

"And I did. And I do. Eoghan." She pressed against him, burrowed into him. "There is such joy."

But she wept.

He stroked, soothed, then eased her away to see her face in the pale moonlight. "We must go back. Go back to Mayo."

"Soon. Soon. I'm sorry —"

"No." He touched his lips to hers, stilled her words. "You will not say so to me. Did you not hear my words?"

"How could I know? Even when you spoke them, when I felt them capture my heart, how could I know I would feel like this? I would wish with all I am to stay, just stay. To be here with you, to leave all the rest behind and away. And I can't. I can't give us that. Eoghan, our children."

"Nothing will touch them." Again he laid a hand on her belly. "Nothing and no one. I swear it."

"You must swear it, for when the time comes I must leave them and face Cabhan with my brother and sister."

"And with me." He gripped her shoulders as fire and fierceness lit his eyes. "Whatever you face, I face."

"You must swear." Gently she drew his hands back down to her belly where their son kicked. "Our children, Eoghan, you must swear to protect them above all. You and Teagan's man must protect them against Cabhan. I could never do what I must do unless I know their father and their uncle guard and protect them. As you love me, Eoghan, swear it."

"I would give my life for you." He rested his brow on hers, and she felt his struggle — man, husband, father. "I swear to you, I would give my life for our children. I will swear to protect them."

"I am blessed in you." She lifted his hands from her belly to her lips. "Blessed in you. You would not ask me to stay?"

"All that you are," he reminded her. "You took an oath, and that oath is mine as well. I am with you, *mo chroi.*"

"You are the light in me." On a sigh, she rested her head on his shoulder. "The light that shines in our children."

She would use all she was to protect that light, all that came from it, and at last, at last, vanquish the dark.

She bided, taking each day, holding it close. When her children rested, when the one inside her insisted she rest as well, she sat by the fire with her mother's spell book. Studied, added her own spells, her own words and thoughts. This, she knew, she would pass down as she passed the amulet. To her children, and to the child who came from her who would carry the purpose of the Dark Witch should she and Eamon, Teagan fail.

Their mother had sworn they — or their blood — would destroy Cabhan. She had seen, with her own eyes, one of their blood from another time, had spoken to him. And she dreamed of another, a woman with her name, who wore the amulet she wore now, who was, as she was, one of three.

Sorcha's three would have children, and they would have children in turn. So the legacy would continue, and the purpose with it, until it was done. She would not, could not, turn away from it.

She would not, could not, turn away from the stirrings in her own blood as summer drew down.

But she had children to tend, a home to tend in turn, animals to feed and care for, a garden to harvest, the little goat to milk. Neighbors and travelers to heal and help.

And magicks, bright, bright magicks, to preserve.

So with her children napping — and oh,

Brin had put up a battle heroic against closing his eyes — she stepped outside for a breath.

And saw her sister, her bright hair braided down her back, walking up the path with a basket.

"You must have heard me wishing for your company, for I'm after some conversation with someone more than two years of age."

"I've brown bread, for I baked more than enough. And I was yearning for you as well."

"We'll have some now, as I'm hungry every minute of every day." Laughing, Brannaugh opened her arms to her sister.

Teagan, so pretty with her hair like sunlight, her eyes like the bluebells their mother had prized.

Brannaugh gathered her close — then immediately drew her back again.

"You're with child!"

"And you couldn't give me the chance to say so to you myself?" Glowing, beaming, Teagan grabbed hold for another strong embrace. "I was only just sure of it this morning. I waked, and I knew there was life in me. I haven't told Gealbhan, for I needed first to tell you. And to be sure of it, absolutely sure. Now I am. I'm babbling like a brook. I can't stop."

"Teagan." Brannaugh's eyes welled as she

kissed her sister's cheeks, as she remembered the little girl who'd wept on that dark morning so long ago. "Blessed be, *deirfiúr bheag.* Come inside. I'll make you some tea, something good for you and the life in you."

"I want to tell Gealbhan," she said as she went in with Brannaugh, took off her shawl. "By the little stream where he first kissed me. And then tell Eamon he'll again be an uncle. I want music and happy voices. Will you and Eoghan bring the children this evening?"

"We will, of course, we will. We'll have music and happy voices."

"I miss Ma. Oh, it's foolish, I know, but I want to tell her. I want to tell Da. I'm holding a life inside me, one that came from them. Was it so with you?"

"Aye, each time. When Brin came, and then my own Sorcha, I saw her for a moment, just for a moment. I felt her, and Da as well. I felt them there when my babes loosed their first cry. There was joy in that, Teagan, and sorrow. And then . . ."

"Tell me."

Her gray eyes full of that joy, that sorrow, Brannaugh folded her hands over the child within her. "The love is so fierce, so full. That life that you hold, not in your womb, but in your arms? The love that comes over you? You think you know, then you do, and what you thought you knew is pale and weak against what is. I know what she felt for us now. What she and Da felt for us. You'll know it."

"Can it be more than this?" Teagan pressed a hand to her middle. "It feels so huge already."

"It can. It will." Brannaugh looked out at the trees, at the rioting gardens. And her eyes went to smoke.

"This son in you, he will not be the one, though he'll be strong and quick to power. Nor will the son that comes from you after him. The daughter, the third, she is the next. She will be your one of the three. Fair like you, kind in her heart, quick in her mind. You will call her Ciara. One day she will wear the sign our mother made for you."

Suddenly light-headed, Brannaugh sat. Teagan rushed over to her.

"I'm well; I'm fine. It came over me so quick I wasn't ready. I'm a bit slower these days." She patted Teagan's hand.

"I never looked. I didn't think to."

"Why should you think to? You've a right simply to be happy. I wouldn't have spoiled that for all the worlds."

"You haven't. How could you spoil anything by telling me I'll have a son, and another, and a daughter? No, sit as you are. I'll finish the tea."

They both glanced toward the door as it opened.

"Sure he has the nose for fresh bread, has Eamon," Teagan said as their brother walked in with his brown hair tousled, as always, around a heartbreakingly handsome face.

With a grin he sniffed the air like a hound. "I've a nose, for certain, but didn't need it to make my way here. You've enough light swirling around the place to turn up the moon. If you're after doing a spell so bright, you might've told me."

"We weren't conjuring. Only talking. We're having a bit of a _céili_ at the cabin this evening. And you can keep Brannaugh company when I leave, so I can have time to tell Gealbhan he's to be a father."

"As there's bread fresh, I can — A father is it?" Eamon's bold blue eyes filled with delight. "There's some happy news." He plucked Teagan off her feet, gave her a swing, then another when she laughed. He set her down in a chair, kissed her, then grinned at Brannaugh. "I'd do the same with you, but it's like to break my back, as you're big as a mountain."

"Don't think you'll be adding my jam to

24

that bread."

"A beautiful mountain. One who's already given me a handsome nephew and a charming niece."

"That might get you a dollop."

"Gealbhan will be overjoyed." Gently, as he was always gentle with Teagan, he brushed his fingers down her cheek. "You're well then, are you, Teagan?"

"I feel more than wonderful. I'm likely to cook a feast, which will suit you, won't it?"

"It will, aye, it will."

"And you need to be finding the woman to suit you," Teagan added, "for you'd make a fine father."

"I'm more than fine with the two of you providing the children so I can be the happy uncle."

"She's hair like fire, eyes like the sea in storms, and a shimmer of power of her own." Brannaugh sat back, rubbing a hand over the mound of her belly. "It comes in waves these days. Some from him, I'm thinking — he's impatient." Then she smiled. "It's good seeing the woman who'd take you, Eamon. Not just for a tumble, but for the fall."

"I'm not after a woman. Or not one in particular."

Teagan reached out, laid a hand on his.

25

"You think, and always have, you're not to have a woman, a wife, as you've sisters to protect. You're wrong, and always have been. We are three, Eamon, and both of us as able as you. When you love, you'll have no say in it."

"Don't be arguing with a woman who carries a child, especially a witch who does," Brannaugh said lightly. "I never looked for love, but it found me. Teagan waited for it, and it found her. You can run from it, *mo dearthair.* But find you it will.

"When we go home." Her eyes filled again. "Ah, curse it, I'm watering up every time I take a breath it seems. This you have to look to, Teagan. The moods come and go as they will."

"You felt it as well." Now Eamon laid a hand on Brannaugh's so the three were joined. "We're going home, and soon."

"At the next moon. We must leave on the next full moon."

"I hoped it would wait," Teagan murmured. "I hoped it would wait until you're finished birthing, though I knew in my head and my heart it would not wait."

"I will birth this son in Mayo. This child will be born at home. And yet . . . This is home as well. Not for you," she said to Eamon. "You've waited, you've bided, you've

26

stayed, but your heart, your mind, your spirit is ever there."

"We were told we would go home again. So I waited. The three, the three that came from us. They wait as well." Eamon ran his fingers over the blue stone he wore around his neck. "We'll see them again."

"I dream of them," Brannaugh said. "Of the one who shares my name, and the others as well. They fought and they failed."

"They will fight again," Teagan said.

"They gave him pain." A fierce light came into Eamon's eyes. "He bled, as he bled when the woman named Meara, the one who came with Connor of the three, struck him with her sword."

"He bled," Brannaugh agreed. "And he healed. He gathers again. He pulls in power from the dark. I can't see where, how, but feel only. I can't see if we will change what's to come, if we can and will end him. But I see them, and know if we cannot, they will fight again."

"So we go home, and find the way. So they who come from us won't fight alone."

Brannaugh thought of her children, sleeping upstairs. Safe, innocent still. And the children of her children's children, in another time, in Mayo. Neither safe, she thought, nor innocent.

"We will find the way. We will go home. But tonight, for tonight, we'll feast. We'll have music. And we three will give thanks to all who came before us for the light. For the lives," she said, with a hand light on his sister's belly, and one on her own.

"And tomorrow." Eamon stood. "We begin to end what took the lives of our father, of our mother."

"Will you bide with Brannaugh? I would speak with Gealbhan now."

"Give him only the joy today." Brannaugh rose with her sister. "Tomorrow is soon enough for the rest. Take today for joy alone, for time is so short."

"I will." She kissed her sister, her brother. "Eoghan must bring his harp."

"Be sure he will. We'll fill the wood with music and send it flying over the hills."

She sat again when Teagan left, and Eamon nudged her tea toward her. "Drink it. You're pale."

"A bit tired. Eoghan knows. I've talked with him, and he's ready to leave — leave all he built here. I never thought it would be hard to go back. Never knew I would be torn in two ways."

"Gealbhan's brothers will tend the land here, for you and for Teagan."

"Aye, and it's a comfort. Not for you, the

land here it's never been for you." Here again was sorrow and joy mixed into one. "You will stay in Mayo, whatever comes. I can't see what we will do, Eoghan and I, the children. But Teagan will come back here, that I see clear. This is her place now."

"It is," he agreed. "She will ever be a dark witch of Mayo, but her home and heart are for Clare."

"How will it be for us, Eamon, not to be together as we have been all our lives?"

His eyes, the wild blue of their father's, looked deep into hers. "A distance in space means nothing. We are always together."

"I'm weepy and foolish, and I dislike it very much. I hope this mood is a brief one or I might curse myself."

"Well, you were given to tempers and sharp words toward the end of carrying young Sorcha. It may be I prefer the weeping."

"I don't, that's for certain." She drank the tea, knowing it would settle her. "I'll add a bit more to the tonic I give Kathel and Alastar, for the journey. Roibeard does well without it yet. He's strong."

"He's hunting now," Eamon said of his hawk. "He goes farther each time. He goes north now, every day north. He knows, as we do, we'll travel soon."

29

"We will send word ahead. We will be welcome at Ashford Castle. The children of Sorcha and Daithi. The Dark Witches will be made welcome."

"I'll see to that." He sat back with his own tea, smiled at her. "Hair like fire, is it?"

As he'd wanted, she laughed. "Oh, and you'll be struck dumb and half blind, I promise you, when you meet."

"Not I, my darling. Not I."

2

For the children it was an adventure. The idea of a long journey, of the traveling to a new place — with the prize of a castle at the end of it, had Brin especially eager to go, to begin.

While Brannaugh packed what they'd need, she thought again of that long-ago morning, rushing to do her mother's bidding, packing all she was told to pack. So urgent, she thought now, so final. And that last look at her mother, burning with the power left in her, outside the cabin in the woods.

Now she packed to go back, a duty, a destiny she'd always accepted. Eagerly wished for — until the birth of her first child, until that swamping flood of love for the boy who even now raced about all but feverish in his excitement.

But she had a task yet to face here.

She gathered what she needed — bowl,

candle, book, the herbs and stones. And with a glance at her little boy, felt both pride and regret.

"It is time for him, for this," she told Eoghan.

Understanding, he kissed her forehead. "I'll take Sorcha up. It's time she was abed."

Nodding, she turned to Brin, called him.

"I'm not tired. Why can't we leave now and sleep under the stars?"

"We leave on the morrow, but first there are things we must do, you and I."

She sat, opened her arms. "First, come sit with me. My boy," she murmured, when he crawled onto her lap. "My heart. You know what I am."

"Ma," he said and cuddled into her.

"I am, but you know, as I've never hidden it from you, what I am besides. Dark witch, keeper of magicks, daughter of Sorcha and Daithi. This is my blood. This is your blood as well. See the candle?"

"You made the candle. Ma's make the candles and bake the cakes, and Da's ride the horses."

"Is that the way of it?" She laughed, and decided she'd let him have that illusion for a little while more. "Well, it's true enough I made the candle. See the wick, Brin? The wick is cold and without light. See the

32

candle, Brin, see the wick. See the light and flame, the tiny flame, and the heat, the light to be. You have the light in you, the flame in you. See the wick, Brin."

She crooned it to him, over and over, felt his energy begin to settle, his thoughts begin to join with her.

"The light is power. The power is light. In you, of you, through you. Your blood, my blood, our blood, your light, my light, our light. Feel what lives in you, what waits in you. See the wick, it waits for your light. For your power. Bring it. Let it rise, slow, slow, gentle and clean. Reach for it, for it belongs to you. Reach, touch, rise. Bring the light."

The wick sparked, died away, sparked again, then burned true.

Brannaugh pressed a kiss to the top of his head. There, she thought, there, the first learned. And her boy would never be just a child again.

Joy and sorrow, forever entwined.

"That is well done."

He turned his face up, smiled at her. "Can I do another?"

"Aye," she said, kissed him again. "But heed me now, and well, for there is more to learn, more to know. And the first you must know, must heed, must vow is you harm none with what you are, what you have. Your gift, Brin? An' it harm none. Swear this to me, to yourself, to all who've come before, all who will come after."

She lifted her athame, used it on her palm. "A blood oath we make. Mother to son, son to mother, witch to witch."

Solemn-eyed, he held out his hand to her, blinked at the quick pain when she nicked it.

"An' it harm none," he said when she took his hand, mixed her blood with his.

"An' it harm none," she repeated, then gathered him close, kissed the little hurt, healed it. "Now, you may do another candle. And after, together, we will make charms, for protection. For you, for your sister, for your father."

"What of you, Ma?"

She touched her pendant. "I have what I need."

In the morning mists, she climbed onto the wagon, her little girl bundled at her side. She looked at her boy, so flushed with delight in the saddle in front of his father. She looked at her sister, fair and quiet astride Alastar; her brother, their grand-father's sword at his side, tall and straight on the horse he called Mithra. And Gealbhan steady and waiting on the pretty mare Alastar had sired three summers before.

She clucked to Gealbhan's old plow horse, and with Brin letting out a whoop, began. She looked back once, just once at the house she'd come to love, asked herself if she would ever see it again.

Then, she looked ahead.

A healer found welcome wherever she went — as did a harpist. Though the baby heavy in her belly was often restless, she and her family found shelter and hospitality along the wild way.

Eoghan made music, she or Teagan or Eamon offered salves or potions to the ailing or the injured. Gealbhan offered his strong back and calloused hands.

One fine night they slept under the stars as Brin so wished, and there was comfort in knowing the hound, the hawk, the horse guarded what was hers.

They met no trouble along the way, but then she knew the word had gone about. The Dark Witches, all three, journeyed through Clare and on to Galway.

"The word would reach Cabhan as well," Eamon said as they paused in their travels to rest the horses, to let the children run free for a time.

She sat between him and Teagan while

Gealbhan and Eoghan watered the horses and Eamon dropped a line into the water.

"We're stronger than we were," Teagan reminded him. "We journeyed south as children. We go north children no more."

"He worries." Brannaugh stroked her belly. "As you and I carry more than we did."

"I don't doubt your power or your will."

"And still you worry."

"I wonder if it must be now," Eamon admitted, "even knowing it must be now. I feel it as both of you, and yet would be easier if there was time for both of you to have proper lyings-in before we face what we must face."

"What's meant is meant, but in truth I'm glad we'll break our journey for a day or so with our cousins. And by all the gods I'll be happy to have a day off that bloody wagon."

"I'm dreaming of Ailish's honey cakes, for no one has a finer hand with them."

"Dreaming with his belly," Teagan said.

"A man needs to eat. Hah!" He pulled up the line, and the wriggling fish who'd taken the hook. "And so we will."

"You'll need more than one," Brannaugh said, and reminded them all of those same words their mother spoke on a fine and happy day on the river at home.

They left the rugged wilds of Clare, pushed by fierce winds, sudden driving rains. They rode through the green hills of Galway, by fields of bleating sheep, by cottages where smoke puffed from chimneys. Roibeard winged ahead, under and through layers of clouds that turned the sky into a soft gray sea.

The children napped in the wagon, tucked in among the bundles, so Kathel sat beside Brannaugh, ever alert.

"There are more cottages than I remember." Teagan rode beside her on the tireless Alastar.

"The years pass."

"It's good land here — I can all but hear Gealbhan thinking it."

"Would you plant yourself here then? Does it speak to you?"

"It does. But so does our cabin in the woods in Clare. And still, the closer we come to home, the more I ache for it. We had to put that aside for so long, all of us, but now . . . Do you feel it, Brannaugh? That call to home?"

"Aye."

"Are you afraid?"

"Aye. Of what's to come, but more of failing."

"We won't." At Brannaugh's sharp look,

Teagan shook her head. "No, I've had no vision, but only a certainty. One that grows stronger as we come closer to home. We won't fail, for light will always beat the dark, though it take a thousand years."

"You sound like her," Brannaugh murmured. "Like our mother."

"She's in all of us, so we won't fail. Oh, look, Brannaugh! That tree there with the twisted branches. It's the very one Eamon told our cousin Mabh came to life each full moon, to scare her. We're nearly to Ailish's farm. We're all but there."

"Go on, ride ahead."

Her face lit so she might've been a child again, Teagan tossed back her head and laughed. "So I will."

She rode to her husband, let out a fresh laugh, then set off in a gallop. Beside Brannaugh, Kathel whined, quivered.

"Go on then." Brannaugh gave him a stroke.

He leaped out of the wagon, raced behind the horse with the hawk flying above them.

It was a homecoming, for they'd lived on the farm for five years. Brannaugh found it as tidy as ever, with new outbuildings, a new paddock where young horses danced.

She saw a young boy with bright hair all but wrapped around Kathel. And knew when the boy smiled at her, he was Lughaidh, the youngest and last of her cousin's brood.

Ailish herself rushed over to the wagon. She'd grown a bit rounder, and streaks of gray touched her own fair hair. But her eyes were as lively and young as ever.

"Brannaugh! Oh look at our Brannaugh! Seamus, come over and help your cousin down from the wagon."

"I'm fine." Brannaugh clambered down herself, embraced her cousin. "Oh, oh, it does my heart good to see you again."

"And mine, seeing you. Oh, you're a beauty, as ever. So like your mother. And here's our Eamon, so handsome. My cousins, three, come back as you said you would. I've sent the twins off to get Bardan from the field, and Seamus, you run over and tell Mabh her cousins are here."

Teary-eyed, she embraced Brannaugh again. "Mabh and her man have their own cottage, just across the way. She's near ready to birth her first. I'm to be a granny! Oh, I can't stop my tongue from wagging. It's Eoghan, aye? And Teagan's Gealbhan. Welcome, welcome all of you. But where are your children?"

"Asleep in the wagon."

Nothing would do but for Ailish to gather

them up, to ply them with the honey cakes Eamon remembered so fondly. Then Conall, who'd been but a babe in arms when last she'd seen him, took her children off to see a new litter of puppies.

"They'll be fine, my word on it," Ailish said as she poured out tea. "He's a good lad, is Conall — one you helped bring into the world. We'll let the men see to the horses and that, and you'll both take your ease awhile."

"Praise be." Brannaugh sipped the tea, let it and the fire warm her, soothe her. "I'm sitting in a chair that's not moving."

"Eat. You've another in you who needs the food as well."

"I'm starving all the day and half the night. Teagan's not as hungry — yet. But she will be."

"Oh, are you carrying?" Delight glowed on her face as Ailish stopped her fussing with tea, laid her hands over her own heart. "My sweet little Teagan, to be a mother. The years, where do they go? You were but a babe yourself. Will you stay? Will you stay until your time comes?" she asked Brannaugh. "It's still a distance to Mayo, and you're close. I can see you're close."

"A day or two only, and so grateful for it. The babe will be born in Mayo. It's meant.

It's what must be."

"Must it?" Ailish gripped Brannaugh's hand, then Teagan's in turn. "Must it? You've made your lives in Clare. You're women, mothers. Must you go back to the dark that waits?"

"We're women, and mothers, and more. We can turn our back on none of it. But don't fret, cousin. Don't think of it. We have today, with tea and cakes and family."

"We will come back again." When they looked at her, Teagan pressed a hand to her heart. "I feel it so strong. We will come back again. Believe that. Believe in us. I think faith only makes us stronger."

"If that's so, you'll have all of mine."

They had music and feasting and family. And for a night and a day peace. Still Brannaugh found herself restless. Though her man slept in the bed Ailish had provided them, she sat by the fire.

Ailish came in, wearing her night-robes and a thick shawl.

"You need some of the tea you always made for me when I was so close to the end, and the babe so heavy in me I couldn't sleep."

"I look for her in the fire and smoke," Brannaugh murmured. "I can't help the looking, I miss her so. More as we near home. I miss my father; it's an ache. But my mother is a kind of grieving that won't end."

"I know it." Ailish sat beside her. "Does she come to you?"

"In dreams. There are moments, but only moments. I long to hear her voice, to have her tell me I'm doing right. That I'm doing what she'd want of me."

"Oh, my love, you are. You are. Do you remember the day you left us?"

"I do. I hurt you by leaving."

"Leaving always hurts, but it was what was right — I've come to know it. Before you left you told me of Lughaidh, the babe I carried. You said he must be the last, for neither I nor a babe would live through another birthing. And you gave me a potion to drink, every moon until the bottle was empty. So there would be no more children for me. It grieved me."

"I know." And knew it more poignantly now that she had her own children. "You are the best of mothers, and were one to me."

"I would not have lived to see my children grown, to see my oldest girl ripe with her own child. To see, as you told me, Lughaidh, so bright and sweet, with a voice — as you said — like an angel."

Nodding, Ailish studied the fire in turn, as if seeing that day again in the smoke and flame. "You laid protection over me and mine, gave me the years I might not have had. You are what she would want. Even as it grieves me that you will go, you will face Cabhan, I know you must. Never doubt she is proud of you. Never doubt, Brannaugh."

"You comfort me, Ailish."

"I will have faith, as Teagan asked. Every night I will light a candle. I will light it with the little magick I have so that it shines for you, for Teagan, for Eamon."

"I know you fear the power."

"It's my blood as well. You are mine as you were hers. This I will do, every sunset, and in the small light I'll put my faith. Know it burns for you and yours. Know that, and be safe."

"We will come back. In that I will have faith. We will come back, and you will hold the child now inside me."

They journeyed on. With a little spotted pup given the children with much ceremony, and with promises for a longer visit when they returned.

The air grew colder, the wind brisk.

More than once she heard Cabhan's voice, sly and seductive, trailing on that wind.

I wait.

She would see Teagan look out over the hills, or Eamon rubbing his fingers over his pendant — and know they heard as well.

When the hawk veered off, and Alastar strained to follow, Kathel leaped out of the wagon, trotted off on a fork in the road.

"It's not the way." Eoghan pulled his horse up by the wagon. "We would make Ashford by tomorrow, but that is not the way."

"No, not the way to Ashford, but the way we must go. Trust the guides, Eoghan. There's something we must do first. I feel it."

Eamon drew up on the other side. "Near home," he said. "All but near enough to taste. But we're called."

"Aye, we're called. So we answer." She reached out, touched her husband's arm. "We must."

"Then we will."

She didn't know the way, yet she did. With her mind linked with the hound's she knew the road, the turns, the hills. And oh, she felt him reaching out, that darkness, hungry and eager to take what she was, and more.

The hazy sun slid down toward the western hills, but still they rode. Her back ached from the hours in the wagon, and a thirst rose up in her. But they rode.

She saw the shadow of it in the oncoming dark — the rise of it with fields around. A place of worship, she thought, she could feel that.

And a place of power.

She stopped the wagon, breathed the air.

"He can't get through. It's too strong for him to push through."

"Something here," Eamon murmured.

"Something bright," Teagan said. "Strong and bright. And old."

"Before us." Grateful for the help, Brannaugh let her husband lift her from the wagon. "Before our mother. Before any time we know."

"A church." Gealbhan reached up to lift Teagan from the saddle. "But no one's here."

"They're here." Weary, Teagan leaned against him. "Those who came before us, those who sanctified this ground. They will not let him pass. This is a holy place."

"Tonight, this is ours." Brannaugh stepped forward, lifted her hands. "Gods of light, goddesses bright, we call to you across the night. By the power you have given, by the purpose we are driven, we seek your blessing. A night within your walls before whatever fates befall, this respite, this resting. We are Sorcha's three. Dark witches come to thee. By thy will, so mote it be."

Light bloomed like sun, shining through the windows, the doors that opened with a wind like breath. And warmth poured out.

"We are welcome here." Smiling, she lifted her daughter, and all the fatigue from the long journey fell away. "We are welcome."

Brannaugh settled the children to sleep on pallets she made on the floor of the church. And was grateful to find both of them too weary to whine or argue, for her momentary energy already flagged.

"Do you hear them?" Eamon whispered.

"Even I hear them." Eoghan scanned the church, the stone walls, the wooden seats. "They sing."

"Aye." Gealbhan picked up the pup to soothe it. "Soft, lovely. As angels or gods might sing. This is a holy place."

"It offers more than sanctuary for the night." A hand pressed to her back, Brannaugh rose. "It offers the blessing, and the light. We were called by those who've come before us, to this place, on this night."

Teagan touched her fingers lightly, reverently, to the altar. "Built by a king for a kindness given. A promise kept. Built here near a pilgrim's walk. This abbey called Ballintubber."

She lifted her hands, smiled. "This much

I see." She turned to her husband. "Aye, this is a holy place, and we'll seek the blessing of those who called us."

"Like the king," Brannaugh said, "we have a promise to keep. Eoghan, my love, would you fetch me my mother's book?"

"I will, aye — if you will sit. Just sit, Brannaugh. You're too pale."

"I'm weary, in truth, but I promise you this must be done, and we will all be better for it. Teagan —"

"I know what we need. I'll —"

"Sit," her brother insisted. "I'll get what we need, and the both of you will take your ease for a moment. Gealbhan, I swear by the gods, sit on the pair of them if they don't rest for a bit."

Gealbhan had only to touch his wife's cheek, to take Brannaugh's hand to have them heed. "What must be done?" he asked Teagan.

"An offering. An asking. A gathering. He cannot come here. Cabhan cannot come here, or see here. Here he has no power. And here, we can gather ours together."

"What do you need?"

"You are the best of us." She kissed his cheek. "If you would help Eamon, I promise you Brannaugh and I will bide here, will rest."

When he'd gone, she turned quickly to Brannaugh. "You have pain."

"It's not the birthing pains. You'll learn the babe often gives you a bit of a taste of what's coming. This will pass. But the rest is welcome. What we will do here will take strength."

They took an hour, to rest, to prepare.

"We must cast the circle," she told Eoghan, "and make the offering. Do not fear for me."

"Would you ask me not to breathe?"

"It is your love, your faith, and Gealbhan's with yours we need."

"Then you have it."

They cast the circle, and the cauldron floated over the fire they made. Water flowed from Teagan's hands into the cauldron. Brannaugh added herbs, Eamon crushed stones.

"These come from the home we made."

"And these." Teagan opened a pouch, poured in the precious. "From the home we seek. Small things, a dried flower, a pebble, a bit of bark."

"More than gold or silver treasured. We offer to you. Here, a lock of hair from my firstborn."

"A feather from my guide." Eamon added it to the now bubbling cauldron.

"This charm my mother made me."

"Ah, Teagan," Brannaugh murmured.

"She would wish it." Teagan added it to the offering.

"To you we give what we hold dear, and add to them this witch's tear. And seal with blood this brew to show our hearts are true."

And each with a sacred knife offered their blood, and with it the bubbling cauldron boiled and smoked.

"Father, mother, blood of our blood and bone of our bone, we orphans have faith forever shown. Grant us here in this holy place, in this holy hour the might and right of your power. With your gift we cannot fail and over Cabhan will prevail. Imbue us now, we witches three. As we will, so mote it be."

The wind had stirred inside the walls. The candlelight gone brilliant. But at the final words the three spoke together, the wind whirled, the light flashed.

The voices that had murmured, rang out.

With her siblings Brannaugh clasped hands, with them she dropped to her knees.

It ripped through her, the light, the voices, the wind. And the power.

Then came silence.

She rose again, and with Teagan and Eamon turned.

"You were alight," Eoghan said in wonder. "Like candles yourselves."

"We are the three." Teagan's voice rose and echoed in the humming silence. "But there are many. Many before us, many who come after."

"Their light is ours; ours is theirs." Eamon lifted his arms, his sisters' high. "We are the three, and we are one."

Filled with light, fatigue vanished, suffused, Brannaugh smiled. "We are the three. We cast our light over the dark, we seek it out of its shadows. And we will prevail."

"By our blood," they said together, "we will prevail."

In the morning, in the soft light of day, they set out again. They traveled the road with green hills rising, with water shining blue under a welcoming sun. Toward the grand gray stones of Ashford they rode, where the gates were open for them, the bridge drawn down, and the sun shined bright over the water, over the land of their birth.

And so Sorcha's children came home.

3

Winter 2013

Branna O'Dwyer woke to a gray, soggy, relentless rain. And wished for nothing more than to burrow in and sleep again. Mornings, she had always felt, came forever too soon. But like it or not, sleep was done, and with its leaving came a slow and steady craving for coffee.

Annoyed, as she was often annoyed by morning, she rose, pulled thick socks over her feet, drew a sweater over the thin T-shirt she'd slept in.

Through habit and an ingrained tidiness, she stirred up the bedroom fire so the licks of flame would cheer the room, and with her hound, Kathel, having his morning stretch on the hearthrug, she made her bed, added the mounds of pretty pillows that pleased her.

In her bath, she brushed out her long fall of black hair, then bundled it up. She had work, and plenty of it — after coffee. She frowned at herself in the mirror, considered doing a bit of a glamour, as the restless night surely showed. But didn't see the point.

Instead, she walked back into the bedroom, gave Kathel a good rub to get his tail wagging.

"You were restless as well, weren't you now? I heard you talking in your sleep. Did you hear the voices, my boy?"

They walked down together, quiet, as her house was full as it was too often these days. Her brother and Meara shared his bed, and her cousin Iona shared hers with Boyle.

Friends and family all. She loved them, and needed them. But God be sweet, she could've done with some alone.

"They stay for me," she told Kathel as they walked down the steps of the pretty cottage. "As if I can't look after myself. Have I not put enough protection around what's mine, and theirs, to hold off a dozen Cabhans?"

It had to stop, really, she decided, heading straight toward her lovely, lovely coffee machine. A man of Boyle McGrath's size could hardly be comfortable in her cousin Iona's little bed. She needed to nudge them along. In any case, there had been no sign nor shadow of Cabhan since Samhain.

"We almost had him. Bugger it, we nearly finished it."

The spell, the potion, both so strong, she thought as she started the coffee. Hadn't they worked on both hard and long? And the power, by the gods, the power had risen like a flood that night by Sorcha's old cabin.

They'd hurt him, spilled his blood, sent him howling — wolf and man. And still . . .

Not done. He'd slipped through, and would be healing, would be gathering himself.

Not done, and at times she wondered if ever it would be.

She opened the door, and Kathel rushed out. Rain or no, the dog wanted his morning run. She stood in the open doorway, in the cold, frosty December air, looking toward the woods.

He waited, she knew, beyond them. In this time or in another, she couldn't tell. But he would come again, and they must be ready.

But he wouldn't come this morning.

She closed the door on the cold, stirred up the kitchen fire, added fuel so the scent of peat soothed. Pouring her coffee, she savored the first taste, and the short time of quiet and alone. And, a magick of its own, the coffee cleared her head, smoothed her mood.

We will prevail.

The voices, she remembered now. So many voices rising up, echoing out. Light and power and purpose. In sleep she'd felt it all. And that single voice, so clear, so sure.

We will prevail.

"We'll pray you're right about it."

She turned.

The woman stood, a hand protectively over the mound of her belly, a thick shawl tied around a long dress of dark blue.

Almost a mirror, Branna thought, almost like peering into a glass. The hair, the eyes, the shape of the face.

"You're Brannaugh of Sorcha. I know you from dreams."

"Aye, and you, Branna of the clan O'Dwyer. I know you from dreams. You're my blood."

"I am. I am of the three." Branna touched the amulet with its icon of the hound she was never without — just as her counterpart did the same.

"Your brother came to us, with his woman, one night in Clare."

"Connor, and Meara. She is a sister to me." Now Branna touched her heart. "Here. You understand."

"She saved my own brother from harm, shed blood for him. She is a sister to me as well." With some wonder on her face, Sorcha's Brannaugh looked around the kitchen. "What is this place?"

"My home. And yours for you are very welcome here. Will you sit? I would make you tea. This coffee I have would not be good for the baby."

"It has a lovely scent. But only sit with me, cousin. Just sit for a moment. This is a wondrous place."

Branna looked around her kitchen — tidy, lovely, as she'd designed it herself. And, she supposed, wondrous indeed to a woman from the thirteenth century.

"Progress," she said as she sat at the kitchen table with her cousin. "It eases hours of work. Are you well?"

"I am, very well. My son comes soon. My third child." She reached out; Branna took her hand.

Heat and light, a merging of power very strong, very true.

"You will name him Ruarc, for he will be a champion."

It brought a smile to her cousin's face. "So I will."

"On Samhain, we — the three and three more who are with us — battled Cabhan.

Though we caused him harm, burned and bled him, we didn't finish him. I saw you there. Your brother with a sword, your sister with a wand, you with a bow. You were not with child."

"Samhain is yet a fortnight to come in my time. We came to you?"

"You did, at Sorcha's cabin where we lured him, and in your time, as we shifted into it to try to trap him. We were close, but it wasn't enough. My book — Sorcha's book — I could show you the spell, the poison we conjured. You may —"

Brannaugh held up a hand, pressed the other to her side. "My son comes. And he pulls me back. But listen, there is a place, a holy place. An abbey. It sits in a field, a day's travel south."

"Ballintubber. Iona weds her Boyle there come spring. It is a holy place, a strong place."

"He cannot go there, see there. It is sacred, and those who made us watch over it. They gave us, Sorcha's three, their light, their hope and strength. When next you face down Cabhan, we will be with you. We will find a way. We will prevail. If it is not to be you, there will come another three. Believe, Branna of the O'Dwyers. Find the way."

"I can do nothing else."

"Love." She gripped Branna's hand hard. "Love, I have learned, is another guide. Trust your guides. Oh, he's impatient. My child comes today. Be joyful, for he is another bright candle against the dark. Believe," she said again, and vanished.

Branna rose, and with a thought lit a candle for the new light, the new life.

And with a sigh, accepted her alone was at an end.

So she started breakfast. She had a story to tell, and no one would want to hear it on an empty stomach. Believe, she thought — Well, she believed it was part of her lot in life to cook for an army on nearly a daily basis.

She swore an oath that when they'd sent Cabhan to hell she'd take a holiday, somewhere warm, sunny — where she wouldn't touch a pot, pan, or skillet for days on end.

She began to mix the batter for pancakes — a recipe new to her she'd wanted to try — and Meara came in.

Her friend was dressed for the day, a working day at the stables, in thick trousers, a warm sweater, sturdy boots. She'd braided back her bark brown hair, sent Branna a cautious look with her dark gypsy eyes.

"I promised I'd see to breakfast this morning."

"I woke early, after a restless night. And have already had company this morning."

"Someone's here?"

"Was here. Drag the others down, would you, so I'll tell my tale all at once." She hesitated only a moment. "Best if Connor or Boyle rings up Fin, and asks if he'd come over as well."

"It's Cabhan. Is he back?"

"He's coming, right enough, but no."

"I'll get the others. Everyone's up, so it won't take long."

With a nod, Branna set bacon sizzling in a pan.

Connor came first, and her brother sniffed the air like Kathel might do.

"Be useful," she told him. "Set the table."

"Straightaway. Meara said something happened, but it wasn't Cabhan."

"Do you think I'd be trying my hand with these pancake things if I'd gone a round with Cabhan?"

"I don't." He fetched plates from the cupboard. "He stays in the shadows. He's stronger than he was, but not full healed. I barely feel him yet, but Fin said he's not full healed."

And Finbar Burke would know, Branna thought, as he was Cabhan's blood, as he bore the mark of Sorcha's curse.

58

"He's on his way," Connor added.

When she only nodded, he went to the door, opened it for Kathel. "And look at you, wet as a seal."

"Dry him off," Branna began, then sighed when Connor simply saw to the task by gliding his hands over the wet fur. "We've towels in the laundry for that."

Connor only grinned, a quick flash from a handsome face, a quick twinkle in moss green eyes. "Now he's dry all the faster, and you don't have a wet towel to wash."

Iona and Boyle came in, hand in hand. A pair of lovebirds, Branna thought. If anyone had suggested to her a year before that the taciturn, often brusque, former brawler could resemble a lovebird, she'd have laughed till her ribs cracked. But there he was, big, broad-shouldered, his hair tousled, his tawny eyes just a little dreamy beside her bright sprite of an American cousin.

"Meara will be right down," Iona announced. "She had a call from her sister."

"All's well?" Connor asked. "Her ma?"

"No problems — just some Christmas details." Without being asked she got out flatware to finish what Connor started, and Boyle put the kettle on for tea.

So Branna's kitchen filled with voices, with movement — and she could admit now that she'd had coffee — with the warmth of family. And then excitement as Meara dashed in, grabbed Connor and pulled him into a dance.

"I'm to pack up the rest of my mother's things." She did a quick stomp, click, stomp, then grabbed Connor again for a hard kiss. "She's staying with my sister Maureen for the duration. Praise be, and thanks to the little Baby Jesus in his manger!"

Even as Connor laughed, she stopped, pressed her hands to her face. "Oh God, I'm a terrible daughter, a horrible person altogether. Dancing about because my own mother's gone to live with my sister in Galway and I'll not have to deal with her on a daily basis myself."

"You're neither," Connor corrected. "Are you happy your mother's happy?"

"Of course, I am, but —"

"And why shouldn't you be? She's found a place where she's content, where she has grandchildren to spoil. And why shouldn't you kick up your heels a bit, as she won't be ringing you up twice a day when she can't work out how to switch out a light-bulb?"

"Or burns another joint of lamb," Boyle added.

"That's the bloody truth, isn't it?" So

Meara did another quick dance. "I'm happy for her, I am. And I'm wild with joy for my own self."

When Fin came in Meara launched herself at him — and gave Branna a moment to adjust herself, as she had to do whenever he walked in her door.

"You've lost a tenant, Finbar. My ma's settled once and done with my sister." She kissed him hard as well, made him laugh. "That's thanks to you — and don't say you don't need it — for the years of low rent, and for holding the little cottage in case she wanted to come back to Cong."

"She was a fine tenant. Kept the place tidy as a church."

"The place looks fine now, it does, with the updates we've done." As Iona took over the table setting, Connor grabbed his first coffee. "I expect Fin will have someone in there, quick as you please."

"I'll be looking into it." But it was Branna he looked at, and into. Then saying nothing, took Connor's coffee for himself.

She kept her hands busy, and wished to bloody hell she'd done that little glamour. No restless night showed on his face, on that beautiful carving of it, in the bold green eyes.

He looked perfect — man and witch —

with his raven black hair damp from the rain, his body tall and lean as he shed his black leather jacket, hung it on a peg.

She'd loved him all her life, understood, accepted, she always would. But the first and only time they'd given themselves to each other — so young, still so innocent — the mark had come on him.

Cabhan's mark.

A Dark Witch of Mayo could never be with Cabhan's blood.

She could, would, and had worked with him, for he'd proven time and again he wanted Cabhan's end as much as she. But there could never be more.

Did knowing it pained him as it did her help her through it? Maybe a bit, she admitted. Just a bit.

She took the platter heaped with pancakes she'd already flipped from the skillet out of the warmer, added the last of them.

"We'll sit then, and eat. It's your Nan's recipe, Iona. We'll see if I did her proud."

Even as she lifted the platter, Fin took it from her. And as he took it, his eyes met and held hers. "You've a story to go with them, I'm told."

"I do, yes." She took a plate full of bacon and sausage, carried it to the table. And sat. "Not an hour ago I sat here and had a

62

conversation with Sorcha's Brannaugh."

"She came here?" Connor paused in the act of sliding a stack of pancakes onto his plate. "Our kitchen?"

"She did. I'd had a restless night, full of dreams and voices. Hers among them. I couldn't be sure of the place as it was vague and scattered as dreams can be." She took a single pancake for herself. "I was here, getting my first cup of coffee, and I turned around. There she was.

"She looks like me — or I like her. That was a jolt of surprise, just how close we are there — though she was heavily pregnant. Her son comes today — or not today, as in her time it was still a fortnight to Samhain."

"Time shifts," Iona murmured.

"As you say. They'd gone to Ballintubber Abbey on the way here. That's where the dream took me."

"Ballintubber." Iona shifted to Boyle. "I felt them there, remember? When you took me to see it, I felt them, knew they'd gone there. It's such a strong place."

"It is, yes," Branna agreed. "But I've been there more than once, as has Connor. I never felt them."

"You haven't been since Iona's come," Fin pointed out. "You haven't been there since the three are all in Mayo."

"True enough." And a good point, she was forced to admit. "But I will, we will. On your wedding day, Iona, if not before. She said the others, those before us, guard the place, so Cabhan's barred from it. He can't go in, see in. It's a true sanctuary if we find we need one. They, who came before, gave light and strength to the three. And hope — I think she needed that most."

"And you," Iona said, "all of us. Hope wouldn't hurt us either."

"I'm more for doing than hoping, but it gave her what she needed. I could see it. She said — in the dream, and here — we will prevail. To believe that, and they'll be with us when we face Cabhan again. To find the way. To know, if it isn't for us to finish, another three will come. We will prevail."

"Though it takes a thousand years," Connor added. "Well then, I'm fine with hope, fine with doing. But I'll be buggered if I wait a thousand years to see the end of Cabhan."

"Then we find the way, in the here and the now. I had pancakes once when I went to Montana in the American West," Fin commented. "They called them something else . . ."

"Flapjacks, I bet," Iona suggested.

"That's the very thing. They were brilliant.

These are better yet."

"You've rambled far and wide," Branna said.

"I have. But I'm done with rambling until this is done. So, like Connor, a thousand years won't suit me. We find the way."

Just like that? Branna thought and struggled against annoyance. "She said they'd be with us, next time we faced him down. But they were there on Samhain, and still he got away from us."

"Only just there, or barely," Connor remembered. "Shadows like? Part of the dream spell we cast, that could be. How would we bring them full — could it be done? If we could find *that* way, how could we not end him? The first three, and we three. And the three more with us."

"Time's the problem." Fin sat back with his coffee. "The shifts. We were there on Samhain, but from what you say, Branna, they were not. So they were but shadows, and unable to take part. We have to make the times meet. Our time or theirs, but the same. It's interesting, an interesting puzzle to solve."

"But what time and when?" Branna demanded. "I've found two, and each should have worked. The solstice, then Samhain. The time should have been on the side of light. The spells we worked, the poison we created, all done to mesh with that specific time and place."

"And both times we wounded him," Boyle reminded her. "Both times he bled and fled. And the last? It should've been mortal."

"His power's as dark as ours is light," Iona pointed out. "And the source of it heals him. Longer this time. It's taking longer."

"If we could find his lair." Connor's face turned grim. "If we could go at him when he's weakened."

"I can't find him. Even the two of us together failed," Fin reminded him. "He has enough, or what feeds him has enough to hide. Until he slithers out again, and I — or one of us — can feel him, we wait."

"I'd hoped by Yule, but that's nearly on us." Branna shook her head. "I'd hoped we could take him on by Yule, though that was more from a wanting it done than a know-ing it was the time. I haven't found it in the stars. Not yet anyway."

"It seems to me we have an outline of the work needed." Boyle lifted a shoulder. "Finding the day, the time. Finding the way to bring the first three into it, if that's a true possibility."

"I believe it is." Fin looked at Branna.

"We'll study on it, work on it."

"I've time this morning."

"I have to go into the shop, take stock in. I'm barely keeping up with the holidays."

"I can help tomorrow, my off day," Iona offered.

"I'll take it."

"I want to finish a little shopping myself," Iona added. "My first Christmas in Ireland. And Nan's coming. I can't wait to see her, and to show her the house — well, what there is of it." She leaned into Boyle. "We're building a house in the woods."

"She changed her mind on the tiles in the big bath again," Boyle told the room at large.

"It's hard to decide. I've never built a house before." She looked at Branna. "Help me."

"I told you there's little I'd love more. Give me tomorrow, and we'll spend an hour or so over wine at day's end for looking at tile and paint samples and so on."

"Connor and I start talking about what we might want our place to look like, sitting in the field above the cottage here. And my brain goes to mush instantly." Meara swirled a bite of pancake in syrup. "I can't really get my mind around the building of a place, and the knowing down to the color of paint on the walls."

"Well, come for the wine and we'll play with yours as well. And speaking of houses," Branna added as she saw the door opening to her early-morning thoughts. "The lot of you have places — Boyle's, Meara's. There's no need for all of you to pack yourself in here every night."

"We're better together," Connor insisted.

"And there wouldn't be the idea that sleeping at Meara's flat would mean oatmeal for breakfast most mornings?"

He grinned. "It would be a factor."

"I've a fine way with oatmeal." Meara poked him.

"That you do, darling, but did you taste these pancakes?"

"I confess even my famous oatmeal can't rise up to them. You're after a bit of space," Meara said to Branna.

"I wouldn't mind some, now and again."

"We'll work on that as well."

"It seems we've plenty to be working on." Boyle rose. "I'd say we have to start with clearing up Branna's kitchen, and getting to the work that makes our living."

"When will you be back from your shop business?" Fin asked Branna.

She'd hoped the divergence of talk had distracted him off that, and should have known better. More, she admitted, avoiding working with him couldn't be done. Not for the greater good.

"I'll be back by two."

"Then I'll be here at two." He rose, picked up his plate to take it to the sink.

Making a living had to be done, and in truth, Branna enjoyed the making of hers. Once her house was empty and quiet, she went up to dress for the day, banked her bedroom fire to a simmer.

Down in her workshop she spent the next hour wrapping the fancy soaps she'd made the day before. Adding the ribbons and dried flowers to the bottles of lotions she'd already poured.

Candles she'd scented with cranberry she tucked into the fancy gift boxes she'd bought for the holiday traffic.

After a check of the list her manager had given her, she added salve, bath oil, various creams, noted down what needed replenishing, then began to carry boxes out to her car.

She'd intended to leave the dog home, but Kathel had other plans and jumped right in the car.

"After a ride, are you? Well, all right then." After one last check, she slid behind the wheel, and took the short drive to the village of Cong.

The rain and the cold discouraged any tourists pulled to the area in December. She found the steep streets empty, the abbey ruins deserted. Like a place out of time, she thought, with a smile.

She loved it, empty in the rain, or full of people and voices on a fine day. While she sold straight out of her workshop from time to time — especially to those who might come in hoping for a charm or spell — she'd chosen to place her shop in the village where the tourists and locals could easily breeze in. And as she was ever practical, where they might exchange some euros for what she made herself.

She parked in front of the whitewashed building, the corner shop on the pretty side street where the Dark Witch was housed.

Kathel jumped out behind her, waited patiently despite the rain while she unloaded the first box of stock. She elbowed open the door to a cheery ring of bells, walked into the lovely scents, the pretty lights of what she'd made herself, for herself.

All the lovely bottles, bowls, boxes on shelves, candles flickering to add atmosphere — and that lovely scent. Soft colors to soothe and relax, bold ones to energize, hunks of crystal placed just so for power.

And of course, the fuss for the holiday with the little tree, the greenery and berries, some ornaments she bought from a woman in Dublin, the jeweled wands and stone pendants she bought from a Wiccan catalog because people expected such things in a shop called the Dark Witch.

And there was Eileen, her pixie-sized body up on a step stool, cleaning a high shelf. Eileen turned, her bold green glasses slipping down her pug of a nose.

"Well now, it's the lady herself, and glad I am to see you, Branna. I hope you've come with more of those cranberry candles, for I sold the very last of them not fifteen minutes ago."

"I have two dozen more, as you asked. I would've thought too many, but if we're fully out, you were right again."

"It's why you made me manager." Eileen stepped down. She wore her dark blond hair in a scoop, dressed always smart — today in tall boots under a pine green dress. She was barely five feet altogether, and had borne and raised five strapping sons.

"More in the car then? I'll go fetch them in."

"You won't, no, as there's no need for both of us to be drenched." Branna set the first box down on the spotless counter. "You

71

can unpack and keep Kathel company, for he insisted on coming along."

"He knows where I keep special treats for lovely, good dogs."

His tail wagged as she spoke, and he sat politely, all but grinned at her.

Branna went out into the rain again, Eileen's laugh trailing behind her.

It took three trips, and a truly thorough drenching.

She waved her hands, down from her hair to her feet, drying herself as Connor had dried the dog that morning. Something she would have done for few outside her own circle.

Eileen didn't so much as blink, but continued to unpack the stock. Branna had chosen Eileen to run her shop, and manage the part-time clerks, for many practical reasons. But not the least of them was the wisps of power she sensed in the woman, and Eileen's acceptance of all Branna was.

"I had four hearty tourists — in from the Midlands — come to see *The Quiet Man* museum, have lunch at the pub. They stopped in, and dropped three hundred and sixty euros among them before they headed out again."

And not the least of those practical reasons, Branna thought now, was Eileen's knack of guiding the right customer to the right products.

"That's fine news on a rainy morning."

"Will you have some tea then, Branna?"

"No, but thanks." Instead, Branna pushed up her sleeves and helped Eileen unpack and place the stock. "And how's it all going?"

As she'd hoped, Eileen kept her mind off her troubles by catching her up with village gossip, with news of her sons, her husband, daughters-in-law (two, and another in June), grandchildren, and all else under the sun.

A scatter of customers came in during the hour she worked, and didn't leave empty-handed. And that was good for the spirit as well as the pocketbook.

She'd built a fine place here, Branna reminded herself. Full of color and light and scent, and all tidily arranged as her organized soul demanded — and as artfully displayed as her sense of style could wish.

And she thanked the gods again for Eileen and the others who worked for her, that they dealt with the customers, and she could have her time in her workshop to create.

"You're a treasure to me, Eileen."

Eileen's face flushed with pleasure. "Ah now, that's a lovely thing to say."

"A true one." She kissed Eileen's dimpled cheek. "How fortunate are we as we both get to do what we love and are bloody good at, every day? If I had to work the counter and such as I did in the first months I opened, I'd be mad as a hatter. So you're my treasure."

"Well, you're mine in turn, as having an employer who leaves me to my own ways is a gift."

"Then I'm leaving you to it now, and we'll both go on with what we love and do bloody well."

When she and Kathel left, Branna felt refreshed. A trip to her shop tended to lift her mood, and today's had lifted it higher than most. She drove through the rain on roads as familiar as her own kitchen, then sat a moment outside her cottage.

A good morning, she thought, despite the dreariness of the day. She'd spoken to her cousin, one of the first three, and at her own kitchen table. She would think and think long and hard on the hope and faith needed.

She'd taken good stock into her shop, spent an hour and more with a friend, watched people take away things she'd made with her own hands. Into their homes those things would go, she mused. Or to others as gifts and mementos. Good, useful

things, and pretty besides, for she valued
the pretty as much as the useful.

And thinking just that, she lifted a hand
and had the tree in her front window, the
lights around the windows of her shop
twinkling on.

"And why not add some pretty and some
light to a dreary day?" she asked Kathel.
"And now, my boy, we've work to do."

She went straight to her workshop,
boosted the fire while Kathel made himself
comfortable on the floor in front of it.

She'd told Fin she'd be back by two,
knowing she'd planned to return by noon.
A bit later than her plan, she noted, but she
still had near to two hours of quiet and
alone before she had him to deal with.

After donning a white apron, she made
ginger biscuits first because it pleased her.
While they cooled and their scent filled the
air, she gathered what she needed to make
the candle sets on the new list Eileen had
given her.

It soothed her, this work. She wouldn't
deny she added a touch of magick, but all
for the good. All in all it was care, it was
art, and science.

On the stove she melted her acid and wax,
added the fragrance oils, the coloring she
made herself. Now the scents of apple and

cinnamon joined the ginger. With a dollop she fixed the wicks in the little glass jars with the fluted edges, held them straight and true with a slim bamboo stick. The pour required patience, stopping to use another stick to poke into the apple-red wax to prevent pockets of air from forming. So she poured, poked until the little jars were filled and set aside for cooling.

A second batch, white and pure and scented with vanilla, and a third to make the scent — for three was a good number — green as the forest and perfumed with pine. Seasonal, she thought, and the season on them, so a half dozen sets should do.

The next she made perhaps she'd bring in spring.

Satisfied with the work, she glanced at the clock, saw it was nearly half-two. So the man was late, but that was fine as she'd had time to finish as she'd wanted.

But she'd be damned if she'd wait for him on the next job of work.

She took off her apron, hung it up, made herself some tea, and took two biscuits from the jar. With them, she sat, opened Sorcha's book, her own, her notebook, her laptop.

In the quiet alone, she began to study all they'd done before, and how they might do it better.

He came in — fully thirty-five minutes late — and drenched. She barely spared him a glance, and said, firmly, "Don't track up my floor."

He muttered something she ignored, dried himself quickly. "There's no point in being annoyed I'm later than I said. One of the horses took sick and needed tending."

She often forgot he had work of his own. "How bad?"

"It was bad enough, but she'll be all right. It's Maggie, and a sudden stable cough. The medicine might have righted her, but . . . well, I wouldn't risk it."

"You wouldn't, no." And there, she knew him. His softest spot was for animals, for anything and anyone who needed tending. "And couldn't." And it had been bad enough, she could see that now as well in the fatigue in his eyes.

"Sit. You need some tea."

"I wouldn't mind it, or a couple of those biscuits I smell. The ginger ones?"

"Sit," she said again, and went to turn up the heat on the kettle.

But he wandered around, restless.

"You've been working, I see. New candles not yet set."

"I've a shop to fill. I can't spend every moment of my day on bloody Cabhan."

"You can spend it taking offense from me where none was meant. And as it happens I want some candles for myself."

"Those just made are for gift sets."

"I'll have two of those then, as I've gifts to buy, and for more . . ." He wandered over to some shelves. "I like these you have here in the mirror jars. They'd shine in the light." He lifted one, sniffed at it. "Cranberries. It smells of Yule, so that suits, doesn't it? I'd have a dozen."

"I don't have a dozen of those, exactly, on hand. Just the three you see there."

"You could make the rest."

She made the tea, slanted him a look. "I could. You'll have to wait for them until tomorrow."

"That'll do. And these tapers as well, the long white ones, the smaller red."

"Did you come to work or to shop?"

"It's a fine thing to do both in one place, at one time." He took what he wanted, set it all on her counter for later.

After he sat, lifted his tea, he looked directly into her eyes. Her heart might have skipped, just once, but she ignored it.

"On the other side of the river, as we knew before. He gathers in the dark, in the deep. A cave, I think, but when and where I don't know, not for certain."

"You looked for him. Bloody, buggering hell, Fin —"

"Through the smoke," he said, coolly. "No point thrashing about on a filthy day like this. I looked through the smoke, and like smoke, it hazed and blurred. But I can tell you he's not as weak as he was, even days ago. And something's with him, Branna. Something . . . else."

"What?"

"Whatever, I think, he bargained with to be what he is, to have what he has. It's darker yet, deeper yet, and I think . . . I don't know," he murmured, rubbing his shoulder where the mark dug into him. "I think it plays him, I think it uses him as much as he uses it, and in his weakness I could see that much. More than I have before. It's a sense only, this other. But I know, and for certain, he heals, and he will come again before much longer."

"Then we'll be ready. What did we miss, Fin? That's the question. So, let's find the answer."

He bit into a biscuit, smiled for the first time since he'd come in. "I might need more than two of these to sustain me while going over these bloody books again."

"There's more in the jar if you need them.

Now." She tapped her book. "The potion first."

4

It pained him to look at her — so close, but distant as Saturn. It sustained him, far more than ginger biscuits, to see her face, hear her voice, catch her scent, just hers, among the others wafting through her workshop.

He'd tried everything he knew to kill his love for her. He reminded himself she'd turned from him, cast him aside. He'd taken other women, tried to fill the abyss she'd left in him with their bodies, their voices, their beauty.

He'd left his own home, often for months at a go, just to put himself away from her. Traveling, rambling, to places near and far, foreign and familiar.

He'd made his fortune, and a good, solid one, with work, with time, with wit and grit. He'd built a fine home for himself, and had seen to it his parents had all they needed, though they'd moved to New York City to be near his mother's sister. Or, he often thought, to be away of any talk or thought of magicks and curses. For that he couldn't blame them.

No one could say he'd wasted his life or his skills — magickal or otherwise. But nothing he'd done had eroded even a fraction of that love.

He'd considered a potion, a spell, but he knew love magick, to bring it or remove it — held consequences far beyond the single person who wished for it, or wished it gone.

He would not, could not, use his gift to ease his heart.

Was it worse or better, he often wondered, knowing she loved him as well, she suffered as well? Some days, he admitted, he found some solace in that. Other days it buggered the living hell out of him.

But for now neither of them had a choice. They must be together, work together, join together for the single purpose of destroying Cabhan, for defeating him, for ending him.

So he worked with her, through argument and agreement, in her lovely workshop over endless cups of tea — and finally a bit of whiskey in it — poring over the books, writing out a new spell neither of them was satisfied with, and again, going over every step of the two previous battles.

And neither of them devised anything new, found another answer.

She was the canniest witch he knew — and all too often the strictest in her ethics. And beautiful with it. Not just the face and form, all that glorious hair, those warm gray eyes. What she was, the power and presence of it, added more, and her unstinting devotion to her craft, to her gift — to family — more still.

He was doomed to love her.

So he worked with her, then paid for the candles — full price, he thought with amusement, for the gods knew Branna O'Dwyer was a practical witch, and left her to drive home through the steady rain.

He checked on Maggie first, pleased with her progress. He gave the sweet-natured mare half an apple and some of his time and attention. He visited the rest of the horses, giving them time as well. He had pride in what he'd built here, in what he and Boyle had built here and at the rental stables. Pride, too, in the falconry school nearby.

Connor ran it like a dream, Fin thought.

If not for Cabhan, he could leave tomorrow for India or Africa, for America or Istanbul, and know Boyle and Connor would take care of all they'd built.

Once Cabhan was done, he'd do just that. Pick a spot on the map, and go. Get away, see something new. Anything but here for a bit, for here was all he loved far too deeply.

He gave the little stable dog Bugs a treat, then on impulse picked him up, took him along to the house. Fin imagined they'd both enjoy the company.

He liked his quiet and alone as much as Branna did hers — or nearly. But the nights were so bleeding long in December, and the chill and dark so unrelenting. He couldn't pop up to Boyle's above the garage as he'd often done in the past, and he expected Boyle and his Iona would end up at Branna's even though she tried to discourage it.

They would guard her, as he could not.

That alone stirred rage and frustration he had to shove back down.

He set the dog down inside the house, flicked a hand to the fire to have the flames snapping, another toward the tree he'd put in the big front window.

The dog pranced around, his joy at being inside so palpable, Fin smiled and settled a little. Yes, they'd both do well with the company.

He wandered back toward the kitchen, its light bright on all the gleaming surfaces, got himself a beer.

She'd only been in his home once, and only as Connor was there, and hurt. But he could see her there. He'd always seen her there. It ground his pride to admit he'd built the place with her in mind, with the dreams they'd once woven together in mind.

He carried a few of her candles into the dining room, put the tapers in silver holders, set out some of the mirrored ones. Yes, they caught the light well, he decided. Though she'd be unlikely to see her work in his space.

He thought of making some food, but put it off as he purely hated to cook. He'd slap something together later, he decided, as a trip to the pub for a meal didn't appeal with the rain thrashing.

He could go downstairs, wile away some of the evening with sports on the big TV, or kill time with a game or two. He could stretch out with another beer in front of the fire with a book that wasn't all magicks and spells.

"I can do whatever I bloody well please," he told Bugs. "And it's my own fault, isn't it, that nothing pleases me. Maybe it's just the rain and the dark. What would please me is a hot beach, some blasting sun, and a willing woman. And that's not altogether true, is it?"

He crouched, sent Bugs into paralytic joy by giving him a belly rub. "Would we were all so easily happy as a little stable dog. Well, enough of this. I'm tired of myself. We'll go up and work, for the sooner this is done, the sooner I'll find if that hot beach is the answer after all."

The dog followed him, slavishly devout, as he walked back, then up the wide stairs to the second floor. He thought of a hot shower, maybe a steam as well, but turned directly into his workroom. There he lit the fire as well, flames shimmering in a frame of deep green tourmaline while the dog explored.

He'd designed every inch of the room — with some help from Connor — the black granite work counters, the deep mahogany cabinetry, the wide plank cypress floors that ran throughout the house. Tall, arched windows, with the center one of stained glass that created the image of a woman in white robes bound by a jeweled belt. She held a wand in one hand, a ball of flame in the other while her black hair swirled in an unseen wind.

It was Branna, of course, with the moon full behind her and the deep forest surrounding her. The Dark Witch watched him with eyes, even in glass, full of power and light.

He had a heavy antique desk — topped by a state-of-the-art computer. Witches didn't fear technology. A cabinet with thick and carved doors held weapons he'd collected the world over. Swords, a broadaxe, maces, foils, throwing stars. Others held cauldrons, bowls, candles, wands, books, bells, athames, and still others various potions and ingredients.

She would have liked the room, he thought, for when it came to work as well as living, he was nearly as ruthlessly tidy as she.

Bugs looked up at him, tail wagging hopefully. Reading him, Fin smiled.

"Go ahead then. Make yourself at home."

The dog wagged more fiercely, then ran over and leaped onto a curved divan, circled about, and settled down with a sigh of utter contentment.

Fin worked into the night, dealing with practical matters such as charms — protection needed refreshing with regularity — on tonics and potions. Something specifically for Maggie. He cleansed some crystals — what he thought of as housework — as that needed doing as well.

He'd have forgotten supper altogether, but

he felt the dog's hunger. He went down, Bugs on his heels, put together a sandwich, some crisps, sliced up an apple. As he'd neglected to bring in any food for the dog, he simply shared the meal, amusing them both by tossing bits of sandwich for Bugs to snatch out of the air as handily as he did the bugs from which he'd earned his name.

Considering the practical again, he let the dog out, kept his mind linked with Bugs so he'd know if the little hound headed back to the stables after the practical was seen to.

But Bugs pranced right back to the kitchen door, sat, and waited until Fin opened it for him.

"All right then, it seems you're spending the night. And that being the case, it's God's truth you could use a shower even more than I. You carry the stables with you, little friend. Let's take care of that."

In the bath, the shower nearly had Bugs scrambling off, but Fin was quick. And laughing, carted the dog in with him. "It's just water. Though we're going to add soap all around."

Bugs trembled, lapped at the spray coming out of the many jets, wiggled against Fin's bare chest when Fin rubbed in some of the liquid soap.

"There you see, not so bad now is it?" He

stroked gently to soothe as well as clean. "Not so bad at all."

He gestured toward the ceiling. Lights streamed, soft colors, music flowed in, soft and lilting. He set the dog down, gave himself the pleasure of the hot jets while the dog lapped at the wet tiles.

Fin was quick, but not quite quick enough to dry the dog before Bugs shook himself, shooting drops all over the bath. His own laugh echoed in the room as the little dog shot him a look of satisfaction.

With that mess sorted out, he moved into the bedroom, tossed down one of the big pillows that grouped on the sofa in his sitting area. But the dog, fully at home now, jumped onto the big, high bed, stretched out like a potentate at his ease.

"Well, at least you're clean."

He climbed in himself, decided on a book rather than TV to ease him toward sleep.

By the time Fin turned off the light, Bugs was quietly snoring. Fin found the sound of it a small comfort, and wondered how pathetic it was when a snoring dog eased the lonely.

In the dark, with the fire down to glowing embers, he thought of Branna.

She turned to him, her hair a black curtain, all silk spilling over her bare shoulders.

The fire flickered now, gold flames that turned her eyes to silver with that gold dancing in them.

And she smiled.

"You yearn for me."

"Day and night."

"And here you want me, in your big bed, in your fancy house."

"I want you anywhere. Everywhere. You torture me, Branna."

"Do I?" She laughed, but the sound wasn't cruel. It was warm as a kiss. "Not I, Finbar, not I alone. We torture each other." She trailed a finger down his chest. "You're stronger than you were. As am I. Do you wonder, would we be stronger together?"

"How can I think, how can I wonder, when I'm so full of you?"

He took her hair in his hands, pulled her to him. And God, oh God, the taste of her after so long, after a lifetime, was like life after death.

He rolled over, pressing her under him, going deeper into the wonder of it. Her breasts, fuller, softer, sweeter than he remembered, and her heart drumming under his hands as she arched up to him.

A blur and storm of the senses — the feel of her skin, silk like her hair and warm, so warm, chasing away all the cold. The shape of her, the lovely curves, the sound of her breathing his name, moving, moving under him, chasing away all the lonely.

His blood beat for her; his own heart pounded as she tangled her hands in his hair as she used to, as she ran them down his back. Gripped his hips, arched up. Opened.

He plunged in. The light exploded, white, gold, sparking like fire — all the world afire. Wind whipped in a torrent to send that fire into a roar. For an instant, one breath, the pleasure struck.

Then came the lightning. Then came the dark.

He stood with her in the storm, her hand gripped in his.

"I don't know this place," she said.

"Nor do I. But . . ." Something, something he knew, somewhere deep. Too deep to reach. Thick woods, whirling winds, and somewhere close the rush of a river.

"Why are we here?"

"Something's close," was all he said.

She turned up her hand, held a small ball of flame. "We need light. Can you find the way?"

"Something's close. You should go back. It's the dark that's close."

"I won't go back." She touched her amulet, closed her eyes. "I feel it."

When she started forward, he tightened his hold on her hand. He would find a way to shield her, if needed. But the urgency to move on pulled him.

Thick trees, deep shadows that seemed to glow with the dark. No moon, no stars, only that wind that sent the night screaming.

In it, something howled, and the howl was hungry.

Fin wished for a weapon, dug deep for power, drew a blade, and set the blade on fire.

"Dark magicks," Branna murmured. She, too, seemed to glow, alight with her own power. "All around. This is not home."

"Not home, but near enough. Not now, but long ago."

"Yes, ago. His lair? Could it be? Can you tell?"

"It's not the same. It's . . . other than that."

She nodded as though she'd felt the same. "We should call the others. We should have our circle in full. If this is his place."

"There." He saw it, dark against dark, the mouth of a cave hunched in a hillside.

He would not take her in, Fin thought. Would not take her there, for within was death. And worse.

Even as he thought it, the old man stepped out. He wore rough robes, worn hide boots. Both his hair and beard were a long tangle of gray. Both madness and magick lived in his eyes.

"You are too soon. You are too late." As he spoke he held up a hand. Blood dripped from it, blood spread over his rough robes.

"It's done. Done, as I am done. You are too soon to see it, too late to stop it."

"What is done?" Fin demanded. "Who are you?"

"I am the sacrifice. I am the sire of the dark. I am betrayed."

"I can help you." But as Branna started forward, power roared out of the cave. It swept her back, Fin with her, sent the old man falling to the ground where his blood pooled black on the earth.

"Dark Witch to be," he said. "Cabhan's whelp to come. There is no help here. He has eaten the dark. We are all damned."

Fin pushed to his feet, tried to shove Branna back. "He's in there. He's in there. I can feel him."

But as he made to leap toward the cave, she grabbed at him. "Not alone. It isn't for you alone."

He whirled toward her, all but mad himself. "He is mine; I am his. Your blood made it so. It's your curse I carry, and I *will* take my vengeance."

"Not for vengeance." She wrapped herself around him. "For that would damn you. Not for vengeance. And not alone."

But he woke alone, covered with sweat, the mark on his arm burning like a fresh brand.

And could still smell her on the sheets, on his skin. In the air.

The dog quivered against him, whining.

"It's all right now." Absently, he stroked. "It's done for now."

He showered off the sweat, grabbed pants, an old sweater, pulling the sweater on as he went downstairs. He let the dog out, barely noticed the rain had stopped and weak winter sunlight trickled down.

He needed to think, and clearly, so started for coffee. Cursed at the banging on his front door.

Then thought of Maggie, hurried to answer even as he thought her out, settled himself the mare was doing well.

He opened the door to Branna.

She walked through it, shoving him back with both hands.

"You had no right! Bloody bastard, you had no right pulling me into your dream."

He grabbed her hands by the wrists before

she could shove him again. And he thought again she all but glowed, but this was pure fury.

"I didn't — or not by intent. For all I know you pulled me into yours."

"I? What bollocks. You had me in your bed."

"And willing enough while you were." As he had her hands she couldn't slap him, but she had power free enough, and shot him back two full steps with it. It burned a bit as well. "Stop it. You'd best cool yourself off, Branna. You're in my home now. I don't know if I pulled you, you pulled me, or if something else pulled us together. And I can't shagging think as I haven't had so much as a cup of fucking coffee."

With that, he turned, strode off toward the kitchen.

"Well, neither have I." She strode after him. "I want you to look at me."

"And I want my fucking coffee."

"Look at me, Finbar, damn it. Look at me and answer this. Did you pull me into your dream, into your bed?"

"No." He shoved a hand through his hair. "I don't know, I just don't know, but if I did, I did it in my fecking sleep and not meaning to. Bugger it, Branna, I wouldn't bespell you. Whatever you think of me you shouldn't think that. I'd never use you that way."

She took a breath, then a second. "I do know it. I apologize, for of course I know it when I calm myself. I'm sorry, I am. I was . . . upset."

"Small wonder. I'm not doing so well myself."

"I could do with coffee myself, if you don't mind."

"Right."

He walked over to the coffeemaker — the type she'd been toying with indulging in, as it did all the fancy coffees and teas and chocolates besides.

"Will you sit?" He lifted his chin toward the little glassed-in bump where she imagined he took his coffee in the morning.

She slid onto one of the benches thickly padded in burnt orange, studied the turned wooden bowl — as glossy as glass — full of sharp red apples.

They were adults, she reminded herself, and couldn't shy away from discussing what had happened in that big bed.

"I won't, and can't, blame you or any man for where his mind goes in sleep," she began.

"I won't, and can't, blame you or any woman for where hers goes." He set her coffee, served in an oversized white mug, on

96

the table in front of her. "For it could've been you as easily as me."

She hadn't thought of it, and found herself baffled into silence for a moment. To give herself time to think, she tried the coffee, found it doctored exactly as she liked.

"That's fair enough. Fair enough. Or, as I didn't give myself the chance to think of it before this, it could've been other powers entirely."

"Others?"

"Who can say?" More frustrated than angry now, she threw up her hands. "What we know is I came or was brought to your bed, and in this dreaming state we began what healthy people might begin."

"Your skin's as soft as rose petals."

"Hardly a wonder," she said lightly, "as I use what I make, and I make fine products."

"For those moments, Branna, it was as it once was with us, and more besides."

"For those moments, both bespelled. And what happened, Fin, when we joined? In that moment? The lightning, the storm, the light then the dark, and we were thrown into another place and time. Can it be clearer, the price paid for those moments?"

"Not to me, not clear at all. What did we learn, Branna? Go back to it."

She folded her hands on the table, deliberately, firmly, set emotion aside. "All right. Into the dark, thick woods, no moon or stars, great wind moaning through the trees."

"A river. The rush of it somewhere behind us."

"Yes." She closed her eyes, took herself back. "That's right, yes. The river behind, power ahead. The dark of it, and still we went toward it."

"The cave. Cabhan's lair, I know it."

"We saw nothing of him."

"I felt him, but . . . it wasn't as it is now. Something else." He shook his head. "It isn't clear at all, but though I don't know where we were, I sensed something familiar all the same. As if I should have known. Then the old man was there."

"I didn't know him."

"Nor did I, but again it felt as if I should. We were too soon to see, he said, and too late to stop it. Riddles. Just fecking riddles."

"A time shift, I'm thinking. We weren't in the now, but not when we could know more. He called himself the sacrifice."

"And the sire of the dark. He bled and bled. Mad and dying, but there was power in him. Fading, but there."

"Cabhan's sacrifice?" Branna wondered, then sat rod straight. "Cabhan's sire?" she said even as she saw the same thought in Fin's eyes. "Could it be?"

"Well, he was whelped from someone. Ah, Cabhan's whelp, he called me, and you Dark Witch to be. He knew us, Branna, though we'd yet to be born in his time. He knew us."

"He didn't make Cabhan what he is." She shook her head, let herself feel again what she'd felt. "There wasn't enough in him for that. But . . ."

"In the cave, there was more." Calmer now, Fin relaxed the hand he'd fisted on the table. "Did the old man conjure more than he could deal with, bring the dark in, give it a source?"

"Cabhan's blood — his sire. And the sire's blood spilling out. His life spilling onto the ground. In sacrifice? God, Fin, did Cabhan kill his own father, sacrifice his own sire to gain the dark?"

"It must be blood," Fin murmured. "It must always be blood. The dark demands it; even the light requires it. Too soon to see. If we had stayed, would we have found him, just coming into the power he has? Just coming in, and not fully formed?"

"It happened then, as the old man lay dying. It erupted, didn't it, heaving us back, breaking whatever spell had taken us. And it was cold, do you remember, did you feel? It was brutally cold for an instant before it was done, and I woke in my own bed."

Fin pushed up, restless, pacing. "He couldn't have wanted us there — Cabhan. Couldn't have wanted us anywhere near his lair, or to have us gain any knowledge of his origin."

"If we've the right of it."

"He didn't bring us there, Branna. Why would he? The more we know, the more we can use to end him. Other powers you said. And I say other powers sent us there, whether those powers are without or within us."

"Why only we two? Why not the six of us?"

"Dark Witch to be, Cabhan's whelp?" He shrugged. "You know very well you can't always logic out magicks. We need to go back, learn more."

"I'm not after having sex with you so we can travel back in time to Cabhan's cave."

"But you'd give your life for it." He waved her off before she could speak. "I don't want sex as a magickal tool, even with you. And I want to be full in control on the next journey, not taken by other forces or means. I have to think on it."

"I'll have your oath."

"What?" Distracted, he glanced back,

watched her rise from the table, her hair long, loose, a bit wild. Her eyes somehow calm and fierce at once.

"Your oath, Finbar. You won't go back alone. You won't move on this without me, without our circle. You aren't alone and won't act alone. Your word on it, here and now."

"Do you see me so reckless, so hell-bent on my own destruction?"

"I see you as I did on Samhain when you would have left our circle and safety to go after Cabhan alone, even at the risk of never coming back to your own place and time. Do you think so little of us, Fin? So little you'd step away and leave us behind?"

"I think everything of you, and the others, but he's my blood, not yours." The words held a bitter taste, but were all truth. "And still I won't act alone. I won't because if I go wrong I'd risk you, and the others. Everything."

"Your hand on it." She held out her own. "Your hand on it, to seal the oath."

He took her hand in his. Light streamed out between their fingers, sizzled and snapped like a wick just fed the flame.

"Well. Well, now," he said quietly. "That hasn't happened in some time."

She felt the heat, the spread of it through

her — both comfort and torment. Would it grow, she wondered, if she moved to him, if she reached for him?

She drew her hand from his, stepped back.

"I need to tell the others before they scatter for the day. You're welcome to come."

"You'll deal with it." And he needed some distance from her. "I've things to do."

"All right then." She started back, him with her, to his front door. "I'll be working with Iona today, and we'll see what we can do. It might be best for us to meet, all of us, but not tonight. A little time more to sort through it all. Tomorrow night if it suits you."

"You'll be cooking."

"My lot in life."

He wanted to run his hand over her hair, just feel it as he'd felt it in the dream. But he didn't touch her. "I'll bring wine."

"Your lot in life." She stepped through the door when he opened it for her, then turned, stood for a moment with the morning mists around her. "You've built a good house, Fin. Handsome for certain, but it has a fine, strong feel to it."

"You've seen hardly more than the kitchen."

"Well now, that's the heart of a home. If you could come tomorrow at around three, we could work before the others come for supper."

"I'll work it out, and be there."

He waited while she walked to her car, surprised when she stopped, looked back again with a quick, saucy smile.

"I should've mentioned, your skin's not far off from rose petals, but in a manly way, of course."

When he laughed, the tension in his belly eased even as she drove away from him.

5

After Branna told her tale, asked her circle to think on its meanings, she put in another request.

"I'd like the house cleared of men tonight, if you don't mind, and to spend it with my women here, with wine and paint samples and such. If you could do me a favor, Connor, Boyle, would you invade Fin's house, and stay there? Do whatever men do with an evening free of females. I don't want to know what that might be."

When Connor hesitated, she drilled her finger in his belly. "And don't be after thinking the three of us need the protection of men. Two of us are witches same as you, and the other could kick your arse into next week if you riled her."

"I take pains not to rile her. All right then. What do you say, Boyle, we'll drag Fin off to the pub, then stagger back to his place?"

"I'm for it. He'll want the company, I

expect," he said with a glance at Branna.

"Want it or not, he needs it. I'll be in the workshop. Iona, when you're done here, I'll put you to work."

"I'll be here by six," Meara told her, and waited until Branna left the room. "A terrible hard thing for both of them. I don't know how they stand up to it. So let's give them some fun and ease tonight at least."

"That we can do." Boyle rubbed a hand on Meara's shoulder, turned to Iona. "It's good you'll be with her today."

She hoped she could help, would know what to say — what not to say. And when Iona went into the workshop, Branna was already at the stove, with a dozen mirrored bowls set out on the counter.

"I've an order for these, so want to get them done straight off, and I've a mind to make up some sets — the small bottles — of hand lotion and scrubs and soaps. Put them together in the red boxes they sent me too many of, tie them with the red-and-green-plaid ribbon. Eileen can put them on special, as the company didn't charge me for the overstock as it was their mistake. Some will wait till the final moment for the holiday shopping, so they should move well enough."

Iona went with instinct, crossed over, and,

saying nothing, put her arms around her cousin.

"I'm all right, Iona."

"I know, but only because you're so strong. I wouldn't be. Just so you know, I'd get behind you if you just needed to cut loose."

"Cut what loose?"

On a half laugh, Iona eased back. "I mean rant, rave, curse the heavens."

"No point in it."

"The ranting, raving, cursing *is* the point. So whenever you need to, I've got your back. I'll get the bottles, the boxes. I know where they are."

"Thanks for that — for all of that. Would you mind running the little sets into the shop once we've done them? I'd like them out as soon as we can."

"Sure. But do you just want them in stock, or do you want me out of here?"

Her cousin, Branna thought, had finely honed instincts. "Both, but you, just for a little while. I'm glad to have you, but for just a little while I could do with some alone. And when you come back, we can begin the more essential work between us."

"All right." Iona got out the boxes, began to assemble them. "How many of these?"

"Half dozen, thanks."

"I think you're right if you want my opinion."

"About the boxes?"

"No, not about that. About what happened. About it being another power that pulled you and Fin together."

"I'm not sure I'm right, or I've concluded just that."

"It's what I think." She brushed at her cap of bright hair, glanced up. "Maybe — I hope I don't push too hard on a sore spot — but maybe both you and Fin want to be together, maybe that wanting stirs up from time to time, and maybe last night, for whatever reason, was one of those times."

"A lot of maybes in your certainty, cousin."

"Circling around the sore spot, I guess. There's no maybe in the wanting or the stirring. I'm sorry, Branna, it's impossible not to see it or feel it, especially the more we all bind together for this."

Branna kept her hands busy, her voice calm. "People want all manner of things they can't have."

Sore spot, Iona reminded herself, and didn't push on it. "What I mean is, it's very possible the two of you were a little vulnerable last night, that your defenses or shields were lowered some. And that opened the door, so to speak, to that other power. Not Cabhan, because that absolutely makes no sense."

"It hurt us." And left a terrible aching behind. "He lives to hurt us."

"Yes, but . . ." Iona shook her head. "He doesn't understand us. He doesn't understand love or loyalty or real sacrifice. Lust, sure. I don't doubt he understands you and Fin are hot for each other, but he'd never understand what's under it. Sorcha would."

Branna stopped working on the candles, stared at Iona. "Sorcha."

"Or her daughters. Think about it."

"When I think about it, I'm reminded Sorcha's the very one who cursed all that came from Cabhan, which would be Fin."

"That's true. She was wrong, but that's true. And sure, maybe, considering he killed her husband, tore her from her own children, she'd do the same thing again. But she knew love. She understood it, she gave her power and her life for it. Don't you think she'd use it if she could? Or that her children would?"

"So she, or they, cast the dreaming spell? Where we were together, and all defenses down, so we came together."

She began to walk about, deliberately, running it over in her mind. "And when we did,

108

used the power of that to send us back. But both too soon and too late."

"Okay, think about that. Sooner, whatever happened in that cave might have pulled you in, beyond what you could fight. Later, you wouldn't have spoken with the old man — potentially, and I think right again — Cabhan's father."

Iona got out the ribbon, the bottles as Branna worked in silence.

"I think you saw what you were meant to see, that's what I'm saying. I think we need to find a way to see more — that's the work. They can't hand it to us, right? And I think — sore spot — it had to be only you and Fin together because the two of you need to resolve — not gloss over or bury or ignore — your feelings."

"Mine are resolved."

"Oh, Branna."

"I can love him and be resolved to living without him. But I see now too much of it was hazed in my mind. All that feeling I couldn't quite set down. You have good points here, Iona. We saw what we were meant to see, and we work from that."

She glanced over, smiled before she poured more scented wax. "You've learned a great deal since the day you came to that door, in all that rain, in that pink coat, babbling away with your nerves."

"Now if I could only learn to cook."

"Ah well, some things are beyond our reach."

She finished the candles, and together she and Iona made up the half dozen pretty gift sets. When her cousin set off to Cong, Branna took her solitude with tea by the fire, with Kathel's head in her lap.

She studied the flames, let her thoughts circle. Then with a sigh, set her tea aside.

"All right then, all right." She held her hands out to the fire. "Clear for me and let me see, through the smoke and into the fire, take me where the light desires."

Images in the flames, voices through the smoke. Branna let herself drift toward them, let them pull her, surrendered to the call she'd felt in the blood, in the bone.

When they cleared, she stood in a room where another fire simmered, where candles flickered. Her cousin Brannaugh sat in a chair singing softly to the baby at her breast. She looked up, her face illuminated, and said, "Mother?"

"No." Branna stepped out of the shadows. "No, I'm sorry."

"I wished for her. I saw her when my son came into the world, saw her watching, felt her blessing. But only that, and she was gone. I wished for her."

"I asked the light to take me where it willed. It brought me here." Branna moved closer, looked down at the baby, at his down of dark hair, and soft cheeks, his dark, intense eyes as he suckled so busily at his mother's breast.

"He's beautiful. Your son."

"Ruarc. He came so quick, and the light bloomed so bright with his birthing. I saw my mother in it even as Teagan guided him out of me and into the world. I thought not to see you again, not so soon."

"How long for you?"

"Six days. We stay at Ashford, are welcome. I have not yet gone to the cabin, but both Teagan and Eamon have done so. Both have seen Cabhan."

"You have not."

"I hear him." She looked toward the window as she rocked the baby. "He calls to me, as if I would answer. He called to my mother, now to me. And to you?"

"He has, will again, I imagine, but it will do him no good. Do you know of a cave, beyond the river?"

"There are caves in the hills, beneath the water."

"One of power. A place of the dark."

"We were not allowed beyond the river.

Our mother, our father both forbade it. They never spoke of such a place, but some of the old ones, at gatherings, I heard them speak of Midor's cave, and would make the sign against evil when they did."

"Midor." A name, at least, Branna thought, to work from. "Do you know of Cabhan's origins? There is no word of it in the book, in Sorcha's book."

"She never spoke of it. We were children, cousin, and at the end, there was no time. Would it help to know?"

"I'm not sure, but knowing is always better than not. I was there, in a dream. With Fin. Finbar Burke."

"Of the Burkes of Ashford? No, no," she said quickly. "This is the one, the one of your circle who is Cabhan's blood. His blood drew him to this place, and you with him?"

"I don't know, nor does he. He is not Cabhan, he is not like Cabhan."

Now Sorcha's Brannaugh looked into her own fire. "Does your heart speak, cousin, or your head?"

"Both. He's bled with us. You saw yourself, or will on Samhain night. And you will judge for yourself. Midor," she repeated. "The light brought me here, and it may be for only this. I've never heard of Midor's cave. I think this may be buried in time, but I know how to pick up a shovel and dig."

They both looked toward the tall window as the howling rose up outside.

"He hunts and stalks." Brannaugh held her son closer. "Already since we've come home a village girl's gone missing. He pushed the dark against the windows, swirls his fog. Beware the shadows."

"I do, and will."

"Take this." Shifting the baby, she held out her hand, and in it a spear of crystal clear as water. "A gift for you, and a light."

"Thank you. I'll keep it with me. Be well, cousin, and bright blessings to you and your son."

"And to you. Samhain," she murmured as Branna felt herself pulled away. "I will tip my arrows with poison, and do all in my power to end him."

But you won't, Branna thought as she sat in front of her own fire again, studying the crystal in her hand. Not on Samhain.

Another time, gods willing, but not on Samhain.

She rose, tucking the gift into her pocket. Choosing her laptop over the books, she began to search for Midor's cave.

"I couldn't find a bloody thing that applied

to this." Branna sat, poking at the salad she'd made to go with a pretty penne and a round of olive bread.

"I'm not sure you can Google the cave of a sorcerer from the twelfth or thirteenth century." Meara slathered butter on the bread.

"You can Google near to every bleeding thing."

"Is it an Irish name? Midor?" Iona wondered.

"Not one I've heard. But he might've come from anywhere, from the bowels of hell for all we know, and ended up dying in front of that cave."

"What about the mother?" Iona gestured with her wine. "Midor had to sire Cabhan — if we've got that right — with someone. Where's the mother? Who's the mother?"

"There's nothing, just nothing about any of this in Sorcha's book, in my great-grandmother's. Maybe it's not important after all." Branna fisted her chin on her hand. "And bollocks to that. Some of it must be or Fin and I wouldn't have gone to that shagging cave."

"We'll figure it out. Ah, this pasta's brilliant," Meara added. "We will figure it out, Branna. Maybe it's Connor's absolute faith rubbing off, but I believe it. Things are starting up again, you see? You having visits with Sorcha's Brannaugh, you and Fin going on dreamwalks after a bit of a dream shag."

Iona hunched her shoulders, then relaxed them again when she saw from Branna's face Meara handled it just right.

"Wasn't much of a shag," Branna admitted. "It took premature ejaculation to a new level entirely. Fate's a buggering bitch, I say. It's all, Here you are, Branna, remember this? Then it's, Well, remembering's all you'll get. And it's back to the blood and the dark and the evildoings for you."

"You're tired of it." Iona reached over, rubbed her arm.

"Tonight I am, that's for certain. No one's ever touched me like Fin, and I'm tired enough of it tonight to say so out loud. No one, not my body or my heart or my spirit besides. And no one will. Knowing that, well, it can make you tired."

Iona started to speak, but Meara shook her head, silenced her.

"I didn't need to be reminded of it. It was cruel, but magick can be. Here's a gift, and oh, look what you are, what you have. But you can never be sure what you'll pay for it."

"He's paid as well," Meara said gently.

115

"Sure I know it. More than any other. It was easier when I could be angry or feel betrayed. But what needs doing can't be done with anger and hard feelings. Letting them go brings back so much. Too much. So I have to ask how do I do what needs doing when I feel all this? It needs to be let go as well."

"Love's power," Iona said after a moment. "I think even when it hurts, it's power."

"That may be. No, that *is,*" Branna corrected. "But how to use it and not be swallowed by it, that's a fine, thin line, isn't it? And right now I feel weighed and unbalanced and . . ."

She trailed off, laid a hand lightly on Iona's, the other on Meara's. "Beware the shadows," she murmured, looking out the window where they dug deep pockets in the wall of fog.

"No, sit easy," she said when Meara started to rise. "Just sit easy. He can't come in to what's mine, try as he might. But I'm sitting here in my own kitchen acting the gom. Sitting here, sniveling away so he can slide around my walls and windows, feeding on my self-pity. Well, he's fed enough."

She shoved away from the table, ignoring Iona's quick, "Wait!" Striding straight to the window, she flung it open, and hurled out a ball of fire, then another, then two at once while the fury of her power snapped around her.

Something roared, something inhuman. And the fog lit like tinder before it vanished.

"Well now." Branna closed the window with a little snap.

"Holy shit." Iona standing, a ball of fire on her palm, let out a shaky breath. "Holy shit," she repeated.

"I don't think he liked the taste of that. And I feel better." After dusting her hands, palm to palm, she came back, sat, picked up her fork. "You should put that fire out now, Iona, and finish your pasta." She sampled her first bite. "For it's brilliant if I say so myself. And, Meara, if you wouldn't mind texting Connor. Just letting them know to have a care, though I don't think Cabhan's up to tangling with them tonight."

"Sure I'll do that."

"He thought to take a little swipe at the women," Branna said as she ate. "He'll forever underestimate women. And he thought to lap up some of my feelings. Now he'll choke on them. It's light he can't abide." With a flick of her fingers the light in the room glowed just a little brighter. "And joy, and we'll have some of that, for it's not much makes me happier than picking out colors and finishings and the like."

She scooped up more pasta. "So, Iona, have you thought of travertine for the master bath?"

"Travertine." Iona let out another breath, and managed, "Hmmm."

"And we've still details on your wedding to see to, and have barely talked of yours, Meara. There's joy here." She took her friends' hands again. "The kind women know. So let's have more wine and talk of weddings and making stone and glass into homes."

Connor read the text from Meara. "Cabhan's been at the cottage. No," he said quickly as both his friends pushed back from the table. "He's gone. Meara says Branna sent him off with his tail burning between his legs."

"I'll see better outside, out of the light and noise. We'll be sure," Fin added, and rose, walked out of the warmth of the pub.

"We should go back," Boyle insisted.

"Meara says not to. Says that Branna needs her evening with just the women, and swears they're safe, tucked up inside. She wouldn't brush it off, Boyle."

He opened himself, did what he could to

block out the voices, the laughter around him.

"He's not close." He looked to Fin for verification when Fin came back.

"He's that pissed, and still on the weak side," Fin said. "Away from the cottage now, away from here. I should've felt him. If we'd been there . . ."

"Only shadows and fog," Connor put in. "It's all he'd risk yet. But the pub's done for us, isn't it? Back to your house?"

"Easy enough to keep watch from there, whether Branna likes it or not."

"I'm with you. No, I've got this." Boyle dug out some bills, tossed them down. "You never got around to talking to Connor as you wanted."

"About what?" Connor asked.

Fin merely swung on his jacket, and bided his time as half the pub had something to say to Connor before he left. The man drew people like honey drew flies, Fin thought, and knew he himself would go half mad if he had that power.

Outside, they squeezed into Fin's lorry as they'd decided — after considerable discussion — one would do them.

"It's the school I wanted to discuss," Fin began.

"There are no problems I can think of. Is

119

it adding the hawking on horseback, as I've given that considerate thought?"

"We can talk about that as well. I've had partnership papers drawn up."

"Partnership? Is Boyle going into it with you?"

"I've got enough on my plate with the stables, thanks all the same," Boyle said, and tried to find space to stretch out his legs.

"Well, who'd you partner with then? Ah, tell me it's not that idjit O'Lowrey from Sligo. He knows his hawks sure enough, but on every other point he's a git."

"Not O'Lowrey, but another idjit altogether. I'm partnering with you, you git."

"With me? But . . . Well, I run the place, don't I? There's no need for you to make me a partner."

"I'm not having the papers for need but because it's right and it's time. I'd've done it straight off, but you were half inclined to building, as much as you're for the hawks. And running the school might not have suited you, the paperwork of it, the staffing and all the rest of the business. But it does, otherwise you could've just done the hawk walks, and the training. But the whole of it's for you, so well, that's done."

Connor said nothing until Fin stopped in

front of his house. "I don't need papers, Fin."

"You don't, no, nor do I with you. Nor does Boyle or me with him. But the lawyers and the tax man and all of them, they need them. So we'll read them over, sign them, and be done with it. It'd be a favor to me, Connor."

"Bollocks to that. It's no favor to —"

"Would the pair of you let me out of this bloody lorry if you're going to fight about it half the night as I'm stuck between you?"

Fin got out. "We'll pour a couple more pints in him, and he'll be signing the papers and forgetting he ever did."

"There aren't enough pints in all of Mayo for me to forget a bloody thing."

The edge in Connor's voice had Boyle shaking his head, leaving them to it. And had Fin laying his hands on Connor's shoulders.

"*Mo dearthair,* do you think I do this out of some sense of obligation?"

"I don't know why you're doing it."

"Ah, for feck's sake, Connor. The school's more yours than mine, and ever was. It wouldn't *be* but for you, as much as I wanted it. I'm a man of business, am I not?"

"I've heard tell."

"And this is business. It's also the hawks,

121

which are as near and dear to me as you." He lifted his arm, gloveless. In moments Merlin, his hawk, landed like a feather on his wrist.

"You care for him when I'm away."

"Of course."

Fin angled his head so the hawk rubbed against him. "He's part of me, as Roibeard is part of you. I trust you to see to him, and Meara to see to him. When this is done, with Cabhan, I can't stay here, not for a while in any case."

"Fin —"

"I'll have to go, for my own sanity. I'll need to go, and I can't say, not now, if I'll come back. I need you to do this favor, Connor."

Annoyed, Connor gave Fin a hard poke in the chest. "When this is over, you'll stay. And Branna will be with you, as she once was."

"Ending Cabhan won't take away the mark." Fin lifted his arm again, sent Merlin lifting off, spreading his wings in flight. "She can't be mine, not truly, while I bear it. Until I can rid myself of it I can't ask her to be mine. And I can't live, Connor, I swear to you, knowing she's hardly more than a stone's throw away every night and never to be mine. Once I thought I could. Now I know I can't."

"I'll sign your papers if it's what you want. But I'm telling you now, looking eye to eye, when this is done — and it will be done — you'll stay. Mark it, Finbar. Mark what I say. I'll wager you a hundred on it, here and now."

"Done. Now." He slung an arm around Connor's shoulders. "Let's go have a pint and see if we can talk Boyle into making us something to eat as we didn't get that far at the pub."

"I'm for all of that."

She couldn't sleep. Long after the house was quiet, Branna wandered through it, checking doors and windows and charms. He was out there, lurking. She felt him like a shadow over a sunbeam. As she walked back upstairs, she trailed a hand over Kathel's head.

"We should sleep," she told him. "Both of us. There's more work to be done tomorrow."

In the bedroom she built up the fire, for warmth, for the comfort of its light. She could walk through those flames in her mind, she considered, but knew whatever visions came might not bring warmth and comfort.

She'd had enough of the chill for now.

Instead, once Kathel settled, she took out her violin. He watched her as she rosined her bow, thumping his tail as if in time. That alone made her smile as she walked to the windows.

There she could see out, toward the hills, toward the woods, into the sky where the moon floated in and out of clouds, and stars flickered like distant candles.

And he could see in, she thought, see her standing behind the glass, behind the charms. Out of his reach.

And that turned her smile potent.

Look all you want, she thought, for you'll never have what I am.

She set the violin on her shoulder, closed her eyes a moment while the music rose up in her.

And she played, the notes lifting out of her heart, her spirit, her blood, her passions. Slow, lilting, lovely, power sang through the strings, shimmered its defiance against the glass, against the dark.

Framed in the window, the firelight dancing behind her, she played what both lured and repelled him while her hound watched, while her friends slept, while the moon floated.

In his bed, alone in the dark, Fin heard

her song, felt what lifted out of her heart pierce his own.

And ached for her.

6

She took the morning for domestic tasks, tidying and polishing her house to what Connor often called her fearful standards. She considered herself a creature of order and sense, and one happiest when her surroundings echoed not only that order, but her own tastes.

She liked knowing things remained where she wanted them, a practical matter to her mind that saved time. To be at her best, she required color and texture and the pretty things that brightened the heart and appealed to the eye.

Pretty things and order required time and effort, and she enjoyed the housewifely duties, the simple and ordinary routine of them. She appreciated the faint scent of orange peel once the furniture was polished with the solution she made for herself and the tang of grapefruit left behind once she'd scrubbed her bath.

Fluffed pillows offered welcome as a soft, pretty throw arranged just so offered comfort and eye appeal.

Once done she refreshed candles, watered plants, filled her old copper bucket with more peat for the fire.

Meara and Iona had set the kitchen to rights before they'd gone off to the stables, but . . . not quite right enough to suit her.

So while laundry chugged away in the machines, she fussed, making a mental list of what she wanted at the market, a secondary list of potential new products for her shop. Humming while she planned, she finished the last of the housework with mopping the kitchen floor.

And felt him.

Though her heart jumped she made herself turn slowly to where Fin stood in the doorway that led to her shop.

"A cheerful tune for scrubbing up."

"I like scrubbing up."

"A fact that's always been a mystery to me. As is how you manage to look so fetching doing it. Am I wrong? Did we agree to work this morning?"

"You're not wrong, just early." Deliberately she went back to her mopping. "Go put the kettle on in the workshop. I'm nearly done."

She'd had her morning, Branna reminded herself, her time alone to do as she pleased. Now it was time for duty. She'd work with Fin as it needed to be done. She accepted that, and had come to accept him as part of her circle.

Duty, she thought, couldn't always be easy. Reaching a goal as vital as the one sought required sacrifice.

She put away her mop and bucket, put the rag she'd tucked in the waistband of her pants in the laundry. After taking just one more minute to gird herself for the next hours, went into her workshop.

He'd boosted the fire, and the warmth was welcome. It wasn't as odd as it once had been to see him at her workshop stove, making tea.

He'd shed his coat, stood there in black pants and a sweater the color of forest shadows with the dog standing beside him.

"If you're wanting a biscuit we'd best clear it with herself first," he told the dog. "I'm not saying you didn't earn one or a bit of a lie-down by the fire." He stopped what he was doing, grinned down at the dog. "Afraid of her, am I? Well now, insulting me's hardly the way to get yourself a biscuit, is it?"

It disconcerted her, as always, that he could read Kathel as easy as she.

And as she had with him in the kitchen, he sensed her, turned.

"He's hoping for a biscuit."

"So I gather. It's early for that as well," she said with a speaking look to her dog. "But he can have one, of course."

"I know where they are." Fin opened a cupboard as she crossed the room. Taking out the tin, he opened it. Before he could offer it, Kathel rose up, set his paws on Fin's shoulders. He stared into Fin's eyes for a moment, then gently licked Fin's cheek.

"Sure you're welcome," Fin murmured when the dog lowered again, accepted the biscuit.

"He has a brave heart, and a kind one," Branna said. "A fondness and a great tolerance for children. But he loves, truly loves a select few. You're one of them."

"He'd die for you, and knows I would as well."

The truth of it shook her. "That being the case we'd best get to work so none of us dies."

She got out her book.

Fin finished the tea, brought two mugs to the counter where she sat. "If you're thinking of changing the potion we made to undo him, you're wrong."

"He's not undone, is he?"

"It wasn't the potion."

"Then what?"

"If I knew for certain it would be done already. But I know it brought him terror, gave him pain, great pain. He burned, he bled."

"And he got away from us. Don't," she continued before he could speak. "Don't say to me you could have finished him if we'd let you go. It wasn't an option then, and will never be."

"Has it occurred to you that's just how it needs to be done? For me, of his blood, for me, who bears his mark, to finish what your blood, what cursed me, to end him?"

"No, because it isn't."

"So sure, Branna."

"On this I am. It's written, it's passed down, generation by generation. It's Sorcha's children who must end him. Who will. For all those who failed before us, we have something they lacked. And that's you."

She used all her will to keep her mind quiet as she spoke, to keep her words all reason.

"I believe you're essential to this. Having one who came down from him working to end him, working with the three, this is new. Never written of before in any of the books. Our circle's the stronger with you, that's

130

without question."

"So sure of that as well?"

"Without question," she repeated. "I didn't want you in it, but that was my weakness, and a selfishness I'm sorry for. We've made our circle, and if broken . . . I think we'll lose. You gave me your word."

"That may have been a mistake for all, but still I'll keep it."

"We can end him. I know it." As she spoke, she took the crystal from her pocket, turned it in the light. "Connor, Iona, and I, we've all seen the first three. Not in simple dreams, but waking ones. We've connected with them, body and spirit, and that's not been written of before."

He heard the words, the logic in them, but couldn't polish away the edges of frustration and doubt. "You put great store in books, Branna."

"So I do, for words written down have great power. You know it as I do." She laid her hand on the book. "The answers are here, the ones already written, the ones we'll write."

She opened the book, paged through. "Here I wrote you and I dream-traveled to Midor's cave, and saw his death."

"It's not an answer."

"It will lead to one, when we go back."

"Back?" Now his interest kindled. "To the cave?"

"We were taken there. We'd have more, learn more, see more, if we took ourselves. I can find nothing about this man. The name meant nothing to Sorcha's Brannaugh. We need to seek him out."

He wanted to go back, thought of it every day, and yet . . . "We have neither the place nor the time. We'd have no direction, Branna."

"It can be done, it can be worked. With the rest of our circle here to bring us back if needed. Cabhan's sire, Fin, how many answers might he have?"

"The answers of a madman. You saw the madness as well as I."

"You'd go back without me if you could. But it must be both of us."

He couldn't deny it. "There was death in that cave."

"There's death here, without the answers. The potion must be changed — no, not the essence of it, in that you're right. But what we made, we made specific to Samhain. Would you wait until Samhain next to try again?"

"I would not, no."

"I can't see the time, Fin, can you? I can't see when we should try for him again, and without that single answer, we're blind." She pushed up, wandered the room. "I thought the solstice — it made good logic. The light beats back the dark. Then Samhain, when the veil thins."

"We saw them, the first three. The veil thinned, and we saw them with us. But not fully," he added before she could.

"I thought, is it the solstice, but the winter? Or the spring equinox? Is it Lammas or Bealtaine? Or none of those at all."

Temper, the anger for herself in failing, bubbled up as she whirled back to him. "I see us at Sorcha's cabin, fighting. The fog and the dark, Boyle's hands burning, you bleeding. And failing, Fin, because I made the wrong choice."

On a half laugh — just a touch of derision in it, he arched his eyebrows. "So now it's all yours, is it?"

"The time, that choice, *was* mine, both of them. And both of them wrong. All my careful calculations, wrong. So more's needed to be certain this time. This third time."

"Third time's the charm."

Huffing out a breath, she smiled a little. "So it's said. What we need may be there, for the taking, if we go back. So, will you go dreaming with me, Fin?"

To hell and back again, he thought.

"I will, but we'll be sure of the dream spell first. Sure of it, and of the way back. I won't have you lost beyond."

"I won't have either of us lost. We'll be sure first, of the way there, and the way back. It's Cabhan's time, his origins — we agree on that?"

"We do." So Fin sighed. "Which means you'll be after bleeding me again."

"Just a bit." Now she lifted her eyebrows. "All this fuss over a bit of blood from a man who so recently claimed he'd die for me?"

"I'd rather not do it by the drop."

"No," she said when he started to pull off his sweater. "Not from the mark. His origins, Fin. He didn't bear the mark at his beginning."

"The blood from the mark's more his."

She did what she did rarely, stepped to him, laid a hand over the cursed mark. "Not from this. Yours from your hand, mine from mine, so our blood and dreams entwine."

"You've written the spell already?"

"Just pieces of it — and in my head." She smiled at him, forgetting herself enough to leave her hand on his arm. "I do considerable thinking when I clean."

"Come to my house and think your fill, as your brother left the room he uses there a small disaster."

"He's the finest man I know, along with the sloppiest. He just doesn't see the mess he makes. It's a true skill, and one Meara will have to deal with for years to come."

"He says they're thinking the solstice — the summer — for the wedding, and having it in the field behind the cottage here."

"They're both ones for being out of doors as much as possible, so it suits them." She turned away to fetch a bowl and her smallest cauldron.

"They suit each other."

"Oh, sure they do, however much that surprised the pair of them. And with Boyle and Iona before them, we'll have spring and summer weddings, new beginnings, and the gods willing, the rest far behind us."

She got out the herbs she wanted, already dried and sealed, water she'd gathered from rain on the full moon, extract distilled from valerian.

Fin rose, got down a mortar and pestle. "I'll do this," he said, measuring herbs.

For a time they worked in easy silence.

"You never play music in here," he commented.

"It distracts me, but you can bring in the iPod from the kitchen if you're wanting some."

"No, it's fine. You played last night. Late

135

in the night."

Startled, she looked up from her work. "I did. How do you know?"

"I hear you. You often play at night, late in the night. Often sad and lovely songs. Not sad last night, but strong. And lovely all the same."

"It shouldn't carry to you."

His gaze lifted, held hers. "Some bonds you can't break, no matter how you might wish it, no matter how you might try. No matter how far I traveled, there were times I'd hear you play as if you stood beside me."

It tugged and tore at her heart. "You never said."

He merely shrugged. "Your music brought me home more than once. Maybe it was meant to. Bowl or cauldron?" he asked.

"What?"

"The herbs I've crushed. For the bowl or the cauldron?"

"Bowl. What brought you home this last time?"

"I saw Alastar, and knew he was needed. I bargained and bought him, arranged for him to be sent. But it wasn't time for me. Then I saw Aine, and knew she was for Alastar, and . . . more. Her beauty, her spirit, called to me, and I thought, she must come home, but it wasn't time for me. Then

Iona came to Ireland, came to Mayo, walked by Sorcha's clearing through the woods to you. In the rain, she walked in a pink coat, so full of excitement and hope and magicks yet untapped."

Stunned, Branna stopped her work. "You saw her."

"I saw she came home, and came to you, and knew so must I. He would see, and he would know. And he would come, and with the three I might finally end him."

"How did you see Iona — even to her pink coat?" Flummoxed, Branna pushed her hands at her hair, loosened pins she had to fix in again. "She's not your blood. Do you ask yourself how?"

"I ask myself many things, but don't always answer." He shrugged again. "Cabhan knew her for of the three, so it may be through him I saw, and I knew."

"It should remind you, when you doubt, the blood you share makes our circle stronger." She lit the candles, then the fire under the little cauldron. "Slow heat builds to a steady boil. We'll let that simmer while we write the spell."

When Connor came in he kept his silence, as magicks swam through the air. Branna and Fin stood, hands outstretched over the cauldron while smoke rose pale blue.

"Sleep to dream, dream to fly, fly to seek, seek to know." She spoke the words three times, and Fin followed.

"Dream as one, as one to see, see the truth, truth to know."

Stars flickered through the smoke.

"Starlight guide us through the night and safe return us to the light." Branna lifted a hand, and with the other gestured toward a slim, clear bottle.

Liquid rose from the cauldron, blue as the smoke, shining with stars, and in one graceful flow, poured into the bottle. Fin capped it.

"That's done it. We've done it." She let out a breath.

"Another dreaming spell?" Now Connor crossed the room. "When do we go for him?"

"It's not for that, not yet." Branna shoved her hands through her hair again, muttered a curse at herself, and this time just pulled the pins out. "What time is it? Well, bloody hell, where did the day go?"

"Into that." Fin pointed to the bottle. "She nearly ate my head when I was so bold as to suggest we take an hour and have lunch."

"She'll do that when she's working," Connor agreed, giving Fin a bolstering pat on the shoulder. "Still, there's always supper."

He gave Branna a hopeful smile. "Isn't there?"

"Men and their bellies." She took the bottle to a cupboard so it could cure. "I'll put something together as it's best we all talk through what Fin and I worked out today. Get out of my house for a bit."

"I've only just got into the house," Connor objected.

"You're after a hot meal and wanting me to make it, so get out of the house so I can have some space to figure on it."

"I just want a beer before —"

Fin took his arm, grabbed his own coat. "I'll stand you one down the pub as I could use the air and the walk. And the beer."

"Well then, since you put it that way."

When Kathel trotted to the door with them, Branna waved at the three of them. "He could use the walk himself. Don't come back for an hour — and tell the others the same."

Without waiting for an answer, she turned and walked through to her kitchen.

Spotless, she thought, and so beautifully quiet — a lovely thing after hours of work and conjuring. She would've enjoyed a glass of wine by the fire, and that hour without a single thing to do, so she had to remind herself she enjoyed the domestic tasks.

She put her hands on her hips, cleared her head of clutter.

All right then, she could sauté up some chicken breasts in herbs and wine, roast up some red potatoes in olive oil and rosemary, and she had green beans from the garden she'd blanched and frozen — she could do an almondine there. And since she hadn't had time to bake more yeast bread, and the lot of them went through it like ants at a picnic, she'd just do a couple quick loaves of beer bread. And that was good enough for anyone.

She scrubbed potatoes first, cut them into chunks, tossed them in her herbs and oil, added some pepper, some minced garlic and stuck them in the oven. She tossed the bread dough together — taking a swig of beer for the cook, and with plenty of melted butter on top of the loaves, stuck them in with the potatoes.

As the chicken breasts were frozen, she thawed them with a wave of her hand, then covered them with a marinade she'd made and bottled herself.

Satisfied things were well under way, she poured that wine, took the first sip where she stood. Deciding she could use some air, a little walk herself, she got a jacket, wrapped a scarf around her neck, and took her wine outside.

Blustery and cold, she thought, but a change from all the heat she and Fin had generated in the workshop. As the wind blew through her hair, she walked her back garden, picturing where her flowers would bloom, where her rows of vegetables would grow come spring.

She had some roses still, she noted, and the pansies, of course, who'd show their cheerful faces right through the snow or ice if they got it. Some winter cabbage, and the bright orange and yellow blooms of Calendula she prized for its color and its peppery flavor.

She might make soup the next day, add some, and some of the carrots she'd mulched over so they'd handle the colder weather.

Even in winter the gardens pleased her.

She sipped her wine, wandered, even when the shadows deepened, and the fog teased around the edges of her home.

"You're not welcome here." She spoke calmly, and took out the little knife in her pocket, used it to cut some of the Calendula, some hearty snapdragons, a few pansies. She'd make a little arrangement, she thought, of winter bloomers for the table.

"I will be." Cabhan stood, handsome,

smiling, the red stone of the pendant he wore glowing in the dim light. "You'll welcome me eagerly into your home. Into your bed."

"You're still weak from your last *welcome*, and delusional besides." She turned now, deliberately sipped her wine as she studied him. "You can't seduce me."

"You're so much more than the rest of them. We know it, you and I. With me, you'll be more yet. More than anyone ever imagined. I will give you all the pleasure you deny yourself. I can look like him."

Cabhan waved a hand in front of his face. And Fin smiled at her.

And oh, it stabbed her heart as if she'd turned the little knife on herself. "A shell only."

"I can sound like him," he said in Fin's voice. *"Aghra, a chuid den tsaol."*

The knife twisted as he said the words Fin used to say to her. *My love, my share of life.*

"Do you think that weakens me? Tempts me to open to you? You are all I despise. You are why I am no longer his."

"You chose. You cast me away." Suddenly he was Fin at eighteen, so young, so full of grief and rage. "What would you have me do? I never knew. I never deceived you. Don't turn from me. Don't cast me aside."

"You didn't tell me," Branna heard herself say. "I gave myself to you, only you, and you're his blood. You're his."

"I didn't know! How could I? It came on me, Branna, burned into me. It wasn't there before —"

"Before we loved. More than a week ago, and you said nothing, and only tell me now, as I saw for myself. I am of the three." Tears burned the back of her eyes, but she refused to let them thicken her voice. "I am a Dark Witch, daughter of Sorcha. You are of Cabhan, you are of the black and the pain. You're lies, and what you are has broken my heart."

"Weep, witch," he murmured. "Weep out the pain. Give me your tears."

She caught herself standing in front of him, on the edge of her ground, and his face was Cabhan's face. And that face was lit with the dark as the red stone glowed stronger.

Tears, she realized, swam in her eyes. With all her will she pulled them back, held her head high. "I don't weep. You'll have nothing from me but this."

She jabbed out with the garden knife, managed to stab shallowly in his chest as she grabbed for the pendant with her other hand. The ground trembled under her feet;

the chain burned cold. For an instant his eyes burned red as the stone, then the fog swirled, snapped out with teeth, and she held nothing but the little knife with blood on its tip.

She looked down at her hand, at the burn scored across her palm. Closing her hand into a fist she drew up, warmed the icy burn, soothed it, healed it.

Perhaps her hands trembled — there was no shame in it — but she picked up the flowers, the wineglass she'd dropped.

"A waste of wine," she said softly as she walked toward the house.

But not, she thought, a waste of time.

She'd stirred the potatoes, taken the bread from the oven, and had poured a fresh glass of wine before the rest of her circle began wandering in.

"What can I do," Iona asked as she washed her hands, "that won't give anyone heart-burn?"

"You could mince up that garlic there."

"I'm good at mincing, also chopping."

"Mincing will do."

"Are you all right?" Iona said under her breath. "You look a little pale."

"I'm right enough, I promise you. I have something to tell all of you, but I'd as soon wait until I have this all done."

"Okay."

She focused on cooking, on letting the voices flow around her while she worked. She didn't have to ask for help — others set the table, poured wine, arranged food on platters or in bowls.

"Do you have a marketing list?" Meara asked as those bowls and platters made their way around the table. "And if not, if you could make one, I'll be doing the marketing for you — unless you object."

"You're doing my marketing?"

"The lot of us will be taking turns on it, from now on. Well, as long as you're stuck doing most of the cooking. It's gone past cleaning up after being a fair trade-off. So we'll see to the marketing."

"I have a list started, and planned to go to the market tomorrow."

"It'll be my turn for that, if that's all right with you."

"Sure it's fine with me."

"If there's anything you want taken into your shop, I can haul it in for you at the same time."

She started to speak, then looked around the table, narrowed her eyes. "What's all this then, doing the marketing, taking in my stock?"

"You look tired." At Connor's eye-roll and

145

sigh, Boyle scowled. "Why dance around it?"

"Thank you so much for pointing it out to me," Branna snapped back.

"You want the truth or want it fancied up?" Boyle's scowl only deepened. "You look tired, and that's that."

Eyes narrowed still, she ran her hands down her face, did a glamour. Now she all but glowed. "There, all better."

"It's under it where you're tired."

She started to round on Fin, and Connor threw up his hands. "Oh leave off, Branna. You're pale and heavy-eyed, and we're the ones looking at you." He jabbed a finger when she started to rise, sent a little shove across the table to put her back in her chair.

She didn't need the glamour now to bring the flush to her cheeks. "Want to take me on, do you?"

"Just stop it, both of you," Iona ordered. "Just stop. You have every reason to look tired, with all you're doing, and we have every right to take some of the load off. It's just marketing, for God's sake, and cleaning up and *chores.* We're doing it so you can have some time to breathe, damn it. So stop being so snarly about it."

Branna sat back. "Doesn't seem so long ago it was an apology coming out of your mouth every two minutes or less. Now it's orders."

"I've evolved. And I love you. We all love you."

"I don't mind the marketing," Branna said, but calmly now. "Or the chores — very much. But I'm grateful to pass some of it on for the time being as we'll all be busy with more important matters, and Yule's all but on us. We should have light and joy for Yule. We will have."

"Then it's settled," Iona stated. "If anybody wants to say anything else about it, I'm cooking tomorrow." She forked up some chicken, smiled. "I thought that would close the subject."

"Firmly." Branna reached over to squeeze her hand. "And there's another subject entirely needs discussion. Cabhan was here."

"Here?" Connor shoved to his feet. "In the house?"

"Of course not in the house. Be sane. Do you think he could get through the protection I've laid — and you as well? I saw him outside. I went out in the back garden to check on the winter plantings, and to get some air as I'd been working inside all day. He was bold enough to come to the edge of the garden, which is as far as he can step.

147

We spoke."

"After Connor and I went down to the pub." Fin spoke coolly. "And you're just telling us of it now?"

"I wanted to get supper on as there's enough confusion in that with the kitchen full of people. And once we sat, the conversation began on my haggard self."

"I never said haggard," Boyle muttered.

"In any case, I'm telling you now, or would if Connor would stop checking out all the windows and come back to the table."

"And you wonder I don't like leaving you on your own."

She shot arrows at her brother with the look. "Mind yourself or you'll be trying to make such insulting remarks with a tongue tied in knots. I was wandering the garden, with a glass of wine. The light changed, the fog came."

"You didn't call for us."

This time she pointed a warning finger at her brother. "Leave off interrupting. I didn't call, no, because I wanted to know what he had to say, and I wasn't in trouble. He couldn't touch me, and we both knew it. I wouldn't risk my skin, Connor, but more, you — all of you — should know I'd never risk the circle, what we have to do. Not for curiosity, not for pride. For nothing would I risk it."

"Let her finish." Though Meara was tempted to give Connor's leg a kick under the table, she gave it a comforting squeeze instead. "Because we do know it. Just as we knew he'd try for Branna before it was done."

"A poor try, at least this time," Branna continued. "The usual overtures. He'd make me his, give me more power than I could dream of and more bollocks of the same sort. He was still hurting a bit, hiding it, but the red stone was weaker. But he still has power up his sleeve. He changed to Fin."

In the silence, Fin lifted his gaze from his wineglass, and the heat of it clashed with Branna's. "To me?"

"As if his illusion of you would shatter all my defenses. But he had a bit more. He's canny, and he's been watching us for a lifetime. He changed again, back to when you were eighteen. Back to the day . . ."

"We were together. The first time. The only time."

"Not that day, no, but the week after. When I learned of the mark. All you felt and said, what I felt and said, all there as it had been. He had enough to make me feel

149

it, to draw me to the edge of my protection. He fed on that so the stone glowed deeper, as did his arrogance, as he didn't understand I had more than enough to take out my garden knife and give him a good jab with it. As I did I grabbed the chain of the stone, and I saw fear. I saw his fear. Back he went to fog, so I couldn't hold it, couldn't work fast enough to break the chain.

"It's ice. So cold it burns," she murmured, studying her palm. "And holding it, for that instant, I felt the dark of him, the hunger, and most I felt the fear."

Connor snatched her hand.

"I saw to it," she assured him as he scanned for injuries. "You could see the links of the chain scored across my palm."

"But you wouldn't risk yourself."

"I didn't. Connor, he couldn't touch me. And had he been quick enough to lay a hand on me when I grabbed the chain, the advantage would have been mine."

"Certain of that, are you?" Fin rose, came around the table, held out his hand. "Give it to me. I'll know if there's any of him left."

Without a word, Branna put her hand in his, stayed quiet as she felt the heat run under her skin, into her blood.

"And if he'd gotten the knife from you?" Boyle asked. "If he'd used it against you, sliced at your hand or arm when you held the chain?"

"Gotten the knife from me?" She picked up her table knife. And held a white rose. "He gave me an opportunity. I took it, and gave him none." She looked at Fin. "He put nothing in me."

"No." He released her hand, walked back and sat. "Nothing."

"He fears us. I learned this. What we've done, the harm we caused him, gives him fear. He gained some strength from my emotions, I won't deny it, but he bled for it, and he ran."

"He'll come back." Fin kept his eyes on hers as he spoke. "And fear will have him strike more violently at the source of the fear."

"He'll always come back until we end him. And while he may strike more violently, the more he fears, the less he is."

7

He thought to go off hawking. He'd saddle Baru, Fin decided over his morning coffee with dawn barely broken in the eastern sky. Saddle up his horse, whistle up his hawk, and go off. A full morning for himself.

They had the dream potion, and though there was more work, he needed — God he needed some time and distance from Branna. One bleeding morning could hardly matter.

"We'll take it, won't we?" he said to Bugs, who sprawled on the floor joyfully gnawing on a rawhide bone Fin had picked up at the market in a weak moment. "You can go along so I'll have the full complement. Horse, hound, hawk. I'm in the mood for a long, hard gallop."

And if Cabhan was drawn to him, well, it wasn't as if he'd gone out looking. Precisely.

He glanced toward the door at the knock. One of the stablemen, he expected, as they'd come to the back. But he saw Iona through the glass.

"An early start?" he said as he opened the door to her.

"Oh yeah, bright and." Her smile shone bright as Christmas. "I'm picking Nan up at the airport."

"Of course, I'd forgotten she was coming. From now till the New Year, is it?"

"For Christmas — Yule — and staying until the second of January. I wish it was longer."

"You'll be glad to see her. So will we all. And she'll be back, won't she, in the spring for your wedding?"

"That's an absolutely. I couldn't convince her to stay straight through, but that's probably for the best anyway. Considering."

"Out of harm's way."

"Still. And she won't be talked into staying at Branna's while she is here. I'm taking her to her friend Margaret Meeney. Do you know her?"

"She taught me my letters and sums, and will still tell me not to slouch if she spots me in the village. A born teacher was Mrs. Meeney. Do you want coffee?"

"Thanks, but I've had my quota. Oh, there's Bugs. Hey, Bugs."

When she crouched down to give the dog

153

a rub, Fin struggled with mild embarrassment. "He comes wandering in now and again."

"It's nice to have the company. Mrs. Meeney didn't teach me my letters and sums." She looked up at Fin. "I didn't grow up with you like the others. I don't have the same history."

"It doesn't change what we are now."

"I know, and that's a constant miracle to me. This family. You're my family, Fin, but I don't have the history with you or Branna the others do, so maybe I can say what the others can't, or say it in a different way. He used you, what happened between you, to try to get to her. That hurt you as much as her."

She straightened. "It would be easier to walk away, leave this to the three. But you don't. You won't. Part of it's because of your own need to right a wrong — a wrong done to you. Part's for family, for your circle, your friends. And all the rest, all the parts of the rest, that's for Branna."

He leaned back against the counter, slipped his hands into his pockets. "That's a lot of parts."

"There are a lot of parts to you. I didn't grow up with you, didn't watch you and Branna fall in love, or go through the pain of what pulled you apart. But I see who you are now, both of you. And from where I'm standing, she's wrong not to let herself have love, have joy. It makes all the sense in the world, but it's still wrong. And you're wrong, Fin. You're wrong for believing — and deep down you do — she's doing it to punish you. If that were true, Cabhan couldn't have used you to hurt her.

"I should go."

"You've such kindness in you." He pushed off the counter, then cupped her chin, kissed her. "Such light. If you could cook I swear I'd turn Boyle into a mule and steal you away for my own."

"I'm keeping that in reserve. We'll have Christmas, we'll have family. I know you, and Branna, too, would rather move on this dream spell right away. But Connor was right last night. We'll take our family time, have the holiday with color and light and music. Throw that in his face first."

"We were outvoted on it, and I can see it from your side."

"Good." She reached for the door, turned back. "You need to have a party. This fabulous house begs for it. You should have a party for New Year's Eve."

"A party?" The quick switch unbalanced him. "Here?"

"Yes, a party; yes, here. I don't know why I didn't think of it before. Time to sweep out the old, ring in the new. Definitely a New Year's Eve party. I'll text Boyle. We'll help you throw it together."

"I —"

"Gotta go."

She shut the door, and quickly, leaving him frowning after her. "Well, Christ, Bugs, it looks like we're having a party."

He decided to think about it and all that entailed later. He still wanted that ride. He'd get out, give Baru his head, let Merlin soar and hunt. Give little Bugs the time of his young life.

And on the way home, he'd stop by the stables, and stop again by the falconry school, put some time in each. If there was enough of the day left after all of that, he'd check to see if he could be of use in Branna's workshop. Though he assumed she'd be as pleased as he to have a full day apart.

Out in the stables while he saddled his big black, he had a conversation with Sean that ranged from horses, a feed order, to women, to football, and back to horses.

He paused as he led Baru out. "It may be I'm having a party for New Year's Eve."

Sean blinked, pushed back his cap. "At the big house here?"

"Sure that would be the place."

"Hah. A party at the big house — fancy-like?"

"Not altogether fancy." He hadn't thought of it either way — and supposed he should have consulted Iona since it was her doing. "Just scrape the horse shite off your boots."

"Hah," Sean said again. "And would you be having music then?"

Fin blew out a breath. "It seems only right there'd be music. And there'd be food and drink as well before you ask. Nine o'clock seems right." He scooped Bugs off the ground, swung into the saddle.

"A party at the big house," Sean said as Fin kicked Baru straight into a gallop.

When Fin glanced back, he saw his long-time stable hand, hands on hips, studying the house as if he'd never seen it before.

Which said, Fin supposed, it was long past time for a party.

Bugs vibrated excited delight as they thundered off, the horse sent out waves of pleasure at the chance to run, and overhead the hawk called out, high and bright, as it circled.

And long past time for this, he realized.

Though part of him yearned for the woods, the smell of them, the song of the trees in the breeze, he headed for open. So

157

he took to the fields, the gentle rise of hill, let the horse run over the green while the hawk soared the blue.

He pulled out, put on his glove. He and Merlin wouldn't need it, but it was best if someone rambled by. He lifted his arm, lifted his mind. The hawk dived, did a pretty, show-off turn that made Fin laugh, then glided like a feathered god to the glove.

The dog quivered, watched them both.

"We've taken to each other, you see. That's the way of it. So you're brothers now as well. Will you hunt?" he asked Merlin.

In answer the hawk rose up, calling as he circled the field.

"We'll walk a bit." Fin dismounted, set Bugs down.

The dog immediately rolled in the grass, barked for the fun of it.

"He's young yet." Fin patted Baru's neck when the horse gave the hound a pitying glance.

Here's what he'd needed, Fin thought as he walked with the horse. The open, the air. A cold day for certain, but clear and bright for all that.

The hawk went into the stoop, took its prey.

Fin leaned against Baru, gazing out over the green, the brown, the slim columns of smoke rising from chimneys.

And this, he thought, he missed like a limb when he was off wandering. The country of his blood, of his bone, of his heart and spirit. He missed the green, the undulating hills, the gray of the stone, the rich brown of earth turned for planting.

He would leave it again — he would have to when he'd finished what he needed to finish. But he would always come back, pulled to Ireland, pulled to Branna, pulled . . . Iona had said it. Pulled to family.

"They don't want you here."

Fin continued to lean on the horse. He'd felt Cabhan come. Maybe had wanted him to.

"You're mine. They know it. You know it. You feel it."

The mark on his shoulder throbbed.

"Since the mark came on me, you've tried to lure me, draw me. Save your promises and lies, Cabhan. They bore me, and I'm after some air and some open."

"You come here." Cabhan walked across the field on a thin sea of fog, black robes billowing, red stone glowing. "Away from them. You come to me."

"Not to you. Now or ever."

"My son —"

"Not that." Anger he'd managed to tamp down boiled up. "Now or ever."

"But you are." Smiling, Cabhan pulled the robe down his shoulder, exposed the mark. "Blood of my blood."

"How many women did you rape before you planted your seed, a seed that brought you a son?"

"It took only the one destined to bear my child. I gave her pleasure, and took more. I will give Branna to you, if she is what you want. She'll lie with you again, and as often as you choose. Only come to me, join with me, and she can be yours."

"She's not yours to give."

"She will be."

"Not while I breathe." Fin held out a hand, palm forward, brought the power up. "Come to me, Cabhan. Blood to blood, you say. Come to me."

He felt it, that tug-of-war, felt the heat as his power burned. Saw, as Branna had, a flicker of fear. Cabhan took a lurching step forward.

"You do not summon me!"

Cabhan crossed his arms, wrenched them apart. And broke the spell. "They will betray you, shun you. When you lie cold, your blood on the ground, they will not mourn you."

He folded into the fog, lowered, hunched, formed into the wolf. Fin saw his sword in his mind's eye, in its sheath in his workshop. And lifting his hand, held it.

Even as he called the others, called his circle, the wolf lunged.

But not at him, not at the man holding a flaming sword and burning with power. It lunged at the little dog quivering in the high grass.

"No!"

Fin leaped, swung. Then met, sliced only fog, and even that died away with the dog bleeding in the grass, his eyes glazed with shock and pain.

"No, no, no, no." He started to drop to his knees. The hawk called; the horse trumpeted. Both struck out at the wolf that had re-formed behind Fin.

With a howl, it vanished again.

Even as he knelt, Branna was there.

"Oh God." He reached down, but she took his hands, nudged them away.

"Let me. Let me. My strength is healing, and hounds are mine."

"His throat. It tore his throat. Harmless, he's harmless, but it went for him rather than me."

"I can help. I can help. Fin, look at me, look in me. Fin."

"I don't want your comfort!"

"Leave it to her." Connor crouched down beside him, laid a hand firmly on his shoulder. "Let her try."

Already grieving, for he felt the life slipping away, he knelt in helpless rage and guilt.

"Here now, here." Branna crooned it as she laid her hands on the bloodied throat. "Fight with me now. Hear me, and fight to live."

Bugs's eyes rolled up. Fin felt the dog's heart slow.

"He suffers."

"Healing hurts. He has to fight." She whipped her gaze to Fin, all power and fury. "Tell him to fight, for he's yours. I can't heal him if he lets go. Tell him!"

Though it grieved him to ask, Fin held his hands over Branna's. *Fight.*

Such pain. Branna felt it. Her throat burned with it, and her own heart stuttered. She kept her eyes on the eyes of the little hound, poured her power in, and the warmth with it.

The deep first, she thought. Mend and mend what was torn. In the cold field, the wind blowing, sweat beaded on her forehead.

From somewhere, she heard Connor tell

her to stop. It was too much, but she felt the pain, the spark of hope. And the great grief of the man she loved.

Look at me, she told the dog. *Look in me. In me. See in me.*

Bugs whimpered.

"He's coming back, Branna." Connor, still scanning the field, still guarding, laid a hand on Branna's shoulder, gave her what he had.

The open wound narrowed, began to close.

Bugs turned his head, licked weakly at her hand.

"There now," she said gently. "Yes, there you are. Just another moment. Just a bit more. Be brave, little man. Be brave for me another moment."

When Bugs wagged his tail, Fin simply laid his brow against Branna's.

"He'll be all right. He could do with some water, and he'll need to rest. He . . ."

She couldn't help it, couldn't stop herself. She wrapped her arms around Fin, held him.

"He's all right now."

"I owe you —"

"Of course you don't, and I won't have you say it, Fin." She eased back, framed his face with her hands. For a moment they knelt, the dog gamely wagging his tail between them.

"You should take him home now."

"Yes. Home."

"What happened?" Connor asked. "Can you tell us? We told Iona not to come. Christ, she's driving her grandmother from the airport in Galway."

"Not now, Connor." Branna pushed to her feet. "We'll get the details of it later. Take him home, Fin. I have some tonic that would do well. I'll get it for you. But rest is all he really needs."

"Would you come with me?" He hated to ask, to need to ask, but still feared for the little dog. "Look after him for just a bit longer, just a bit to be sure?"

"All right. Of course. Connor, you could ride Baru back, and take the hawks, take Kathel. I'll be home soon."

"Well, I —"

But Branna put her hand in Fin's. She, Fin, and the little dog winked away together.

"Well, as I was saying." Connor ran his fingers through his hair, looked up to where Fin's hawk and his own Roibeard circled. He gave Kathel's head a pat, then swung onto Baru. "I'll just see to the rest."

In his kitchen, the dog snuggled in his arms, Fin tried to sort out what to do next.

"I should bathe this blood off him."

"Not in there," Branna said, all sensibilities shocked when he walked to the kitchen sink. "You can't be washing up a dog in the same place you wash up your dishes. You must have a laundry, a utility sink."

Though he didn't see the difference, Fin changed directions, moved through a door and into the laundry with its bright white walls and burly black machines. Opening a cupboard, he reached for laundry soap.

"Not with that, for pity's sake, Fin. You don't bathe a dog with laundry soap. You're wanting dish soap — the liquid you'd use for hand washing."

He might have pointed out the bloody dish soap was under the bloody kitchen sink where he'd intended to wash the dog in the first place. But she was bustling about, pulling off her coat, notching it on a peg, pushing up her sleeves.

"Give me the dog; get the soap."

Fine then, he thought, just fine. His brain was scattered to bits in any case. He fetched the soap, stepped back in.

"You're doing fine," she murmured to Bugs, who stared up at her with adoration. "Just tired and a little shaky here and there. You'll have a nice warm bath," she continued as she ran water in the sink. "Some tonic, and a good long nap and you'll be right as rain."

"What's right about rain, I've always wondered." He dumped soap in the running water.

"That's enough — enough, Fin. You'll have the poor thing smothered in bubbles."

He set the bottle on the counter. "I've something upstairs — a potion — that should do for him."

"I'll get him started here if you'll get it."

"I'm grateful, Branna."

"I know. Here now, in you go. Isn't that nice?"

"He's fond of the shower."

With the dog sitting in the sea of bubbles looking, to Fin's eye, ridiculous, Branna turned.

"What?"

"Never mind. I'll get the tonic."

"The shower, is it?" she murmured when Fin left, rubbing her hands over the dog. Bugs lapped at the bubbles, at her hand, and brought on a very clear image of Fin, wearing nothing but water, laughing as he held the dog in a glass-walled shower where the jets streamed everywhere and steam puffed.

"Hmmm. He's kept in tune, hasn't he? Still some of the boy in there though,

166

showering with a dog."

It amused her, touched her, which wasn't a problem. It stirred her, which was.

Fin brought back a pretty bottle with a hexagon base filled with deep green liquid. At Branna's crooked finger, he unstopped it, held it out for her to sniff.

"Ah, yes, that's just what he needs. If you have a little biscuit, you'd add three — no, let's have four — drops to it. It'll go down easier that way, and he'll think it a treat."

Without thinking, Fin reached in his pocket, took out a thumb-sized dog biscuit.

"You carry those in your pocket — what, in case you or the dog here get hungry?"

"I didn't know how long we'd be out," he muttered, and added the drops.

"Set it down to soak in. We could use an old towel."

He set off again, came back with a fluffy towel the color of moss.

"Egyptian cotton," Branna observed, and smoothly lifted the dog out, bundled him up before he could shake.

"I don't have an old towel. And it'll wash, won't it?"

"So it will." She rubbed the dog briskly, kissed his nose. "That's better now, isn't it? All clean and smelling like a citrus grove. An Egyptian one. Give him his treat, Fin,

167

for he's a good boy, a good, brave boy."

Bugs turned those adoring, trusting eyes on Fin, then gobbled down the offered treat.

"He could do with some water before . . ." She glanced down, and stared. Truly horrified. "Belleek? You're using Belleek bowls for the dog's food and water."

"They were handy." Flustered, he took the dog, tossed the towel on the counter, then set Bugs down by the water bowl.

The dog drank thirstily, and noisily, for nearly a full minute. Let out a small belch then sat, stared up at Fin.

"He only needs a warm place to sleep for a while," Branna told him.

Fin picked the dog up, snagged a pillow from the sofa in the great room, tossed it down in front of the fire.

Egyptian cotton, Belleek bowls, and now a damask pillow, Branna thought. The stable dog had become a little prince.

"He's tired." Fin stayed crouched down, stroking Bugs. "But he doesn't hurt. His blood's clear. There's no poison in him."

"He'll sleep now, and wake stronger than he was. I had to give him a boost to bring him back. He'd lost so much blood."

"He'll have a scar here." Gently, Fin traced a finger over the thin, jagged line on the dog's throat.

"As Alastar carries one."

Nodding, Fin rose as the dog slept. "I'm in your debt."

"You're not, and insult us both by saying it."

"Not insult, Branna, gratitude. I'll get you some wine."

"Fin, it can't be two in the afternoon."

"Right." He had to scrub his hands over his face, try to find his balance again. "Tea then."

"I wouldn't say no." And it would keep him busy, she thought as he walked back into the kitchen, until he settled a little more.

"He's for the stables. It's been two years, thereabouts, since he wandered in. I wasn't even here. It was Sean cleaned him up, fed him. And Boyle who named him."

"Could be he wandered here for a reason, more reason than a bed of straw and scraps and some kind words. He's in your home now, sleeping on a damask pillow in front of the fire. You took him on Samhain."

"He was handy, like the bowls."

"More than that, Fin."

He shrugged, measured out tea. "He has a strong heart, and I never thought Cabhan would pay him any mind. He's . . ."

"Harmless. Small and harmless and sweet-natured."

"I brought him in one night. He has a way of looking at you, so I brought him in."

Yes, still some of the boy, she thought, and all the kindness born in him. "A dog's good company. The best, to my mind."

"He chases his tail for no good reason but it's there. I haven't any biscuits," he realized after a quick search. "Of the human sort."

"Tea's fine. Just the tea."

Understanding he'd want to be close to the dog, she took a chair in view of the fire, waited until he'd brought the tea, sat with her.

"Tell me what happened."

"I wanted a ride, a good, fast ride. The hills, the open."

"As I wanted to walk in my garden. I understand the need."

"You would. I thought to ride, to do some hawking, and took Bugs along to give him an adventure. Christ Jesus."

"Your horse, your hawk, your hound." She could almost see the guilt raging around him, hoped to smooth it down again. "Why wouldn't you? You're the only one of us who can link to all three."

"I wasn't looking for Cabhan, but in truth, I was more than pleased he found me."

"As I was, walking in my garden. I understand that as well. Did he attack?"

"He started with his blather. I'm his blood, the lot of you will betray me, shun me, and so on. You'd think he'd be as bored with all that as I, but he never stops. Though this time out he promised to give you to me, should I want you, and that was fresh."

Branna angled her head, and her voice was dry as dust. "Oh, did he now?"

"He did. He understands desire well enough. Understands the hungers of lust, but nothing of the heart or spirit. He knows I want you, but he'll never understand why. I turned it on him. Began to draw him to me. It surprised him I could, for a moment, I could, and it threw him off. I called for the three — for we'd promised that — and as he became the wolf I pulled the sword from the cupboard upstairs, enflamed it."

He paused a moment, got his bearings. "I could have held him off, I'm sure of it. I could have engaged him, with Baru and Merlin with me, until you came and we went at him together. But he didn't come at me. He streaked to the side, had Bugs by the throat. All so fast. I went at him, struck at him, but he shifted away. He went for the dog who barely weighs a stone, tore his throat, then vanished away before I could strike a single blow. He never came at me."

171

"But he did. He struck at your heart. Baru, Merlin, yourself? There's a battle. The little dog, a strike at you with no risk to himself. A fecking coward he's always been, will always be."

"He rounded behind me when I went to the dog."

Because, Branna knew, Fin thought of the dog before his own safety. "He knew you would go to the hurt and the helpless. Go to what's yours."

"I would have faced him man to man, witch to witch." Now Fin's eyes fired, molten green, as rage overcame guilt. "I wanted that."

"As we all do, but that's not his way. You may come from him, but you're not of him. He keeps at you, as he can't conceive you'd make the choice not to be."

"You left me because I'm of him."

"I left you because I was shocked and hurt and angry. And when that cleared, because I'm sworn." She closed a hand around her pendant. "I'm sworn by Sorcha and all who came after her, down to me, and Connor and Iona, to use all we are to rid the world of him."

"And all who come from him."

"No. No." Outrage would have come first at any other time, but she still felt his guilt under everything else he felt. "You come from him, but you're one of us. I've come to know that was meant. I've come to believe none who've come before us succeeded because none who came before had you. Had his blood with them. None of them had you, Fin, with your power, your loyalty, your heart."

He heard the words, believed she meant them. And yet. "I'm one of you, but you won't be with me."

"How can I think of that, Fin? How can I think of it when even now I can feel the urgency of what we're sworn to do building again? I can't see beyond that, and when I do, when I let myself think about what might be once this is done, I can't see any of the life we once thought we'd make together. We were so young —"

"Bollocks to that, Branna. What we felt for each other was older than time. We weren't the young and foolish playing at love."

"How much easier would it have been if we had been? How much easier now? If we only played at it, Fin, we wouldn't be bound to think of tomorrows. What future could we have? What life, you and I?"

He stared into the fire, knowing again she spoke the truth.

And yet.

"None, I know it, and still that feels like more than either of us have without the other. You're the rest of me, Branna, and I'm tired enough right now to stop pretending you're not."

"You think I don't mourn what might have been?" Hurt radiated through her, into the words. "That I don't wish for it?"

"I have thought that. I've survived thinking that."

"Then you've been wrong, and it may be I'm too tired as well to pretend. If it was only my heart, it would be yours."

She took an unsteady breath as he turned his gaze from the fire to her face.

"It can't be anyone else's. It's already lost. But it isn't only that, and I can't act on *might be.* When my father gave me this?" She held up the pendant. "I had a choice. He told me I had a choice, to take it or not. But if I took it, the choice was done. I would be one of the three, and sworn to try, above all, to end what Sorcha began. I won't betray you, Fin, but neither will I betray my blood. I can't think of wants and wishes, I can't reach for *might be*s. My purpose was set before I was born."

"I know that as well." There were times the knowing it emptied him out. "Your purpose takes your head, your power, your spirit, but you can't separate your heart from the rest."

"It's the only way I can do what needs to be done."

"It's a wonder to me you believe all who've come before you would want you unhappy."

"I don't, of course, I don't. It's that I believe all who've come before need me to do what must be done, what each of us have sworn. I . . ." She hesitated, not at all sure she knew how to say what was in her. "I don't know, Fin, I don't, if I know how to do what I must and be with you. But I can swear it's not wanting to hurt or punish you. It may have been long ago when I was so young and so hurt and frightened. But it's not that, not at all."

He sat silent for a time, then looked back at her. "Tell me this. This one thing. Do you love me?"

She could lie. He would know it for a lie, but the lie would serve. And a lie was cowardly.

"I've loved no one as I loved you. But —"

"It's enough. It's enough to hear you say what you haven't said to me in more than a dozen years. Be grateful I owe you a debt." There was fire behind his eyes, burning hot.

"I owe you for what lies sleeping there, else I'd find a way to get you into my bed, and put an end to this torment."

"Seduction? Persuasion?" She tossed back her hair, rose. "I go to no man's bed unless and until it's my clear choice."

"Of course, and one made only with your head. For such a clever woman you can be amazingly thick."

"Now that you're back to insulting me, I'll be on my way. I've work I'm neglecting."

"I'll drive you. I'll drive you," he said even as she prepared to blast him. "There's no point giving Cabhan another target today should he still be around. And I'll stay and work with you, as agreed. The purpose, Branna, is mine as well, however different our thoughts on the life we live around that purpose."

She might still have blasted him — she could work up a head of steam quickly and keep it pumping. But she caught the quick and concerned glance he sent the dog.

Bugger it.

"That's fine then, as there's plenty of work. Bring the dog. He'll sleep through the ride, then Kathel can look after him."

"I'd feel better about it. Oh, and there's another thing. Iona tells me I'm having a party here for New Year's Eve. So there's that."

"A party?"

"Why does everyone say it back to me as if I've used a foreign tongue?"

"That may be because I don't recall you ever having a party."

"There's a first time," he muttered, and got the dog.

8

She blamed the dog. He'd softened her up, and Fin, with his fancy towels and bowls and utter love for a stable dog, had marched right through her defenses.

She'd said more than she'd meant to, and more than she'd admitted to herself. Words had as much power as deeds to her mind, and now she'd given them to him when it might have been more rational, more practical to keep them to herself.

But that was done, and she knew well how to shore up her defenses. Where Finbar Burke was concerned she'd been doing so for more than a decade.

And in truth, there was too much to do, too much going on around her, to fret about it.

They'd had a lovely, quiet Yule, made only more special by Iona's grandmother joining them. As they observed the solstice and the longest night, she could begin looking toward spring.

But Christmas came first.

It was a holiday she particularly enjoyed — all the fussiness of it. She liked the shopping, the wrapping, the decorating, the baking. And this year in particular, all the work of it gave her a short respite from what she'd termed to Fin her *purpose*.

She'd hoped they'd host a big *céili* during the season, but it seemed too mixed with risks with Cabhan lurking. Next year for certain, she promised herself. Next year, she'd have her parents and other cousins, neighbors and friends and the rest.

But this year, it would be her circle, and Iona's Nan, and that was a fine thing, and a happy one.

With her breads and biscuits baked, along with mince pie she'd serve with brandy butter, she checked the goose roasting in the oven.

"Your kitchen smells of my childhood." Mary Kate, Iona's grandmother, came in. Her face, still flushed from cold, beamed as she crossed the room to kiss Branna's cheek. "Iona's slipping some gifts under the tree, and likely shaking a few as well. I thought I'd see what I could do to help."

"It's good to see you, and I'm more than

grateful to have a pair of skilled hands in here."

Trim and stylish in a bright red sweater, Mary Kate walked over to sniff at pots. "I'm told you've taught Iona to cook a thing or two, which was more than I could do."

"She's willing, and getting better at the able. We'll have some wine first, before we get down to it. It's Christmas, after all. Did you get by to see the new house?"

"I did. Oh, it's going to be fine, isn't it? And finished, they tell me, by the wedding — or near enough. It's a light in my heart to see her so happy."

She took the wine Branna offered. "I wanted a moment alone with you, Branna, to tell you what it means to me you and Connor gave her a home, a family."

"She's family, and a good friend as well."

"She's such a good heart. It was hard for me to send her here. Not to Ireland, not to you." Mary Kate glanced toward the front of the house. "But to what it would all mean. To send her, knowing what it could mean, and what I know it does. I thought to write to you, to tell you she was coming, and then I thought no, for that would be in the way of asking you, an obligation, to take her in, to help her hone her gifts. And it should be a choice."

Once more Branna thought of Fin. "Do we have one?"

"I believe we do. I chose to give her the amulet, though it grieved me to do it. Once done it can't be taken back. But it was hers to wear, hers to bear. I knew the first time I held her. I held you and Connor when you were only babes. And knew, as your father knew, and your aunt. And now the three of you are grown, and the time's here, as it wasn't with me and your father, your aunt."

She walked to the window, looked out. "I feel him. He won't bother with me — Iona frets over that, but he won't bother with me. I'm nothing to him now. But I've power enough to help if help's needed."

"We may, when the day comes."

"But that isn't today." Mary Kate turned again, smiled again. "So today I'll help in the kitchen." She took a long sip of wine. *"Nollaig Shona Duit."*

"We'll see it is." Branna tapped her glass to Mary Kate's. "A very happy Christmas."

It took a little magick to expand the table to fit seven people and all the food, but she'd wanted a feast — and no more talk of Cabhan.

"We won't be eating like this tomorrow at my sister's," Meara announced as she sampled Branna's stuffing. "Between Maureen and my mother, we may be in a runoff for the worst cook in Ireland."

"So we'll fill up tonight, eat careful there, and be back here for leftovers." Connor stabbed a bite of goose.

"It's my first major holiday with Boyle's family." Happiness rolled off Iona as she looked around the table. "I'm taking bread pudding — and I won't be in the runoff, as Nan walked me through it. We're going to pick a holiday, Boyle, for us to host. Make a tradition. How're things going on New Year's, Fin?"

"They're coming."

"I could make bread pudding."

He smiled, adoring her. "I'm having it catered."

"Catered?"

He flicked a glance at Branna's instant shock. "Catered," he said firmly. "I look at a menu, say, this, and that, and some of these, hand over the money, and it's done."

"You'll enjoy the party more without having to fuss," Mary Kate said lightly.

"It's for certain everyone will, as they'd enjoy it less if I'd tried my hand at making the food."

"God's truth," Boyle said, with feeling. "He's hired Tea and Biscuits for the music."

"You hired a band?"

This time Fin shrugged at Branna. "People want music, and they're a good band. If guests want to pick up a fiddle or pipe or break out in song, that's fine as well."

"It'll be good *craic,*" Connor decreed.

"How many are coming?" Branna wondered.

"I don't know, precisely. I just set the word out."

"You could have half the county there!"

"I didn't set word that far out, but if that's the case, the caterer will be busy."

"Patrick and I used to have parties that way," Mary Kate remembered. "Oh, we couldn't afford a caterer in those days, but we'd just set the word out with friends and neighbors. It's friendly. A good *céili.*"

"Branna's not happy with the idea altogether," Connor put in. "She'd rather we didn't have any sort of party until we've done with Cabhan."

"We won't bring him to the table tonight," Branna said in a tone that brooked no argument. "Did I hear Kyra got a ring for Christmas, Connor?"

"You did, and you've ears to the ground, as she only got it last night, I'm told. She's flashing what there is of it everywhere." Thinking of their office manager, he wagged his fork at Fin. "Be sure you get into the school and make over it like it was the Hope Diamond. She gets her nose out of joint easy."

"I'll be sure to do that. My ear to the ground tells me that Riley — you remember Riley, Boyle, as his face ran into your fist some months back."

"He earned it."

"He did, and it seems he earned the same again from one Tim Waterly, who owns a horse farm in Sligo. I've had some dealings with Tim, and we've dealt together well. You'd think him a mild-mannered sort of man, but in this case, Riley's face ran into Tim's fist during a lively discussion on if trying to pass off moldy hay was good business practice."

"He's a fucker is Riley, right enough. I'm begging your pardon, Nan."

"No need, for a man who'd try to sell moldy hay, or worse, mistreat a horse as he did your sweet mare Darling, is a fucker indeed. Would you pass me those potatoes, Meara? I think I've room for another bite of them."

They ate their way through the feast, and some groaned their way through the cleanup, but somehow managed pie or trifle or some of both. There was Fin's champagne, and gifts exchanged. Delighted hugs, and a pause as carolers wandered by.

And no sign of Cabhan, Branna thought as she checked out the windows yet again.

When she slipped out to the kitchen to check from there, Fin followed her.

"If you don't want Cabhan brought up, stop looking for him."

"I'm after another bottle of champagne."

"You're after worrying yourself to distraction. He's burrowed in, Branna. I've my own way of looking."

He got out the bottle himself, set it on the counter.

"I just want tonight to be . . . unspoiled."

"And it is. I've something for you."

He turned his hand, empty, turned it again, and held out a box wrapped in gold paper and topped with an elaborate silver bow.

"We've exchanged our gifts."

"And one more yet. Open it, and I'll open this." He turned to the champagne.

Thrown off yet again, she unwrapped the box, opened it as Fin drew the cork with a muffled *pop.*

She knew the bottle was old — and beautiful. Its facets streamed with light, shimmering with it so it seemed to glow in her hand. It had held power once, she thought, long ago. Then traced a finger over the glass stopper. A dragon's head.

"It's stunning. It's old and stunning and still hums with power."

"I found it in a fussy antiques shop in New Orleans, though it didn't come from there. It had passed from hand to hand long before it came to that fussy shop where they had no idea what it was. I knew it for yours as soon as I picked it up. I've had it a few years now as I wasn't sure how to give it so you'd accept it."

She stared down at the bottle. "You think I'm hard."

"I think nothing of the sort. I think you're strong, and that makes it hard for both of us. Still, I couldn't leave it in that shop where they didn't know what they had, and not when I knew it for yours."

"And you know when I look at it, I'll think of you."

"Well, there is that advantage to it. All the same, it's for you."

"I'll keep it in my room, and despite my better sense I'll think of you when I look at it." She couldn't risk her lips on his, but brushed hers to his cheek, and for a moment rested her cheek to his as she'd once done so often, so easily. "Thank you. I — Oh, she had it made very particularly. I have

186

a glimmer here," she murmured, staring at the bottle. "The dragon was hers, I think. And she had this made, just so, to hold . . . to hold tears. A witch's tears — so precious and powerful when shed for joy, when shed in sorrow."

"Which did this hold?"

"I can't see it, but I'll think joy, as it's Christmas, and a beautiful gift. It should hold joy." She set it carefully on the counter. "We should have champagne, and we should have music. And I won't check the windows any more tonight."

That night, late, she put the bottle on her dresser, and, sliding into bed, watched it catch all the golds of the fire.

And thought of him. And thinking of him, laid a charm under her pillow to block dreams. Her heart was too full to risk dreams.

Things needed doing, Branna thought as she spent the day — happily alone — in her workshop. She'd enjoyed every minute of Yule, of Christmas. Gathering with her circle, preparing the food, making music together. She'd loved the trip to Kerry on Christmas Day, didn't feel the least guilty she'd magickly flown to see her parents, to spend time with them and other family. And had felt warmer yet, as Connor did the same, with Meara.

It had done her spirit good to see her parents so happy with this new phase of their lives. Boosted her confidence to recognize their complete faith in her, in Connor.

But now it was back to practical matters again. To the work that earned her living. To the work that was her destiny, that was life or death.

She replenished some of her most popular lotions and creams, worked on the pretty travel candles that all but flew off her shop's shelves.

Then she gave herself the pleasure of experimenting with new scents, new colors, new textures. She could focus her mind on her senses, how did this look, what mood did this scent evoke, how did this feel on the skin?

She glanced up when the door opened, found herself happy to see Meara come in.

"Well now, this is perfectly timed. Take off your gloves, would you, and try this new cream."

"It's an ugly day out there, all cold, blowing rain." She pulled off her cap, unwound her scarf — tossed her thick brown braid behind her back. "And in here it's warm and smells like heaven. A fine change from the damp and the horse shite."

She hung up her coat, walked over to Branna, held out bare hands. "Oh, that's lovely." She rubbed in the cream, sniffed at her hands. "Just lovely and cool, and it smells like . . . air. Just fresh air, like you'd find on the top of a mountain. I like the color of it in the bowl, too. Pale, pale blue. Like blue ice."

"A perfect name for it. Blue Ice, it is. It's made for working hands and feet. I thought to do it in a sturdy sort of jar. The sort men wouldn't fuss about having for themselves. I'm thinking of doing a line of it. A scrub as well, a gel for the shower, cake and liquid soap. Again with packaging women will like, but men won't feel insults their testicles."

"I don't know how you think of all of it."

"If I didn't, I might have spent the day in the cold rain and horse shite with you." She walked over to put on the kettle. "And I feel as we come to the end of the year, it's time to think of new. Just yesterday my mother asked if I couldn't create some products exclusive for their little B and B. Some they could use as amenities for the guests — then sell in full size. And after year's end, I'm going to see what I can do about that."

"It was lovely seeing your mother yesterday, and your father as well, and the rest. Connor sprang it on me all at once. Why don't we fly down and see my ma and da for a bit before we're off to Galway? I'm saying how I'd love to see them, and shouldn't we ring them up first, but he just takes my hand, and *pop* we're there." She laid a hand on her belly. "I don't think I'll ever get used to that mode of traveling."

"It meant a lot to them, and to me, to have you both there for a few hours."

"Christmas means family, and if we're lucky, friends as well."

"And yours? Your family?"

"Ah, Branna, my mother's thriving at Maureen's. She's happier than I've seen her in years. Roses in her cheeks, a sparkle in her eye. She showed me her bedroom, and I have to give Maureen full marks there, as it's as fussy and pretty as Ma would want."

Meara sighed, but it was a sound of contentment. "Having us all in one place meant the world to her, that I could see. And didn't Maureen take me off to a corner to tell me how good it is for Ma to be there — I even let her go on about it, as if it had been her notion all along."

"It's a weight off you."

"A heavier one than I knew. And she's so pleased I won't be having sex with Connor much longer outside Holy Matrimony." Laughing, Meara sat by the fire. "She's already talking more grandchildren."

"And you?" Branna brought over a tray with steaming tea and sugar biscuits.

"I want them, of course, but likely not as quickly as will suit her. A bridge to cross at a later time." She sipped at her tea. "I'm glad you said I'd timed it well, coming in on you. I wanted to talk to you. Just you and me."

"Is there a problem?"

"That's what I want to ask you. I don't remember a time we weren't friends as it all started when we were still in nappies."

Branna took a bite of a sugar biscuit, grinned. "And may be in nappies again before we're done."

Meara snorted out a laugh. "That's a thought. As we're forever, you and I, we can say things maybe others can't. So I want to say this to you. Could it be good for you, Branna, this dream linking you're about to do with Fin?"

"We all agreed —"

"No, no, I'm not asking as part of the circle. I'm asking only as your friend, your sister. Nappie to nappie, we'll say."

"Ah, Meara."

"I'm thinking only of you now, as it's only

you and me here. It's intimate, this dreaming together. I know and understand that well. It's a lot to ask of yourself, Branna, of your heart, your feelings."

"Dealing with Cabhan comes ahead of all that."

"Not for me. Not between me and you. I know you'll do it regardless, but I want to know how you feel about it all — friend to friend, and woman to woman besides. How you feel, and what I can do to help you."

"How I feel?" Branna loosed a long breath. "I feel it must be done, that it's the best way we have. And I know there'll be hurt, for it is intimate as you say. I know Fin and I must work together for the good of all, and I've accepted that."

"But?"

She sighed, knowing she could tell Meara whatever she held in her heart. "Since he came back months ago, since he's stayed all these months, and I've seen him fight and bleed with us, it's harder to hold back what I feel for him, and always have felt. It's harder to set aside what I know he feels for me, and always has felt. What we do next will make it harder still, on both of us. And I can only be grateful knowing you're there, you understand."

"Couldn't Connor go with him, or Boyle,

or any of us?"

"If it was meant to be Connor or Boyle or any of us, it wouldn't have been me pulled into the dream that took us to Midor's cave. I can deal with it, Meara, as he can, though I know it's no easier for him than for me."

"He loves you, Branna, as deep as any man can love. I know it hurts you for me to say it."

"No, you don't hurt me." Branna rubbed a hand on Meara's thigh. "I know he loves me, or some part of him does. Some part always will. Love's powerful, and it's vital, but it's not all."

"Do you blame him still for his lineage?"

"It was easier when I did, when I was so young, so shattered, I could. But not blaming him doesn't change the facts of it all. He's Cabhan's blood. He bears the mark, and that mark came on him, manifested after we'd been together. If there's any of that lingering in me that blames him, well, it blames myself as well."

"I wish you wouldn't," Meara replied. "I wish you wouldn't take on blame, either of you."

"My blood, his blood. He bears the mark as much because of Sorcha as Cabhan, doesn't he? I think now that we're older and know more than we did, we both understand

193

we're not meant to be together."

"If we defeat Cabhan, would you still feel that way? Still believe you couldn't be with him, and happy?"

"How can I say? How can I know? It's fate that drew us together, and fate pulled us apart. Fate decides these things."

"I don't believe that for a minute," Meara said, with heat. "We decide our own fate, by our choices, our actions."

Branna smiled, sat back. "You've a point there. Of course we're not merely puppets. But fate deals the hand, to my way of thinking. How we play the cards matters, but we only have the ones we're dealt. What would I do if fate hadn't dealt me you? I wouldn't have a friend who'd know to come give me her shoulder."

"It's always here for you."

"I know it. I'm built to stand on my own, but God, it's good to lean now and then. I can wish I didn't love him. I can wish I could look back at the girl I'd been and say, well now, she had her fling and her disappointment, her bit of heartbreak. Now she's moved on. But whatever cards I hold, he's one of them. And ever will be."

"We could take more time, try to find another way."

"We've waited too long already. We deserved to take the time for family and friends, but it's time to turn back to duty. I'm prepared for it, I promise you."

"Would you want me to stay after it's done? I mean after all of it, for me to stay. Me and Iona?"

"We'll see how it all goes. But it's a comfort to me to know, should I be needing you, you and Iona would be here. Before we worry if I'll be needing comfort, we go back, Fin and I, and find what this Midor is to Cabhan and Cabhan to him. And if the fates deal the cards, we learn how and when to stop him."

She tipped her head to Meara's shoulder. "I know Fin to be a good man, and that steadies me. I once tried to believe he wasn't, because it made it simpler, but that was wrong and foolish. At the end of it all, if I can know I've loved a good man, I can be satisfied with that."

9

She'd prepared for it, emotionally, mentally. Branna told herself the spell, the dream-walk, was not only a necessary step, but could and should go forward without personal issues.

She and Fin had reached a place, hadn't they, over the past months where they could work together, talk together without anger or heartache?

They were adults now, far from the starry-eyed children they'd been. She had a duty to her bloodline. And Fin, to his credit, had unstinting loyalty to their circle.

It would be enough.

And still as they gathered together in her workshop, long after dark settled, she had to hold back trepidation.

"Are you sure about this?" Connor brushed a hand down her back, earned a quick look and a mental push.

Stay out of my head.

He left his hand warm on the small of her back. "There's still time to find another way."

"I'm completely sure, and this is the best way. Fin?"

"Agreed."

"Cousin Mary Kate, are you certain you don't want to join the circle?"

"You should go as you've been, and know I'll be here to help should you need it."

"Nan's our backup." Iona gave her grand-mother's hand a squeeze, then stepped forward.

They cast the circle, for ritual and respect, for protection and unity. Together Branna and Fin stepped inside it. He wore his sword on his belt, she a ritual knife.

This time, this deliberate time, they wouldn't go unarmed.

"From this cup we drink this brew so together in dreams we ride." Branna sipped the potion, handed the cup to Fin.

"With this drink we travel through another time and place side by side." Fin drank, handed off the cup to Connor.

"Within our circle, hand in hand, we travel over sky and land." They spoke together, eyes locked, as Branna felt the power rising up.

"Into dreams, willingly, there to seek,

there to see Cabhan's origin of destiny. Full faith, full trust in thee and me, as we will, so mote it be."

Fin held out his hand; Branna put hers in it.

In a flash of light, in a burst of bright power, they flew.

Through the wind and the whirling, fast, so fast it whisked the breath from her lungs. She had a moment to think they'd made the potion too strong, then she stood, swaying a little, in the starry dark. Her hand still gripped in Fin's.

"A bit too much essence of whirlwind."

"Do you think so?"

She shot him a smirking glance. His hair looked as wild as hers felt. Though his sharp-featured face seemed grim, satisfaction mixed with it.

She felt about the same herself.

"There's no point in sarcasm, as you had as much to do with the formula as I." Branna shook her hair out of her eyes. "And it got us here, for that's the cave."

In the cold, starry dark, the mouth of the cave pulsed with red light. She heard a low hum, like a distant storm at sea from within. But without, nothing moved, nothing stirred.

"He's in there," Fin told her. "I can feel it."

"He's not alone. I can feel that. Something wicked, that brings more than a pricking of thumbs."

"I should go in alone, assess things."

"Don't insult me, Finbar. Side by side or not at all."

To settle it, she started forward. Fin kept a firm grip on her hand, laid the other on the hilt of his sword. "If it turns on us, we break the spell. Without hesitation, Branna. We don't end here."

She might have swayed toward him, such were the needs the dream spell stirred. But she steadied herself, stood her ground. "I've no intention of ending here. We've work to do in our own time and place."

They stepped into the mouth of the cave, the pulsing light. The hum grew louder, deeper. Not like a storm at sea, Branna realized. But like something large, something alive, waiting at rest.

The cave widened, opened into tunnels formed with walls damp enough to drip so the steady *plop* of water on stone became a kind of backbeat to the hum. Fin bore left, and as Branna's instincts said the same, they moved quietly into the tunnel.

His hand, she thought, was the only link

to the warm and the real, and knew he felt the same.

"We can't be sure when we are," Branna whispered.

"After the last time we dreamed." He shook his head at her look. "I don't know how I know, but I know. It's after that, but not long after."

Trust, she reminded herself. Faith. They continued on with the humming growing deeper yet. She could all but feel it inside her now, like a pulse, as if she'd swallowed the living dark.

"It pulls him," Fin murmured. "It wants to feed. It pulls me through him, blood to blood." He turned to her, took her firmly by the shoulders. "If it — or he — draws me in, you're to break the spell, get out, get back."

"Would you leave me, or any of us, to this?"

"You, nor any of the others come from him. You'll swear it, Branna, or I'll break it now and end it before it's begun."

"I'll end it, I swear it." But she would drag him back with her. "I'll swear it because they won't draw you in. You won't allow it. And if we stand here arguing over it, we won't have to break the spell, it'll end on its own time without us learning a bloody thing."

Now she took his hand. A spark shot between their palms before they moved forward.

The tunnel narrowed again, and turned into what she recognized as a chamber — a workshop of sorts for dark magicks.

The bodies of bats, wings stretched, were nailed to the stone walls like horrific art. On shelves skeletal bird legs, heads, the internal organs of animals, others she feared were human, bodies of rats, all floated in jars filled with viscous liquid.

A fire burned, and over it a cauldron bubbled and smoked in sickly green.

To the left of it stood a stone altar lit by black tallows, stained by the blood of the goat that lay on it, its throat slit.

Cabhan gathered the stream of blood in a bowl.

He looked younger, she realized. Though his back was to them as he worked, he struck her as younger than the Cabhan she knew.

He stepped back, knelt, lifted the bowl high.

"Here is blood, a sacrifice to your glory. Through me you feed, through you I feed. And so my power grows."

He drank from the bowl.

The hum throbbed like a beating heart.

"It's not enough," Fin murmured. "It's pale and weak."

Alarmed, Branna tightened her grip on his hand. "Stay with me."

"I'm with you, and with him. Goats and sheep and mongrels. If power is a thirst, quench it. If it's hunger, eat it. If it's lust, sate it. Take what you will."

"More," Cabhan said, raising the bowl again. "You promised more. I am your servant, I am your soldier. I am your vessel. You promised more."

"More requires more," Fin said quietly, his eyes eerily green. "Blood from your blood, as before. Take it, spill it, taste it, and you will have more. You will be me, I will be thee. And no end. Life eternal, power great. And the Dark Witch you covet, yours to take. Body and power to our will she must bend."

"When? When will I have more? When will I have Sorcha?"

"Spill it, take it, taste it. Blood from your blood. Into the cup, through your lips. Into the cauldron. Prove you are worthy!"

All warmth had drained from Fin's hand. Branna pressed it between hers, gave him what she could.

"I am worthy." Cabhan set the bowl down, rose to take up a cup. He turned.

For the first time Branna saw the woman in the shadows. An old woman, shackled and shivering in the bitter cold.

He walked to her, taking the cup.

"Have mercy. On me, on yourself. You damn yourself. He lies. He lies to you, lies to all. He has chained you with lies as you have chained me with iron. Release me, Cabhan. Save me, save yourself."

"You are only a woman, now old, your puny powers leaking. And of no value but this."

"I am your mother."

"I am already born," he said, and slit her throat.

Branna cried out in shock and horror, but the sound drowned in the rising roar. Power swam in the air now, black as pitch, heavy as death.

He filled the cup, drank, filled it again. This he carried to the cauldron, poured through the smoke. And the smoke turned red as the blood.

"Now the sire's with it," Fin said, and Cabhan went to a bottle, poured its contents into the cauldron.

"Say the words." Fin's fingers, icy in Branna's, flexed, unflexed. "Say the words, make the binding."

"Blood unto blood I take so the hunger I will slake and the power here we make. From the dam and from the ram mix and smoke and call dark forces to invoke my name, my power, my destiny. Grant to me life eternal and sanctuary through this portal. I am become both god and demon and reign hereby over woman and man. Through my blood and by my power, I will take the Dark Witch unto me. I am Cabhan, mortal no more, and by these words my humanity I abjure."

He reached through the smoke, into the cauldron, and with his bare hand, pulled out the amulet and its bloodred stone.

"In this hour by dark power I am sworn."

He lifted the amulet over his head, laid the glowing stone on his chest.

The wind whirled into a roar as Cabhan, his eyes glowing as red as the stone, lifted his arms high. "And I am born!"

From the altar leaped the wolf, black and fierce. It sprang toward Cabhan, sprang into him with a deafening scream of thunder.

Something howled in triumph, and even the stones trembled.

He turned his head. Through the dark, through the shadows, his eyes, still glowing, met Branna's.

She lifted a hand when his arms shot out toward her, prepared to block whatever magicks he hurled. But Fin spun her around, wrapped around her. Something crashed, something burned.

And he broke the spell.

Too fast, too unsteady. Branna clung to Fin as much to warm him — his body burned so cold — as to keep herself from spinning away.

She heard the voices first — Connor's steady as a rock and calm as a summer lake — guiding her. Then Iona's joining his.

Don't be letting go now, Connor said inside her head. *We've got you. We've got both of you. Nearly home now. Nearly there.*

Then she was, dizzy and weak-limbed, but home in the warmth and the light.

Even as she drew a breath, Fin slipped out of her grip, went down to his knees.

"He's hurt." Branna went down on her own. "Let me see. Let me see you." She took his face, pushed back his hair.

"Just knocked the wind out of me."

"The back of his sweater's smoking," Boyle said, moving in and quickly. "Like Connor's shirt that time."

Before Branna could do so herself, Boyle pulled the sweater up and off. "He's burned. Not so deep as Connor's, but near the whole of his back."

"Get him down, face-first," Branna began.

"I'm not after sprawling down on the floor like a —"

"Have a nap." With that snapped order, Branna laid a hand on his head, put him under. "Face-first," she repeated, and had Connor and Boyle laying him out on the workshop floor.

She passed her hands over the scorching burns covering his back. "Not deep, no, and the poison can't mix with his blood. Just the cold, the heat, the pain. I'll need —"

"This?" Mary Kate offered her a jar of salve. "Healing was my strongest art."

"That's it exactly, thanks. We'll be quick. It hasn't had time to dig into him. Iona, would you take some? I've a bit of a burn on my left arm. It's nothing, but we'll want to keep it nothing. You know what to do."

"Yes." Iona shoved up Branna's sleeve. "It's small, but it looks angry."

But it cooled the moment Iona soothed on the salve. The faint dizziness passed as well as her cousin added her own healing arts. Steadier, she could focus fully on Fin.

"That's better, isn't it? Sure that's better. We could do with a whiskey, if you don't mind. We went a little faster than I'd calculated, and coming back was like tumbling off a building."

"I've already got it," Meara told her. "He looks all clear again."

"We'll just be making sure." With her hands on him, Branna searched for any deeper injury, any pocket of dark. "He'll do." Relief stung the back of her throat, rasped through her voice. "He's fine." She laid her hand on his head again, lingered just a moment. "Wake up, Fin."

His eyes opened, looked straight into hers. "Fuck it," he said as he pushed up to sit.

"I'm sorry for it, as it's rude to give sleep without permission, but I wasn't in the mood to argue."

"She was burned, too," Iona said, knowing it would shift Fin's temper. "On her left arm."

"What? Where?" He'd already grabbed Branna's arm, shoved her sleeve up.

"Iona saw to it. It was barely there at all, as you shoved me behind you, covered over me as if I wasn't capable of blocking an attack."

"You couldn't have, not that one. Not with the new power so full and young, and him flying on it like an addict on too much of a hard drug. He had more in that moment than he has now, or I think ever since. And he hungers for that wild high again."

Connor crouched down. "I'll say this. Thank you for looking after my sister."

"Now I'm ungracious." Branna sighed. "I'm sorry for that as well. I'm still turned around. I do thank you, Fin, for sparing me."

She took the whiskeys from Meara, handed him one.

"He took you for Sorcha. In the dark, near to hallucinating, he felt you — when the power came full, he felt you, but took you for Sorcha. He meant to . . ."

"Drink some of that."

"So I will." Fin tapped his glass to hers, drank. "He meant to disfigure you if he could, so no one would see your beauty, so your husband, he thought, would turn from you. I saw his mind in that moment, and the madness in it."

"A man would have to be mad to slit his own mother's throat, then drink her blood."

"That's purely disgusting," Meara decided. "And still if we're going to hear about it, I'd rather hear all at once, and when we're all sitting down."

"That's the way. Fin, put on your sweater now so you can sit at the table like a civilized man." Mary Kate handed him the sweater. "I'll just look around the kitchen, Branna, see what you might have I can put together, as I'll bet everyone could do with a bit of food."

While Mary Kate put together a wealth of leftovers from the Christmas feast, Branna sat — relieved not to be doing the fixing — so she and Fin could tell the story.

"His own mother." Shaking his head, Boyle picked up one of the pretty sandwiches Mary Kate put together.

"Just a woman, and old, so he said. He had no feelings for her. There was nothing in him for her. There was nothing in him," Fin continued, "but the black."

"You heard what spoke to him."

Frowning, Fin turned to Branna. "You didn't?"

"Only a humming, as we heard when we got there, when we went into the cave. A kind of . . . thrumming."

"I heard it." Absently, Fin rubbed at his shoulder, at the mark. "The promises for more power, for eternal life, for all Cabhan could want. But to gain it, he had to give more. Sacrifice what was human in him. It started with the father."

"Do you know it or think it?" Connor asked him.

"I know it. I could see inside his head, and I could feel the demon trapped in the stone, and its needs, its avarice. Its . . . glee at knowing it would soon be free again."

"Demon?" Meara picked up the wine she'd opted for. "Well now, that's new — and terrifying."

"Old," Fin corrected. "Older than time, and it waited until it found a vessel."

"Cabhan?"

"It's still him," Fin told Boyle. "It's Cabhan right enough, but with the other a part of him, and hungry always for power and for blood."

"The stone's the source, as we thought," Branna continued. "It came from the blood of the father and the mother Cabhan sacrificed for power. Conjuring it, pledging to it, he took in this . . . well, if Fin says demon, it's a demon right enough."

"Why Sorcha?" Iona wondered. "Why was he so obsessed with her?"

"For her beauty, and her power, and . . . the purity, you could say, of her love for her family. He wanted, craved the first two, and wanted to destroy the last."

Fin rubbed his fingers on his temple, attempting to ease the pounding still trapped inside his head.

"She rejected him, time and again," he continued, though the pounding refused to be abated. "Scorned him and his advances. So he . . ."

Surprised when Mary Kate stepped behind him, stroked her hands along temples, along the back of his neck where he hadn't realized more pain lodged, he lost his thread.

And the headache drifted away.

"Thank you."

"You're more than welcome."

She gave him a grandmotherly kiss on the top of the head before she sat again. It flustered him, and showed him just where Iona got her kind and open heart.

"Ah. His lust for her, woman and witch, became obsession. He would turn her, take what she had, and he believes no spell, no magicks can stop him, can touch him. Her power could cause him harm, threaten his existence, and her rejection burned his pride."

"Then there were three," Branna calculated. "And with the three the power, and the threat, increases. We can end him."

"In that moment, in the cave, when he took in the demon, and the black of it, he believed nothing could or ever would. But what's in him knows better. It lies to him, as his mother warned him. It lies."

"We can hurt him, bloody him, burn him to ash, but . . ." Connor shrugged. "Unless we destroy the amulet as well, unless we can destroy the demon joined with him, he'll heal, he'll come back."

"It's good to know." Iona spread some cheese on a cracker. "So how do we destroy the stone, the demon?"

"Blood magick against blood magick," Branna decided. "White against dark. As we have been, but perhaps with a different focus. We have to find the right time, and be sure of it. I'm thinking it must be Sorcha's cabin, as before, to draw what she had into it, but we need to find a way to trap him, to keep him from escaping again so it can be finished. And if we can do that, it would be Fin who needs to destroy the stone, the source."

"I felt the pull, of the demon, of the witch. And the far stronger one when they united. I felt the . . . appeal, the lust for what they'd give me."

"And feeling that, risked yourself to shield me. It's for you to do when the time comes," Branna said briskly. "We've only to figure out the hows and the whens. Mary Kate, are you certain you have to go back to America, for it's a joy to me to have someone else fixing a meal around here."

Understanding the need to shift the conversation, Mary Kate smiled. "I do, I'm afraid, but I'll be back for Iona's wedding, and before it enough to help with some of the doings. And it might be, I'm thinking, I'll stay."

"Stay?" Iona reached around the table, grabbed her hands. "Nan, do you mean you'd stay in Ireland?"

"I'm doing some thinking about it. I stayed in America after your grandda died for your mother, then for you. And I love my house there, my gardens, the views out my window. I have good friends there. But . . . I can have a house here, and gardens, and pretty views out my windows. I have good friends here. And I have you. I have all of you, and more family besides."

"You could live with us. I showed you where we're putting on the room for you to have when you visit. You could just live there, with us." Iona looked at Boyle.

"Of course, and we'd love that."

"You've a sweet heart," Mary Kate said to Iona, "and you've a generous one, Boyle. But if I come to stay, to live, I'll take my own place. Close by, be sure of that. In the village most like, where I can walk to the shops and see my good friends, and visit with you in your fine new home as often as you please."

"I've a cottage and no tenant," Fin commented, and had Mary Kate lifting her eyebrows.

"I've heard as much, but it's some months till April."

"It's easy to rent it to tourists for short spells who want something in the village, something self-catering. You might have a look at it before you go back to America."

"I'll do just that, and should confess I've already had a peek in the windows." She grinned. "It's cozy as a kitten, and so nicely updated."

"I'll see you get a key, and you can go in, look around whenever you like."

"I'll do that. I should go. Margaret will start worrying if I'm much later."

"I'll drive you in." Boyle started to rise.

"I'll do it." Fin stood instead. "I'll give you the key, and drop you round your friend's. I need to be home myself."

"I'll get my coat. No, the lot of you stay where you are," Mary Kate insisted. "I don't mind being escorted from the house by a handsome young man."

When they'd left, Iona got to her feet. "I'm going to draw you a bath."

Branna's eyebrows shot up. "Are you?"

"A bath with some of your own relaxation salts, and Meara's going to make you a cup of tea. I'd like to send Connor and Boyle to

Fin's to do the same for him —"

"I'm not drawing a bath for Fin Burke," Boyle said, definitely.

"But the two of them are going to clean up in here, just the way you like it. So you can get some rest, good rest, and put all this out of your mind for the rest of the night."

"I wouldn't argue with her once she gets the steam up," Boyle advised.

"I wouldn't mind a bath, or the tea."

"That's settled then." Iona walked out.

"And I wouldn't mind you leaving the kitchen as it is if one of you would go check on Fin," Branna said. "This was more of a strain on him than it was on me, and I'll confess, I'm worn through from it."

"I'll give him a few minutes, then go over," Connor told her. "I'll stay if that's what he needs, or stay till I'm sure he's settled. We can still see to the kitchen. Go on up now, don't worry."

"Then I will. Good night."

Meara waited until Branna was out of earshot, Kathel by her side, then walked over to put the kettle on. "You're the one who's worrying, Connor."

"She didn't eat, not a thing." He glanced toward the kitchen doorway, stuck his hands in his pockets as if he couldn't quite figure out what to do with them. "She only pretended to eat. There were shadows under her eyes that weren't there at the start of the spell. Then letting you and Iona fuss over her without putting up a fight? She's worn to the bone, that's what.

"You'll look after her, won't you, Meara? You and Iona will see to her. I won't be long at Fin's unless I'm needed. And we'll stay here tonight."

"Give Fin what he needs, and we'll see to Branna."

"Without making it like you're seeing to her."

She shot the fretting brother a glance. "I've known her near as long as you, Connor. I think I know how to handle Branna O'Dwyer as much as any can. We'll give her a bit of female time, then leave her alone. She'll do best with the quiet and alone."

"True enough. I'll run over to Fin's, and be back as soon as I can."

"If you need to stay, you've only to let us know." She turned her face for a kiss when he came over, smiled at his quick, hard hug.

She finished up Branna's tea while Connor put on his outdoor gear, and turned to Boyle when they were alone. "It looks like you're left with the dirty dishes." Meara gave him a quick pat on the shoulder as she sailed out.

He looked around the empty kitchen, sighed. "Ah, well." And rolled up his sleeves.

Connor walked straight into Fin's as he had since the day the front door went up. Before, come to that, as he'd installed the door himself.

He found Fin with another whiskey in front of the living room fire, the little stable dog Bugs curled up sleeping at his feet.

"I've orders to check in on you," he announced, and thought it was good he had. Fin looked as worn and bruised as Branna.

"I'm fine, as you can see plain enough."

"You're not, as I see plain enough," Connor corrected, and helped himself to a whiskey, then a chair. "Iona's after drawing Branna a bath, and Meara's making her tea. She's letting them, which tells me she needs the fussing. What do you need?"

"And if I ask it, you'll give it?"

"You know I will, though it's a mortifying thought I may be drawing your bath and tucking you up."

Fin didn't smile, only shifted his gaze from whatever he saw in the fire, met Connor's eyes. "It was a hard pull, a bloody brutal pull. For a moment I could feel all it promises. That power beyond what any of us hold. It's black and it's cold, but it's . . . seductive. And all I have to say is, I'll take it."

"You didn't. And you won't."

"I didn't, this time. Or times before, but it's a call to the blood. And to the animal that's inside all of us. So I'll ask you for something, Connor, as you're my friend as near as much a brother to me as you are to Branna."

"I'm both."

"Then you'll swear to me, on your own blood, on your heart where your magick roots, if I turn, if the pull is too much and I fall, you'll stop me by whatever means it takes."

"You'd never —"

"I need you to swear it," Fin interrupted, eyes fierce. "Otherwise I'll need to go, I'll need to leave here, leave her — leave all of you. I won't risk it."

Connor stretched out his legs, crossed his boots at the ankles, stared at them for several moments.

Then slowly, he lifted his gaze to Fin's.

"Listen to yourself. You want his end more than the three, more than the three we come from, but you'd step away, on the chance you've put in your block of a head you could fall when you've stood all this time."

"You weren't in the cave. You didn't feel what I felt."

"I'm here now. I've known you near to all our lives, before the mark came on you and after. I know who you are. And because I do, I'll swear it to you, Fin, if that's what you need. What I have comes from my heart, as you said, and my heart knows you. So you'll have your brood, and I'll say you've earned it. And tomorrow we'll be back to it."

"All right then." Steadier now, Fin sipped his whiskey. "I have earned a brood."

"That you have, and I'll brood with you until I finish my whiskey." Connor sipped and sat awhile in silence. "We both love her," he said.

Fin leaned back, shut his eyes. "That's the fucking truth."

And love, Connor knew well, pulled stronger than any dark promises.

10

Fin considered himself sociable enough. He knew when to stand a round in the pub, was a good guest who could make conversation at dinner. If he had mates over to watch a match or play some snooker, he provided plenty of beer and food and didn't fuss about the mess made.

He hadn't been raised in a barn, after all, so he understood as well as any man the basic expectations and duties when hosting a party.

Iona reeducated him.

In midafternoon on the last day of the year, she came to his door with her sunlight crown of hair tucked into a bright blue cap he remembered her Nan had knit her for Christmas. And loaded down with shopping bags.

"Didn't we just have Christmas?"

"Party supplies." She pushed some bags in his hand, carried the rest with her as she walked back to his kitchen. After dumping them on the center island, she pulled off her coat, scarf, hat, gloves, then her boots — and took all of them into his laundry room.

"We've got candles," she began.

"I have candles. I bought some from Branna not long before Yule."

"Not enough, not nearly." Both firmness and pity lived in Iona's shake of the head. "You need them everywhere."

She dug into a bag, started taking things out. "These are for the living room mantel. You'll get a twelve-hour burn, so you want to light them about a half hour before you expect people to start coming."

"Do I?"

"You do," she said definitely. "They'll set a pretty, celebrational yet elegant atmosphere. These are for the powder room up here, and for the bathroom downstairs, and the main bath upstairs. No one should go into your master suite unless invited, but there's extra so you should put some there, just in case. And these are guest towels — pretty, simple, and disposable."

She laid out a wrapped stack of white napkins embossed with silver champagne flutes.

"So people don't have to dry their hands

221

on the same cloth towel someone else dried their hands on."

Fin let out a quick laugh. "Seriously now?"

"Fin, look at my face." She pointed to it. "Deadly serious. I got some extra candles for your dining room in case you didn't have enough there, and others for the mantel on your lower level. Now, it's essential you make sure there's plenty of TP in the bathrooms. Women hate, loathe, and despise when they're sitting there and there's no TP."

"I can only imagine. Fortunately."

"I plan to do an hourly check on the bathrooms, so it shouldn't be a problem."

"You're a comfort to me, Iona."

She laid her hands on his cheeks. "I got you into this, and I said I'd help. I'm here to help. Now. The caterers will pretty much take over the kitchen, and they'll know what they're doing. I checked on them, and they're supposed to be stellar. Good choice."

"Thanks. I do what I can."

She only smiled. "We'll just want to be sure the servers understand they'll need to cover your lower level with food and drink because you're going to have a lot of people gathering down there to play games, dance, and hang out. You'll have fires going, of course."

"Well, of course."

"I know everyone will have plenty to eat and drink. It's not called The Night of the Big Portion or . . . wait." She closed her eyes a moment. "Or *Oiche ne Coda Moire,* for nothing."

Now he grinned at her. "You handled the Irish brilliantly."

"I've been practicing. We don't have to get into the New Year's Eve tradition of cleaning the house — I read up on Irish traditions — because yours is already spotless. You're as scary as Branna there, so I'm going to put these candles where they belong, and the guest towels, and oh —" She reached into another bag. "I picked up these pretty mints and these candied almonds. The colors are so pretty, and it's a nice thing to have here and there in little bowls. Oh, and Boyle's picking up the rolling rack I borrowed from Nan's friend's daughter."

"A rolling rack?" For reasons he didn't want to explore, he got the immediate image of a portable torture device.

"For hanging coats. You have to do something with people's coats, so we're borrowing the rack. It should work fine in the laundry room. One of us will take people's coats as they come in, hang them up, get them when people want to leave. You can't just toss them on the couch or on a bed."

"I hadn't given it a thought. I'm lucky to have you."

"You are, and it's also good practice. I'm already planning a blowout party next summer when our house is finished and furnished, and we're settled in."

"I'm already looking forward to it."

"We'll have finished Cabhan by then. I believe it. We won't be working every day as we are now on how and when. We'll just be living. I know it's been a hard week, on you and Branna especially."

"It's not meant to be easy."

Carefully, Iona tidied the stacks of guest towels. "Have you seen her today?"

"Not today, no."

"This morning she said she was going to try some calculations on finishing this a year from the day I arrived — the day I first went to the cottage to meet her."

He considered. "There's a thought."

"And she looked as doubtful it's right as you do, but it's something to consider. So we will. But not tonight. Tonight is party time."

"Hmm. What's in this other bag here?"

"Ah, well . . . some people like silly party

hats and noisemakers."

He opened the bag, stared in at colorful paper hats, sparkly tiaras. "I'm going to tell you right out of the gate. Though I adore the very ground you walk on, I won't be wearing one of these."

"Completely optional. I thought we could put them in a couple big baskets for anyone who wants them. Anyway, I'm going to set all this up, then I'm going to work with Branna for an hour or two before I deck myself out in my party clothes. I'll be here an hour early for finishing touches."

She carted out candles, and he looked deeper into the bag full of paper hats. No, he wouldn't be wearing one, but he'd put himself up as her second in command now, help her with her candles and fussing.

Then he'd take an hour himself for some calculations of his own.

Later, when the caterers invaded and he'd answered dozens of questions, made far too many decisions on details he hadn't considered, he closed himself off in his room for a blessed half hour to dress in the quiet. He wondered what his odds were of staying closed in, considered Iona's cheerful determination and calculated them at nil.

Where had he been this time last year? he

wondered. The Italian Alps, near Lake Como. He'd spent three weeks or so there. He'd found it easier to spend holidays away from home, to celebrate them in his own way with strangers.

Now he'd see how he managed not only to be home, but to have those he knew in his home.

Maybe he dawdled a little longer than necessary, then dressed in black jeans and black sweater, started downstairs.

He heard voices, music, laughter. Glanced at his watch to see if he'd completely miscalculated the time. But no, he had forty minutes yet before guests were due.

Candles in red glass holders glowed on his mantel above a crackling fire. His tree shined. A bouncy reel played out of his speakers. The massive candlestand he'd bought in some faraway place stood in a corner, cleverly filled with votives that radiated more light.

Light and music, he thought, his circle's weapon against the dark.

Iona had been right. She'd been perfectly right.

He started back, noted she'd set more candles in his library, still more in the space he'd fashioned into a music room.

She'd come up with flowers as well —

little glass jars of roses tied with silver ribbons.

He found her and Meara, along with some of the catering staff, busy in the dining area.

Another fire, more candles, more roses, silver trays and crystal dishes filled with food, chafing dishes holding more.

And all the sweets displayed on his buffet — the cakes and biscuits and pastries. Offerings of cheeses under a clear dome.

Iona, in a short sheath of dark, deep silver, had her hands on her hips as she took — he had no doubt — eagle-eyed stock. Beside her, Meara had her hair tumbling loose over the shoulders of a gown the color of carnelian that clung to her curves.

"I think I've made a mistake," he said and had both his friends turning to him. "Why have I invited people here tonight when I could have two beautiful women all to myself?"

"That's just the sort of charm that will have all your guests talking about this party for months," Iona told him.

"I was going to say bollocks, but it's charming bollocks," Meara decided. "Your home looks absolutely amazing on top of it all."

"I didn't have much to do with it."

"Everything," Iona corrected. "You just

let me play with fire." Laughing, she walked over, hooked her arm in his. "And Cecile and her team are the best. Honestly, Cecile, the food looks too good to eat."

Cecile, a tall blonde in black pants and a vest over a crisp white shirt, flushed with pleasure. "Thanks for that, but eating it's just what we want everyone to do. We did some stations downstairs as Iona suggested," she told Fin. "And have a bar set up there as well. We'll have servers passing through regularly up here, down there, to be sure all your guests are well seen to."

"It all looks brilliant."

"You haven't seen downstairs." Iona led him to the stairs and down. "I went a little mad with the candles, and got nervous, so I did a protection spell. They can't burn anything or anyone."

"You think of everything."

More candles and greenery, pretty food and flowers. He walked to the bar, to the fridge behind it and took out a bottle of champagne.

"You should have the first drink."

"I'll take it."

He opened the champagne with a muffled *pop,* poured her a flute, then poured one for himself. "It was a happy day when you came into our lives, *deirfiúr bheag.*"

228

"The happiest of my life."

"To happy days then."

She tapped her glass to his. "To happy days, for all of us."

Within the hour it seemed he had half the village in his house. They swarmed or gathered, gawked or settled right in. They filled plates and glasses, sat or stood in his living room or, as Iona had predicted, wandered downstairs where the band he'd hired began their first set.

He found himself happy enough with a beer in his hand to move from conversation to conversation. But of all the faces in his house, there was one he didn't see.

Then as if he wished it, she was there.

He came back upstairs to do his duty with his main-floor guests, and she was there, standing in his kitchen chatting with the caterers.

She'd left her hair down, a black waterfall that teased the waist of a dress of velvet the color of rich red wine. He thought Iona could have found a hundred more candles and still not achieved the light Branna O'Dwyer brought into his home.

He got a glass of champagne, brought it to her. "You'll have a drink."

"I will indeed." She turned to him, eyes smoky, lips as red as her dress. "You throw a fine party, Fin."

"I do, as I follow Iona's orders."

"She's been half mad with excitement and anxiety over tonight, having pushed you into it. And all but bought me out of candles. I see she made good use of them."

"They're everywhere, as she commanded."

"And where is our Iona?"

"She's downstairs. Meara's down there as well, and Boyle and Connor, and Iona's Nan." But he guided her toward the dining area as he spoke. "Will you eat?"

"Sure I will as it looks delicious, but not just yet."

"Do you still have a weakness for these?" He picked up a mini cream puff drenched in powdered sugar.

"A terrible one, which I usually deny. But all right, not tonight." She took it, tried a small bite. "Oh, that's a sinful wonder."

"Have two. *Oiche na Coda Moire.*"

She laughed, shook her head. "I'll come back for the second."

"Then I'll take you down to your circle, and the music."

He offered a hand, waited until she put hers in it. "Will you dance with me, Branna? Put yesterday and tomorrow aside, and dance with me tonight?"

She moved with him toward the music,

the warmth, the glowing light.

"I will."

She nearly hadn't come. She tried to find reasons to stay away, or failing that to simply pay a courtesy visit, then slip out again. But every reason devised rang the same way in her ears.

As cowardice. Or worse, pettiness.

She couldn't be so petty, so cowardly as to snub him because it distressed her to be in his home, to see, to feel the life he'd built himself without her.

Her choice, without him. Her duty, without him.

So she'd come.

She'd spent a great deal of time on her hair, her makeup, the whole of her appearance. If she was to celebrate the end of one year, the beginning of another in his house, in his company, she'd bloody well look amazing doing it.

She found the downstairs of his home, what she thought of as a play area, so very him. Good, rich colors mixed with neutrals, old refurbished furniture mixed with the new. Small pieces obviously bought on his rambles. And plenty of entertainment.

The absurdly big wall TV, the snooker table, the old pinball machine and jukebox along with a gorgeous fireplace of Conne-mara marble topped by a thick, rough plank for a mantel.

The musicians played lively tunes near a mahogany bar he told her he found in Dublin. Though the space was roomy, furniture had been pushed back to make more room yet for dancing.

When he drew her into a dance, it was yesterday with all its innocent joy, with its simplicity and possibilities. But she pushed aside the pang it brought, told herself to let this one night be a time out of time.

She looked up at him laughing. "Now you've done it."

"What's that I've done?"

"Hosted the party of the year and now will be expected to do the same next. And next."

Mildly horrified, he glanced around. "I thought to pass that torch to Iona and Boyle."

"Oh no, they'll have their own. But I'm thinking you own New Year's Eve now. I see your Sean wearing a party hat, over there kicking up the heels of clean and shiny boots, and Connor's Kyra and her boyfriend — fiancé now — with him wearing a shirt that matches the color of her frock and a cardboard king's crown on his head. And there's my Eileen dancing with her husband as if they were but sixteen, and the years, the children with them yet to come. You built a house that can hold most of the village for a party, and now you've done it."

"I never thought of that."

"Sure it's too late now. And there I see Alice giving you the seductive eye, as she's resigned to Connor being lost to her. You should give her a dance."

"I'd rather dance with you."

"And you have. Do your duty, Finbar, give her a twirl. I've people I should talk with."

She stepped back from him, turned away. If she danced with him again, and too often, the people she should talk with would begin talking about them.

"Isn't it great?" Iona grabbed her, did a quick circle. She'd donned a pink tiara that announced 2014 in sparkles. "It's such a good party. I just have to do my hourly bathroom sweep and I'll be back."

"Bathroom sweep?"

"Checking TP and guest towel supplies, and so on."

"I'm putting you in charge of every party I may have."

"You're a natural with parties and gatherings," Iona countered. "Fin's new at it. So am I, but I think I have a knack."

"God help us," Boyle said, and kissed the top of her head.

Branna enjoyed the music, the bits of conversation. After she slipped back upstairs, she enjoyed some of the food, and some time with those who sought more quiet in Fin's living room or the great room.

It gave her time to see more of his house, to feel the flow of it. And the chance to check out the windows, to open herself enough to search for any sense of Cabhan.

"He won't come."

She turned from the tall French doors of his library toward Fin, who stepped through the doorway.

"You're so sure?"

"Maybe there's too much light, too many people, the voices, the thoughts, the sounds, but he won't come here tonight. Maybe he's just burrowed in, waiting for the year to pass, but he won't come tonight. I wish you wouldn't worry."

"Being vigilant isn't the same as worrying."

"You worry. It shows."

Instinctively, she reached up to rub her fingers between her eyebrows where she knew a line could form. And made him smile.

"You're perfectly beautiful. That never

changes. It's in your eyes, the worry."

"If you say he won't come tonight, I'll stop worrying. I like this room especially." She ran her hand over the back of a wide chair in chocolate leather. "It's for the quiet, and a reward."

"A reward?"

"When work's done, it's for settling down in a good chair like this with a book and the fire. With rain pattering down, or the wind blowing, or the moon rising up. A glass of whiskey, a cup of tea — what's your pleasure — and a dog at your feet."

She did a turn, holding out a hand. "All these books to choose from. A good warm color for the walls — you did well there — with all the dark wood to set it off."

She angled her head when he gave her a half smile. "What?"

"I built it with you in mind. You always used to say, when we were building our dream castle, how it had to have a library with a fire and big chairs, with windows the rain could drip down or the sun could creep through. It should have glass doors leading out to a garden so on a bright day you'd step out, and find a spot outside to read."

"I remember." And saw it now. He'd made one of her imaginings come to life.

"And there should be a room for music,"

Fin added. "There would be music through-out the house, but a room just for it where we'd have a piano and all the rest. The children could take their lessons there."

He glanced back. "It's just over there."

"Yes, I know. I saw it. It's lovely."

"There was part of me thought if I built it, if I kept you in mind, you'd come. But you didn't."

So clear now that she let herself see, the house was what they'd dreamed of making together.

"I'm here now."

"You're here now. What does that mean for us?"

God, her heart was too full of him, here in this room he'd conjured out of dreams.

"I tell myself what it can't be. That's so clear, so rational. I can't see what it can or might."

"Can you say what you want?"

"What I want is what can't be, and that's harder than it was, as I've come to believe that's through no fault of yours or my own. It was easier when I could blame you or myself. I could build a wall with the blame, and keep it shored up with the distance when you spent only a few days or few weeks here before you went off again."

"I want you. Everything else comes behind that."

"I know." She let out a breath. "I know. We should go back. You shouldn't be so long away from your guests."

But neither of them moved.

She heard the shouting, the rise of voices, the countdown. Behind her, the mantel clock began to strike.

"It's going onto midnight."

Only seconds, she thought, between what was and what is. And from there what would be. She took a step toward him. Then took another.

Would she have walked by him? she asked herself when he pulled her to him. No. No, not this time. At least this one time.

Instead she linked her arms around his neck, looked into his eyes. And on the stroke of midnight met his lips with hers.

Light snapped between them, an electric jolt that shocked the blood, slammed into the heart. Then shimmered into an endlessly longed-for warmth.

Oh, to feel like this, to finally feel like this again. To finally have her body, her heart, her spirit united in that longing, that warmth, that singular wild joy.

His lips on her lips, his breath with her breath, his heart on her heart. And all the sorrow blown away as if it never was.

He'd thought once what he felt for her was all, was beyond what anyone could feel. But he'd been wrong. This, after all the years without her, was more.

The scent of her filling him, the taste of her undoing him. She gave as she once had, everything in a simple kiss. Sweetness and strength, power and surrender, demand and generosity.

He wanted to hold on to her, hold on to that moment until the end of his days.

But she pulled back, stayed a moment, brushed a hand over his cheek, then stepped back from him.

"It's a new year."

"Stay with me, Branna."

Now she laid a hand on his heart. Before she could speak, Connor and Meara turned into the room.

"We were just —"

"Going," Meara finished Connor's sentence. "Going back right now."

"Right. Sure, we weren't even here."

"It's all right." Branna left her hand on Fin's heart another moment, then let it fall away. "We're coming back now. Fin's been too long away from his own party. We'll go toast the New Year. For luck. For light. For what may be."

"For what should be," Fin said, and walked out ahead of them.

"Go with him," Meara suggested, and moved into Branna. "Are you all right then?"

"I am. But it's God's truth I could do with a drink, and as much as it goes against my nature, a lot of noise and people."

"We'll get all of that."

When she put an arm around Branna's waist, Branna leaned into her a moment. "How could I love him more now than once I did? How could it be so much more in me for him when what was, was everything?"

"Love can fade and die. I've seen it. It can grow and build as well. I think when it's real and meant, it can only grow bigger and stronger."

"It's not meant to be a misery."

"No. It's what we do with it that's the misery or the joy, I think, not the love."

Branna sighed, gave Meara a long look. "When did you get so bloody wise about it?"

"Since I let myself love."

"Let's go toast to that then. To you letting yourself love, to Iona's party skills, to the New bloody Year, to the end of Cabhan. I feel I might want to get a wee bit snackered."

"What kind of friend would I be if I didn't get snackered right along with you? Let's find some champagne."

11

He was more than done with people. At half-two in the morning, far too many of them lingered in his house, cozied up as if they'd stay till spring. He considered just going upstairs, shutting himself in, leaving them to it. He was brutally tired, and more, that moment — that incredible moment with Branna had cross-wired his emotions so he didn't know what he felt.

So it seemed easier all around to shut it all off and feel nothing at all.

She seemed perfectly content to sit, sip champagne, chat with whoever remained. But that was Branna, wasn't it? Strong as steel.

The best thing for him would be a few hours' escape in sleep. They'd be back to Cabhan in the morning — or later in the morning. And the sooner the better. Ending him would fulfill his obligations. Ending

Cabhan would end his own personal torment.

So he'd slip away — no one would miss him by this point.

Then Iona stepped up, as if she'd read his mind, twined her arm with his, took his hand.

"The problem with throwing a really great party is people don't want to leave."

"I do."

She laughed, squeezed his hand. "We're down to the diehards, and we'll start nudging them along. Your circle won't leave you alone with them. Give it about twenty minutes. What you should do is go around, start gathering up the empties since the caterers left a couple hours ago. It's a sign it's time to go."

"If you say."

"I do." To demonstrate, she began picking up bottles and glasses, gave Boyle a telling look that had him doing the same.

In moments a handful of those diehards readied to go with many thanks and wishes for a happy and prosperous New Year. And in the case of a few, such as Sean, heartfelt if somewhat sloppy hugs.

Party magicks, Fin decided, and started on discarded tea and coffee cups.

He carted them up to the kitchen, said

good-bye to another handful. Two birds, he decided, he'd have the party debris dealt with, and move out the stragglers.

Though it took thirty minutes rather than Iona's predicted twenty, he wouldn't complain.

"That's the last of them," Iona announced.

"Thank the gods."

"You gave a lot of people a fun and memorable evening." She tipped onto her toes to kiss his cheek. "And you had one yourself."

"I'm happy to remember it now that it's done. And thank you for all you did."

"Couldn't have had a better time of it." She glanced around the living room, nodded. "And we're not leaving you with much of a mess. Branna, I can ride with you if you want, just leave my car here. I'm not taking Nan to the airport until afternoon tomorrow, so I can come back for it easily."

"Best you ride with Boyle."

"We'll make a caravan of it," Connor said as he shrugged into his coat. "A short drive for certain, but it's still the dead of night. Branna can follow you and Boyle out, and Meara and I will come up behind."

"I'm not driving home tonight at all. I'm staying here."

Branna looked at Fin as she spoke. He wasn't sure how he kept his feet when she'd rocked him back so stunningly on his heels.

"Well then!" Brightly, Meara smiled, and jammed her cap on her head. "We'll be off. Good night, and happy New Year."

"But," Connor began as she all but dragged him to the door with Iona pushing Boyle behind him.

"Would you let me get my coat on?" Boyle complained even as Iona firmly closed the door behind the four of them.

Fin stood exactly where he was. Only one thought managed to eke through the logjam in his mind. "Why?"

"I decided for this time, this place, I wouldn't think about yesterday or about tomorrow. It may be we'll both come to regret it, but I want to be with you. I always have, likely always will, but this is only tonight. There can't be any promises or building dream castles this time around, and we both know that. But there's need, and there's finally trust again."

"You're content with that?"

"I find I am, and God knows I've turned it all over a hundred different ways, but I find I am content with that. We're both entitled to make this choice. You asked me to stay with you. I'm saying I will."

244

So much of the turmoil inside him settled into calm even as all the resignation he'd carried for years dropped away to make room for a tangle of joy and anticipation.

"Maybe I changed my mind on it."

She laughed, and he saw the light sparkle in her smoky eyes. "If that's the case, I wager I can change it back again quick enough."

"It seems the least I can do is give you that chance." He held out a hand. "I won't kiss you here or we'd end up on the floor. Come to bed, Branna."

She put her hand in his. "We've never been in a bed together, have we? I'm curious about yours. I resisted going upstairs and poking around during the party. It took heroic willpower."

"You've never lacked that." He brought her hand to his lips. "I've imagined you here a thousand times. A thousand and a thousand times."

"I couldn't do the same, as even my heroic will wouldn't have held up against the imagining." Amazed at her own calm, she kissed his hand in turn. "I knew when Iona walked into my workshop you'd come back. You'd be a part of this, a part of me again. I asked why, why, when I'd found my life, made myself content with it, fate should put

245

you back into it again."

"What was the answer?"

"I've yet to get one, and still can't stop the asking. But not tonight. It's so grand, your home. All these rooms, and the all but heartbreaking detail of every centimeter of space."

And none of it, he thought, so much home as the kitchen of her cottage.

He opened the door of his bedroom, kissed her hand again, then drew her in. Rather than turn on the lights, he flicked his wrist.

The fire kindled in the hearth, and candles flickered to life.

"Again grand," she said. "A grand male sanctuary, but warm and attractive instead of practical and Spartan. Your bed's glorious." She moved to it, trailed fingers over the massive footboard. "Old, so old. Do you dream of those who've slept here?"

"I cleansed it so I wouldn't feel I shared the bed with strangers from other times. So, no, I don't dream of them. I've dreamed of you when I've slept here."

"I know it, as I had a moment in that bed with you in dreams."

"Not just then. A thousand and a thousand times."

She turned to him, looked at him in the

light and shadow of dancing flames. The heart she'd lost to him so many years before swelled inside her. "We won't dream tonight," she said, and opening her arms, went to him.

The nerves that had hummed just under her skin dissolved. Body to body with him, mouth to mouth with him, her world simply righted.

This, of course, the single missing link in the chain of her life.

For tonight, if it could only be tonight, she would give herself a gift. She would only feel. She would open herself, heart, body, mind, and feel what she'd struggled against for so long.

Tomorrow, if need be, she'd tell herself it was only the physical, only a way to relieve the tension and strain between them for the greater good. But tonight, she embraced the truth.

She loved. Had always loved, would always love.

"I've missed you," she murmured. "Ah, Finbar, I've missed you."

"Ached for you." He brushed his lips over her cheeks, brought them back to hers.

She clung as they lifted inches off the floor, then a foot, circling. With a laugh, she flung her arms up, scattered stars above them.

"By firelight and starlight, by candle flame, tonight, what I am, is yours."

"And what you are, is cherished."

He lowered them to the bed, sank into the kiss.

With her, at last with her, free to drink deep and deep from her lips, free to feel her body under his, to see her hair spread out.

The gift she gave them both, too magnificent to rush. So he would savor her gift, and give all he had in return.

He took his hands slowly up her body, gently captured her breasts. No longer the budding girl etched in his memory, but the bloom.

New memories here to layer over what had been.

He pressed his lips to her throat, lingered over the scent of her caught there, just there, that had haunted his days and nights. His again, to take in like breath.

As he slid the dress down her shoulders, she arched to ease his way. Her skin, white as milk, caught the gold of his firelight, the silver of her stars. He undressed her as if uncovering the most precious of jewels.

Her heart fluttered under his touch. Only he had ever been able to bring her that sensation, one of both nerves and pleasure. Each time he kissed her, it was slow and deep, as if worlds could spin away and back again while he savored.

"You've more patience than you did," she managed as her blood began to sing under her skin.

"You're more beautiful than you were. I never thought it possible."

She caught his face in her hands a moment, fingers skimming up into his hair, then she shifted to rise above him with stars sparkling over her head.

"And you." She drew his sweater up, off. "Witch and warrior. Stronger than the boy I loved." She spread her hands over his chest. "Wounded, but ever loyal. Valiant."

When he shook his head, she brought his hands up, pressed them to her own heart. "It matters to me, Fin, more than I can tell you. It matters." She lowered to press her lips to his lips, to press her lips to his heart.

She'd broken his heart, as he'd broken hers. She didn't know what fate would grant them, even if those hearts could be truly mended. But tonight she wanted him to know she knew his heart, and valued it.

To change the mood she danced her fingers along his left ribs. Fin jumped like a rabbit.

"Bloody hell."

"Ah, still a weakness there, I see. That one small spot." She reached for it again, and he caught her wrist.

"Mind yourself, as I recall a weakness or two of yours."

"None that make me squeal like a girl, Finbar Burke." She shifted again as he reared up, wrapped her legs around his waist, her arms around his neck. "Still would rather a fist in the face than a tickle along the ribs."

"The one's less humiliating."

She shook back her hair, laughed up at the ceiling.

"Do you remember —"

She looked back at him, met his eyes. It was all there, in that instant, looking out at her. His craving for her, and the love wrapped around it. Past and present collided, rushed through her like a hot wind, sparking her own terrible, burning need.

"Oh God, Fin."

No more patience, no more careful explorations. They came together in a fury, all wild need and desperation. Rough hands rushed over her, took greedily while her own yanked and pulled to free him of the rest of his clothes.

Nothing between them, she thought now.

She couldn't bear even air between them. Their mouths came together in heat and hunger as they rolled over the bed to find more of each other.

She closed her teeth over his shoulder, dug her fingers into his hips.

"Come inside me. I want you inside me."

When he drove into her, the world stopped. No breath, no sound, no movement. Then came thunder, a hoarse roar of it, charging like a beast from the hills. And lightning, a flash that lit the room like noon.

With her eyes locked on his, she gripped his hands.

"It's for us to say tonight," she said. "It's for us tonight." She arched toward him. "Love me."

"Only you. Always you."

He gave himself over to the need, to her demand, to his own heart.

When they came together, they were the thunder, they were the lightning. And over their heads her stars shone the brighter.

When he woke, the sun was up and streaming. A bright day for the start of a new year. And Branna lay sleeping beside him.

He wanted to wake her, to make love with her in that streaming sunlight as they had in the dark and through to the soft kiss of dawn.

But shadows haunted her eyes. She needed sleep, and quiet, and peace. So he only touched her hair, and smiled, reminding himself she could be annoyed at best, ferocious at worst, on waking.

So he got out of bed, pulled on his pants, and slipped out of the room.

He'd work. He wanted work, wanted to find the way to end all of it, to resolve it once and for all. And to find the way to break the curse a dying witch had laid on him, so long before.

If he could break the curse, remove the mark, he and Branna could be together, not for a night, but a lifetime.

He'd given up believing that could be. Until this New Year, until the hours spent with her. Now that hope, that faith was back inside him, burning bright.

He would find a way, he told himself as he went to his workshop. A way to end Cabhan and protect the three, and all that came from them. A way to erase the mark from his body, and purge his blood of any trace of Cabhan.

Today, the first day of the New Year, he'd renew that quest.

He considered the poison they'd created

for the last battle. Strong and potent, and they'd come close. The injuries to Cabhan — or what inhabited him — had been great. But not mortal. Because what empowered Cabhan wasn't mortal.

A demon, Fin thought, paging through his own books. One freed by blood sacrifice to merge with a willing host. A host with power as well.

Blood from the sire.

He sat to make notes of his own.

Blood from the dam.

Shed by the son.

He wrote it all down, the steps, the words, what he'd seen, and what he'd felt.

The red stone created by blood magicks of the darkest sort, of the most evil of acts. The source of power, healing, immortality.

"And a portal," Fin murmured. "A portal for the demon to pass through, and into the host."

They could burn Cabhan to ash as Sorcha had, but wouldn't end him without destroying the stone, and the demon.

A second potion, he considered, and rose to pace. One conjured to close this portal. Trap the demon inside, then destroy it. Cabhan couldn't exist without the demon, the demon couldn't exist without Cabhan.

He pulled down another book, one of the

journals he kept when he traveled. With his hands braced on the work counter, he leaned over, reading, refreshing himself. Considering what might be done.

"Fin."

Engrossed, his mind on magicks dark and bright, he glanced over. She wore one of his oldest shirts, a faded chambray he sometimes tossed on to work in the stables. Bare feet, bare legs, tumbled hair, and a look in her eyes of astonished sorrow.

His heart skipped — just the sight of her — even before he followed her gaze to the window, to the stained-glass image of her.

He straightened, hooked his thumbs in his front pockets. "It seemed right somehow, to have the Dark Witch looking over my shoulder when I worked here. Reminding me why I did."

"It's a constant grief to love like this."

"It is."

"How do we go on, as that may never change?"

"We take what we have, and do whatever we can to change it. Haven't we lived without each other long enough?"

"We are what we are, Fin, and some of that is through no choice of our own. There can't be promises between us, not for tomorrows."

"Then we take today."

"Only today. I'll see to breakfast." She turned to go, glanced back. "You've a fine workshop here. Like the rest of the house, it suits you."

She went down. Coffee first, she told herself. Of a morning, coffee always made things clearer.

She'd begun the New Year with him, something she'd sworn would never happen. But she'd made that oath in a storm of emotion, in turmoil. And had kept it, she admitted, as much for self-preservation as duty.

And now, for love, she'd broken it.

The world hadn't ended, she told herself as she worked Fin's very canny machine. Fire hadn't rained from the sky. They'd had sex, a great deal of lovely sex, and the fates appeared to accept it.

She'd woken light and bright and loose and . . . happy, she admitted. And she'd slept deeper and easier than she had since Samhain.

Sex was energy, she considered, gratefully taking those first sips of coffee. It was positive — when done willingly — a bright blessing and a meeting of basic needs. So sex was permitted, and she could thank the goddesses for that, and would.

But futures were a different matter. She wouldn't make plans again, let herself become starry-eyed and dreaming. Today only, she reminded herself.

It would be more than they'd had before, and would have to be enough.

She hunted in his massive fridge — oh, she'd love having one so big as this — and found three eggs, a stingy bit of bacon, and a single hothouse tomato.

Like today only and sex, it would have to be enough.

She heard him come in as she finished cobbling together what she thought of as a poor man's omelette.

"Your larder is a pitiful thing, Fin Burke. A sad disgrace, so you'll make do with what I could manage here, and be grateful."

"I'm very grateful indeed."

She glanced around. He'd put on a black long-sleeved tee, but his feet remained as bare as hers. And he had a smile on his face.

"You seem very happy for a miserly bit of bacon and tomato scrambled up with a trio of eggs."

"You're wearing only my old shirt and cooking at my stove. I'd be a fool not to smile."

"And a fool you've never been." She stuck a second mug on his coffee machine, pressed the proper buttons. "This one here is far better than mine. I should have one. And your jam was old as Medusa, and just as ugly. You'll make do with butter for your toast. I've started you a list for the market. You'll need to —"

He whirled her around, lifted her to the tips of her toes, and ravished her mouth. When she could think, she thought it fortunate she'd taken the eggs off the heat, or they'd have been scorched and ruined.

But since she had, she gave as good as she got in the kiss.

"Come back to bed."

"That I won't as I've taken the time and trouble to make a breakfast out of your pitiful stores." She pulled back. "Take your coffee. I'm plating this up before it goes cold. How do you manage breakfast on your own?"

"Now that Boyle's rarely available for me to talk into frying one up, I get whatever's handy. There's the oatmeal packs you make up in the microwave."

"A sad state of affairs." She put a plate in front of him, sat with her own. "And with such a lovely spot here to have your breakfast. I think, once Boyle and Iona are in their house, you'd be able to see their lights through the trees from here. It meant something to them, you selling them the land."

"He's a brother to me, and he's lucky for all that, as otherwise I might have snatched Iona up for my own. Though she can't cook for trying."

"She's better than she was. But then she had nowhere to go but up in that department. She's stronger every day. Her power's still young and fresh, but it has a fierceness to it. It may be why fire's hers."

This was good, she thought, and this was sweet. Sitting and talking easy over coffee and eggs.

"Will her grandmother take your cottage to rent?" she asked him.

"I think she will."

Branna toyed with her eggs. "There's connections everywhere between you and me, and us. I put it all out of my mind for a very long time, but I've had to ask myself in these last months, why so many of them? Beyond you and me, Fin. There's always been you and Boyle and Connor, and Meara as well."

"Our circle," he agreed, "less one till Iona came."

"That she would come as fated as the rest. And didn't you have that cottage when Meara's mother needed it, and now for Iona's Nan? You and Boyle and the stables, you and Connor with the falconry school. Land you owned where Boyle and Iona will live their life. You've spent more time away than here these past years, and still you're so tightly linked. Some may say it's just the way of things, but I don't believe that. Not anymore."

"What do you believe?"

"I can't know for certain." Poking at the eggs on her plate, she stared off out the window. "I know there are connections again, the three now, the three then. And each of us more closely linked to one of them. And didn't Eamon mistake our Meara for a gypsy he knew — name of Aine as you named the white filly you brought back to breed with Alastar? I feel Boyle has some connection there as well, some piece of it, and if we needed we'd find that connection to Teagan of the first three."

"It's no mystery." He rubbed his shoulder. "It's Cabhan for me."

"I think it's more, somewhere. You're from him, of his blood, but not connected in the way I am with Sorcha's Brannaugh, or Connor with Eamon and so on. If you were, I can't see how you'd have known to bring Alastar back for Iona, and Aine back for Alastar."

"I didn't bring Aine back for Alastar, not altogether, or not only. I brought her back for you."

The mug she'd lifted stilled in midair. "I . . . I don't understand you."

"When I saw her, I saw you. You used to love to ride, to fly astride a horse. I saw you on her, flying through the night with the moon bursting full in the sky. And you, lit like a candle with . . ."

"What?"

"As you are in the window upstairs, just as I saw you years before when I had it done. A wand in one hand, fire in the other. It came and went like a fingersnap, but was clear as day. So I brought her back for you, when you're ready for her."

She said nothing, could say nothing for a moment. Then she rose, went to the door, and let in the little dog she'd sensed waiting.

Bugs wagged around her feet, then dashed to Fin.

"Don't feed him from the table," she said absently as she sat again. "It's poor manners for both of you."

Fin, who'd been about to do just that, looked down at the hopeful dog.

You know where the food is, little man. Let's not ruffle the lady's feathers.

Happy enough, Bugs raced off to the laundry, and his bowls.

"I'll ride her when we next face Cabhan, and be the stronger for it. You brought us weapons, for both Alastar and Aine are weapons against him. You've bled with us, conjured with us, plotted with us, to end him. If your connection was with him, strongest with him, how could you do these things?"

"Hate for him, and all he is."

Branna shook her head. Hate didn't make courage or loyalty. And what Fin had done took both.

"I was wrong to try to block you out in the beginning of this, and it was selfishly done. I wanted to believe that connection, you to Cabhan, but it's not there. Not in the way he'd want, not in the way he needs. Your connection is with us. I don't understand the why of it, but it's truth."

"I love you."

Oh, her heart warmed and ached at the words. She could only touch his hand. "Love is powerful, but it doesn't explain, in a logical way, why your feelings for me link you so tight with the others."

She leaned forward now, her breakfast forgotten. "Between the first three and us, I've found no others who've been so tightly

261

woven together. No others who've gone back dreaming to them, or had them come. Others have tried and failed, but none have come so close as we to ending him. I've read no tales in the books of one of the three riding on Alastar into battle, with Kathel and Roibeard with them. And none that speak of a fourth, of one who bears the mark, joining them. It's our destiny, Fin, but you're the change in it. I believe that now. It's you who make our best chance to finish it, you who bear his mark and come from his blood. And still, I can't see the why of it."

"There are choices, you know well, to be made with power, and with blood."

"I feel there's more, but that alone may be enough."

"It won't be enough to destroy Cabhan. Or I mean to say we won't succeed in destroying him, no more than Sorcha could, without destroying what he took into him."

She nodded, having come to the same conclusion. "The demon he bargained with."

"The demon who used him to gain freedom. Blood from his sire, from his mother, shed by him, drunk by him, used by him with the demon's demands and promises, to create the stone."

"And the power source."

"Not just a power source, I think. A portal, Branna, the entry into Cabhan."

"A portal." She sat back. "There's a thought. Through the stone conjured with the blackest of blood magicks, into the sorcerer who made the bargain. There sits the power, and the way into the world. If a portal can be opened . . ."

"It can be closed," Fin finished.

"Yes, there's a thought indeed. So it becomes steps and stages. Weaken and trap Cabhan so he can't slip away and heal again. And as he — the host — is weak and trapped, close the portal, trapping the demon, who *is* the source. Destroy it, destroy Cabhan for good and all."

She picked up her fork again, and though the eggs had gone cold, ate. "Well then, all that's left is figuring out how it's to be done, and when it can be done, and doing it."

"I've a few thoughts, and may have more when I finish reading up. I spent some time with a Shaolin priest some years ago."

"A . . . You worked with a Shaolin priest? In China?"

"I wanted to see the wall," he said with a shrug. "He had some thoughts on demons, as a kind of energy. And I've spent some time here and there with shamans, other witches, a wise man, an Aborigine. I kept journals, so I'll be reading through."

"It seems you've had quite the education in your travels."

"There are places in the world of such strong energy, such old power. They call to people like us. Only today," he said, reaching over for her hands. "But if there are ever tomorrows, I'd show you."

Since she couldn't answer, she only squeezed his hands, then rose to clear the plates. "It's today that needs us. I've never given a thought to destroying demons, and in truth never believed they existed in our world. Which is, I see now, as shortsighted as those who can't believe in magicks."

"I'll see to the clearing up here. It's the rule in your own house, and a fair one."

"All right then. I should get home, and start reading up on demons myself."

"It's the first day of the New Year," he said as he walked to her. "And a kind of holiday."

"Not for the likes of us, with what's coming. And I've work besides to earn my living. You may have staff and all that to see to most, but I'd think you've a living to earn as well."

"We've no lessons today, and the guided rides and hawk walks are a handful only between them both. And I've a couple hours yet before I'm to meet with Boyle, then Connor."

She angled her face up to his. "It's a fortunate man you are to have such leisure time."

"Today it is. I'm thinking you may have an hour yet to spare."

"Well, your thinking isn't —" She broke off, narrowed her eyes as the shirt she'd worn winked away, leaving her naked. "That was rude and inhospitable."

"I'll show you great hospitality, *aghra*." Closing his arms around her, he flew them both back into bed.

12

She didn't leave until midday, and found Kathel outside playing run and tumble with Bugs. She ignored the fact that those who worked in the stables would have seen her car still parked when they'd arrived that morning.

The juice would begin to flow from the grapevine, but it couldn't be helped. She gave Bugs a quick rub, told him he was welcome to come with Fin anytime at all and play with Kathel.

Then she whistled her own dog into the car, and drove home.

She went straight upstairs to change out of her party dress and into warm leggings, a cozy sweater, and soft half boots. After bundling her hair up, she considered herself ready to work.

In her workshop, she put the kettle on, lit the fire. And feeling a shift in the air, whirled around.

Sorcha's Brannaugh stood, a quiver on her back, her own Kathel at her heel.

"Something changed," she said. "A storm came and blew through the night. Thunder raged, lightning flamed even through a fall of snow. Cabhan rode the storm until the stones of the castle shook."

"Are you harmed? Any of you?"

"He could not get past us, and will not. But another maid is missing, and a kinswoman, and I fear the worst for her. Something changed."

Yes, Branna thought, something changed. But first there were questions. "What do you know of demons?"

Sorcha's Brannaugh glanced down as Branna's Kathel went to hers, and the hounds sniffed each other.

"They walk, they feed, they thirst for the blood of mortals. They can take many forms, but all but one is a lie."

"And they search out, do they not," Branna added, "those willing to feed them, to quench that thirst? The red stone, we've seen its creation, and we've seen the demon Cabhan bargained with pass through it and into him. They are one. Sorcha couldn't end Cabhan because the demon lived, and healed him. They healed, I think, each other."

"How did you see?"

"We went in a dream spell, myself and Finbar Burke."

"The one of Cabhan's blood. You went with him, to Cabhan's time, to his lair. How can there be such trust?"

"How can there not? Here is trust," she said, gesturing to the dogs who'd gone to wrestling on the floor. "I know Fin's heart, and would not know all we do now without him."

"You've been with him."

"I have." And though she felt her cousin's concern, even disapproval, she wouldn't regret it. "The storm came to you. I heard it when I joined with Fin, and I thought fate clashed at the choice we made. But you say it was Cabhan who rode the storm, and you felt it was his power, or rage, that shook the stones. It may be the joining angered him — this speaks true to me. What angers him only pleases me."

"I know what it is to love. Have a care, cousin, on how that love binds you to one who carries the mark."

"I've had a care since the mark came on him. I won't shirk my duty. My oath on it. I believe Fin may be the true change, the weapon always needed. With him, as no three has before, we will end this. Cabhan, and what made him what he is now. It must be both, we believe that, or it will never end. So, what do you know of demons?"

Brannaugh shook her head. "Little, but I will learn more. You will call him by his name. This I have heard. You must use his name in the spell."

"Then we'll find his name. How long since last we talked in your time?"

"Today is La nag Cearpairi."

Day of the Buttered Bread, Branna realized. New Year's Day. "As it is here. We are on the same day, another change. This will be our year, cousin, the year of the three. The year of the Dark Witch."

"I will pray for it. I must go, the baby's waking."

"Wait." Branna closed her eyes again, brought the image into her mind from the box in her attic. Then held out a small stuffed dog. "For the baby. A gift from his cousins."

"A little dog." As she petted it, Sorcha's Brannaugh smiled. "So soft it is, and clever."

"It was mine, and well loved. Bright blessings to you and yours this day."

"And to you and yours. I will see you again. We will be with you when it's needed, in that I will have faith, and trust." She laid her hand on her dog's head, and they faded away.

Branna lowered her hand to her own dog's head, stroked. "Once I thought to give the little dog to my own baby. But since that's not to be, it seemed a fine gift for my cousin's." Kathel leaned his great body against her in comfort. "Ah, well, we've work to do, don't we? But first I think you've earned a biscuit for being so welcoming to our cousin's hound."

She got one for him, smiled when he sat so politely. "How lucky am I to have so many loves in my life." She leaned down, pressed a kiss to the top of his head, then offered the biscuit.

Content in the quiet, she made her tea, and she sat with her spell books, looking for whatever she might find on demons.

She had the whole of the afternoon to herself, a precious thing, so mixed work and reading with some baking to please herself. She put a chicken on the boil, thinking chicken soup with chunky vegetables and thick egg noodles would go well. If she didn't have a houseful, she could freeze most of it for when she did.

With dusk she shifted her books to the kitchen so she could continue to work as she monitored her soup. She'd just rewarded herself with a glass of wine when Iona came in.

"Boy, I could use one of those. I took Nan back, got weepy — sad she had to go home, so happy she's coming back. And I thought I was done for the day." She poured the wine. "But Boyle texted me they'd had a group of twelve who'd celebrated New Year's at Ashford, decided they'd finished feeling hungover and wanted guided rides. So it was back to work."

She took her first sip. "And I'm babbling about all that — can babble about more if necessary — to keep from asking about you and Fin if you don't want to be asked."

"You may have gleaned we had sex."

"I think we all gleaned that was a strong probability. Are you happy, Branna?"

Branna went to stir the soup. "I can say, without question, I've had a long-nagging itch thoroughly scratched, and I'm not sad about it. I'm happy," she said when Iona just waited. "Today, I'm happy and that's enough."

"Then I'm happy." She stepped closer, gave Branna a hug. "What can I do to help? In any area."

"I've dinner under control. You could sit there, read over my notes, see what you think of it all."

"Okay. Boyle and I were going to eat out, and stay at his place — and Connor and Meara the same. We thought you'd have plans with Fin and wanted to give you room. But you've got that vat of soup going, so . . ."

"Don't change plans on my account. I'd already thought of freezing the bulk of it. I was in the mood to make soup, and give my head time to think that way." She didn't mention she'd made no plans with Fin — and wouldn't mind a night alone.

"You're planning to keep seeing him — being with him, I mean."

"A day at a time, Iona. I won't think on it further than that."

"All right, but I may as well tell you Fin was by to talk through some business with Boyle and he looked . . . happy. Relaxed."

"Sex will relax you in the aftermath. We've an understanding, Fin and I. We're both content with it."

"If you are, I am." Iona sat, started to read.

Branna tested the soup, considered, then added more rosemary.

At the table, Iona said, "A portal! It makes so much sense. It's an evil stone, created from human sacrifice — through patricide, matricide — what better way for a demon to transport into Cabhan? It *all* makes sense. Sorcha burned him to ash. We had him on the ropes — we had him bleeding under the damn ropes, but we didn't deal with the demon. How do we?"

"Read on," Branna suggested. She considered having her soup in her pajamas. Maybe even on a tray in her room while she read a book that had nothing to do with magicks, evil, or demons.

"A second poison," Iona muttered, "a kind of one-two punch. And a spell that closes the portal. How do we close a portal opened through human sacrifice? That's going to be tricky. And . . . Call the demon by his name." She looked up and over at Branna. "You know its name?"

"I don't, not yet. But it was the advice given me by Brannaugh of the first three. She came to me today. And I've written all that down as well, but the most important part to my thinking is it was the same day for her as it is for us. For her today was the first day of the year. I think if we can somehow stay balanced that way, we'll draw more from each other."

"Do we know any demonologists?"

"Not offhand, but . . . I suspect we could find one should we need one. I think it might be more simple and basic than that."

"What's simple and basic about finding

out a demon's name?"

"Asking it."

Iona flopped back in the chair, gave a half laugh. "That would be simple. We could all come here, or all meet in the pub if you want to go over this tonight."

"I think you can pass it all on well enough."

"Then I will. When's Fin coming by? I don't want to be in the way."

"Oh . . ." Branna went back to the soup. "We didn't set any specific time. It's best if we keep it more casual-like."

"Gotcha. I'm going to go up, grab a shower, and change. I'll just ask Boyle to swing by and get me. The four of us can put our heads together on it, and talk it to death with you and Fin later."

"That would suit me very well."

Evasive, Branna thought when alone again. She preferred evasive to deceptive. She hadn't absolutely said she expected Fin. And it would give her brain a rest not to have to talk it all through, to give it all a day or two to stir around in her head first.

Maybe she'd rest her brain with the telly instead of a book. Watch something fun and frivolous. She couldn't think of the last time she'd done only that.

"I'm heading out!" Iona called back. "Text

me if you need me."

"Have a good time."

Branna waited until she heard the door close, then, smiling to herself, got out a container to freeze all but a bowl of the soup.

A bowl of soup, a glass of wine, followed by a bit of the apple crumble she'd baked earlier. A quiet house, old pajamas, and something happy on the telly.

Even as she thought what a lovely idea it all was, the door opened.

Fin, with Bugs on his heel, came in with a ridiculously enormous bouquet of lilacs. The scent of them filled the air with spring and promise. She wondered where he'd traveled for them, and arched her eyebrows.

"And I'm supposing you're thinking a forest of flowers buys your way into dinner and sex?"

"You always favored lilacs. And both Boyle and Connor did mention going off tonight to give us the cottage to ourselves. Who am I to disappoint my mates?"

She got out her largest vase, began to fill it while Bugs and Kathel had a cheerful bout of wrestling. "I'm after a bowl of soup in front of the telly."

"I'd be more than happy with that."

She took the lilacs, breathed them in —

remembered doing the same on a long-ago spring when he'd brought her an equally huge bouquet of them.

"I baked an apple crumble to follow."

"I'm fond of apple crumble."

"So I recall." And so, she thought, this explained why she'd had a yen to bake one. "I had myself a fine plan for the evening. An all but perfect one for me." She laid the flowers aside a moment, turned to him. "All but perfect, and now it is. It's perfect now you're here."

She walked into his arms, pressed her face into his shoulder. "You're here," she murmured.

Branna thought of it as refocusing. Weeks and weeks of studying, charting, calculating had brought her no closer to a time and date for the third and, please the gods, last battle with Cabhan. She rarely slept well or long, and she had eyes to see the lack of sleep had begun to show.

Pure vanity if nothing else demanded a change of direction.

Now that she was bedding Fin and being bedded by him, very well, thank you very much, she couldn't say she'd gotten more sleep, but she'd rested considerably better in those short hours.

Still, she'd gotten no further, not on the when or precisely the how. So, she'd refocus.

Routine always steadied her. Her work, her home, her family, and the cycle that spun them together. A new year meant new stock for her shop, meant seeds to be planted in her greenhouse flats. Negative energies should be swept out, and protection charms refreshed.

Added to it she had two weddings to help plan.

She spent the morning on her stock. Pleased with her new scents, she filled the containers she'd ordered for the Blue Ice line, labeled all, stacked them for transport to the village with the stack of candles she'd replenished from the stock Iona had decimated for Fin's party.

After a check of her list, she made up more of the salve Boyle used at the stables. She could drop that by if the day went well, and thinking of it, added a second jar for the big stables.

A trip to the market as well, she decided. Despite it being Iona's turn for it, Branna thought she'd enjoy a trip to the village, a drive in the air. The dinner with the rest of her circle after their night away hadn't accomplished much more than emptying her container of soup, so the stop by the market was necessary.

With a glance at the clock she calculated she could be back in two hours, at the outside. Then she'd try her hand at creating a demon poison. Wrapped in her coat, a bold red and blue scarf, and the cashmere fingerless gloves she'd splurged on as a Yule gift to herself, she loaded up her car.

As Kathel was nowhere in sight, she sent her mind to his, found him spending some quality time with Bugs and the horses. She gave him leave to stay till it suited him, then drove herself to Cong.

She spent half her allotted time in the village, loitering with Eileen in the shop. More time in the market, buying supplies and exchanging gossip with Minnie O'Hara, who knew all there was to know — including the fact that on New Year's Eve Young Tim McGee (as opposed to his father Big Tim, and his grandfather Old Tim) had gotten himself drunk as a pirate. And so being had serenaded Lana Kerry — she who had broken off their three-year engagement for lack of movement — below her flat window with songs of deep despair, sadly off key.

It was well known Young Tim couldn't sing a note without causing the village dogs to howl in protest. He had begun this at near to half-three in the morning, and until the French girl in the flat below — one Violet Bosette who worked now in the cafe — opened her own window and heaved out an old boot. For a French girl, Minnie considered, her aim was dead-on, and she clunked Young Tim right upside the head, knocking him flat on his arse where he continued to serenade.

At which time Lana came out and hauled him inside. When they'd emerged near to dinnertime the next day, the ring was on Lana's finger once more, and a wedding date set for May Day.

It was a fine story, Branna thought as she drove out of the village again, especially as she knew all the participants but the French girl with good aim.

And it had been worth the extra time spent.

She took the long way around just for the pleasure of it, and was nearly within sight of the stables when she saw the old man on the side of the road, down on his knees and leaning heavily on a walking stick.

She pulled up sharply, got out.

"Sir, are you hurt?" She started toward him, began to search for injuries or illness with her mind.

Then stopped, angled her head. "Have you fallen, sir?"

"My heart, I think. I can bare get my breath. Will you help me, young miss?"

"Sure and I'll help you." She reached out a hand for his, and punched power into it. The old man flew back in a tumble.

"Do you think to trick me with such a ploy?" She tossed back her hair as the old man lifted his head, to look at her. "That I couldn't see through the shell to what's inside?"

"You stopped, outside your protection." As the old man rose, he became Cabhan, smiling now as the red stone pulsed light.

"Do you think I'm without protection? Come then." She gestured with an insulting wiggle of her fingers. "Have a go at me."

The fog spread, nipping like icy needles at her ankles; the sky darkened in a quick, covering dusk. Cabhan dropped to the ground, became the wolf, and the wolf gathered itself, leaped.

With a wave of hands, palms out, Branna threw up a block that sent the wolf crashing against the air, falling back.

Poor choice, she thought, watching it as it stalked her. For in this form she could read Cabhan like the pages of a book.

She probed inside, searched for a name, but sensed only rage and hunger.

So when he charged as wolf from the

right, she was prepared for the man rushing in from the left. And she met fire with fire, power with power.

It surprised her the earth itself didn't crack from the force that flew out of her, the force that flashed out at her. But the air snapped and sizzled with it. She held, held, while the muscles of her body, the muscles of her power ached with the effort. While she held, the brutal cold of the fog rose higher.

Though her focus, her eyes, her magicks locked with his, she felt his fingers — its fingers — crawl up her leg.

Sheer insult had force. She swung what she had out at him so it struck like a fist. Though it bloodied his mouth, he laughed. She knew she'd misjudged, let temper haze sense, when he lunged forward and closed his hands over her breasts.

Only an instant, but even that was far too much. Now she merged temper, intellect, and skill and called the rain — a warm flashing flood that washed away the fog and burned his skin where the drops fell.

She braced for the next attack, saw it coming in his eyes, then she heard, as he did, the thunder of hoofbeats, the high, challenging cry of the hawk, the ferocious howl of the hound.

"Soft and ripe and fertile. And in you I'll plant my seed and my son."

"I'll burn your cock off at the root and feed it smoldering to the ravens should you try. Oh, but stay, Cabhan." She spread her arms, stopped the rain, held a wand of blinding light and a ball of fire. "My circle comes to greet you."

"Another time, Sorcha, for I would have you alone."

Even as Fin slid from his still-racing Baru, his sword flaming, Cabhan swirled into mists.

Fin and Kathel reached her on a run, and Fin gripped her shoulders.

"Did he hurt you?"

"I'm not hurt." But as she said it she realized her breasts throbbed, a dark throb like a rotted tooth. "Or not enough to matter."

She laid one hand on Fin's heart, the other on Kathel's head. "Be easy," she said as the others came up on horseback or in lorries. The hawks — Roibeard and Merlin — landed together on the roof of Boyle's lorry. Before she could speak through the rapid-fire questions, she saw Bugs running for all he was worth down the road to her.

"Brave heart," she crooned, and crouched to gather him up when he reached her. "It's too open here," she told the others. "And I'm right enough."

"Connor, will you see to Branna's car? She'll ride with me. My house is closest."

"I can drive perfectly well," Branna began, but he simply picked her up, set her in the saddle, then swung up behind her.

"You take too much for granted," she said stiffly.

"And you're too pale."

She held Bugs safe as Baru lunged forward.

If she was pale, Branna thought, it was only because it had been an intense battle, however short. She'd get her color back, and her balance with it quickly enough.

No point in arguing, she decided, as the lot of them were worried for her — as she'd have been for any of them in the same case.

When they reached the stables, Fin swung down, plucked her off, and called out to an openmouthed Sean, "See to the horses."

Since she deemed it more mortifying to struggle, Branna allowed him to carry her into his house.

"You've made a scene for no reason, and will have tongues wagging throughout the county."

"Cabhan going at you in the middle of the road in the middle of the day is reason enough. You'll have some whiskey."

"I won't, but I'd have some tea if it's no trouble to you."

He started to speak, then just turned on his heel, leaving her on his living room sofa as he strode off to the kitchen.

In the moment alone, she tugged at the neck of her sweater, looked down at herself. She could clearly see the imprint of Cabhan's fingers on her skin over the top of her bra. She rose, deciding the matter would be best dealt with in private.

And the rest of her circle, along with her dog, crowded in.

"Don't start. I want the powder room a moment first." She sent a look at Meara, at Iona, the request clear in her eyes.

So they followed her into the pretty little half bath under the stairs.

"What is it?" Iona demanded. "What don't you want them to see?"

"I'd as soon my brother and your fiancé don't get a gander of my breasts." So saying she stripped off the sweater. And on Meara's hiss of breath, the bra.

"Oh, Branna," Iona murmured, lifted her hands. "Let me."

"If you'd lay your hands over mine." Branna covered her own breasts. "I could do it myself, but it'll be faster and easier with your help."

Branna searched inside herself, brought up the warmth of healing, sighed into it when Iona joined her, and again when Meara just put an arm around her waist.

"It's not deep. He only had me for a fraction of a second."

"It hurts deep."

Branna nodded at Iona. "It does, or did. It's easing already, and my own fault for giving him even that small opening."

"I think it'll go faster, hurt less if you look into me. If you boost what I can do with what you have. Just for this, okay? Look at me, Branna. Look into me. The hurt lifts out, let it go. The bruising eases. Feel the warm."

She let it go, opened herself, twined what she had with Iona.

"It's clear. He's left no mark on or in you. You're . . ." Iona paused, still searching for injury. And her eyes widened.

"Oh, Branna."

"Ah, well, I supposed that's next." She unhooked her pants, let them fall to reveal the streaks of bruising up her inner thighs.

"Bloody bastard," Meara muttered and took Branna's hand in a strong grip.

"It was the fog, a kind of sly attack. More a brush than a squeeze, so it's not as dark or painful. Have at it, Iona, if you wouldn't mind."

She let herself go again, let herself drift on the warmth Iona gave her until even the echo of pain faded.

"He wanted to frighten me, to attack me on the level women fear most. But he didn't frighten me." Calmly Branna hooked her pants again, slipped into her bra, then her sweater. "He enraged me, which gave him the same chance to rush my defenses and find that one small chink. It won't happen a second time."

She turned to the mirror over the sink, gave herself a hard look — and a very light glamour.

"There, that's done the job. Thank you, both of you. I'll see if Fin's made a decent cup of tea and tell you all what happened."

She stepped out. Connor stopped pacing the foyer, strode straight to her, caught her up against him.

"I'm fine, I promise. I . . . No prying into my head, Connor, you'll only annoy me."

"I've a right to be certain my sister's unharmed."

"I've said I am."

"He left the mark of his hands, black as pitch, on her breasts."

At Meara's words, Branna twisted around,

astonished by the betrayal.

"There's no holding things back." Meara stiffened her spine. "It's not fair or right, and not smart, either. You'd say so yourself if it was me or Iona."

When Connor started to pull up her sweater, Branna slapped his hands away. "Mind yourself! Iona and I took care of it. Ask her yourself if you can't take my word."

"There's not a trace of him in or on her," Iona confirmed. "But he'd put his marks on her, up her thighs, on her breasts."

"He put his hands on you." Fin spoke with a quiet that roared like thunder.

Branna closed her eyes a moment. She hadn't sensed him come up behind her. "I let him rile me, so it's my own fault."

"You said you weren't hurt."

"I didn't know I was until I got back here and had a look. It was nothing near what Connor dealt with, or Boyle, or you. He bruised me, and where he did is a violation as he meant it to be."

Fin turned away, walked to the fire, stared into it.

It was Boyle who moved to Branna, put an arm around her waist. "Come on now, darling. You'll sit down and have your tea. You'd do better with some whiskey in it."

"My sensibilities aren't damaged. I'm not

so delicate as that. But thank you. Thank all of you for coming so quickly."

"Not quick enough."

She gave Connor's arm a squeeze when he sat beside her. "That's likely my doing as well, and I'll confess it, as Meara — and rightfully — has shamed me into bare truth. I wanted just a moment or two, and took it before I called for you. And before you all rain down on my head, it *was* but a moment or two, and I had good reason."

"Good reason?" Fin turned back. "Not to call your circle?"

"For a moment," she repeated. "I'm well protected."

Rage, pure and vicious, burned in his eyes. "Not so well he couldn't put his hands on you, and leave marks behind."

"My own fault. I'd hoped he'd change into the wolf, and he did. The hound is mine, and a wolf is the same. I thought I might be able to pull out the name of the demon, now that we know we're looking for one. But it wasn't long enough, and all I found was the black, and the greed. I need longer. I believe, I promise you, I could dig out the name if I had longer."

She picked up her tea, sipped, and found it strong enough to battle a few sorcerers on its own. And that was fine with her.

"He came as an old man, looking ill and sick on the side of the road. He thought to trick me, and did — but only for a handful of seconds, and only because I'm a healer and it's my call and my duty to help those who need it."

"Which he knew very well," Connor said.

"Of course. But he persists in thinking of women, whatever their power, as less, as weak, and as foolish. So I turned the trick on him, pretended I thought him an old helpless man, then knocked him head over arse.

"It's true I should have called for you right at that moment, and you have my word on it, I won't take even that little time again before I do. He did what I hoped, as I said, came at me as the wolf."

She took them through it, left out no detail, then set the tea aside.

Connor drew her tight against him. "Feed his cock to the ravens, will you?"

"It's what came to me at the time."

"And the stone?"

"Brilliantly bright at the start of it. And bright again when he took hold of me. But when my rain burned him, it went muddy."

She took another breath. "And there came a kind of madness in his eyes. He called me Sorcha. He looked at me, and he saw her,

289

as Fin said when he saw me in the cave. It's still Sorcha for him."

"Centuries." Eyes narrowed, Boyle nodded. "Being what he is, wanting what he wants and never getting it. It would breed a madness, and she's the center of it for him."

"And now you are," Fin finished. "You have the look of her. I've enough to see his thoughts to know he sees her in you."

"She is in me, but there was a confusion in that madness. And confusion is a weakness. Any weakness is an advantage for us."

"I saw him, glimpses when I took out a guided this morning," Meara said.

"I saw him, too, on one of mine. I didn't have a chance to tell anyone." Iona puffed out a breath. "He's feeling strong again, and getting bolder."

"Easier to end him when he's not hiding," Boyle pointed out. "I have to get back to the stables. I can spare either Meara or Iona if you need, Branna."

"I'm fine now, and I . . . Oh bloody hell!" She pushed to her feet. "I'd been marketing, and all I bought is still in the car."

"I'll see to it," Connor told her.

"And put everything where I won't find it? I bought a fine cut of beef, and had in mind to roast it."

"With the little potatoes and carrots and

onions all roasting with it?"

Meara cast her eyes to the ceiling. "Connor, only you would think of your stomach when your sister's barely settled."

"As he knows I'm fine, and if I wasn't, cooking would settle me the rest of the way."

"We'll bring it in here." Fin spoke in a tone that brooked no argument. "If you've a mind to cook, you can cook here. If you need something I don't have, we'll get it. I've some work in the stables, and more upstairs, but someone will be close."

He walked out, she assumed to bring in her groceries.

"Give him a break." Iona spoke quietly, got up herself, rubbed a hand on Branna's arm. "Giving him a break doesn't make you weak, won't make him think you are. It'll just give him a break."

"He might have asked what I wanted to do."

Connor kissed her temple. "You might have asked the same of him. We'll be off then, and back in time for dinner. If you need anything, you've only to let me know."

When they all left, Branna sat back down and had a good brood into the fire.

13

Branna decided, given the circumstances, she'd just call what she needed to her. It seemed the best place to work on her research and studies would be the breakfast nook in his kitchen, and that way all would be close to hand when the roast was in the oven.

He kept his distance from her, and his silence — and both, she knew bloody well, were deliberate acts. Let him have his temper, she thought. She had one of her own, and the cold shoulder he offered only kept it stirred on a simmer.

On top of it all, it irritated her not to be able to stamp out the pleasure of cooking a real meal in his kitchen. It had such a nice flow to it, such fine finishes, such canny little bits of businesses such as the pot filler near the cooktop should she have a big pot to fill and not want to haul it from sink to stove.

And the cooktop she coveted. Then she might've had a six-burner commercial grade herself if she'd envisioned cooking for so many so often.

It didn't seem right a man who didn't cook himself should have a kitchen superior to hers — and she'd considered her own a dream of style and efficiency.

So she brooded about that while she let the meat marinate, and set up her temporary desk in his nook.

Another cup of tea, a couple of biscuits — store-bought, of course — and her dog along with Bugs snoring under the table. She passed the time working on the formula for the second poison — ingredients, words, timing — sent a long email to her father in case he knew, or knew anyone who knew, more of demons than she could uncover.

By the time Fin came in, grubby from the stables, she'd abandoned her books and sat at his counter peeling carrots.

He got out a beer, said nothing.

"You're the one who put me in this kitchen." She didn't snap, but the edge of one colored her tone. "So if you're going to cling to your anger with me, take yourself elsewhere."

He stood in a ragged jacket and sweater more ragged yet, jeans giving way at one knee and boots that had seen far better days. His hair mussed and windblown around the cool expression on his face.

It only egged on her own temper he could look so bloody sexy.

"I'm not angry with you."

"You've an odd way of showing your cheerful feelings then, as you've been in and out of the house twice and said not a word to me."

"I'm buying a couple more hacks for the guideds and working a deal on selling one of the young hawks to a falconer. It's my business, one that keeps all this running, and I came in and up to my office so I wouldn't be talking terms in front of the hands and the young girl in for her afternoon lesson."

He tipped the beer toward her, then drank. "If it's all the same to you."

"It's all the same, and still the same I'm saying to take your temper somewhere else. It's a bloody big house."

"I like them big." He walked over, stood on the other side of the island. "I'm not angry with you, so don't be a fecking idjit."

She felt the very blood kindle under her skin. "A fecking idjit is it now?"

"It is from where I'm standing."

"Then if you insist on standing there, it's

me who'll go elsewhere." She slapped down the peeler, shoved back, and got halfway to the doorway before he took her arm.

She gave him a jolt that would've knocked him back to the opposite side of the room if he hadn't been ready for it. "Cool yourself down, Branna, as I've been working on doing these past hours."

Her eyes were smoke, her voice a fire simmering. "I won't be called an idjit, fecking or otherwise."

"I didn't say you were, only advised you not to be." His tone was cool as January rain. "And for the third time, I'm not angry with you. And *rage* is too tame a word for what I hold in me for him, for the bastard who put his hands on you."

"He poisoned Connor, near to killed Meara, and Iona, he's burned Boyle's hands black and laid you out on my kitchen floor. But you're more than raged because he now knows the shape of my teats?"

He took her shoulders, and she saw now he spoke the truth. What lived in his eyes was more than rage. "Battle wounds, and fair or foul they're won in battle. This wasn't any of that. You've only just let me touch you again, and he does this? You can't see the deliberation, the timing? Doing this so you'd think of my blood, of my origins when next I want to touch you?"

"That's not —"

"And you can't see, can't think with that clever brain that he had contact with you? Physical contact, and with it might have pulled you out of the here and now to where he willed?"

She started to speak, then held up both hands until he released her. And she went back, sat again. "You can call me a fecking idjit now, as I've earned it. I didn't think of either, but I can see it clear enough now. I didn't think of the first, as you have nothing to do with what he did, what he tried to do to me. I wouldn't think of him when you touched me, Fin. That's where you have it wrong. He meant you to think it, and there it seems he succeeded."

She reached for his beer, then shook her head. "I don't want beer."

Saying nothing, he turned, took the wine stopper out of the bottle of Pinot Noir she'd used in the marinade. When he poured her a glass, she sipped slowly.

"As for the second, I'm well rooted. He may think he has enough to pull me when and where he wills. I can promise you he doesn't. I took precautions there when he tried luring Meara, and we fully understood how he can shift in time. You can trust me on this."

"All right."

She lifted her eyebrows. "Just that?"

"It isn't enough?"

"He meant to frighten and humiliate me, and did neither. Perhaps he did also mean to twist my sensibilities so I wouldn't want your touch, but he failed there as well. But he appears to have well succeeded in enraging you. This he understands, the rage. You're bedding me now, and you won't have me touched by another."

"It's not that, Branna." Calmer — marginally — he shoved his fingers through his hair. "Well, not just that. It's what touched you."

"He'd only understand the possession. He'd never understand your remorse, your guilt, for no matter how many times you show him you reject his part of you, it's all he sees there. He can't see past your blood. You must. We all must. I do or however I felt about you, I couldn't have let you touch me."

"It's his blood I want. I want it dripping from my hands."

"I know it." Understood it, she admitted, and had felt the same herself more than once. "But that's vengeance, and vengeance won't defeat him. Or not vengeance alone, for whatever we are, we're human, too, and he's more than earned that thirst from us."

"I can't be calm about it. I don't know how you can be."

"Because I looked in his eyes today, closer than you are now to me. I felt his hands burning cold on me. And it wasn't fear running through me. It has been; there's been fear mixed in, even with the power so full and bright. But not today. We're stronger, each one of us alone, stronger than he is, even with what's in him. And together? We're his holocaust."

He skirted the counter, laid his hands on her shoulders again. Gently now. "We must stop him this time, Branna, whatever it takes."

"And I believe we will."

Whatever it takes, he thought again, and brushed his lips to her brow. "I need to keep you from harm."

"Do you think I need protection, Fin?"

"I don't, no, but that doesn't mean I won't give it. It doesn't mean I don't need to give it."

He kissed her brow again.

Whatever it takes.

He had businesses to run, and the work didn't wait until it was convenient for him.

Ledgers had to be balanced, calls had to be made or returned, and it seemed there was forever some legal document to read and sign.

He'd learned early that owning a successful business required more than the owning of it, and the dream. He could be grateful Boyle and Connor handled the day-to-day demands — and all the paperwork, time, and decision-making on the spot that engendered. But it didn't leave him off the hook.

Even when he traveled, he stayed keyed in — via phone or Skype or email. But when he was home, he felt obliged to get his hands dirty. That held the pleasure of grooming horses as he prized that physical contact and mental bond. More than using a currycomb or hoof pick, the grooming or feeding or exercising gave him an insight into each horse.

Nor did he mind cleaning up for the birds at the school or spending time carefully drying wet feathers. He'd gained a great deal of satisfaction in having a hand training the younger ones, and had found himself bonding particularly with a female they'd named Sassy — as she was.

Though the days grew slowly longer, there rarely seemed enough hours in them to do all he wanted or needed to do. But he knew where he wanted to be, and that was home.

Nearly a year now, he thought as he stood with Connor in the school enclosure, kicking a blue ball for Romeo, their office manager's very enthusiastic spaniel. The longest straight stretch for him since he'd been twenty.

Business and curiosity and the need for answers would call him away again, but no more, he hoped, for months at a time. For the first time since the mark had come on him, he felt home again.

"I'm thinking the winter, and the slower demand, makes the best time to experiment with the hawk rides we talked of before."

"We'd offer something more than special to those who come here for some adventure." Connor gave the ball a kick, sent the dog racing. "I've worked out the pricing on it, should we give it a go, and Boyle grumbled as he does so it seemed in line."

"As do I. It'll require a different waiver, and some adjustment on the insurance end of things, and I'll see to that."

"Happy not to pick up that torch."

Fin took his turn to boot the ball. "The other end is scheduling, which I'll leave to you and Boyle to coordinate. We've got Meara and yourself as experienced riders and hawkers, and Iona's done well with the hawking."

"And none better on a horse. So that gives us three who could take the point on a combination. You'd be four."

Fin glanced over as Connor grinned at him. "I haven't run a guided since . . . not since the first few months Boyle and I were getting it all off the ground."

"Sure you could go out anytime, I'm certain, with one of the others, as a kind of apprentice."

Connor set to kick, and for the hell of it Fin blocked, took the ball himself, added some footwork remembered from boyhood before he sent it flying.

"After a match then?" Connor asked.

"I'll take you on when I've time, and that'll be after I've done a draft of a new brochure for you and Boyle to have a look at. Meanwhile, you should have another who can hawk and ride and handle a small group — as I think we'd keep this combination, at least at the start to groups of six and under. Who strikes you?"

"I've some with more hawking experience, but I'd say our Brian. He's the most eager to learn the new, try the different."

"Then you'll speak to him, and if he's keen on it, he can start training, see how it all goes. We'll want to try it a few times, with just staff or friends. If *that* all goes well, we'll begin to offer the package in March, we'll say. By the equinox, as a goal."

"A good time to work out any kinks in the wire."

"And now, I'm after taking Sassy out for a bit. I'll go to the stables, get a mount, and we'll see how she does with a horse and rider. Merlin will come along as he'll keep her in line. And I want to see how they get on. I think to breed them."

Connor grinned. "I was going to speak to you about just that. It's the right match, to my mind. They're well suited — his dignity and her sassiness. I think they'd produce a grand clutch for us."

"We'll let them decide."

Fin got a baiting pouch as the female still looked for the reward, and pulling on a glove, fixed Sassy's jesses. She preened a bit, pleased to be chosen, and cocked her head, eyeing him with a look he could only deem flirtatious.

"Sure you're a fetching one, aren't you now?" He walked out the gates with her, and turning toward the stables, called for Merlin.

His hawk soared overhead, then went into a long, graceful swoop Fin could only deem a bit of showing off. On his arm, Sassy spread her wings.

"Want to join him, do you? Then I'll trust you to behave and go where I lead you." He loosened the jesses, lifted his arm, and watched her lift into the sky.

They circled together, added a few playful loops, and he thought, yes, he and Connor had the right of it. They matched well.

He enjoyed the walk, the familiar trees, the turn of the path, the scents in the air. Though he'd hoped he would, he felt nothing of Cabhan, and traveled from school to stables with only the hawks for company.

He thought the stables made a picture, spread as they were with the paddock, the lorries and cars, and Caesar's majestic head lifted out the open stall window. The horse sent Fin a whinny of greeting so he went directly over to stroke and rub, have a short conversation before going inside.

He found Boyle in the office, glowering at the computer.

"Why do people ask so many stupid questions?" Boyle demanded.

"You only think they're stupid as you already know the answers." Fin sat on a corner — about the only clear area — of the desk. "I've just come from Connor at the school," he began, and spoke with Boyle about the plans for the new package.

"Iona's keen on it, that's for certain. And Brian, well, he's young, but from what I've seen and heard, he works hard, and I know he rides well enough. I'm willing to give it a go."

"Then we'll smooth out the details. Unless you need me here, I'm taking Caesar. We'll try a hawk ride as I've Merlin and a young female along with me. I'll map out a potential route."

"Have a care. Iona and I went by the new house to see the progress early this morning. She saw the wolf, the shadow wolf, slinking through the trees."

"You didn't?"

"No, I was turned away, and talking with one of the carpenters. She said it came closer than it had before, though she's put protection around the house."

"I'll have a look myself."

"I'd be grateful."

Fin saddled Caesar, who was eager to be off as he understood he'd get a run out of it instead of the usual plod. After he'd led the horse out, mounted, he walked a distance away, then baited his glove, called to Sassy.

She landed prettily, gobbled the bit of chicken as if she'd been starved for a month, then settled into it. She and Caesar exchanged one long stare, then the horse turned his head away as if the hawk was nothing to do with him.

"That's a fine attitude," Fin decided, and to test both horse and hawk, kicked into a gallop.

It startled the hawk, who spread her wings — another picture — and would have risen off the glove if Fin hadn't soothed her.

"You're fine. It's just another way to fly." She fidgeted some, not entirely convinced, but stayed on the glove. Satisfied, Fin dropped into a canter, turned toward the woods before he signaled her to lift.

She soared to a branch where Merlin already waited.

"Well done, well done indeed. You'll lead, Merlin, and we'll follow."

His hawk looped through the trees; the female followed. Keeping to a dignified walk, Fin led the horse through.

For the next half hour he took her through the paces, bringing her back to the glove, letting her go again.

The chilly, damp air opened for a thin drizzle of rain, but none of them minded it. Here was freedom for all in a kind of game.

He mapped out the route in his head, thought it would make a fine loop for the package, showing off how the hawks could dance through the trees, and return time and time to the glove without breaking the horse's easy pace.

Close enough here to hear the river murmur, far enough there to feel as though you rode hawking into another time. And he could smell snow coming. By nightfall, he thought, and it would grace the greens and browns, lie still and quiet for a time.

And come spring, the blackthorn would bloom, and the wildflowers Branna gathered for pleasure and for magicks.

Come spring, he thought — he hoped — he could walk through the woods with her, in peace.

And thinking of her, he changed direction. The hawks and horse could settle down outside her cottage awhile while he worked with her.

When he moved onto a clear path, he let Caesar canter again, then laughed as he saw Bugs running, tongue lolling.

"Now with the hound I've all three. We'll just go by, stop in Branna's. She might have something for all of you. Then we'll take a look at Boyle's new house before going on home."

Apparently fine with that plan, Bugs raced along beside the horse.

Fin slowed again as they approached the big downed tree, and the thick vines that barred most from the ruins of Sorcha's cabin.

Bugs let out a low growl.

"Oh aye, he's coming around now. I feel him as well."

Fin ordered Sassy to stay in the air, called Merlin to the glove.

Fog snaked through the vines. Fin held out his free hand, levitated the dog up to sit in front of him in the saddle.

He felt the pull, the almost cheerful invitation to come through, to bask in all that could be, all the dark gifts offered.

"If that's the best you have . . ." With a shrug, Fin started to turn the horse.

The wolf burst out of the vines, gleaming black, red stone pulsing. Caesar shied, reared, but Fin managed to keep his seat, and snatched the dog before Bugs lost his.

To Fin's surprise, Sassy went into a stoop, swooped over the wolf, then up again where she perched in a tree, staring down at it.

Clever girl, he thought. Fierce and clever girl.

"I'll say again, if that's the best you have . . ."

Fin took Caesar into a charge, and shot down a hand to split the earth open under the wolf. As the horse leaped over it, the wolf vanished.

Fin heard the laughter behind him, turned the horse.

Cabhan floated above the open earth on a blanket of fog.

"Far from the best, boy. You've yet to taste my best. Spare yourself, for in the end you'll come to me. I know your blood."

Fin fought the urge to charge again, but he'd been in business long enough to know a turned back could pack a harder punch.

So he simply turned Caesar, walked away without hurry.

"Spare yourself." It came as a whisper, not a shout. "And when I've finished with you, I will bind the dark witch you lust for to you for eternity."

The urge to turn and charge grew with fury.

Without looking back, Fin healed the earth, and moved forward and out of the woods.

Fin tethered the horse outside the cottage and, dismounting, pressed his cheek to Caesar's. "You earned your name today, as you never hesitated to charge when I asked it of you." Like a magician, he held out his hand, showed it empty, then turned his wrist and produced an apple.

While Caesar crunched his treat, Fin called Sassy to glove. "And you, so brave for one so young. You'll hunt." He signaled to Merlin. "You'll hunt together in Branna's field, and you can stay awhile in Roibeard's lean-to. And you." He bent to rub Bugs. "I'll wager there's a biscuit inside for the likes of you."

With the dog, Fin walked to the workshop and in.

"There's my reward," he said as Branna took a tray of biscuits out of the little workshop oven.

"You timed that exceedingly well." She laid the tray on the top of the stove, turned. "Something happened," she said immediately.

"Not of great import, but here's a hound who's earned a biscuit if you have one."

"Of course." She got two from the jar, as Kathel had already stirred himself from his nap by the fire to greet his small friend.

"I'd rather this sort," Fin said and plucked up one of the human variety she already had cooled on a rack. "I had business to see to at home, then at the school and around to the stables. We're doing the hawk-and-horse package come spring."

"That's all well and good, but what happened?"

"I took hawk and horse out myself. Caesar and Merlin and a pretty female name of

Sassy who will mate with Merlin when she's ready for it."

"And how does she feel about that?" Branna put the kettle on as Fin already grabbed a second biscuit.

"She likes the look of him, and he of her. I was after mapping out a couple of routes that might suit the package, and Bugs joined in as we passed near the big stables. With them I turned this way, thinking to work with you for an hour or two, and passed by the entrance to Sorcha's cabin."

"You could've avoided that spot."

"True enough. I didn't want to avoid it. And because I didn't, I learned the hawk I chose for Merlin will be his match."

He told her, accepted the tea, and actively considered trying for a third biscuit.

"He grows more arrogant," Branna said.

"Enough to taunt, which is all this business was. He wanted me to come at him again, and it occurred to me that denying him that was more of an insult."

"He wants us to know none of us can take a simple walk in the woods without risk. Taunting," Branna agreed, "in hopes to destroy our morale, close us in."

"He's more confident than he was, or so it strikes me."

"We've bloodied him twice, more than

twice, and the last time nearly destroyed him."

"But we didn't," Fin pointed out. "And he heals, and knows he's only to reach his lair again to heal. Knows he can battle us time and time again, and come back time and time again. If you're a gambling man, the odds would be at some point we'll lose the day. It's time again, Branna, and he has that in his pocket."

"He doesn't believe he can be destroyed — or he doesn't believe what's in him can. But I'm working on that."

She walked over, tapped her finger on her notebook. "I called on my father, and he called on others, and I've put together ingredients and the mixing of them I think will take the demon. I've been working on the words of the spell along with it. We need the name. I don't believe this will work without calling the demon by name, and those who consulted with my father confirm that."

Fin palmed the third biscuit, then stepped closer to read over her shoulder.

"Dried wing of bat — best from Romania?"

"I'm told."

"Tail hairs from a pregnant yak." Fin arched a brow. "No eye of newt or tongue of dog. Apologies," he said to both Kathel and Bugs.

"You may joke about the English bard's witches three, but I've formulated this from the best sources I can find."

"Wolfsbane, Atropa belladonna berries — crushed — tincture of Amazonian angel's trumpet, conium petals from Armenia, sap from the manchineel tree. I know some of these."

"All poisons. All of them natural poisons. We have some of this in what we've devised for Cabhan, but there are a number of ingredients here that are more exotic than I've worked with before. I'll have to send for some, obviously. It requires water blessed by a priest, which is easy enough. Blood remains the binding agent. It's yours we'll need. Your blood, some of your hair, and nail clippings."

He only grunted.

"I'd started on the amounts, and the orders. My sources conflict somewhat on both, but we'll find the right mix. And the words need to be right. The potion will be black and dense when we have it right. It will hold no light, reflect no light."

He reached up, massaged her shoulders. "You're knotted up. You should be pleased, not tense. This is brilliant progress, Branna."

"None of it will have a hope of working unless we choose the right time, and there I've made no progress at all."

"I've thought on it. Ostara? The equinox. We tried the summer solstice, for light. Ostara is light as well, the balance of it tipping to the light."

"I come back to it, again and again." She pushed her hands through her hair to secure loosened pins. "But it won't hold for me as the other tries did. It should be right; maybe it is and I just can't see it through the other elements."

He turned her, still rubbing her shoulders. "We might try devising the spell, and the potion with Ostara as the time, and see if it holds then. Providing we find a pregnant yak."

She smiled as he'd hoped. "My father tells me he knows a man who can acquire anything, for a price."

"Then we'll pay the price, and we'll begin. I've still got an hour or so, and I'll help with the spell. But tonight, I think you could use a distraction, having your mind off all this."

"Is that what you think?"

"I think you should come out to dinner with me. I've a place in mind you'll like, very much."

"Out to dinner? And what sort of place

would this be?"

"A very fancy place. Romantic and elegant, and where the food is a god." He twined some of her loosened hair around his finger. "You could wear the dress you wore New Year's Eve."

"I've more than one dress, and would consider going skyclad to be served food fit for gods that I don't make myself."

"If you insist, but I'd rather see to getting you skyclad myself after dessert."

"Are we having a date, Finbar?"

"We are. Dinner at eight, though I'll pick you up at seven so you'll have some time to enjoy the city before we eat."

"The city? What city?"

"Paris," he said, and kissed her.

"You want us flying off to Paris for a meal?"

"A brilliant meal — in the City of Light."

"Paris," she repeated, and tried to tell herself it was frivolous and foolish, but just couldn't. "Paris," she said again, and kissed him back.

14

"What was it like? Paris," Iona added. "We haven't had a chance to talk about it without the guys around since you went."

"It was lovely. A bit breathtaking really. The lights, the voices, the food and wine, of course. For a few hours, another world altogether."

"Romantic?" Iona tied pretty raffia bows around softly colored soaps, and boldly colored ones.

"It was."

"I wonder why that part of it worries you."

"I'm not after romance. It's the sort of thing that weakens resolve and clouds sense." Branna measured out ground herbs. "It's not something I can risk now."

"You love each other."

"Love isn't always the answer." While Iona helped with store stock, Branna focused on more magickal supplies. Another battle would come, other attacks were likely. She wanted a full store of medicinals on hand, for any contingency.

"It is for you, and I'm glad of it." She added precisely six drops of extract of nasturtium to the small cauldron. "It adds to what you are, strengthens your purpose."

"You think it weakens yours."

"I think it can, and now more than ever that can't be allowed. Both Fin and I know we can live without each other. We have done so, and well enough. We know what we have now may only be for now. Whatever the rest, with or without, waits until Cabhan is finished."

"You're happier with him," Iona pointed out.

"And what woman isn't happier when she can count on a good shag with some regularity?" After Iona's snort, she held up a finger for silence, then holding her hands over the cauldron, brought the brew to a fast boil. Murmuring now, drawing light down with one hand, a thin shower of blue rain with the other. For an instant a rainbow formed, then it, too, slid into the pot.

Branna took the brew down to the slowest of simmers.

Satisfied, she turned, found Iona studying her.

"Watching you work," Iona explained.

"It's all so pretty, so graceful, with power just flowing all around."

"We'll want this restorative on hand, as well as the balms and salves I've been stocking up." Branna tapped the door to a cupboard she thought of as her war chest.

"Hope for the best, but prepare for the worst."

"A good policy."

"It's what you're doing with Fin?"

"Being with him — and not just for the sex — lets me remember all the reasons I fell in love with him. He has such kindness — and I wanted to forget that of him. His humor, his focus, his loyalty. I want to remember all that now, for the comfort of it, and for the unity. Remembering who he is means I can give him all my trust in this. All of it. And I'm not sure, no matter how I tried, I did before. Because I can and do, there'll always be some best to hold on to."

"Is he coming today?"

"I told him no need. We're still shy some of the ingredients so we can't begin to make the poison as yet. He has his work as I have mine. And I appreciate you giving me so much of your off day."

"I like playing with your store stock — and the more I can do, the more time you have for demon poisons. I want to take

Alastar out later, and was hoping you'd want to go for a ride with us."

"A ride?"

"I've seen you ride, and Meara mentioned you don't take much time for it, the way you once did."

She hadn't, Branna thought, as it reminded her of Fin. But now . . . He'd brought Aine for her, and she hadn't given herself the pleasure of testing the bond with the horse.

"If what needs doing is done, I would. And if the pair of us rode out for pleasure, it's a nose-thumbing in Cabhan's direction."

"We're seeing him every day now." Idly, Iona stacked the pretty soaps into colorful towers. "Skulking around."

"I know it. I see him as well. He tests my borders often now."

"I dreamed of Teagan last night. We talked."

"And you're just telling me of it?"

"It was like a little visit. Sitting in front of the fire, drinking tea. She's showing, and she let me feel the baby kick. She told me about her husband, and I talked about Boyle. And it struck me — what you'd said about all of us being connected — her husband and Boyle are so alike. In temperament, his love of horses and the land."

"Boyle's connected to the three through the man Teagan married? Yes, that could be."

"We didn't talk of Cabhan, and isn't that odd? We just drank tea and talked of her husband, the baby to come, Boyle, the wedding plans. At the end of the dream, she gave me a little charm, and said it was for Alastar."

"Do you have it?"

"I put it on his bridle this morning before I came. I had a charm in my pocket, one I'd made for Alastar, so I gave it to her."

"We've exchanged tokens, each of us with each of them. I think it's more than courtesy. Something of ours in their time, and something of theirs in ours. We'll want all three gifts with us when we face Cabhan again."

"We're still not sure when."

"It's a frustration to me," Branna admitted. "But it can't be done until we have all we need to destroy the demon. I have to believe we'll know when we must."

"Demons and visits in dreams with cousins from centuries ago. Battles and whirlwinds and weddings. My life is so different from what it was a year ago. I've been here nearly a year now, and it feels as if the life I led before was barely there. Is it silly — and unrealistic — for me to plan and cook a kind of anniversary dinner for Boyle? Surprise him with it — and I mean something he can actually eat without pretending it doesn't suck."

Both amused and touched, Branna glanced over while Iona rearranged her towers. "Of course it's not."

"I can still see him just the way it was when he first rode up on Alastar. The way both of them just shot straight into me. Now they're mine. I want to mark the day."

"So you will."

Something brushed the edge of her thoughts. Branna paused, waited for it to come, and the door jangled open.

One of her neighbors, a cheerful, grandmotherly type, stepped inside.

"Good day to you, Mrs. Baker."

"And to you, Branna, and here's Iona as well. I hope I'm not a bother to you."

"Not at all. Would you have some tea?" Branna offered.

"I wouldn't mind it, if it's no trouble. It's tea I've come for — if you've the blend you make for head colds. It would save me a trip to the village if you've some on hand I can buy from you."

"I do, of course. Here, take off your coat,

and sit by the fire. Have you a cold coming on?"

"Not me, but my husband has one full blown, and is driving me mad with his complaints. I swear a cup of tea by your fire here with women who know better than to think their life's finished because they've got a cold in the head would save my sanity. Oh, and aren't these soaps as pretty as candy in a jar."

"I can't decide which is my favorite, but this one's leading the charge." Iona held up a bold red cake for Mrs. Baker to sniff.

"That's lovely. I'm going to treat myself to one of these as a reward for not knocking himself unconscious with a skillet."

"You deserve it."

"A bit of the sniffles and men are more work than a brood of babies. You'll be finding that out for yourself soon enough, with the wedding coming."

"I'm hoping to get a good skillet as a wedding gift," Iona said, and made Mrs. Baker laugh until she wheezed.

Accepting the invitation, she took off her coat, her scarf, and settled herself by the fire. "And here's your Kathel — it's a fine thing, a dog, a fire, a cup of tea. I thought I saw him when I started over, prowling along the edge of the woods, even called out a greeting to him before I saw it wasn't our Kathel at all. A big black dog for certain, and for a moment I thought: Well, God in heaven, that's a wolf. Then it was gone." She snapped her fingers. "Old eyes, I imagine, playing tricks."

After a quick glance at Iona, Branna brought over tea and biscuits. "A stray perhaps. Have you seen it before?"

"I haven't, no, and hope not to again. It gave me gooseflesh, I admit, when it turned its head toward me after I called out, thinking it was Kathel. I nearly turned round and went back inside — which should prove it gave me the shivers, as inside I've Mr. Baker's whining.

"Oh, Branna, what a treat! I couldn't be more grateful."

"You're very welcome. I've a tonic you could add to Mr. Baker's tea. It's good for what troubles him, and will help him sleep."

"Name your price."

They entertained Mrs. Baker, rang up the sale of tea and tonic, and gave the pretty soap as a gift. And Branna sent Kathel out with her, to be certain she got home safe.

"Did he show himself to her," Iona said the minute they were alone, "or is his . . . presence — would that be it — just more tangible?"

"I'm wondering if he got careless, as that's another possibility. Prowling around as she said, hoping to trouble us, and he didn't shadow himself from others. As he doesn't want the attention of others, I think it was carelessness."

"He's impatient."

"It may be, but he'll just have to wait until we're ready. I'm going to finish this restorative, then we'll take ourselves off. We'll have that ride."

"You're hoping he'll take a run at us."

"I'm not hoping he won't." Branna lifted her chin in defiance. "I'd like to give him a taste of what two women of power can do."

Branna wasn't disappointed Fin had business elsewhere. If he'd been at home or in the stables, he wouldn't have cared for the idea of her and Iona going out at all, or would have insisted on going with them.

She wore riding boots she hadn't put on in years, and had to admit it felt good. And what felt even better was saddling Aine herself.

"We don't know each other well as yet, so I hope you'll let Iona know if you've any problems with me." She took a moment to come around the filly's head, stroke her cheeks, look into her eyes.

"He'd have wanted you for your beauty and grace alone, for you have both in full measure. But he sensed you were for me, and I for you. If that's the way of it, I'll do my best for you. That's an oath. I made this for you today," she added, and braided a charm into Aine's mane with a bright red ribbon. "For protection, as mine or not, I'll protect you."

"She thinks you're nearly as pretty as she is," Iona told Branna.

With a laugh, Branna stepped over to adjust the stirrups to her liking. "Now then that's a fine compliment."

"With you on her back, you'll make a picture — which is something she's happy to make for Alastar."

"Let's make one then." With Iona she led the horses out of the stables, vaulted into the saddle as if it had been only yesterday.

"Do we have a plan?" Iona leaned over the saddle to pat Alastar's neck.

"Sometimes it's best to take things as they come."

They walked to the road, with Kathel and Bugs prancing along with them.

"I can't call the hawk," Iona said.

"They'll come if needed. Though that would've been a thought, wouldn't it, to ride out with all the guides. What do you say to a canter?"

"I say yay."

Graceful, Branna thought again when Aine responded and broke into a bright canter. And flirtatious, Branna added, as she didn't need to have Iona's gift to interpret the way Aine tossed her mane.

She glanced back, saw that the faithful Kathel slowed his own pace to stay with Bugs, felt her lips curve at the happiness beaming from both of them.

So she let herself just enjoy.

The cool air, with a sharpness in it that told her more snow would come. The scent of the trees and horses, the steady beat of hooves.

Maybe she had taken too little time for too long a time if a little canter down the road brought her such a lift in spirit.

She felt in tune with the horse. Fin would be right, she admitted, as he was never wrong on such matters. For whatever reason, Aine would be hers, and the partnership between them began now.

They turned onto the path into the trees where the air was cooler yet. Small pools of snow lay in shadows where they'd formed in a previous fall, and a bird chattered on a bough.

They slowed to an easy trot.

"She's hoping, and so's Alastar, we'll head to some open before it's done for a gallop."

"I wouldn't mind it. I haven't gone this way in more than a year. I'd nearly forgotten how lovely it can be in winter, how hushed and alone."

"I'll never get used to it," Iona told her. "Could never take any of it for granted. I don't know how many guideds I've done through here this last year, and still every one is a wonder."

"It doesn't bore you, a horsewoman of your skills, just plodding along?"

"You'd think it would, but it doesn't. The people are usually interesting, and I'm getting paid for riding a horse. Then . . ." Iona wiggled her eyebrows. "I get to sleep with the boss. It's a good deal all around."

"We could circle around on the way back, go by your house."

"I was hoping you'd say that. They were supposed to — maybe — start putting up drywall today. Connor's been a champ, making time to get over there and pitch in."

"Sure he loves the building, and he's clever with it."

In unison they turned to walk the horses along the river.

The air chilled, and Branna saw the first fingers of fog.

"We've company," she murmured to Iona.

"Yeah. Okay."

"Keep the horses calm, won't you, and I'll do the same with the hounds."

He came as a man, handsome and hard, dressed in black with silver trim. Branna noted he'd been vain enough to do a glamour as his face glowed with health and color.

He swept them a deep bow.

"Ladies. What a grand sight you make on a winter's day."

"Do you have so little to occupy yourself," Branna began, "that you spend all your time sniffing about where you're not welcome."

"But you see I've been rewarded, as here are the two blooms of the three. You think to wed a mortal," he said to Iona. "To waste your power on one who can never return it. I have so much more for you."

"You have nothing for me, and you're so much less than him."

"He builds you a house of stone and stick when I would give you a palace." He spread his arms, and over the cold, dark water of the river swam a palace shining with silver and gold. "A true home for such as you, who has never had her own. Always craved her own. This I would give you."

Iona dug deep, turned the image to black. "Keep it."

"I will take your power, then you will live in the ashes of what might have been. And you." He turned to Branna. "You lay with my son."

"He isn't your son."

"His blood is my blood, and this you can never deny. Take him, be taken, it only weakens you. You will bear my seed one way or the other. Choose me, choose now, while I still grant you a choice. Or when I come for you, I will give you pain not pleasure. Choose him, and his blood, the blood of all you profess to love, will be on your hands."

She leaned forward in the saddle. "I choose myself. I choose my gift and my birthright. I choose the light, whatever the price. Where Sorcha failed, we will not. You'll burn, Cabhan."

Now she swept an arm out, and over that cold, dark river a tower of fire rose, and through the flame and smoke the image of Cabhan screamed.

"That is my gift to you."

He rose a foot off the ground, and still Iona held the horses steady. "I will take the greatest pleasure in you. I will have you watch while I gut your brother, while I rip your cousin's man in quarters. You'll watch me slit the throat of the one you think of as sister, watch while I rape your cousin. And only then when their blood soaks the ground will I end you."

"I am the Dark Witch of Mayo," she said simply. "And I am your doom."

"Watch for me," he warned her. "But you will not see."

He vanished with the fog.

"Those kind of threats —" Iona broke off, gestured toward the flaming towers, the screams. "Would you mind?"

"Hmm. I rather like it, but . . ." Branna whisked it away. "They're not threats, not in his mind, but promises. We'll see he breaks them. I'd hoped he'd take wolf form, at least for a few moments. I want the name of what made him."

"Satan, Lucifer, Beelzebub?"

Branna smiled a little. "I think not. A lesser demon, and one who needs Cabhan as Cabhan needs it. The pair of them left a stink in the air. Let's have that gallop now, and go by and see your house."

"The sticks and stones?"

"Are solid and strong. And real."

Iona nodded. "Branna, what if . . . if while you're with Fin you got pregnant?"

"I won't. I've taken precautions." With that she urged Aine into a gallop.

She gave Aine a carrot and a rubdown, so

when Fin came into the stables he found both her and Iona.

"I'm told you went for a ride."

"We did, and it reminded me how I enjoy it." She leaned her cheek to Aine's. "You did say she and I should get acquainted."

"I didn't have in mind you going off alone."

"I wasn't alone. I was with Iona and she with me, with Aine and Alastar and the dogs altogether. Oh, don't try to slither out because he's glowering," she said to Iona. "You're tougher than that. We had a conversation with Cabhan — no more really than a volley of harsh words all around. We'll tell you and the others the whole of it."

"Bloody right you will." He started to grab Branna's arm, and Aine butted him in the shoulder with her head.

"Taking her side now?"

"She's mine, after all. And knows as well as I do we had no trouble, and took no more risks than any of us do when taking a step out of the house. I suppose you'll want a meal with the telling."

"I could eat," Iona said.

"We'll have it all here," Fin told them.

"With what?"

He took Branna's arm now, but casually. "You've given me lists every time I turn around. There's enough in the kitchen to put together a week of meals."

"As it should be. All right then. Iona, would you mind telling the others while I see what I can put together in Finbar's famous kitchen?"

"You went out looking for him," Fin accused.

"I didn't, no, but I didn't go out not expecting to find him."

"You knew he'd come at you."

"He didn't come at us, not in any way as you mean. Only words. A kind of testing ground on his part, I'm thinking. I'd hoped he'd come as the wolf, so I could try to get the name, but he was only a man."

Inside, she took off her coat, handed it to Fin. "And we did have a lovely ride around it, coming back so I could see the progress on Iona's house. It's going to be lovely, just lovely. An open kind of space, and still a few snug little places for the cozy. Coming back here that way, I had a different perspective on this house. That room with all the windows that juts toward the woods. It must be a lovely place to sit and look out, all year long. Private enough, and steps from the trees."

She rummaged in the refrigerator, freezer, cupboards as she spoke.

"I've a recipe for these chicken breasts Connor's fond of. It gives them a bite." Head angled, she sent him a challenging look. "Can you take a bite, Fin?"

"Can you?" He pulled her to him, nipped her bottom lip.

"I give good as I get. And you might get more yet if you pour me some wine."

He turned, found a bottle, studied the label. "Do you understand what it would have done to me if he'd hurt you?"

"None of us can think like that. We can't. What we feel for each other, all of us for each other, is strong and true and deep. And we can't think that way."

"It's not thinking, Branna. It's feeling."

She laid her hands on his chest. "Then we can't feel that way. He weakens us if he holds us back from taking the risks we have to take."

"He weakens us all the more if we stop feeling."

"You're both right." Iona came in. "We have to feel it. I'm afraid for Boyle all the time, but we still do what we have to do. We feel it, and we keep going."

"You've a good point. You feel, but you don't stop," she said to Fin. "Neither can I. I can promise you I'll protect myself as best I can. And I'm very good at it."

"You are that. I'm going to open this wine, Iona. Would you have some?"

"Twist my arm."

"After you've done the wine, Fin, you can scrub up the potatoes."

"Iona," Fin said smooth as butter, "you wouldn't mind scrubbing the potatoes, would you, darling?"

Before Branna could speak, Iona pulled off her coat. "I'll take KP. In fact, whatever you're making, Branna, you could walk me through it. Maybe it'll be the anniversary dinner for Boyle."

"This is a little rough and ready for that," Branna began, "but . . . Well, that's it! For the love of . . . Why didn't I think of it before?"

"Think of what?" Iona asked.

"The time. The day we end Cabhan. Right in front of my face. I need my book. I need my star charts. I need to be sure. I'll take the table here for it — it shouldn't take long."

She grabbed the wine Fin had just poured, and walking toward the dining area, flicked fingers in the air until her spell books, her laptop, her notepad sat neatly on one side. "Iona, you'll need to quarter those potatoes once scrubbed, lay them in a large baking dish. Get the oven preheated now, to three hundred and seventy-five."

"I can do that, but —"

"I need twenty minutes here. Maybe a half hour. Ah . . . then you'll pour four table-spoons, more or less, of olive oil over the potatoes, toss them in it to coat. Sprinkle on pepper and crushed rosemary. Use your eye for it, you've got one. In the oven for thirty minutes, then I'll tell you what to do with them next. I'll be finished by then. Quiet!" she snapped, dropping down to sit before Iona could ask another question.

"I hate when she says more or less or use your eye," Iona complained to Fin.

"I've an eye as well, but I promise it's worse than your own."

"Maybe between us, we'll make one good one."

She did her best — scrubbed, quartered, poured, tossed, sprinkled. And wished Boyle would get there to tell her if it looked right. On Fin's shrug, she stuck it in the oven. Set the timer.

Then she drank wine and hoped while she and Fin studied Branna.

She'd pulled one of her clips from some-where and scooped up her hair. The sweater she'd rolled to her elbows as she worked from book to computer and back again, as she scribbled notes, made calculations.

"What if she's not done when the timer goes off?" Iona wondered.

"We're on our own, as she'd skin us if we interrupted her now."

"That's it!" Branna slapped a hand on her notebook. "By all the goddesses, that's it. It's so fecking simple, it's so bloody *obvious*. I looked right through it."

She rose, strode back, poured a second glass of wine. "Anniversary. Of course. When else could it be?"

"Anniversary?" Iona's eyes went wide. "Mine? The day I came, met you? But you said that hadn't worked. The day I met Boyle? That anniversary?"

"No, not yours. Sorcha's. The day she died. The anniversary of her death, and the day she took Cabhan to ash. That day, in our time, is when we end it. When we will. Not a sabbat or esbat. Not a holy day. Sorcha's day."

"The day the three were given her power," Fin stated. "The day they became, and so you became. You're right. It was right there, and not one of us saw it."

"Now we do." She raised her glass. "Now we can finish it."

15

She felt revived, reenergized. Branna actively enjoyed preparing the meal — and Iona did very well with her end of it — enjoyed sitting around Fin's dining room with her circle, despite the fact that the bulk of the dinner conversation centered on Cabhan.

Now, in fact, maybe because of it.

Because she could see it clear, how it could and would be done. The when and the how of it. Risks remained, and they'd face them. But she could believe now as Connor and Iona believed.

Right and light would triumph over the dark.

And was there a finer way to end an evening than sitting in the steaming, bubbling water of Fin's hot tub drinking one last glass of wine and watching a slow, fluffy snowfall?

"You've been a surprise to me, Finbar."

He reclined across from her, lazy-eyed.

"Have I now?"

"You have indeed. Imagine the boy I knew building this big house with all its style and its luxuries. And the boy a well-traveled and successful man of business. One who roots those businesses at home. I wouldn't have thought a dozen years back I'd be indulging myself in this lovely spot of yours while the snow falls."

"What would you have thought?"

"Considerably smaller, I'd have to say. Your dreams grew larger than mine, and you've done well with them."

"Some remain much as they were."

She only smiled, glided her foot along his leg under the frothy water.

"It feels we could be in some chalet in Switzerland, which I like, but I wonder you didn't put this in that room with all the windows, the way it's situated so private and opening to the woods."

He drank some wine. "I had that room built with you in mind."

"Me?"

"With the hope one day you'd marry me as we planned, live here with me. And make your workshop there."

"Oh, Fin." His wish, and her own, twined together to squeeze her heart.

"You like the open when you work, the

glass so you can look out, the feel of being out, is what appeals to you. Snug enough inside, but with that open to bring the out in to you. So the glass room facing the woods gives you the private and the open at once."

She couldn't speak for a moment, didn't want her voice to shake when she did. "If I had the magicks to change what is, to transform them into what I'd wish them to be, it would be that, to live and to work here with you. But we have this."

She set her wineglass in the holder, flowed over to him, to press body to body. "We have today."

He skimmed a hand down her hair, down to where it dipped and floated over the water. "No tomorrows."

"Today." She laid her cheek against his. "I'm with you, you're with me. I never believed, or let myself believe, we could have this much. Today is the world for me, as you are. It may never be enough, and still." She drew back, just a little. "It's all."

She brushed his lips with hers, slid into the kiss with all the tenderness she owned.

She would give him all she had to give him. And all was love. More than her body, but through her body her heart. It had always been his, would always be, so the gift of it was simple as breathing.

"Believe," she murmured. "Tonight."

Sweetly, for with her practical bent she could forget the sweet, she offered the kiss, to stir, to soothe.

Her only love.

He knew what she offered, and knew what she asked. He would take, and he would give. And setting aside the wish for more, he would believe tonight was everything.

Here was magick in having her soft and yielding, her sigh warm against his cheek as they embraced. The heat rose through him, around him, with the snow a silent curtain to close out all the world but them.

He took her breasts, gently, gently, as he could still see in his mind the violent marks what shared his blood had put on her. He swore as her heart beat against his hand, he would never harm her, would give his life to keep her from harm.

Whatever came tomorrow, he'd never break the oath.

Her hands glided over him, and her fingers brushed against the mark he carried. Her touch, even so light, brought on a bone-deep ache there. A price he'd pay without question.

The water, a steady drumbeat in the hush of the night, swirled around them as their hands drifted under it to give pleasure.

Her breath caught, shaking her heart with the meeting of emotion and sensation, the rise of need and wonder.

How could tenderness cause such heat — a wire in the blood, a fire in the belly — and still have her wish to draw every moment into forever?

So when she straddled him, took him deep, and deep and deep, she knew she would never take another. Whatever the needs of the body, no other could touch her heart, her soul. Combing her fingers through his hair, she held his face as she moved over him so he could see her, see into her, and know.

On their slow climb, the swirling water glowed, a pool of light to bathe them and surround them. As they fell, holding tight, the light flowed out against the dark to illuminate the soft curtain of snow.

Later, lax and sleepy in his bed, she curled against him. As tonight became tomorrow, she held fast to what she loved.

It took more precious days before Branna could acquire all the ingredients, in quantities to allow for experimenting, needed for the poison.

Connor looked on as she sealed them in

individual jars on her work counter.

"Those are dangerous, Branna."

"As well they need be."

"You'll take precautions." His face only went stony when she shot him a withering glance. "So you always do, I know full well. But I also know you've never worked with such as this, or concocted such a lethal brew. I've a right to worry about my sister."

"You do, but you needn't. I've spent the days waiting for all of this to arrive to study on them. Meara, take him off, would you? The pair of you should be off to work, not hovering around me."

"If we can't use the stuff until near to April," Meara argued, "can't you wait to make it?"

"As Connor's so helpfully pointed out, I've never done this before. It may take some time to get it right, and I might even have to send out for more before we're sure of it. It's a delicate business."

"Iona and I should do this with you."

Patience, Branna ordered herself, and dug some out of her depleting stores.

"And if the three are huddled in here, hours a day, maybe for days on end, Cabhan will know we're brewing up something. It's best we all continue our routines." Struggling against annoyance, as his worry

341

for her was from love, she turned to him. "Connor, we talked all this through."

"Talking and doing's different."

"We could mix up the routines a bit," Meara suggested, caught between them. "One of us can stay for an hour or two in the morning, another can come around midday, and another come round early from work."

"All right then." Anything, Branna thought, to move them along. "But not this morning as you're both on the schedule. I'm only going to be making powders, distilling. Preparing the ingredients. And I know what I'm about. Added to it, I expect Fin by midday, so there's two of us at it already."

"That's fair enough," Meara said before Connor could argue, and grabbed his hand. "I've got to get on or Boyle will be down my throat and up my arse at the same time. Branna, you'll let us know if you need any help."

"Be sure I will."

Connor strode over, gave Branna a quick, hard kiss. "Don't poison yourself."

"I thought I would just for the experience, but since you ask so nicely . . ."

She breathed a sigh of relief when the door closed behind them, then found Kathel sitting, staring at her.

"Not you as well? When did I all at once become an idjit? If you want to help, go round on patrol." She marched to the door, opened it. "I'm after cloaking the workshop and locking up besides. It wouldn't do to have someone wander in for hand balm while I'm doing this work. Be helpful, Kathel," she said in a more cajoling tone, "and you'll tell me if you find Cabhan's anywhere near."

Another sigh of relief when she'd shut the door behind him.

She cloaked the glass so none but who she chose could see inside. She charmed the doors so none but who she chose could enter.

And turning back to the counter, began — carefully — with wolfsbane.

It was painstaking work, as one of the precautions involved psychically cleansing each ingredient.

Some said those who practiced the dark arts sometimes imbued poisonous plants with the power to infect strange illnesses by only a touch or an inhale of scent.

She didn't have the time or inclination to fall ill.

After cleansing, she rejarred the entire

343

plant, or crushed petals or berries, or distilled.

From outside, Fin watched her as if through a thin layer of gauze. She'd been wise to cloak her workplace, he thought, as even from here he recognized belladonna, and angel's trumpet — though he could only assume the latter was Amazonian.

She worked with mortar and pestle because the effort and the stone added to the power. Every now and then he caught a quick glimmer of light or a thin rise of dark from the bowl or from a jar.

Both dogs flanked him. He wasn't certain if Bugs had come along for himself or for Kathel, but the little stable mutt sat and waited as patiently as Branna's big hound.

Fin wondered if he'd ever watch Branna through the glass without worry. If that day ever came, it wouldn't be today.

He moved to the door, opened it.

She'd put on music, which surprised him as she most often worked in silence, but now she worked to weeping violins.

Whatever she told the dogs stopped their forward motion toward her so they sat again, waited again. Taking off his coat, so did he.

Then she poured the powder she made through a funnel and into a jar, sealed it.

"I wanted to get that closed up before the dogs began milling around, wagging tails. I wouldn't want a speck of dust or a stray hair finding its way into the jars."

"I thought you'd have banished any speck of dust long before this."

She carried the funnel, mortar, pestle to a pot on the stove, carefully set them inside the water steadily boiling inside.

"I tend to chase them away with rag or broom as it's more satisfying. Is it midday?"

"Nearly one in the afternoon. I was delayed. Have you worked straight through since Connor and Meara left this morning?"

"And with considerable to show for it. No, don't touch me yet." She stepped to her little sink, scrubbed her hands, then coated them with lotion.

"I'm keeping my word," she told him, "and being overly cautious."

"There's no *overly* with this. And now you'll have a break from it, some food and some tea."

Before she could protest, he took her arm to steer her out and into her own kitchen.

"If you're hungry, you might have picked up some take-away while you were out. Here, you'll have a sandwich and be thankful for it."

He only pulled out a chair, pointed. "Sit,"

he said, and put the kettle on.

"I thought you wanted food."

"I said you'd have food, and I wouldn't mind some myself. I can make a bloody sandwich. I make a superior sandwich come to that, as it's what I make most."

"You're a man of some means," she pointed out. "You might hire a cook."

"Why would I do that when I can get a meal here more than half the time?"

When he opened the refrigerator, she started to tell him where he might find the various makings, then just sat back, decided to let him fend for himself.

"Did Connor put a bug in your ear?"

"He didn't have to. It would be better if you worked with someone rather than alone. And better as well if you stopped to eat."

"It seems I'm doing just that."

She watched him build a couple of sandwiches with some rocket, thinly sliced ham, and Muenster, toss some crisps on the side. He dealt with the tea, then plopped it all down on the table without ceremony.

Branna rose to get a knife as he'd neglected to cut hers in half.

"Well, if you have to be dainty about it."

"I do. And thanks." She took a bite, sighed. "I didn't realize I was hungry. This part of it's a bit tedious, but I got caught up all the same."

"What else is to be done?"

"On this first stage, nothing. I have the powders, the tinctures and extracts, some of the berries and petals should be crushed fresh. I cleansed all, and that took time, as did boiling all the tools between each ingredient to avoid any contamination. I think it should rest, and I'll start mixing tomorrow."

"We," he corrected. "I've cleared my days as best I can, and unless I'm needed at the stables or school, I'm with you until this is done."

"I can't say how long it will take to perfect it."

"Until it's done, Branna."

She shrugged, continued to eat. "You seem a bit out of sorts. Did the meeting not go well?"

"It went well enough."

She waited, then poked again. "Are you after buying more horses or hawks?"

"I looked at a yearling, and sealed a deal there as I liked the look of him. With Iona, we've drawn more students for the jumping ring. I thought to have her train this one, as he comes from a good line. If she's willing it may be we can expand that end of things, put her in charge of it."

Branna lifted her eyebrows. "She says she's content with the guideds, but I think she'd be thrilled with this idea. If you're thinking this, she must be a brilliant instructor."

"She's a natural, and her students love her. She's only three young girls regular as yet, but their parents praise her to the skies. And we've two of those students because she started with one, and the word spread around."

Branna nodded, continued to eat as Fin lapsed into silence.

"Will you tell me what's troubling you?" she asked him. "I can see it, hear it, under the rest. If it's something between us —"

"Between us we have today, as agreed." He heard the edge in his own voice, waved the words away. "It's nothing to do with that, with what's between us. Cabhan's coming into my dreams," he told her. "Three nights running now."

"Why haven't you told me?"

"What's to be done about it?" Fin countered. "He hasn't pulled me in. I think he doesn't want that battle and the energy it would cost him, so he slips and slithers into them, making his promises, distorting images. He showed me one of you last night."

"Of me."

"You were with a man with sandy hair and pale blue eyes, an American accent. Together, in a room I didn't know, but a hotel room I'd say. And you laughing as you undressed each other."

She gripped her hands together under the table. "His name was David Watson. It would've been near to five years ago now when he was in Cong. A photographer from New York City. We enjoyed each other's company and spent two nights together before he went back to America.

"He's not the only one Cabhan could show you. There aren't many but more than David Watson. Have you taken no women to bed these past years, Finbar?"

Darkly green, just a bit dangerous, his eyes met hers. "There have been women. I tried to hurt none of them, and still most knew they were solace or, worse, somehow, placeholders. I never thought or expected you'd not had . . . someone, Branna, but it was hard to have no choice than to watch you with another man."

"This is how he bleeds you. He doesn't want you dead, as he hopes to merge what you have with what he has, to hold you up as son, when you're nothing of the kind. So this is how he damages you without leaving a mark."

"I'm already marked, or neither of us would have been with others. I know his purpose, Branna, as well as you. It doesn't make it go down easier."

"We can try to find what will block him out."

Fin shook his head. "We've enough to do already. I'll deal with it. And there's something else, I can't quite see or hear, but only feel there's something else trying to find a way in as well."

"Something?"

"Or someone, and I wouldn't block without knowing. It's like something pushing against him, trying to find room. I can't explain it. It's a feeling when I wake that there's a voice just out of my hearing. So I'll listen for it, see what it says."

"You might do better with a good night's sleep than listening for voices. I can't change the last years, Fin."

He met her eyes. "Nor can I."

"Would it be easier on you if we weren't together now? If we went back to working together only? If he couldn't use me as a weapon against you, it —"

"There's nothing harder than being without you."

She rose, went around the table to curl in

his lap. "Should I give you the names of those I've been with? I could add their descriptions as well, so you'll know what to expect."

After a long moment, he gave her hair a hard tug. "That's a cruel and callous suggestion."

She tipped her head back. "But it nearly made you smile. Let me help you sleep tonight, Fin." She brushed her lips over his cheek. "You'll do better work for it. Whatever's trying to get in along with him can wait."

"There was a redhead name of Tilda in London. She had eyes like bluebells, a laugh like a siren. And dimples."

Eyes narrowed, Branna slid a hand up his throat, squeezed. "Balancing the scales, are we?"

"As you've yet to witness Tilda's impressive agility, I'd say the scales are far from balanced. But I should sleep better tonight for mentioning her."

He dropped his forehead to Branna's. "I won't let him damage me, or us."

Iona rushed in the back door, said, "Oops."

"We're just having some lunch," Branna told her.

"So I see. You'd both better come take a

look at this." Without waiting, she hurried through and into the workshop.

When Branna and Fin joined her, they stood looking out the window at the line of rats ranged just along the border of protection.

Branna laid a hand on Kathel's head when he growled.

"He doesn't like not being able to see in," she said quietly.

"I started to flame them up, but I thought you should see first. It's why I came around the back."

"I'll deal with it." Fin started for the door.

"Don't burn them there where they are," Branna told him. "They'll leave ugly black ash along the snow, then we'll have to deal with that — and it's lovely just now."

Fin spared her a look, a shake of his head, then stepped out coatless.

"The neighbors." On a hiss of frustration, Branna threw up a block so no one could see Fin.

And none too soon, she noted, as he pushed out power, sent the rats scrabbling while they set up that terrible high-pitched screaming. He drove them back, will against will, by millimeters.

Branna went to the door, threw it open,

intending to help, but saw she wasn't needed.

He called up a wind, sent them rolling and tumbling in ugly waves. Then he opened the earth like a trench, whirled them in. Then came the fire, and the screams tore the air.

When they stopped he drew down the rain to quench the fire, soak the ash. Then simply pulled the earth back over them.

"That was excellent," Iona breathed. "Disgusting but excellent. I didn't know he could juggle the elements like that — boom, boom, boom."

"He was showing off," Branna replied. "For Cabhan."

Fin stood where he was, in the open, as if daring a response.

He lifted his arm high, called to his hawk. Like a golden flash Merlin dived down, then, following the direction of Fin's hand, bulleted into the trees.

Fin whirled his arms out, in, and vanished in a swirl of fog.

"Oh God, my God, Cabhan."

"It wasn't Cabhan's fog," Branna said with forced calm. "It was Fin's. He's gone after him."

"What should we do? We should call the others, get to Fin."

"We can't get to Fin as we can't know where he is. He has to let us, and he isn't. He wants to do this on his own."

He flew, shadowed by the fog, his eyes the eyes of the hawk. And through the hawk watched the wolf streak through the woods. It left no track and cast no shadow.

As it approached the river it gathered itself, leaped up, rose up, sprang over the cold, dark surface like a stone from a sling. As it did, the mark on Fin's arm burned brutally.

So Cabhan paid a price, he thought, for crossing water.

He followed the wolf, masked by his own fog until he felt something change in the air, something tremble. He called to Merlin, slowed his own forward motion, seconds before the wolf vanished.

Fin might have wanted to handle things on his own, but Iona called the others anyway. Placidly, silently, Branna brewed a pot of tea.

"You're so calm." Iona paced, waiting for something to happen. "How can you be so calm?"

"I'm so angry it feels my blood's on fire. If I didn't bank it with calm, I might burn the place to the ground."

Stepping over, Iona wrapped her arms around Branna from behind. "You know he's all right. You know he can take care of himself."

"I know it very well, and it changes nothing." She patted Iona's hand, moved to get a dish for biscuits while her angry heart beat fists against her ribs. "I never asked why you're home so early."

"We decided we could start the whole shift rotation today. I have a lesson at the big stables at four, but Boyle could spare me until." Iona rushed to the door. "Here they are now. And, oh! Here's Fin. He's fine."

When Branna said nothing, Iona opened the door. "Get inside," she snapped to Fin. "You don't even have a jacket."

"I was warm enough."

"You'll be warmer yet if I kick your arse," Boyle warned him. "What's all this about taking off after Cabhan on your own, in some fecking funnel of fog."

"Just a little something I've been working on, and an opportunity to test it out." Fin shook back his hair, rolled his shoulders. "Brawling with me won't change anything, but I'm open to it if it helps you."

"I'll be the one holding you down while he does the arse kicking." Connor yanked off his coat. "You've no right going off after him on your own."

"Every right in this world and any."

"We're a circle," Iona began.

"We are." Because it was Iona, Fin tempered his tone. "And each of us individual points of it."

"Those points are connected. What happens to you, affects us all." Meara glanced over at Branna, who continued to fuss with tea and biscuits. "All of us."

"He never knew I was there, couldn't see I was following, watching where he went. I was cloaked. It's what I've been working on, and the point of trying it."

"Without letting any of us know what you were about?" Connor tossed out.

"Well, I didn't know for certain it would work till I tried, did I?"

He walked to Branna. "I used some of what I have of him in me to conjure the fog. It's taken weeks — well, months, come to that — for me to perfect it as I only had bits of time here and there to give to it. Today, I saw a chance to try it. Which isn't so different, if you're honest, from taking a ride out into the woods just to see what may be."

"I wasn't alone."

"Nor was I," he countered just as coolly. "I had Merlin, and used his eyes to follow.

He's taunted us, and you gave him back a bit, for you know, as we all should, if we look to be doing nothing at all, he'll know we're doing a great deal more. Why else did I make such a show of dispatching the rats?"

Irritation vibrating around him, he turned, lifted his hands. "Is there so little trust here?"

"It's not lack of trust," Iona told him. "You scared us. I thought at first Cabhan had ambushed you, but Branna said you'd made the fog yourself. But we couldn't see you, we didn't know where you were. It scared us."

"For that, *deirfiúr bheag,* I'm sorry. I'm sorry for causing you a minute of fear on my account, any of you, but you most especially who stood for me almost before you knew me."

Iona released a sigh. "Is that your way of getting out of trouble?"

"It's only the truth." He moved to her, kissed her forehead. "I admit I followed the moment, saw a chance, took it. And taking it, we know more than we did, if that's any balance to the scales."

"He's right," Branna said before anyone else could speak. "It may take time for me to cool my anger, as it may for the rest of you, but if we're practical — and we can't be otherwise — Fin's right. He used what he has and is. I wondered why you showed off so blatantly for Cabhan. It was a bit embarrassing."

At Fin's cocked brow, she gestured to Connor. "Take this tea tray by the fire, would you? The jars on the work counter are sealed, but I don't want food near them."

"He used the elements, one after the other, fast — zap, zap," Iona explained. "Wind, fire, earth, water. It was pretty awesome."

"Considerable overkill," Branna said tartly, "but I see the purpose now."

"Since it's done, it's done." Boyle shrugged, took a mug of tea. "I'd like to hear what we know that we didn't, and as no one's in a bloody battle, I've only a few minutes for it, as I've work still to do."

"He ran as the shadow wolf, leaving no tracks in the snow. Fast, very fast, but running, not flying. I think he conserves the energy." Fin took a biscuit, then paced as he spoke. "He only flew to get over the river, and as he spanned it, my mark burned. It costs him to cross the water, and now I know when I feel that, as I have before, he's crossed back to our side of it. He took the woods again, turned toward the lake. It tired him, as he ran a long way, then I felt the change, felt it coming so slowed, pulled Merlin back toward me. The wolf vanished. He'd shifted into another time. His own time, I'd say. And his lair."

"Can you find the way back? Sure and you can find the way back," Connor continued, "or you wouldn't look so fecking smug about it."

"I can find the way to where the wolf shifted, and I think we'll find Cabhan's lair isn't far from there."

"How soon can we go?" Meara demanded. "Tonight?"

"I happen to be free," Connor said.

"Not tonight." Branna shook her head. "There are things to prepare for if we find it. Things we could use. What we find, if anything, would be in our time. But . . ."

"You're after going back, once we find it, on going back to his time." Boyle frowned into his tea. "And take him on there?"

"No, not that. We don't have all we need, and the time has to be our choosing. But if we could leave something in his cave — block it from him, use it to see him there. Hear him. We could get the name. And we might learn his plans before he acts on them."

"Not all of us," Fin countered. "It's too

359

risky for all of us to go back. If we were trapped there, it's done for us. Only one goes."

"And you think that should be you."

He nodded at Branna. "Of course. I can go back, leaving no trace in the cloak of the fog, take your crystal, as that's what's best for seeing, and be out again."

"And if he's in there?" Iona gave Fin a light punch on the shoulder. "You could be done."

"That would be why a couple of us — at least a couple," Connor calculated, "find a way to draw him out, keep him busy." He grinned at Meara. "Would you be up for that?"

"I'd be raring for it."

"So . . ." Grabbing a biscuit, and another for his pocket, Boyle considered. "The four of us go where Fin followed today, and hunt from there. Connor and Meara catch Cabhan's attention so he's after them, and the lair's clear of him. If we find it, Fin takes this crystal, shifts in time back to the fecking thirteenth century, plants the thing in the cave, comes back, and we're all off to the pub for a round."

"That's the broad strokes of it." Branna patted his arm. "We'll fix the small, and important details of it. So we don't go until we do. None of us go near the place." She looked directly at Fin. "Is that agreed?"

"It is," he said, "and I've some ideas on a few of the details."

"As have I." Satisfied, and only a little angry still, Branna took a biscuit for herself.

16

It would take nearly a week before Branna was fully satisfied, and those days took precious hours away from perfecting the poison. Still, she considered it all time well spent.

The timing would be tight, and the circle would be separated at several stages — so every step of every stage had to be carefully plotted.

They chose early evening, so routines could hold and they'd still have an hour or more of light before dusk.

In her workshop, Branna carefully placed the crystal she'd chosen and charmed in a pouch.

"You must place it high, facing the altar, where it will reflect what's below," she told Fin. "And you must move there and back quickly."

"So you've already said."

"It bears repeating. You'll be tempted to

linger — as I would be in your place — to see what else you might find, what else you might learn. The longer you're there, in his place and in his time, the more chance there is of you leaving some trace, or of him sensing you."

She placed the pouch in a leather bag, then held up a vial. "Should it go wrong, should he come back before you're done, this should disable him for a few moments, long enough for you to get back to me, Iona, Boyle in our time. It's only if there's no choice."

She pouched the vial, added it to the bag. Stared down at it as she wished what he needed to do didn't need to be done. "Don't risk all for the moment."

"As all includes you, you can be sure I won't."

"Touch nothing of his. Don't —"

"Branna." He cupped her face until their eyes met. "We've been over it all."

"Of course. You're right. And it's time." She handed him the bag, went to get her jacket. "Iona and Boyle will be here any minute."

"When this is done we'll have a window to look in on him as he too often looks in on us. And we'll be able to give all the time needed to the poison that will end it."

"I'm uneasy, that's the truth." She didn't know if it helped to say it, but did know it was foolish, and maybe dangerous, to pretend. "The closer we come to the end of it, and I believe we will end it, there's a pull and tug in me. It's more than confidence and doubt. I don't understand my own feelings, and it makes me uneasy."

"Be easy about this. If for now, only this."

She could only try, as there was no room for doubts, and no time to delay as Iona and Boyle pulled up outside.

She picked up a short sword, fixed the sheath to her belt. "Best be prepared," was all she said as Iona and Boyle came in.

"Connor and Meara are on their way."

"Then we'd best be on ours." Branna reached for Fin's hand, then Boyle's. When Iona took Boyle's other hand, they flew.

Through the cool and the damp, through the wind and over the trees, across the river, then the lake with the castle of Ashford shining behind them.

They landed softly, in a stand of trees, in a place she didn't recognize.

"Here?"

"It's where I lost him. It's been hundreds of years since Midor and his cave," Fin pointed out. "Some houses not far, some roads, but as with Sorcha's cabin, I think the place where Cabhan was made will remain, in some form."

"There's a quiet here." Eyes watchful, Boyle studied the lay of the land. "A kind of hard hush."

Feeling the same, Fin nodded. "We're a superstitious breed, we Irish, and wise enough to build around a faerie hill without disturbing it, to leave a stone dance where it stands. And to keep back from a place where the dark still thrums."

He glanced over at Boyle. "We agreed to stay together, but it's fact we'd cover more ground if we split up."

"Together," Branna said firmly, as she'd expected him to suggest it. "And if the dark still thrums?" She drew out a wand with a tip of glass-clear crystal. "The light will find it."

"I don't recall that being in the plan."

"Best to be prepared," she repeated. She lifted her wand to the sky until the tip pulsed light. And watched Merlin circle above them.

"Between my wand and your hawk, we should find the lair. It pulls north."

"Then we go north." Boyle took Iona's hand in his again, and the four of them headed north.

■ ■ ■ ■

On the other side of the river Connor and Meara walked in the woods. He'd linked with Roibeard, who swooped through the trees, and with Merlin, who watched the rest of the circle travel another wood.

"It's a pleasure to finally have some time to go hawking with you. It's been too long since we just took an hour for it."

"I need to practice more," Meara responded, easy and casual, though her throat was dry. "So I'm full ready when we add the package."

"We could've come on horseback."

"This will do." She lifted a gloved arm for Roibeard, and though the hawking was a ploy, enjoyed having him.

"Would you want a hawk of your own?" Connor asked her.

She glanced at him in genuine surprise. "I've never thought of it."

"You should have your own. A female if you find one who speaks to you. Your hawk and mine could mate."

The idea brought a smile as it seemed a lovely thought, and a normal one. "I've never tended to a hawk on my own."

"I'd help you, but you'd do well with it.

You've helped often enough with Merlin when Fin's gone rambling. We could build a place for them when we build our house. If you're still in the mind to build one."

"I've hardly thought of that either, as I'm barely making strides on the wedding." She let Roibeard fly again. "And there's Cabhan to worry about."

"We won't think of him today," Connor said, though both of them thought of little else. "Today we follow Roibeard's dance. Give us a song, Meara, something bright to lift Roibeard's wings."

"Something bright, is it?" She took his hand, swung his arm playfully as they walked. But she wanted that connection, the physical of it, as they both knew the music could bring Cabhan.

They'd planned on it.

She decided on "The Wild Rover," as it was bright enough, and had a number of verses to give Cabhan time to be drawn in, if it was to happen.

She laughed when Connor joined her on the chorus, and any other day would have prized the walk with him, with the hawk, with the song in the pretty woods where the snowmelt left the ground so soft and pools of white still clung to the shady shadows.

When he squeezed her hand, she knew the

ploy had worked. And it was time for their part of the scheme.

Her voice didn't falter as she saw the first wisps of fog slithering over the ground, nor when Roibeard landed on a branch nearby — a golden-winged warrior poised to defend.

"I could still your voice with a thought."

Cabhan rose from the fog, and smiled his silky smile when Meara stopped singing to draw her sword. "And so I have. You risk your lady, witch, strolling through the woods without your sister to fight for you."

"I've enough to protect my lady, should she need it. But I think you know she does well protecting herself. Still . . ." Connor ran a finger down Meara's blade, set it alight. "A little something more for my lady."

"What manner of man has his woman stand in front of him?"

"Beside him," Connor corrected, and drew a sword of his own, enflamed it.

"And leaves her unshielded," Cabhan said and hurled black lightning at Meara.

Connor sent it crashing to the ground with a hard twist of wind. "Never unshielded."

Across the water, the pulse of Branna's

wand quickened. "Close now."

"There." Fin pointed to a wild tangle of thickets edged with thick black thorns, snaking vines dotted with berries like hard drops of blood. "In there is Midor's cave. I can feel the pull, just as I felt the burn when Cabhan crossed the river. The way's clear."

"It doesn't look clear," Iona said. "It looks lethal." Testing, she tapped the flat of her sword on one of the thorns, listened to the metallic clink of steel to steel. "Sounds lethal."

"I won't be going through them, but through time. Though when this is done we'll come back here, all of us, and burn those thorny vines, salt and sanctify the ground."

"Not yet." Branna took his arm. "Connor hasn't told me Cabhan's taken the bait."

"He has. He's nearly there, and the sooner I'm in and out, the less time Connor and Meara have to stand against him. It's now, Branna, and quick."

Though it filled her with dread, they cast the circle, and she released Fin's hand, accepted it would be done.

"In this place," she chanted with the others, "of death and dark, we send the one who bears the mark through space, through time. Powers of light send him through, let our wills entwine. Send him through, and send him back by the light of the three."

"Come back to me," Branna added, though it hadn't been part of the spell.

"As you will," Fin said, his eyes on hers, "so mote it be."

His fog swirled, and he was gone.

"It won't take long." To comfort, Iona put her arm around Branna's shoulders.

"It's so dark. It's so cold. And he's alone."

"He's not." Boyle took her hand, held it firmly. "We're right here. We're with him."

But he was alone in the cold and the dark. The power here hung so thick and dank he felt nothing beyond it. Black blood stained the ground where Cabhan had shackled and killed his mother.

He scanned the horror of jars, filled with the pieces of the woman who'd birthed him, which Cabhan had preserved for his dark magicks.

The world Fin knew, his world, seemed not just centuries away, but as if it didn't exist. Freeing the demon, giving it form and movement had drawn the cave into its own kind of hell where all the damned burned cold.

He smelled brimstone and blood — old blood and new. It took all his will to resist the sudden, fierce need to go to the altar, take up the cup that stood below a cross of yellowing bones, and drink.

Drink.

Sweat coated his skin though his breath turned to clouds in the frigid air that seemed to undulate like a sea with the fetid drops sliding down the walls and striking the floor in a tidal rhythm.

Something in its beat stirred his blood.

His hand trembled as he forced himself to reach into the bag, open the pouch, take out the crystal.

For a moment Branna was there — warm and strong, so full of light he could slow his pulse again, steady his hands. He rose up within the fog, up the damp wall of the cave. He saw symbols carved in the stone, recognized them from Ogham, though he couldn't read them.

He laid the crystal in a chink, along a fingertip of ledge, and wondered if Branna's charm could be strong enough to hide it from so much dark.

Such deep, fascinating dark, where voices chanted, and those to be sacrificed screamed and wept for a mercy that would never be given.

Why should mercy be given to the less? Their cries and screams of torment were true music, a call to dance, a call to feed.

The dark must be fed. Embraced. Worshipped.

The dark would reward. Eternally.

Fin turned to the altar, took a step toward it. Then another.

"It's taking too long." Branna rubbed her arms to fight a cold that dug into her bones and came from fear. "It's nightfall. He's been more than half an hour now, and far too long."

"Connor?" Iona asked. "He's —"

"I know, I know. He and Meara can't hold Cabhan much longer. Go to Connor, you and Boyle go to Connor and Meara, help them. I'll go through for Fin. Something's wrong, something's happened. I haven't been able to feel or sense him since he went through."

"You'll not go in. Branna, you'll not." Boyle took her shoulders, gave her a little shake. "We have to trust Fin to get back, and we can't risk you. Without you, it ends here, and not for Cabhan."

"His blood could betray him, however much he fights it. I can pull him out. I have to try before. Ah, God, Cabhan, he's coming back. Fin —"

"Can we pull him back, the two of us?"

372

Iona gripped Branna's hand. "We have to try."

"With all of us, we might . . . Oh, thank the gods."

When Fin, his fog thin and faded, fell to his knees on the ground at her feet, Branna dived for him.

"He's coming," Fin managed. "It's done, but he's coming. We have to go, and quickly. I could use some help."

"We've got you." Branna wrapped her arms around him, looked at Iona, at Boyle, nodded. "We've got you," she repeated, and held on to him as they flew.

His skin was ice, and she couldn't warm it as she pulled him over treetops, over the lake, and the castle aglow with lights.

She brought him straight to the cottage, set the fire to roaring before she knelt in front of him. "Look at me. Fin, I have to see your eyes."

They glowed against the ice white of his face, but they were Fin's, and only his.

"I brought nothing back with me," he told her. "Left nothing of me. Only your crystal."

"Whiskey." But even as she snapped it out, Boyle sat beside Fin, cupped Fin's hands around the glass.

"I feel I've walked a hundred kilometers in the Arctic without a single rest." He gulped down whiskey, let his head fall back as Connor and Meara came in.

"Is he hurt?" Connor demanded.

"No, only half frozen and exhausted. Are you?"

"A few singes, and I'll see to them."

"He's already seen to mine." Meara moved straight to Fin. "Clucking like a mother hen over me. What can we do for you, Fin?"

"I'm well enough."

"You don't look it. Should I get one of your potions, Branna?"

"I don't need a potion. The whiskey's fine. And you're doing some clucking yourself, Mother."

Meara dropped into a chair. "The way you are makes a ghost look like it's had ten days in the tropics."

Warming bit by painful bit, Fin smiled at her. "You're not looking rosy yourself."

"He kept going at her," Connor said, and surprised Meara by lifting her up — strapping girl that she was — taking her place, then cuddling her on his lap. "He'd go for me, but that was for show. He wanted our Meara, to hurt her, so kept hammering against her protection, looking for the slightest chink. At first we tried to draw it all out, give the rest of you time, but it went on longer than we thought, and it was get serious about it, or fall back."

"Connor made a tornado." Meara spun a finger in the air. "A small one you could say, but impressive. Then turned it to fire. And that sent Cabhan on his way."

"We couldn't hold him longer," Connor finished.

"It was long enough. We'll all have some whiskey," Branna decided. "Let me see where you're burned, Connor, and I'll tend to it."

"I'll do it." Iona nudged Branna back down. "Stay with Fin."

"I'm well enough," Fin insisted. "It was the cold, that was the most of it. It's so sharp, so bitter it carves the life out of you. Enervates. It's more than it was," he said to Branna. "More than we saw and felt."

She sat on the floor, took one of the glasses Boyle passed around. "Tell us."

"It was darker, darker than it was when we went in the dreamwalk. Colder, and the air thick. So thick you couldn't get a full breath. There was a cauldron on the fire, and it smelled of sulphur and brimstone. And there were voices chanting. I couldn't make out the words, not enough of them, but it was in Latin, and some in old Irish. As were the screams, the pleading that rose up with them. Those being sacrificed. All of that, a kind of echo, in the distance. Still, I could smell the blood."

He took a drink, gathered himself again. "There was a pull to it, from in me. A wanting of it, stronger than before, this pull and tug in two directions. I put the crystal up, a little notch in the stones, high on the wall across from the altar."

Now he turned the glass in his hands, staring down into the amber of the whiskey as if seeing it all again.

"And when I no longer had it with me, the need was more. Bigger. The pull more alluring, you could say. There was a cup on the altar, and in it blood. I wanted it. Coveted it. Innocent blood, that I could smell. The blood of an innocent, and if I only took it, drank it, I would become what I was meant to become. Why was I resisting that? Didn't I want that — my own destiny, my own glory? So I stepped toward the altar, and went closer yet. All the chanting filled the cave, and those screams were almost like music to me. I reached for the cup. I held my hand out to take it. Finally just take it."

He paused, knocked back the rest of the whiskey. "And through all the screaming, the chanting, the pulsing of that thick air, I heard you." He looked down at Branna. "I heard you. 'Come back to me,' you'd said, and what was in me wanted that more than all the rest. Needed that more than the blood I could already taste in the back of my throat.

"So I backed away, and the air, it got colder yet, and was so thick now it was like wet rags in my lungs. I was dizzy and sick and shaky. I think I fell, but I said the words, and I was out, I was back."

He set the glass aside. "You need to know the whole of it, the full of it. How close I came. No more than a fingerbrush away from turning, and once turned, I would have turned again on all of you."

"But you didn't take it," Iona said. "You came back."

"I wanted it. Something in me was near to desperate for it."

"And still you didn't take it," Connor pointed out. "And here you sit, drinking whiskey by the fire."

"I would've broken trust with you —"

"Bollocks," Branna interrupted and surged to her feet. "Bollocks to that, Finbar. And don't sit there saying you came back for me, for you didn't come back for me alone, or for any of us alone. You came back as much for yourself. For the respect you have for who you are, for your gift, and for your abhorrence of all Cabhan is. So bollocks. I didn't let myself trust you in the beginning of this, and you proved me wrong time and time again. I won't have it, I'm telling you, I won't have you sit here after all that and not trust yourself.

"I'm going to heat up the stew. We all need to eat after this."

When she sailed out, Meara nodded, rose. "That says it all and plainly enough. Iona, let's give Branna a hand in the kitchen."

When they left, Boyle went for the whiskey, poured more in Fin's glass. "If you're going to feel sorry for yourself, you'd do better doing it a bit drunk."

"I'm not feeling sorry for myself, for fuck's sake. Did you hear what I said to you?"

"I heard it, we all heard it." Connor stretched out his legs, slouched down in the chair with his own whiskey. "We heard you fought a battle, inward and outward, and won it. So cheers to you. And I'll tell you something I know as easy as I know my own name. You'd slit your own throat before you'd do harm to Branna, or to any one of us. So drink up, brother, and stop acting the gom."

"Acting the gom," Fin muttered, and because it was there, drank the whiskey.

And because they knew him, his friends let him brood.

He waited until they were all in the kitchen, until everyone had taken a seat but himself.

"I'm grateful," he began.

"Shut the feck up and sit down to eat," Boyle suggested.

"You shut the feck up. I'm grateful and have a right to say as much."

"So noted and acknowledged." Branna ladled stew in his bowl. "Now shut the feck up and eat."

He sampled some of the hearty beef and barley stew, felt it slide down to the cold still holding in his belly, and spread warmth again.

"What's in it besides the beef and barley and potatoes?"

Branna shrugged. "There's none of us here couldn't do with a little tonic after this day."

"It's good." Connor spooned some up. "More than good, so here's another, Fin, advising you to shut the feck up."

"Fine and well." Fin reached for the bread on the dish. "Then I won't tell you the rest of it, since you're not interested."

"What rest?" Iona demanded.

It was Fin's turn to shrug. "I've shut the

feck up, as advised."

"I didn't tell you to or so advise you." Meara smiled sweetly. "I'm interested enough so you can talk to me."

"All right then, to your interest, Meara, there were carvings on the walls in the cave. Old ones. Ogham script."

"Ogham?" Connor frowned. "Are you sure of it?"

As it made him feel himself again, Fin ate more stew. "I'm speaking with Meara here."

"Oh, give it over." But Boyle laughed as he helped himself to the bread. "Ogham then? What did it say?"

Fin spared him a long, dry look. "My talents are many but don't stretch far enough to read Ogham. But it tells us the cave's been used, and as the script was high on the walls, and with magickal symbols here and there as well, very likely for dark purposes long before Cabhan's time."

"Some places are inherent for the dark, or for the light," Branna speculated.

"What I felt there was all of the dark, like . . . a rooting place for it. The shadows moved like living things. And on the altar, as I was close enough to see, there were bones in a dish along with the cup of blood. Three black candles, and a book with a hide cover. Carved on it is the mark." He touched his shoulder. "This mark."

"So it goes back, the mark, before Teagan threw the stone and scarred Cabhan. Before Sorcha cursed him." Iona angled her head. "A symbol of the demon in him? Or of his own dark places? I'm sorry," she said quickly.

"No need." Fin picked up his spoon again. "Near the book was a bell, again silver, with a wolf standing on its hind legs as a handle."

"Bell, book, and candle, bones and blood. The symbol of Cabhan's mark, the symbol of the wolf." Branna considered. "So he had these things, symbols of what he became. Old things?"

"Very old, all but the candles. And they . . . made from human tallow mixed with blood."

"Can it get more disgusting?" Meara wondered.

Connor gave her a pat. "I expect it can."

"His tools," Branna speculated, "perhaps passed down from father to son, or mother to son or daughter. Passed down to him, and then used for the dark. Though we can't say if his sire didn't dabble in such, or why he would've chosen the cave for his own."

"He might've been a guardian," Meara suggested. "Someone with power who guarded the demon or whatever it is, and kept it imprisoned."

"True enough," Branna agreed. "Whether or not Cabhan came from light or dark, or something between them, he made his choice."

"There's more," Fin told her. "A wax figure of a woman, bound hand and foot with black cloth, kneeling as in supplication."

"Sorcha." Branna shook her head. "His obsession with her started long ago. But he could never bind her or bring her to her knees."

"Nearly eight hundred years is a long time to hold an obsession or a grudge," Iona pointed out. "I'd say it's been madness that started long ago."

"I'd agree."

"And more," Fin said again. "The figure had blood smeared on its belly, between its legs."

Carefully, Branna set her spoon down. "She lost a child, early that winter. She miscarried, and was never fully well again. She had some terrible illness she couldn't heal. Tearing pains in the belly."

"He killed her child?" Even with centuries of distance, Iona's eyes filled. "Inside her? Could he do that?"

"I don't know." Shaken, Branna rose, got

382

wine for herself and brought the bottle to the table. "If she didn't guard against it, in just the right way? If he found some way to . . . She had three children to tend to, and her husband off with the men of their clan. Cabhan hounding her. She may have given him some vulnerable spot to use, had a moment when she wasn't fully vigilant."

"We will be." Fin touched a hand to hers. "We'll give him nothing, and we'll take all. This is yet more he must answer for."

"She was grieving. You can hear her tears in her book when she wrote of the loss. Yes," Branna said quietly. "He must answer for this, and for all."

17

She increased her efforts. It couldn't be rushed — no, working with a lethal mix couldn't be hurried. But Branna spent every minute she could on concocting the poison.

Whoever from her circle spent time in her workshop took on a task — magickal or otherwise. She herself rarely went out, beyond a walk through her winter gardens to clear her head of formulas and spells and poisons.

Even on those brief walks, Branna obsessed whether five drops of tincture from the angel's trumpet were too much or four too little. Should the crushed berries be freshly used, or allowed to steep in their juices?

"It matters," she muttered, half to herself as she meticulously lined up the jars for the day's attempt. "One drop off, and we start again."

"You said the four drops didn't work

yesterday, so do the five," Connor suggested.

"And if it should be six?" Frustrated, she stared at the jars as if she could will them to tell her the secret. "Or is the other recipe I found the true one, the one that calls for five death cap mushrooms, taken from under an oak?"

"The more poison the better, if you're asking me."

"It can't be more or less. It's not like cooking up a kitchen-sink soup." Though she heard the testiness in her own voice, she simply couldn't smooth it out. "It *must* be right, Connor, and I feel this may be our only chance. If we fail, at best we have to wait another year before trying again. At worst, the demon finds a way to shield himself when he finds we've a way to attack it."

"You're fretting far too much, Branna. It's not your way to fret and second-guess."

He was right, of course, and fretting, she admitted as she pressed her fingers to her eyes, tended to block more than open.

"I feel an urgency, more than I have. A knowing, Connor, this *must* be the time, or our time is done. And the thought we might only go on slapping at Cabhan as we have, for our lifetime, only hold him off until we pass this duty to the next three? It's not bearable. You'll have children with Meara. Would you want to weigh one or more of them with this?"

"I wouldn't, no. Of course, I wouldn't. We won't fail."

He put his hands on her shoulders, rubbed them. "Ease your mind a bit. You'll block your own instincts — and they're a strength — if you pour in all this doubt."

"This will be the third time I've tried creating the brew. The doubt's there for a reason."

"Then put it aside. This recipe, that recipe, put that aside as well. What do you think — how does it feel to you? Maybe it's not like throwing together a soup, but you've been mixing potions since you were four."

Deliberately, he closed the books, knowing full well by now she could recite it all by rote in any case. "What do you say — not just from the head this time, but from the belly?"

"I say . . ." She shoved impatiently at her hair. "Where the devil is Fin? I need his blood for this, and I want it fresh."

"He said he'd be here before noon, so he will. Why don't I work on the order with you, and the words? Then when he comes, you'll bleed him, and begin."

"All right, all right."

Time to stop fussing and fiddling and *do,* she ordered herself.

"The blessed water would be first. I've got 'First we pour the water blest to form the pool for all the rest. Belladonna berries crushed and steeped, stirring juices slow and deep. Hair from a pregnant yak mixed with manchineel tree sap to dissolve the wing of bat. Angel's trumpet, wolfsbane petals, add them in and wait to settle. Then . . .'"

"What do you think, Branna?" Connor prompted.

"Well, I think I rushed it last time. I think this stage needs to work, to boil a bit."

"So . . . Stir and boil and bubble and stir . . ."

"Until the rise of smoke occurs — yes, I rushed it. It should boil and steam a bit. All right." With a firm nod, she wrote more notes. "The mushrooms, we'll try the mushrooms as — what the bloody hell, it feels right."

"There we are now." Connor gave her an elbow poke of encouragement.

"Caps of death soft and white, bring about eternal night. No, no, not for a demon." She crossed it out, started again. "Caps of death three plus two, spread your poison through this brew."

"Better," Connor agreed.

"And the conium petals. Ah, pretty petals sprinkled in, let this lethal magick begin."

"Deadly magick's better, I think."

"Yes, deadly." She made the change. "Blood to bind it, drop by drop, and the demon heart will stop. Power of me, power of three, here fulfill our destiny. As we will, so mote it be."

She dropped the pencil on the counter. "I'm not sure."

"I like it — it sounds right. It's strong enough, Branna, but not fussy. It's death we're dealing, so there's no need for frills."

"You've a point there. Bloody hell, it needs to thicken, go black. I need to add that. Blacken, thicken under my hands . . ."

"To make this poison for the damned," Connor finished.

"I quite like that," she considered. "I want to write it all up fresh."

"If you can't start until Fin's here, why don't you —" He broke off, turning to the door as Fin came in. "Well, here he is now. She's after bleeding you, mate."

Fin stopped in his tracks. "I gave more than enough yesterday, and the day before."

"I want fresh."

"She wants fresh," Fin grumbled and

tossed off his coat. "What are you doing with what's left I bled for you yesterday, and the day before that?"

"It's safe — and you never know when it might be useful. But I want to start it all fresh today. I've changed some of the spell."

"Again?"

"Yes, again," she said in as irritable a tone as he. "It needed work. Connor agreed —"

"I'm not in this." Connor held up his hands. "The two of you sort this out. In fact, now that you're here, Fin, I'm off. It's Boyle, I think, who's coming in a bit later, so he can sweep up the leavings if the two of you battle."

He grabbed his coat, his cap, his scarf, and was out the door with Kathel slipping out with him — as if the dog agreed some distance wouldn't hurt a thing.

"Why are you so cross?" Branna demanded.

"Me? Why are you? You've got that I'm-annoyed-at-every-fecking-thing between your eyebrows."

Only more annoyed, Branna rubbed her fingers to smooth out any such line. "I'm not annoyed — yes, I bloody well am, but not at every fecking thing, or at you. I'm not used to failing so spectacularly the way I am with this damnable brew."

"Not getting it right isn't failing."

"Getting it right is success, so its opposite is failing."

"They called it practicing magicks for a reason, Branna, and you know it full well."

She started to snap, then just sighed. "I do know it. I do. I thought I'd come closer the first few times than I have. If I keep missing by so wide a mark, I'll need to send for the ingredients again."

"So we start fresh." He walked to her, kissed her. "Good day to you, Branna."

She let out a half laugh. "And good day to you, Finbar." Smiling, she picked up her knife. "And so . . ."

She expected him to roll up his sleeve, but he pulled off his sweater.

"Take it from the mark," he told her. "As you did for the poison for Cabhan. From the mark, Branna, as you should have done the first time with this."

"I should have, it's true. It hurts you, it burns you, when I take blood from there."

"Because the purpose is the enemy of the mark. Take it from there, Branna. Then I want a damn biscuit."

"You can have half a dozen."

She stepped to him with the ritual knife and the cup.

"Don't block it." He drew her eyes to him.

"The pain may be part of it. We'll let it come, and let it go."

"All right."

She was quick — quick was best — and scored across the pentagram with the tip of her blade. She caught the blood in the cup — felt the pain though he made no sound, no movement.

"That's enough," she murmured, and set the knife aside to pick up the cloth she had ready, pressed it to the wound.

Then, putting the cup by the jars, turned back to him to gently heal the shallow wound.

Before he knew what she was about — perhaps before she did — Branna pressed a kiss to the mark.

"Don't." Stunned, appalled to the marrow, he jerked back. "I don't know how it might harm you, what it might do."

"It will do nothing to me, as you did nothing to earn it. I spent years trying to blame you for it, and should have blamed Sorcha — or more, her grief. She harmed you — she broke our most sacred oath, and harmed you, and many before you. Innocents. I'd take it from you if I could."

"You can't. Do you think I haven't tried?" He yanked on his sweater again. "Witchcraft, priests, wise women, holy men, magicks black and white. Nothing touches it. I've been to every corner of the world where there was so much of a whisper of a rumor the curse could be broken."

His rambles, she realized. This was their basis. "You never said —"

"What could I say?" he countered. "This visible symbol of what runs inside me can't be changed, it can't be removed by any means I've tried. No spell, no ritual can break the curse she cast with her dying breaths. It can't be burned off, cut off or out of me. Considered lopping my arm off, but feared it would just sear in on another part of me."

"You — Good God, Fin."

He hadn't meant to say so much, but couldn't take back the words. "Well, I was more than a bit drunk at the time, fortunately, as cursed is cursed, two-armed or one, despite what seemed desperately heroic at two and twenty, when shattered on the best part of a bottle of Jameson."

"You won't harm yourself," she said, shaken to the core. "You won't think of it."

"No point in it, as I've been told time and again when all attempts failed. The curse of a dying witch — and one who'd sacrificed herself for her children, to protect them from the darkest of purposes? — it's powerful."

"When this is done, I would help you find a way — all of us —"

"It's for me, if there is a way, and I won't ever stop looking, as because of this you can't give me tomorrows. I can't ask for them or give them to you. We could never have children." He nodded. "I see you know that, too. Neither of us would bring a child into the world knowing he would carry this burden."

"No." Despair, and brutal acceptance, twisted her heart. "And when this is done . . . you'll go again."

"When this is done, could either of us be together as we are, knowing we'd never have the life we once imagined? Knowing this" — he touched his shoulder — "stands between us even after Cabhan's end? As long as I wear it, he doesn't truly end, and Sorcha's curse goes on, in me. So I'll never stop looking for a way."

"So her curse comes back threefold. You, me, and the life we might have had."

"We have today. It's more than I believed I'd have with you again."

"I thought it would be enough." She walked into his arms, held tight.

"We'd best not waste it."

"No, we won't waste it." She lifted her face, lifted her lips to his. "If I could wish it, we'd be ordinary."

He could smile. "You could never be ordinary."

"Just a woman who makes soaps and candles, and has a pretty shop in the village. And you just a man who has the stables and the falconry. If I could wish it. But . . ."

As she did, he looked at the counter, with the spell books, the jars. "If we were ordinary, we couldn't do what has to be done. Best try the spell or you'll be bleeding me again saying the blood's not fresh enough."

Duty, she thought, and destiny. Neither could be shirked.

She got the cauldron, lit its fire low.

The long, painstaking process took precision and power — step by careful step. Branna ordered herself to put all the previous failures aside, to treat this as the first attempt. The toxic brew bubbled and smoked as both she and Fin held their hands over the cauldron to slowly, slowly stir.

She drew a breath as they approached the final step.

"Blacken, thicken under my hands," she said.

Fin followed. "To make this poison for the damned."

"Power of me," they said together as with the words the brew bubbled forcibly. "Power of three, here fulfill our destiny. As we will, so mote it be."

She felt the change, the spread of power and will, from her, from Fin. They reached for each other, linking that power and that will, letting it merge and, merging, increase.

Blocking all else, she focused only on that merging, that purpose, while her heart began a hard, quick tattoo in her breast, while the warmth and scents of her workshop faded away.

All light, bright and brilliant, rising in her, flowing from her. Blooming with what rose and flowed from him.

A meeting, physical, intimate, psychic, potent that built like a storm, ripped through her like a climax.

Her head fell back. She lifted her arms, palms up, fingers spread.

"Here, a weapon forged against the dark. Fired by faith and light. On the Dark Witch's sacrificial ground, three by three by three will stand against the evil born in the black. Blood and death follow. Bring horse, hawk, hound together, and say the name. Ring bell, open book, light candle, say the name. Into fire white, all light, blinding bright, cast the stone and close the door. Blood and death follow. Be it demon, be it mortal, be it witch, blood and death follow."

Her eyes, which had gone black, rolled back white. Fin managed to catch her before she fell, simply folded like a puppet with its strings nipped.

Even as he swept her up, she pressed a hand to his shoulder.

"I'm all right. Just dizzy for a minute."

"You'll sit right here." He laid her on the little sofa in front of the fire, then going to her stock, scanned until he found what he wanted.

He didn't bother to put the kettle on, but made tea with a snap of his fingers, poured six drops of the tonic into it, then brought it to her.

"Drink and don't argue," he ordered. "It's your own potion."

"I was there, all the light and power rising up, and the brew stirring in the cauldron, thickening, bubbling. Then I was watching myself, and you, and hearing the words I spoke without speaking them. I've had flashes of what's to come before — all of us have — but nothing so strong or overtaking as that. I'm all right now, I promise you."

Or nearly, she thought and drank the laced tea.

"It's only when it left me, it was like being emptied out entirely for just a moment."

"Your eyes went black as the dark of the moon, and your voice echoed as if from a mountaintop."

"I wasn't myself."

"You weren't, no. What came in you, Branna?"

"I don't know. But the strength and the light of it was consuming. And, Fin, it was beautiful beyond the telling. It's all that we are, but so brilliantly magnified, a thousand suns all around and inside at once. It's the only way I know to tell you."

She drank more tea, felt herself begin to settle again. "I want to write it down, everything I said. It wouldn't do to forget."

"I won't be forgetting it, not a word."

She smiled. "Best to write it down in any case. A weapon forged — it must have worked then."

"The poison's black and thick as pitch."

"We have to seal it, keep it in the dark, and charm the bottle to hold it."

"I'll take care of it."

"No, no, we conjured it together, and there's something to that, I think. So we should do the rest together as well. I'm altogether fine, Fin, I promise you."

She set the tea aside, got to her feet to prove her words. "It should be done quickly. I wouldn't want the poison to turn and have to go through the whole business again."

He kept an eye on her until he was fully satisfied.

After they sealed the spell, she took two squat bottles, both opaque and black, from the cabinet under her work counter.

"Two?"

"We made enough, as I thought it wise to have a second. If something should happen to the first — before or during — we'll have another."

"Smart and, as always, practical." When she started to get out a funnel, he shook his head. "I don't think this is something we do that way. I understand, again, your practicality, but I think, for this, we stay with power."

"You may be right. One for you, then, one for me. It should be quickly done, then stopped tight, again sealed." She touched one of the bottles. "Yours." Then the other. "Mine." And walked back to stand with him by the cauldron. "Pot to bottle, leaving no trace on the air, no drop on the floor."

She linked one hand with his, held the other out, as he did. Two thin streams of oily black rose out of the cauldron, arched toward the bottles, slid greasily in. When the stream ended, they floated the stoppers up, in.

"Out of light, sealed tight, open only for the right."

Relieved, Branna flashed white fire into the cauldron to burn any trace left behind. "Better safe," she said as she moved to take the bottles, store them deep in a cupboard where she kept the jars of ingredients used, and the poison already prepared for Cabhan. "Though I'll destroy the cauldron. It shouldn't be used again. A pity, as it's served me well." Then she charmed the door of the cupboard. "It will only open for one of our circle."

She went to another cupboard, took out a pale green bottle basketed in silver filigree, then chose two wineglasses.

"And what's this?"

"It's a wine I made myself, and put by here for a special occasion — not knowing what that might be. It seems it's this. We've done what we must, and I'll tell you true, Fin, I wasn't sure we would or could. Each time I thought I was certain of it, we'd fail. But today?"

She poured the pale gold wine in both glasses, offered him one. "Today we haven't failed. So . . ."

Understanding, he touched his glass to hers. "We'll drink to today." He sipped, angled his head. "Well now, here's yet another talent, for this is brilliant. Both light and bold at once. It tastes of stars."

"You could say I added a few. It is good," she agreed. "We've earned good this day. And as I recall, you've earned a biscuit."

"Half a dozen was the offer," he remembered, "but now I think we've both earned something more than biscuits." He swung an arm around her waist. "You'd best hold on to your wine," he warned, and took her flying.

It made her giddy, the surprise and speed of it. Made her hunger as his mouth took hers on the flight. She let out a gasping laugh when she found herself sprawled under him on a huge bed draped with filmy white curtains.

"So this is what we've earned?"

"More than."

"I've lost my wine."

"Not at all." He gestured so she looked over, saw a table holding the glasses. And saw both bed and table floated on a deep blue sea.

"Now who's practical? But where are we? Ah, it's so warm. It's wonderful."

"The South Seas, far away from all but us, and circled so not even the fish might see."

"The South Seas, on a floating bed. There's a bit of madness in you."

"When it comes to you. An hour or two with you, Branna, in our own window into paradise. Where we're warm and safe, and you're naked." And so she was in a finger-snap. Before she could laugh again, he slid his hands up and over her breasts. "By the gods, I love having you naked and under me. We've done what we must," he reminded her. "Now we take what we want."

His mouth came down on hers, hot and possessive, to send the need sizzling through her like a lit fuse. She answered, not with surrender, but equal fire and force.

The magicks merged still pulsed through them, bright and fierce, so each opened to it, and each other.

The crazed rush of his lips over her skin, brewed a storm of lust. The urgency of her seeking hands whipped the storm into a whirlwind. They tumbled over the bed as it rocked over the wide, rolling sea while inside them waves of need rose and broke only to rise again, an endless tide.

If this was his madness, she'd take it willingly, and flood him with her own. Love, beyond reason, simply swamped her. And here, in this window of alone he'd given them, she could ride on it. Here, where there was only the truest of magicks, she could offer it back to him.

Her body quaked, her heart trembled. So much to feel, so much to want. When a cry of pleasure broke from her, it carried across the blue into forever.

To have her, completely, where no one could touch them. To give her the fantasy she so rarely took for herself, and to know she reached for, took, accepted all he felt for her, would ever feel for her. That alone filled him with more than all the powers, all the magicks, all the mysteries.

No words needed. All she felt lived in her eyes, all he felt mirrored back to him from hers.

When he filled her, it was a torrent of pleasure and love and lust. When she closed tight, so tight around him, it was unity.

They drove each other hard and fast, in a world only theirs with the deep blue sea rocking beneath them. She lay with him, lulled by the quiet lap of water against the bed, the warmth of the sun, the scent of the sea. And the feel of him against her, hot, slick skin to skin.

"Why this place," she asked him, "of all

the places?"

"It seemed beyond all we have and know together. We have the green and the wet in us, and wouldn't cast it out. But this? The warm and the blue? A bit of the fanciful for someone who rarely gifts herself with it. And all gods know, Branna, the winter's been cold and hard."

"It has. But at the end of it, we'll have more than spring. We'll have duty done, and the light and breath that comes from it. When it's done . . ."

He lifted his head, looked into her eyes. "Ask."

"Bring me back here again, for both of us, when what's done is done. And before you go wherever you must. Bring me back."

"I will. You'll want to go home now."

"No. No, let's stay awhile." She shifted, sat up, and reached for the glasses. "We'll finish our wine and enjoy the sun and the water. Let's take the fancy of this a little longer. For there'll be little time or chance for it once we return."

She leaned her head on his shoulder, sipped the starry wine, and watched the sea that spread to the far horizon.

18

When the six of them managed to come together, Branna opted for a quietly celebrational meal of rack of lamb, roasted butternut squash, and peas with butter and mint.

"Sure I didn't expect such a fuss," Connor said as he took charge of carving the chops from the rack. "Not that I'm complaining."

"It's the first time we've sat down, the six of us, in near to a week," Branna pointed out. "We've all talked here and there, and we all know what's been done and where we are. The brew's curing well. I checked it only this afternoon." She took a dollop of the squash for her plate, passed the bowl. "Connor and I made a second bottle of the poison needed for Cabhan, so like the demon's brew, we'll have that in case something goes amiss."

"I'm not going to think of misses." Meara

handed off the peas to Boyle. "Near to a year now that evil bastard's been dogging us — longer I know for the three, but in this year he's taunted and attacked with barely a respite. Third time's the charm, isn't it? I'm believing in that — and thinking that every time I see him when I'm out on a guided."

"Today?" Branna asked.

"Today, and every day now, lurking in the woods, even keeping pace for a time. A little closer to the track, it seems. Close enough that twice now, Roibeard's flown in and taken a dive at him. It. Whatever the bloody hell."

"He does it to rattle us," Boyle pointed out. "It's best not to rattle."

"True enough." With the chops severed, Connor took two for himself. "He's getting stronger or bolder, or both. I've seen him skulking about when out on a hawk walk. But today, our Brian mentioned he'd seen a wolf cross the path."

"As Mrs. Baker saw him," Branna added.

"Indeed. Now with Brian, who tends to think an errant wind may be a sign of the apocalypse, it was easy enough to convince him he'd only caught sight of a stray dog. But it's a concern he's showing himself to others."

"Would he hurt them?" Iona demanded. "We can't let him hurt an innocent."

"He would." Fin kept his calm. "It's more likely he'll keep whatever he has for us, but he would and could hurt others. Someone else with power might tempt him, for that would be a kind of feeding."

"Or a woman." Boyle waited a beat, then nodded when no one spoke. "We all know he has needs in that area. So would he take a woman, and if we think he may, how can we stop it?"

"We can spread the protection farther than we have," Branna began. "If he decided to slake that thirst it would be with the young and attractive. The vulnerable. We can do what we can."

"It's not how I'd go about it." Fin sliced lamb from the bone very precisely. "He can shift his times, he can go when and where he likes. Why draw more attention to where he is, and what he plans here? In his place I'd go back, a hundred years or more, take what I wanted, do what I wished, and set no alarm around here."

"So, we can't do anything about it, can't help whoever he'd hurt," Iona said.

"We'll destroy him," Branna reminded her. "And that's doing all there is to do."

"But it's a month before the anniversary

of Sorcha's death."

"He's had eight hundred years to do his worst." Boyle laid a hand over Iona's. "We can only deal with now."

"I know it. I know, and still we can only do so much. There's so much power here, but we're helpless to stop him from doing harm."

"I look through the crystal every morning," Branna told her. "And every night. Often more than that. I've seen him working, and seen some of the spells he conjures. There's blood, always, but I've yet to see him bring a mortal or witch into his cave. I've yet to see or hear anything that would help us."

"It's all we can do now." Connor looked around the table. "Until we do more. It's a month, and that feels long, but in fact, we've more things to gather before that time's up. We need the brew and spell for the cauldron to destroy the stone. With light, as Branna prophesied."

"I've a fine one for that," Branna assured him. "And only need you and Iona to finish it with me. It's for the three to do," she explained to all.

"And so we will," Connor responded. "But we don't yet have the name, and without it, we can't finish it off, no matter the poison, no matter the light."

"Lure out the wolf," Branna considered. "Long enough for me, or Fin come to that, to search its mind and find it."

"We can't know, in that form, if he'd have the name in his mind," Fin pointed out. "Cabhan sleeps, at some point he must sleep."

"You think to go into his dreams?" Connor shook his head. "There's too deep a risk, Fin. And more for you than any of us."

"If Branna watches the crystal, and we know when he sleeps, I might join with him with the rest of you ready to pull me out."

"I won't be a part of it. I won't," Branna said when Fin turned to her. "We can't, and I won't, risk you, and risk all, and for this last piece we've weeks yet to find on our own, another way. You barely pulled yourself away the last time."

"It's not the same as that."

"I'm with Branna on this," Boyle put in. "He'd twist you more than any of the rest of us. If it comes down to it, and we have only that way, it must be someone else. Any one of us here."

"Because you don't trust me."

"Don't play the donkey's arse," Boyle said coolly. "There's not a one at this table who doesn't trust you with their lives, and the lives of those they love."

"You're valued." Scowling, Meara leaned toward Fin. "And that's the why of it. And it's too late not to play the donkey's arse, as you just did."

"Apologies, but it's fact what you see as risk is also advantage, as I could get into his dreams, and out again, quicker than any of us."

"It's off the table." Connor deliberately continued to eat. "And shoving it on again only spoils a fine meal. In any case, I've a thought on all this, if anyone wants to hear it."

"He has thoughts." Smiling now, Meara gave him an elbow nudge. "I've been a witness to the occasion."

"And my thought is, we might try Kathel. We might have Kathel go along with me, or with Meara or Iona during the walks or guideds. It may be Kathel can find what's going on in the mind of the wolf, and then Branna could find it from Kathel."

"That's not as foolish as it sounds," Branna considered.

"Thanks for that." Connor helped himself to another chop.

"I can give him leave to go, then we can see. I've been wondering about the vision I had, the words I spoke that weren't my own when we finished the brew. Three and three and three."

"Well, the three here, the three in their own time," Connor said, "and Fin with Boyle and Meara. It seems clear."

"It felt more. It's hard to say, but it felt more. And even if it's so simple, we've got to bring Sorcha's three together with us, at the time, in that place. It's our time, that *was* clear. Not theirs, but ours, so we have to keep Cabhan closed in to that."

"Bell, book, candle." Iona pushed peas around her plate. "Basic tools. And the need for our guides to be there."

"Blood and death follow." Meara picked up the wine, topped off her glass, then Iona's. "We've known that all along. Witch, demon, or mortal blood and death doesn't change it."

"You're valued." Branna looked from Meara to Boyle. "Sister and brother, for the choice you've made for love and loyalty, for right, and for light. We've always known your worth, but it's clear now so the fates do as well."

A thought wound through her head. Branna drew it back as Connor leaned over to kiss Meara and make her laugh. She kept it there, twirling it like a ribbon as her circle finished the meal.

■ ■ ■ ■

Over the next few days she studied and twirled that ribbon over and over. She saw how it could be done, but had to be certain it should be done. And in the end, whatever her own decision, it had to be a choice for all.

She slipped out of bed, on impulse taking her violin with her. Leaving Fin sleeping, she went down to her workshop where she kept her ball of crystal on a stand. After carrying it to the table, she lit the fire, and three candles. Then she sat, quietly playing while she watched Cabhan sleep in a sumptuous bed of gold in a dark chamber of his cave.

His own fire burned low and red, and she wondered what images he saw in the flames. Blood and death, as had been foretold? Or did he see only his own desires?

She could have sent her music to him, disturbed his sleep as thoughts of him too often disturbed hers. But she wanted to leave no trace for him to follow back to what she loved.

So she played for her own comfort and pleasure as she kept vigil.

She sensed him before he spoke, looked

over as Fin came to sit beside her.

"You don't sleep enough, or rest well enough when you do."

"I'll be doing both when this is finished. See how well he sleeps. Is that a saying? The guilty lose little sleep? Something of the kind, I think."

"But he dreams, I know it."

"Put it away, Finbar. There are five who stand against you there, so the one must bend to the five. I know the wish of it. I thought, well, I could give him a troubled night, by only sending my music into his dreams. But why? What we do, what we send, it can be turned back on us. And we know what we will do, when March winds down."

"What will we do? There's something in here." He tapped her temple. "Something you're not saying to the rest of us. One not bending to five, Branna?"

"Not that at all. I haven't worked it all through yet. I promise you I'll tell you, and all — however I find I stand on it at the end. I only want to be sure where that is first."

"Then come back to bed. He'll give you no name tonight, and cause no harm. He sleeps, and so should you."

"All right." She laid her violin carefully in

its case, took Fin's hand. "Kathel goes out again tomorrow. He's been out with Connor, with Meara, Iona, Boyle, and with you as well. You've all seen the wolf. I see it through Kathel. But all he — or I find — in the mind is a rage and a . . . caginess," she added as they moved through the kitchen, toward the stairs. "That's a different thing than active thought, that caginess, that rage. But it knows its name, as creatures do."

"I'll join Connor tomorrow, with the hawks, and with Kathel. It may be having me with your hound, and Connor to add more power, we'll find what we need."

"It should be you and I," she realized. "He confuses me with Sorcha from time to time, and covets her still — covets you. The two of us, with Kathel. And the two of us who can join with the hound. I should've thought of it."

"You think enough. We'll deal with it tomorrow." He drew her into bed, wrapped around her. "You'll sleep now."

Before she could understand and block, he kissed her forehead, and sent her into slumber.

For a time he lay beside her in a stream of pale moonlight, then he, too, began to drift into sleep.

And from sleep into dreams.

Baru's hooves rang against the hard dirt of the road not yet thawed. He didn't know this land, Fin thought, yet he did. Ireland. He could smell Ireland, but not his home. Not his own place in it.

The dark night, with a few pricks of stars and the wavering light of a moon that flowed in and out of clouds all closed around him.

And the moon showed a haze of red like blood. Like death.

He could smell smoke on the wind, and in the distance thought he saw the flicker of a fire. Campfire.

He wore a cloak. He could hear it snapping in the wind as they galloped — a dead run — along the ringing ground. The urgency consumed him; though he didn't know where he rode, he knew he must ride.

Blood and death follow. The words echoed in his head so he urged more speed out of the horse, took Baru up, into flight under the red-hazed moon.

The wind rushed through his hair, whipped at his cape so the song of it filled his ears. And still, beneath it, came the bright ring of hoofbeats.

He looked down, saw the rider — bright hair streaming — covering the ground swiftly, and well ahead of those who raced behind him.

And he saw the fog swirl and rise and blanket that rider, closing him off from the rest.

Without hesitation, Fin dived down, taking his horse straight into the dirty blanket of fog. It all but choked him, so thick it spread, closing off the wind, the air. The light from the scatter of stars and swimming bloody moon extinguished like candlewicks under the squeeze of fingers.

He heard the shout, the scream of a horse — sensed the horse's fear and panic and pain. Throwing up his hand, Fin caught the sword he brought to him, and set it to flame.

He charged forward, striking, slicing at the fog, cutting through its bitter cold, slashing a path with his flame and his will.

He saw the rider, for a moment saw him, the bright hair, the dark cape, the faintest glint from a copper brooch, from the sword he wielded at the attacking wolf.

Then the fog closed again.

Rushing forward blindly, Fin hacked at the fog, called out in hopes of drawing the wolf off the man and to him. He brought the wind, a torrent of it to tear and tatter the thick and filthy blanket that closed him in. Through the frayed ribbons of it, he saw the horse stumble, the wolf again gather to leap, and threw out power to block the attack as he charged into the battle.

The wolf turned, red stone, red eyes gleaming bright fire. It flew at Fin's throat, so fast, so fleet, Fin only had time to pivot Baru. Claws scored his left arm, shoulder to wrist, the force of it nearly unseating him, the pain a tidal wave that burned like hellfire. Swinging out with his sword arm, he lashed out with blade and flame, seared a line along the wolf's flank — and felt the quick pain of it stab ice through the mark on his shoulder.

He pivoted again, hacking, slicing as the fog once again closed in to blind him. Fighting free, he saw the maneuver had cost him distance. Another charge, another burst of power, but the wolf was already airborne, and though the wounded warrior swung his sword, the wolf streaked over the flash of the blade, and clamped his snapping jaws on the warrior's throat.

On a cry of rage, Fin spurred Baru forward, through the shifting curtains of fog.

Both horse and rider fell, and with a triumphant howl the wolf and fog vanished.

Even as Baru ran, Fin jumped down, fell to his knees beside the man with bright hair and glazed blue eyes.

"Stay with me," Fin told him, and laid his

hand over the gaping, jagged wound. "Look at me. Look in me. I can help you. Stay with me."

But he knew the words were hollow. He had no power to heal death, and death lay under his hands.

He felt it — the last beat of heart, the last breath.

"You bled for him."

With rage, pain, grief all swirling a tempest inside him, Fin looked up, saw the woman. Branna, was his first thought, but he knew almost as soon as that thought formed, he was wrong.

"Sorcha."

"I am Sorcha. I am the Dark Witch of Mayo. It is my husband, dead on the ground. Daithi, the brave and bright."

Her dress, gray as the fog, swayed over the ground as she walked closer, and her dark eyes held Fin's.

"I watch him die, night after night, year after year, century by century. This is my punishment for betraying my gift, my oath. But tonight, you bled for him."

"I was too late. I didn't stop it. Saving him might have saved all, but I was too late."

"We cannot change what was, and still your blood, my love's, Cabhan's lay on this ground tonight. Not to change what was, but to show what can be."

She, too, knelt, then laid her lips on Daithi's. "He died for me, for his children. He died brave and true, as he ever was. It is I who failed. It is I who out of rage harmed you, who cursed you, an innocent, and so many others who came before you."

"Out of grief," Fin said. "Out of grief and torment."

"Grief and torment?" Her dark eyes flashed at him. "These can't balance the scales. I cursed you, and all who came between you and Cabhan, and as it is written, what I sent out into the world, has come back to me threefold. I burdened my children, and all the children who came after them."

"You saved them. Gave your own life for them. Your life and your power."

She smiled now, and though grief lived in the smile, he saw Branna in her eyes. "I held fast to that grief, as if it were a lover or a beloved child. I think it fed me through all the time. I wouldn't believe even what I was allowed to see. Of you or in you. Even knowing not just Cabhan's blood ran in you, I couldn't accept truth."

"What truth?"

She looked down at Daithi. "You are his

as well. More his, I know now, than Cab-han's."

With a hand red with Daithi's blood and his own, Fin gripped her arm. Power shimmered at the contact. "What are you saying?"

"Cabhan healed — what's in him helped him come out of the ashes I'd made him. And healed, he sought vengeance. He couldn't reach my children — they were beyond him. But Daithi had sisters, and one so fair, so fresh, so sweet. He chose her, and he took her, and against her will planted his seed in her. She took her last breath when the child took his first. You are of that child. You are of her. You are of Daithi. You are his, and so, Finbar of the Burkes, you are mine. I've wronged you."

Carefully, she unpinned Daithi's brooch, one she'd made him for protection that held the image of horse, hound, hawk to represent their three children. "This is yours, as you are his. Forgive me."

"She has your face, and I hear her in every word you speak." He looked down at the brooch. "I still carry Cabhan's blood."

With a shake of her head, Sorcha closed Fin's fingers around the copper. "Light covers the dark. I swear to you by all I ever was, if I could break the curse I put on you,

419

I would. But it is not for me."

She rose, keeping his hand in hers so they stood together over Daithi's body. "Blood and death here, blood and death to follow. It is beyond me to change it. I give my faith as I gave my power to my children, to the three who came from them, to the two who would stand with them, and to you, Finbar from Daithi, who carries both the light and the dark. Cabhan's time must end, what joined with him must end."

"Do you know its name?"

"That is beyond me as well. End it, but not to avenge, for there only leads to more blood, more death as I have learned too well. End it, for the light, for love, and for all who come from you."

She kissed his cheek, stepped back. "Remember, love has powers beyond all magicks. Go back to her."

He woke unsteady, disoriented, and with Branna desperately saying his name.

She crouched over him in the thin light of dawn, pressing her hands to his wounded arm. She wept as she spoke, as she pumped warmth into the wound. Some part of him stared at her, puzzled.

Branna never wept.

"Come back, come back. I can't heal this

wound. I can't stop the bleeding. Come back."

"I'm here."

She let out a sobbing breath, looked from the wound to his face with tears running down her cheeks. "Stay with me. I couldn't reach you. I can't stop the bleeding. I can't — Oh, thank God, thank all the gods. It's healing now. Just stay, stay. Look at me. Fin, look at me. Look in me."

"I couldn't heal him. He died with my hands on him. It's his blood on my hands. His blood on me, in me."

"Hush, hush. Just let me work. These are deep and vicious. You've lost blood, too much already."

"You're crying."

"I'm not." But her tears fell on the wound, and closed it more cleanly than her hands. "Quiet, just be quiet and let me finish. It's healing well now. You'll need a potion, but it's healing well."

"I won't need one." He felt steadier, stronger, and altogether clearer. "I'm fine now. It's you who's shaking." He shifted up to sit, brushed his fingers over her damp cheeks. "It may be you who needs a potion."

"Is there pain now? Test your arm. Move it, flex it, so we see if it's as it should be."

He did as she asked. "It's all fine, and no,

there's no more pain." But he glanced down, saw the sheets covered in blood. "Is all that mine?"

Though she trembled still, she rose, changed the sheets to fresh with a thought. But she went into the bath to wash her own hands, needed the time and distance to smooth out her nerves.

She came back, put on a robe.

"Here." Fin held out one of two glasses of whiskey. "I think you need this more than I."

She only shook her head, sat carefully on the side of the bed. "What happened?"

"You tell yours first."

She closed her eyes for a moment. "All right then. You began to thrash in your sleep. Violently. I tried to wake you, but I couldn't. I tried to find a way into the dream, to pull you out, but I couldn't. It was like a wall that couldn't be scaled, no matter what I did. Then the gashes on your arm, the blood flowing from them."

She had to pause a moment, press her hands to her face, gathered back her calm.

"I knew you were beyond where I could reach. I tried to pull you back. Tried to heal the wounds, but nothing I did stopped the blood. I thought you would die in your sleep, trapped in some dream he dragged you into, blocked me out of. You'd die because I couldn't reach you. He'd taken you from me when it seems I've only gotten you back. You'd die because I wasn't strong enough to heal you."

"But you did just that, and I didn't die, did I?" He slid up behind her, pressed a kiss to her shoulder. "You cried for me."

"Tears of panic and frustration."

But when he kissed her shoulder again, she spun around, wrapped around him, rocked. "Where did you go? Where did he take you?"

"He didn't take me, that I'm sure of. I went back to the night Cabhan killed Daithi. I saw Sorcha. I spoke with her."

Branna jerked back. "You spoke with her."

"As I'm speaking to you. You look so like her." He brushed her hair behind her back. "So very like her, though her eyes are dark, they have the same look as yours. It's the strength in them. And the power."

"What did she say to you?"

"I'll tell you, but I think it's best to tell all of us. And the truth is I could use some time to sort through it all myself."

"Then I'll tell them to come."

She dressed, asked him no more questions. In truth, she needed the time herself, to settle, to put on her armor. Not since the day she'd seen the mark on him had she felt the level of fear, of grief she'd known that dawn. She asked herself if feeling so much had blocked her powers to heal him, to bring him out of the dream. And didn't know the answers.

When she went down, she noted he'd put the kettle on, and already had coffee waiting for her.

"You'll think you need to cook up breakfast for the lot of us," he began. "We can fend for ourselves."

"It keeps my hands busy. If you want to fend, scrub and chip up some potatoes. You've skill enough for that."

They worked in silence until the others began to straggle in.

"Looks like a full fry's coming," Connor commented. "But a damned early hour for it. Had an adventure, did you?" he said to Fin.

"You could say it was."

"But you're okay." Iona touched his arm as if checking for herself.

"I am, and also clever enough to turn over the duty dropped on me here to Boyle, who has a better hand with it."

"Nearly all do." Boyle shoved up his sleeves and joined Branna.

With the air of anticipation hanging, they

set the table, brewed tea, made the coffee, sliced the bread.

When all were settled at the table, all eyes turned to Fin.

"It's a strange tale, though some of it we know from the books. I found myself riding Baru at a hard gallop on a dirt road still hard from winter."

He wound his way through it, doing his best to leave out no details.

"Wait now." Boyle held up a hand. "How can you be so sure Cabhan didn't reel you into this? The wolf attacked you, went for your throat, and our Branna couldn't get through to help you, or to bring you back. It sounds like Cabhan's doing."

"I took him by surprise, I can swear to that. The wolf came at me only because I was there, and might interfere with the murder. If Cabhan had wanted to do me harm, why not lie in wait, and come at me? No, his aim was Daithi, and my coming into it something unexpected.

"I couldn't save him, and thinking over it all, was never meant to save him."

"He was a sacrifice," Iona said quietly. "His death, like Sorcha's, gave birth to the three."

"He had eyes like yours, bright and blue. I could see, when I could see, how brave and fierce he fought. But no matter that, no matter what I could bring to help, nothing could change what was done. Cabhan's power was great, more than he has now. Sorcha dimmed that power, though he healed. I think now some of the hunger that drives him is to gain it all back again. And to gain it, he must take it from the three."

"He never will," Branna said. "Tell them the rest. I only know a little of it."

"Daithi fell. I thought I could heal his wound, but it was too late for that. He drew his last breath almost as soon as I put my hands on him. And then she came. Sorcha."

"Sorcha?" Meara set down the coffee she'd started to drink. "She was there with you?"

"We spoke. It seemed a long time there on the bloody road, but I think it wasn't."

He went over it, word by word, her grief, her remorse, her strength. And then the words that changed so much inside him.

"Daithi? You come from him, your blood is mixed with his and Cabhan's?" Shaken, Branna got slowly to her feet. "How could I have not known? How could none of us have known? It's him you carry, it's him and what's in you that beats back Cabhan at every turn. But I didn't see it. Or wouldn't. Because I saw the mark."

"How could you see what I myself couldn't see in me? I saw the mark and let that weigh as heavy as you did. Heavier, I think. She knew, as she said, she knew, but didn't believe or trust. So I think she brought me there, to see what I would do. That last test of what burned strongest in me."

He reached in his pocket. "And in the end, she gave me this." He opened his hand, showed the brooch. "What she made for him, she gave to me."

"Daithi's brooch. Some have searched for it." Branna sat again, studied the copper brooch. "We thought it lost."

"The three guides as one." When Connor held out his hand, Fin gave him the brooch. "As you're the only among us who can speak with all three. It was always yours. Waiting for you, for her to give it to you."

"She sees Daithi die every night, she told me. Her punishment for the curse. I think the gods are harsh indeed to so condemn a grieving woman. Blood and death, she said, as you did, Branna. Blood and death follow, and so she gives us — all of us here, and her children — her faith. We must end him, but not for revenge, and I confess revenge rode high in me before this. We must end him for the light, for love, and all who will come from us. She said love had powers beyond all magicks, then sent me back. She said, 'Go back to her,' and I woke with you weeping over me."

Saying nothing, Branna held out a hand to Connor, then studied the brooch. "She made this for love, as she did what the three wear. It's strong magick here. And as we do, you must never be without it now that it's given to you."

"We can make him a chain for it," Iona suggested, "like ours."

"Yes, we'll do that. That's a fine idea. This all tells me why I've always needed so much of your blood to make a poison. It's never had enough of Cabhan in it."

With a half laugh, Fin decided to eat the eggs that had gone cold on his plate. "Ever practical."

"You're one of us," Iona realized. "I mean, you're a cousin. A really, really distant one, but you're a cousin."

"Welcome to the family then." Connor lifted his tea, toasted. "So it may be written, at some point, that the Cousins O'Dwyer, and their friends and lovers, sent Cabhan the black to hell."

"I'll raise a glass to that."

As Fin did, Boyle gave Iona's hand a squeeze. "I say we all raise them tonight, at the pub, and the new cousin stands the first round."

"I'm fine with that, and the second's on you." Fin lifted his own glass, then drank the coffee that had gone cold as his eggs.

And still he felt a warmth in him.

19

Fin wore the brooch on a chain, felt the weight of it. But when he looked in the mirror, he saw the same man. He was what he ever was.

And while the brooch lay near his heart, the mark still rode on his shoulder. Knowing his blood held both dark and light didn't change that, didn't change him.

It wouldn't change what would be in only a few weeks' time.

He ran his businesses, worked the stables, the school, spent time in his own workshop trying to perfect spells that could be useful to his circle.

He walked or rode with Branna, along with the dogs, hoping to lure out Cabhan, hoping they would find the way to dig out that last piece.

But the demon's name eluded them as February waned and March bloomed.

"Going back to the cave may be the only

way left." Fin said it casually as he and Connor watched a pair of young hawks circle above a field.

"There's time yet."

"Time's passing, and he waits as we wait."

"And you're weary of the waiting, that's clear enough. But going back's not the answer, and you can't know you'll learn the name if you did."

Connor drew the white stone out of his pocket, the one Eamon of the first three had given him. "We all wait, Fin. Three and three and three, for I can't find Eamon in dreams now. I can't find him, and still I know he's there. Waiting as we are."

Fin could admire Connor's equanimity — and curse it. "Without the name, what do we wait for?"

"For what comes, and that's always been an easier matter for me than you. Tell me this, when it's done, when we finish it, and I believe we will, what then for you?"

"There are places in the world I haven't been."

Temper flashed, and Connor was a man slow to temper. "Your place is here, with Branna, with us."

"My home is here, and I can't deny it. But Branna and I can't have the life we wished for, so we take what we can while we can. We can't have the life you'll have with Meara, or Boyle with Iona. It's not meant."

"Ah, bollocks. She thinks too much for her own good, and you blame yourself for things beyond your doing. The past may be written, but the future isn't, and two such clever people should be able to suss out how to make one together."

"Having Daithi's blood in me doesn't change having Cabhan's, or bearing his mark. If we win this, and destroy him, the demon, his lair, what's to say I won't be pulled as he was, a year from now, or ten? I know just how dark and sweet that pull can be, and Branna knows it's in me. We could never have children who would carry that same burden."

"If, can't, doesn't." Connor dismissed all with a wave of his hand. "More bollocks. The pair of you stare into the hard side of things."

"A witch's dying curse may be regretted now, but its power holds. It may be one of the places I haven't been holds the key to breaking it. I won't stop looking."

"Then when this is done, we'll all of us look. Think of all the free time on our hands once we dispatch Cabhan."

Fin smiled, but thought there were lives

to be lived. "Let's keep our minds on dispatching him. And tell me, what sort of house are you thinking of building for yourself and your bride. Something such as . . ."

With a twirl of his finger, Fin floated an image of a glittery faerie palace over a silver lake.

With a laugh, Connor twirled his own. "To start, perhaps more this." And turned the palace into a thatched-roof cottage in a field of green.

"Likely suits you better. And what does Meara have to say about it?"

"That she doesn't want to think about it until Iona and Boyle are wed, and their house finished. At that time, as she's giving up her flat on the first of the month in any case, we thought it might be with Boyle and Iona tucked in their new place, we might give Branna her quiet and tuck ourselves into the flat over your garage."

"You could, indeed. As long as you like, but I think your fingers will be itching to make your own."

"Well, it may be I've drawn up a few ideas on it. I think —"

He broke off as his phone signaled a text.

"It's Branna. No, no, nothing's wrong," he said as Fin lunged to his feet. "She'd like us to come back is all, has something she wants to talk to us and Iona about. Hmm." Connor sent back a quick response. "Witches only, it seems, and I wonder what that's about."

"She's been brewing on something — in her head," Fin added. "She may be finished on the brewing of it."

And with Connor, he called the hawks.

Branna continued to work as she waited. She had indeed finished brewing on it, and felt the time had come to ask if the others were willing or thought the idea had merit.

She'd studied the means to do it, had gone over the ritual needed more times than she cared to count — as it was a great deal to ask, of all.

Was it another answer? she wondered. Another step needed for what they all hoped was the end?

Not an impulse, she assured herself as she filled the last bottles with fragrant oils for the shop. She'd given it far too much thought, considered it from every side and angle for it to be deemed an impulse.

No, it was a decision, a choice, and must be fully agreed to by all.

She washed her hands, wiped her counter, then went over to look into her crystal.

The cave was empty, but for the red glow

of the fire, the dark smoke rising from the cauldron. So Cabhan wandered where he willed. And if he watched, would see nothing that offered him aid or insight. She'd seen to that.

She rose as Iona came in, and did what she always did. Put the kettle on.

"You said no worries, but —"

"There aren't," Branna assured her. "It's just a matter I need to talk over with you and Connor and Fin."

"But not Boyle or Meara."

"Not as yet. It's nothing we would do without them, I promise, only it needs to be discussed among us first. So, have you settled it all then on the wedding flowers?"

"Yes." Iona hung up her jacket and scarf, tried to shift topics as Branna wanted. "You were right about the florist, she's wonderful. We've nailed that all down, and I'm nearly done — I tell myself — changing the menu for the reception. And I'm glad I've left the music in your hands and Meara's or I'd drive myself crazy."

"We're happy to help, and Meara's making notes on what you're doing she might want to turn a bit for herself. Though she claims she's barely thinking of it all yet, she thinks of it quite a bit."

Branna started the tea. "And here come

Fin and Connor now. Let's use the little table so we're all settled in one place."

"It's serious, isn't it?"

"That's for each to decide. Would you get the cups?"

Branna brought the teapot to the table, the sugar, the cream, the biscuits her brother particularly would expect.

And Connor's eyebrows lifted as he came in. "A tea party, is it?"

"A party, no, but there's tea. If we could all sit, I'm more than ready to say what's on my mind."

"And been on your mind for some time." Fin came over, sat.

"I had to be sure of my own thoughts and feelings on it before I asked for yours."

"But not the full circle," Connor pointed out.

"Not yet, you'll see why it's for us first."

"Okay." Iona blew out a breath. "You're killing me now. Spill it."

"I thought of what came through me the day Fin and I made the poison for the demon. What I said, all the words, at the moment all the work we'd done there came to fruition. We have the means to destroy Cabhan, and what's in him, or will when we have the name. And the means to destroy the stone, and close the portal."

"I love that one," Iona commented. "All the light and heat of it."

"It'll take all to close the dark. But there was more that came through me than poisons, than weapons. It's all risk, all duty, and the blood and death may be ours, any of us. And still, even fully myself again, one thing continued to echo in me. Three and three and three."

"And so we are," Connor agreed. "If you've found a way to connect us again with Sorcha's three, I'd like to hear it, for I feel, and all through me feel, they must be a part of it. They must be there."

"And I believe they will, as the shadows of them came on Samhain. To bring them full, it may be another thing. Three and three and three," Branna repeated. "But there are two armed with only courage and sword or fist. They have no magicks. Sorcha's three, we three, and Fin — part of us, part of Cabhan. Then Boyle and Meara. It doesn't truly balance."

"You said we wouldn't leave them out," Iona began.

"And I gave my word I'd never lock her or Boyle away, whatever my wish to protect them." Connor ignored the biscuits, frowned at his sister. "If you think to appeal to others of our blood, to our father or —"

"No. We are a circle, and nothing changes that. We go, three by three by three, as is meant. But that balance can be met, if we're willing. And in turn if Boyle and Meara are willing."

"You'd give them power." Fin sat back as he began to understand. "You would give them, as Sorcha did her children, what we have."

"I would — not near to all as she did, never that. We need what we are, and I would never burden two we loved with so much. But some, from all of us, to them. It can be done. I've studied how Sorcha did it, I've worked on how to pass — gently as we can — some of what we are. It's a risk if I've got any of it wrong, and it must be a choice for all."

"Sorcha's children already had power, through her," Iona pointed out, "through the blood. I'm newer at this than all of you, but I've never heard of transferring magicks into, well, let's say laypeople."

"They're connected. Not just to us, but also through their bloodline. With or without power, that connection is real. And it's that connection that would allow this to work, if it's meant to work."

"They'd have more protection," Connor considered.

"They would, though as much as I love them, my purpose here is balance. It's the fulfillment of what prophecy came through me. But it must be *our* purpose. Ours and theirs. And we can't know, not for certain, what the powers would be for them."

"But in having them," Fin began, "they, with me, become truly another three."

As that was exactly her thought, Branna let out a pent-up breath. "Yes, another three. I've come to believe that. Now each of you must think it through, and decide if you're willing to give them what is both gift and burden. I can show you how it can be done, how I believe it can be done, without draining any of us, or giving them more than they can hold. If any of us aren't sure, aren't willing, then we set it aside. If we are, but they aren't, again it's set aside. A gift like this must be given freely and with a full heart, and taken the same."

"Should any come from me? If there's willing on all sides," Fin continued, "should any come from me, as what I have is tainted?"

"I don't like hearing you say that," Iona replied.

"This is too large a step not to speak plain truth, *deirfiúr bheag.*"

"I'll speak plain truth when I say I asked

myself the same while I worked this through my head." After scanning the table, Branna looked directly at Fin. "Even before we learned you come from Daithi, I had come to believe — again with a full heart — that yes, also from you. They're yours," Branna told him, "as they're ours. And you are of the three. What you have in you isn't pure, but that — to my mind — makes the light in it all the stronger."

"I'll agree to it, if they do. They must be sure they can accept what comes from me."

"You need to take time to think it through," Branna said, and Connor snorted, grabbed a biscuit.

"And didn't I tell you this one thinks too much? Haven't you taxed your brain on this enough for all of us?" he asked Branna. "Fiddled and figured all the little steps, the ways and means, the pros and cons and the good Christ knows what else? If they'll take it, it's theirs." He looked to Iona.

"Absolutely. I'm not sure how Boyle will react to the idea. He accepts all this — we all know. And he'll fight and stand with us. But at the core . . ."

"He's a man with feet planted firm on the ground," Fin said. "That's true enough. We can only ask, as Branna's asked, and leave the rest to him, and to Meara."

"Well, I can see I wasted time making copious notes for the three of you."

Connor grinned at his sister. "Too much thinking," he said, and ate the biscuit.

"When do we ask?" Iona wondered.

"Sooner's better than later," Fin decided. "When the day's work's done?"

"Then I'm cooking for six." Branna shoved at her hair.

"Happens I've the fat chicken you put on the list for me," Fin told her. "And the makings for colcannon."

"As well. Dinner at Fin's then. I'll go over and start on that, but I think it best and fair we tell them what we're thinking before a meal. They'll need time to . . . digest it all, we'll say."

"Let's say they go for it. When would we try it?"

Branna nodded at Iona, finally picked up her own tea. "Sooner's better there as well. You know more than the rest of us, there's a bit of a learning curve."

She did the chicken up with garlic and sage and lemon, put the colcannon together, peeled carrots for baking in butter while the bird roasted. As she'd come up with the scheme, the others had decided she would broach it with Boyle and Meara.

As she worked she considered various ways of putting it all out to them, and finally concluded direct and frank the best possible route. It settled her down, until Meara came in.

"It smells a treat in here. And looks as though you've already done the work when I came soon as I could to give you some help with it."

"No worries."

"Well, I can set the table at least."

"Don't bother with it now." She didn't want plates and such cluttering up the table when they talked. "Just keep me company. Sure let's break into Fin's vast store of wine."

"I'm for that. I tell you it's scraping my nerves raw seeing Cabhan lurking about every time I take a guided through. It must be doing the same with Iona," she added as she pulled a bottle of white from Fin's kitchen cooler. "She was nervy today, at least toward the end of it. She and Boyle will be around soon."

"So he shows himself to you, to Iona, even Connor now and then, but when Fin and I go out, he avoids us. We'll keep at it," Branna decided. "He won't be able to resist trying to bully or taunt for long."

"He doesn't have long, and that's my way

of thinking." Meara drew the cork. "It's good we're getting together, all of us, so regular like this. You never know when another idea might spark."

Oh, I've an idea for you, Branna thought, but only smiled. "You'd be right. But let's put that aside for now. Tell me how your mother's doing."

"Happier than I ever thought she could be. And don't you know she's started taking piano lessons from a woman at the church? All the time on her hands, she tells me, and she can put it to use with the lessons, as she's always wanted to play. As if she didn't have a world of time before she moved in with Maureen, and —"

Meara held up both hands as if calling herself to a halt. "No, I'll say nothing negative about it. She's there, not here, happy not unhappy and flustered, and Maureen herself tells me it's lovely to have her."

"Nothing but good news there then."

"Well, she's marking some of the world of time she now has by sending me a lorry-load of suggestions for the wedding. Photos of gowns that would make me look like a giant princess wearing a wedding cake, and require so much tulle and lace there'd be none left in the whole of Mayo. Here." Meara reached in her pocket, pulled out her phone. "Have a look at her last vision for me."

Branna studied once Meara had scrolled to the image, a dress with an enormous skirt fashioned of stacked layers of tulle, and that decked with lace and beads and ribbons.

"I'd say you're a fortunate woman to be able to choose your own wedding dress."

"I am, and she'll be disappointed when she's learned I've something more like this in mind."

She scrolled to another picture of a fluid column, simple and unadorned.

"It's lovely, just lovely, and couldn't be more Meara Quinn. Worn with a little tiara, I'd see, as you're not the flowers-in-the-hair as Iona is. Just that touch of fancy and sparkle. She won't be disappointed when she sees you."

"A tiara . . . that might suit me, and would give her a bit of the princess she wants."

"You could find three — any of which you'd be happy to wear. Send her pictures, let her choose for you."

Meara picked up her wine. "You're a canny one."

"Oh, that I am."

As Boyle and Iona came in, Branna hoped Meara would think canny a compliment when she'd laid out the choice.

444

She waited while Meara passed out wine, while Fin and Connor came in, then asked everyone to sit around the table as there was something to discuss.

"Did something happen today?" Meara asked.

"Not today. You could say it happened a little while ago, and I've been working it out since." Straight and direct, Branna reminded herself. "I've told you all the words I spoke on the day Fin and I completed the second poison," she began.

And when she finished with, "It can be done, and the four of us are willing. But the choice of it is for you," there was a long, stunned silence.

Boyle broke it. "You're having us on."

"We're not." Iona rubbed a hand over his. "We think we can do it, but it's a big decision for you and for Meara."

"Are you saying you can make witches out of me and Boyle, if only we agree to it?"

"Not exactly that. I believe seeds of power are in us all," Branna continued. "In some, they sprout more than in others. The instincts, the feelings, the sensation of having done something before, of having been somewhere before. What we'd give would feed those seeds."

"Like manure?" Boyle said. "As it sounds

like a barrow-load of it."

"You'd be the same people." Connor spread his hands. "The same people but with some traces of magicks that could be nurtured and honed."

"If you think to add protection for us —"

"There's the benefit of that." Fin interrupted Boyle in calm tones. "But the purpose is as Branna said. The balance, the interpretation of the prophecy."

"I need to walk around with this." Boyle did just that, rising and pacing. "You want to give us something we lack."

"To my mind, you lack nothing. Nothing," Branna repeated. "And to my mind, this was always meant. Always meant, just not seen or known until now. I may be wrong, but even if right, we'll find another way if it feels wrong for you."

"It feels wrong you'd give up something you have, to add to what we have," he said. "Sorcha left herself near to empty by doing the same."

"This is a worry for me as well," Meara put in. "Giving up power is part of what cost her life."

"She was one giving all she had to three. We're four, giving a small part of what we have to two." Connor smiled at her. "It's arithmetic."

"There's another choice, should you accept the first. It may be three into two," Fin added. "What I would give has some of Cabhan in it, so it's another piece to consider."

"It's all or it's none," Boyle snapped back. "Don't insult us."

"Agreed." Meara took a long drink. "All or none."

"Take whatever time you need to think on it." Branna rose. "Ask whatever comes to mind, and we'll try to answer. And know whatever your choice, we value you. We'll eat, if that suits everyone, and put this aside unless you have those questions."

"Eat." Boyle muttered to himself, continued to pace as food was brought to the table. Then Iona simply walked over, put her arms around him.

He heaved a sigh, met Meara's eyes over Iona's head. Meara's response was a simple lifting of shoulders.

"If we agree, how would it be done?" he wanted to know.

"In much the same way Sorcha did with her children," Branna told him. "At the base of it in any case. With some adjustments, of course, to fit our own needs."

"If we agreed," Meara added, "when would it be done?"

"Tonight." Connor waved off his sister's protest. "The ifs they're putting out are smoke. They've both of them decided to agree, because they see, as we do, it's another answer. So it's tonight, a clean, quick step, and giving them time to adjust to what's new in them." He took a heap of colcannon for his plate, before passing the dish to Meara. "Am I wrong?"

"You're a cocky one, Connor, but not wrong. Let's eat, Boyle, and eat hearty, for it's our last meal as we are."

"It doesn't change who you are, even what you are." Iona rubbed a hand on Boyle's arm. "It's . . . Think of it like gaining a new skill or talent."

"Like piano lessons," Meara said, and made Branna laugh and laugh.

So they ate, and talked, they cleared and talked more.

Then all six stood together in Fin's workshop.

"Cabhan mustn't see what we do here," Branna told Fin.

"He won't. I've cloaked my windows and doors to him long since, but another layer wouldn't hurt. Add your own. I have what we'll need. I read your notes," he added. "I'll lay out what's needed, and we'll leave it to you to use them."

"He'll feel something though, won't he?" Iona glanced toward the windows. "Power feels power."

"He may feel, but he won't know." Connor took Meara's hand. "You are the love of my life, before and after."

"That may be, but I'm hoping I get enough of whatever it is to give you a jolt whenever you might need one."

"You give me that already." He swept her back for a dramatic kiss.

"You're easy with it all," Boyle commented.

"I'm nervous as a cat in a dog kennel." Meara pressed her hand to her stomach. "But let's be honest, Boyle, we've seen our lives long what this is, what it means. We've four here who've shown us what this is must be respected and honored, so we will. And the more I think of it, the more I'm liking the idea of having a bit more to turn on Cabhan and his master."

"There is that, for certain, and I can't claim not to consider it. Even if I'd rather just use my fists."

"You're the man you are, so you don't see it's you who's giving tonight, not us." Iona took his face in her hands. "It's you." Then stepped back. "Is there something you need from us, Branna?"

"Three drops of blood from each who gives power. Three only. But first, we cast a circle, we light the fire to ring it. It's your home, Fin. You begin."

"Here and now the circle cast protecting all within, so inside its ring the ritual begin. Flames arise but not to burn, through the light our powers turn. Close the door and seal the locks. Turn away whatever knocks."

Fire flashed to ring them, cool and white.

"We are connected," Branna began. "Are now, have been, will be. If not by blood and bone, but heart and spirit. We seal that connection here with a gift, given and taken willingly.

"So say we all?" Branna asked.

"So say we all," the others answered.

So she began.

"Wine and honey, sweet and dark." She poured both into a bowl. "To help the light within you spark. Oil of herbs and joy-shed tears stirred within to ease your fears. From my heart a drop of blood times three." She pricked her wrist at the pulse, added the three drops to the cup. "Sister, brother, unto me, I share my light with both of thee."

She passed the bowl to Fin. "From heart, from spirit I shed for thee, a drop of blood times three. Sister, brother, unto me, I share my light with both of thee."

When he finished, he handed the bowl to Connor. "And now on a new journey you embark, I give three drops from my heart. Lover, brother, unto me, I share my light with both of thee."

And to Iona.

"You are my heart, you are my light, so that holds fast upon this night. From the beat of my heart, for sister, for love, one, two, and three. I share my light with both of thee."

"Sealed with fire, pure and white, the gift we give upon this night." Branna took the bowl, held it high as white fire flashed within. "Bless this gift and those who take what's given, know by right all here are driven. From bowl to cup for one, for two, pour forth this consecrated brew."

The liquid in the bowl fountained up, split into two with each arch spilling into a waiting cup.

Branna gestured to Connor, to Iona. "Those closest should make the final offering."

"Okay." Iona picked up a cup, turned to Boyle. She touched his cheek, then held out the cup. "In this place and in this hour, we offer you this taste of power. If your choice to take is free, say these words back to me. 'This I take into my body, into my heart, into my spirit willingly. As we will, so mote it be.' "

He repeated the words, hesitated briefly, then looked into her eyes. And drank.

Connor turned to Meara, gave her his words, her own.

She grinned at him, couldn't quite help it, and drank.

"Is that it?" she asked. "Did it work? I don't feel any different." She looked at Boyle.

"No, no different."

"How do we know it worked?" Meara demanded.

The circling fire flashed up in spears to the ceiling. The air quivered with light and heat. A shining beam of it showered over Boyle, over Meara like a welcome.

"That," Connor concluded, "would be an indicator."

"What can we do? What should we do?"

"We give thanks, close the circle." Branna smiled at her lifelong friend. "Then we'll see."

20

They proved nimble students and within a week could both spark a candlewick. Branna moved them on from that most basic skill to test them with other elements.

It didn't surprise her that Meara showed more aptitude with air and Boyle with fire. That connection again, she concluded. Meara to Connor, Boyle to Iona.

They put in a great deal of time training, discovering, and the progress pleased Branna. Meara could create tough little cyclones and found her affinity with horses enhanced. When goaded, Boyle conjured golf-ball-sized fireballs.

Frustrated, he slumped into a chair at Fin's. "What good does it all do? When he comes around, I'm bound by our agreement not to show our hand and left to give him nothing stronger than a hard look. And if I could give a taste of what I have now, he could smack it away like a tennis player returning a lob."

"The player's more likely to end up getting beaned," Connor pointed out, "if the lob comes from an unexpected direction. You've done considerable, you and Meara, with the little you were given, and done considerable in a short time."

"Time's the trouble, isn't it?" Boyle pointed out.

"It is, and that's a hard fact." Fin contemplated his beer. "We thought as he wouldn't know we were looking, we'd find a way into the demon's name. Now I wonder if Cabhan's forgotten it, as the demon's been part of him for so long."

"That's a troubling thought." Connor considered it. "If it's true we can't end it without the demon's name, and if there's no longer a name to find, it may be it's Cabhan's name we have to speak as we poison them."

"Are such matters ever that simple?" Fin asked.

"They haven't proved to be. Still, maybe this will be. Only the name. The rest is complicated enough."

"And only days left to us now," Boyle put in. "Only a few weeks left till our wedding, and Iona isn't able to think of it the way women do. Not with this between."

"You might be grateful for that," Connor commented. "In my experience, from mates who've been through it, some women can go right mad."

"It's outside," Fin said quietly, and Connor came to attention.

"I don't sense him."

"He's shadowed, but I can just feel him out there, trying to watch, trying to get into my thoughts. Biding time, that's what he's doing. The taunting and shadowing, but biding all the same. He has, as he's proved, all the time in all the worlds."

"He's not looking for another fight." Boyle leaned forward now. "Not that he wouldn't take us all on, given the opportunity, but he's waiting us out now. That makes sense to me. Wear down our spirits, wait for the moment when we're careless. We've the wrong strategy, I think, on luring him back to Sorcha's cabin, for then he'll know we're ready for the battle."

"We have to get him there," Connor pointed out. "Everything depends on it."

"But he doesn't have to know we want him to come. What if he thinks we're hiding the fact that we're going from him — but he's so bloody smart and powerful, he got through the shields and sees us?"

"Why would we be going there if not for

battle?" Connor argued.

"To pay our respects." Seeing Boyle's point, Fin nodded. "To honor Sorcha on the day of her death, to hold a ritual of respect — and perhaps try to appeal to her for help. Going under cover of our own fog so he won't stop us from paying those respects or making that appeal."

"And what we're doing is taking the high ground for the battle," Boyle finished, eager now that he could see the fight. "And instead of being taken by surprise, we give the surprise."

"Oh, I'm liking this idea." Connor took a long drink. "This is what comes of talking war with men. And if either of you should repeat that to any of the women, I'll be shocked and amazed at what liars you are."

"Since I want them fully behind this, they won't hear that from me. We set the trap," Fin said, "by letting him think he's set it."

Branna listened to the new plan over pizza in Fin's living room. There had been some talk of an evening out, but no one understood priorities more than Branna O'Dwyer.

"It's clever, sure it's clever," she agreed. "And it annoys me I never thought of it on my own. We don't have much time to change from the plan we've settled on."

"And that one has the benefit of being simple," Meara added. "We transport ourselves there — or you transport the lot of us, along with horses, hawks, and hound, and we call him out. He'd come, as his pride wouldn't allow otherwise. But . . . this is more devious, and I can't help but like it."

"He'd like that we're trying to hide from him," Iona agreed. "That would appeal to his arrogance. And if he thinks we're trying to call on Sorcha, he'd have to come — on the slim chance we could reach her, bring her to us, open her to him again."

"You'd be giving up your own shadow spell," Branna said to Fin. "Something he doesn't know you have. It won't be as useful to you when he does come."

"It will have served. It changes little of what we do once he's there, only the approach."

"We'll gather flowers, wine, bread, honey." Thinking it through, Branna made mental notes. "All the things we'd take to a visit of respect for the dead. We're somber and unsettled, and about to attempt raising the spirit of the witch who cursed one of us. He'd see many advantages to a strike then."

"Could we start the ritual for it?" Iona wondered. "But when it's too late for him, call the first three?"

Boyle laughed, reached over to kiss her soundly. "Who said women can't plan wars?"

Meara angled her head. "Who did?"

"Rhetorical," Connor said with a careless wave. "Well then, let's plan a war."

On the day, Branna gathered all she needed. White roses, wine, honey, bread she made herself, the herbs, all the offerings. In another pouch she placed the poisons, each carefully wrapped.

And separate, to risk no contamination, the bottle of light the three had created.

She'd bathed and anointed herself, had woven charms in her hair, added them to Kathel's collar. Made more for Aine's mane.

Alone, she lit the candles, cast a circle, and knelt inside it to offer her acceptance to what the fates deemed. There was a certainty to her that tonight would end Cabhan or end the three. A sharper certainty that whatever the fates deemed, her life would not be as it had been.

But still her life, and still her choices. She was, and would always be a servant and a child of the light. But she was also a woman.

She rose, certain in purpose. She gathered her things and with her hound, flew to Fin's.

She came to him in his workshop as he

chose weapons from his case.

"You're early."

"I wanted time with you before the others, before we start. I've given myself to the fates, accept whatever comes. I'll fight more fiercely for the acceptance."

"I can only accept his end."

"I hope that's not true." She crossed to him. "Will you accept me, Fin?"

"I do. Of course."

My life, she thought again, my choice. Witch and woman.

"I give myself to you. Will you take me? Will you let me belong to you, and belong to me in turn?"

He touched her cheek, twined a lock of her hair around his finger. "I could never belong to another."

"I never will. Belong to me, and stay with me, for this is home for both of us. I want to live with you here, in this house you built from our young dreams. I want to be married to you, as that's a promise given and taken as well. I want to make my life with you."

As the words squeezed his heart, he laid the sword he'd chosen down. And stepped back from her. "You know we can't. Until I break the curse —"

"I don't know it." She rushed in now —

459

no more thinking. Only feeling. "I know we let what was put on you by light and dark stop us. No more, Fin. We can make no children who would carry it as you do, and this is a grief for us both. But we'd have each other. We can't have the life we once dreamed of, planned for, but we can dream and plan another. I gave myself to the powers greater. I may die this night, and I can accept that. But when I gave myself, the powers didn't say to me — let him go — so I won't."

"Branna." He cupped her face, kissed her cheeks. "I have to find the way to break the curse. I don't know where the search will take me. I don't know, can't know, how long it might take me, if I ever find the answer."

"Then I'll follow you, wherever you go. I'll search with you, wherever it takes us. You can't hide or run from me. I'll follow you, Finbar, track you like a hound, I swear it on my life. I won't go back to living without what I love. I love you."

Overcome, he rested his brow to hers. "You take my breath away. A dozen years you haven't said those words to me. Three words that hold all the power of heaven and earth."

"I would bind you to me with them. We're meant, I know that with all I am. If you can't stay with me, I'll go with you. We can go or stay, but marry me, Fin. Make that vow to me, take that vow from me. Before we face what we have to face, take my love, promise your own."

"Can you live with this, every day?" He rubbed his arm. "Can you live with this, and what we know we can't have?"

She'd given herself to the light, she remembered, and the answer had come. So simple, so clear.

"You do, you live with it every day, and I'm yours. I'll give my life for duty if my life is needed, but I'll no longer close off my heart. Not to myself, not to you. Not to love."

"To have your love is everything to me. We can take it a day at a time, until —"

"No. No more just today. I need this from you." She laid her hands on his chest, on his heart. "I ask this of you. Take my love, and its promise, give yours to me. Whatever comes."

"In my life," he said, his voice quiet as a kiss, "you are all I've wanted. Above all else."

He kissed her lightly, then released her to go to a shelf, opened a puzzle box, took out a ring that flashed light from the fire.

"A circle," he said. "A symbol, a stone of heat and light. I found it in the sea, a warm

461

blue sea where I swam and thought of you. I went to forget you, far away from here, from all. On an island where no one lived, and I swam away from even that, and saw this glint through the water. I knew it for yours, though I never thought to give it to you, never thought you'd take it."

She held out her hand. "Give me the promise, and take mine. If there's tomorrow, Fin, we'll take it as ours."

"I swear to you, I'll find a way to give you all your heart wishes."

"But don't you see, you already have. This is love, and love accepts all."

When he slipped the ring on her finger, the flames in the hearth roared up. Somewhere in the night behind the windows, lightning flashed.

"We'll take it," she said again, and clung to him, clung to the kiss.

Whatever comes, she thought, be it blood and death, they had this.

They gathered, a circle formed from heart and spirit, loyalty and duty, and sealed by magicks. As night grew deep, they took up weapons.

"We don't have the name," Branna began. "Until we do we must keep Cabhan from escaping, keep him within our borders, prevent him from shifting time."

"We build the walls strong, lock the gate," Connor agreed. "And use all we have to draw the demon out, to draw out the name."

"Or thrash it out of him," Boyle countered.

"We each know what's to be done tonight, and how we'll do it," Fin continued. "We're stronger for what's shared among us, and if right's meant to triumph, Cabhan ends tonight. There are none I would rather go into battle with than those in this room. No man ever had truer friends."

"I say we go burn this bastard, then come back here for a full fry." Connor hugged Meara to his side.

"I'm for it." Meara laid a hand on the hilt of her sword. "And more than ready for the first."

"You've given me family, given me home. This has been the best year of my life," Iona continued. "And in this year, I'm going to marry the love of my life, and no demon from hell is going to stop me. So yeah, let's go burn the bastard."

With a laugh, Boyle plucked her off her feet, kissed her. "How can we lose with such as you?"

"We can't." Iona scanned the faces around her. "We won't."

"We have to prepare for —"

"Wait." Iona wiggled away from Boyle, pointed at Branna. "What's this? What *is* this?" She grabbed Branna's hand, gave a tearful laugh. "Oh boy, oh boy!" And launching herself at Branna, squeezed hard. "This is what I've been wishing for. Exactly what I've been wishing for."

"You'd think you'd have said something to the rest of us." Meara grabbed Branna's hand in turn as Iona swung around to wrap around Fin. "This shows right's meant to win. Right here." She pressed her cheek to Branna's, swayed. "It shows it."

"Far past time." Boyle gave Fin a light punch in the chest. "But well done."

Connor waited until Fin met his eyes. "So, you finally listened to me, and all my wisdom."

"I listened to your sister."

"As now you'll have no choice but to do for the rest of your life. And you owe me a hundred."

"What? Ah," Fin said as he remembered the wager. "So I do."

Connor gave Fin a full-on hug, then turned to take Branna's face, to kiss her cheeks. "Now the scales are truly balanced. Love feeds the light."

Branna closed her hands around Connor's

wrists, kissed his cheeks in turn. "Well then, let's go burn the bastard."

"Are we ready then?" Fin waited for assents, and for the circle to form.

"Our place, our time as the hour strikes three," Branna said and drew a breath. "This dawn brings our destiny."

"With fist and light we bring the fight," Boyle continued.

"To end demon-witch on this night," Meara finished.

"Three by three by three we'll ride." Connor took Meara's hand, looked to Iona.

"With horse and hawk and hound our guides," Iona said.

"And while these mists flow from me, Cabhan sees only what we will him see."

Fin spread his arms, circled them, spread them. Branna felt the mists wrap around her — warm and soft. No, she thought, this wasn't Cabhan's cold, bitter cloak.

They went down and out, and into the stables. While Branna braided charms into Aine's mane, Iona stepped over. "She's coming into season."

"Aine?"

"Another day or two. She'll be ready for Alastar if it's what you want."

"It is."

"She isn't afraid; none of the horses are

465

afraid, but they know they'll fly tonight, and why."

"As does the hound. They're ready." Branna looked to Connor.

"And the hawks as well."

"Mind your thoughts and words now," Fin told them, "for I have to let him in, let him see enough to make him believe we go to honor Sorcha and try to raise her."

With a nod Branna crouched to press her head to Kathel's, then she mounted. And with the others, she flew through the dark heart of the night.

"Can we be sure we're cloaked?" she called to Fin.

"I've never done so wide a mist, but it's covered all, hasn't it? And what would Cabhan be doing watching us at this time of the night?"

Though Fin opened, blood calling to blood. As they flew through the trees, with the whisk of the wind rending small gaps in that cloak, he felt the stirring.

And told Branna with no more than a glance.

"It has to hold, give us time to block him out of the clearing, give us the time to pay our respects to Sorcha and work the spell to bring her spirit to us."

"I'd rather fight than try to converse with

ghosts," Boyle muttered.

"She nearly defeated him," Iona pointed out. "She must know something that will help. We've tried everything. We have to try this. If it works . . ."

"It has to work," Meara put in. "It's driving me next to mad having him stalking us day by day."

"She's ours," Connor told her. "We'll reach her, and tonight, on the anniversary of her death, her sacrifice, her curse is our best hope for it."

"We can't wait another year." Branna brought Aine down as they flew through the vines, into the clearing. "We won't."

As agreed, Fin and the three went to the edges of the clearing, each taking a point of the compass. She would begin, with hopes that rather than holding Cabhan out, the ritual would give him time to slip through — and be closed in.

She lifted her arms, called to the north, poured the salt. Iona took the west. It was Connor, at the east, who whispered softly in Branna's head.

He's coming. Nearly here.

As her brother called on the east Branna's heart tripped.

The first step, luring him, had worked.

Fin called on the south, then all four

467

walked the wide circle, salting the ground while Boyle and Meara set out the tools for the next part of the plan.

She felt the change, the lightest of chills as Cabhan's fog mixed with Fin's.

As they closed the barrier that would keep all out, keep all in, she prayed he wouldn't use the swirls and shadows to attack before they were ready.

Struggling not to rush, she lifted the roses, offered the bouquet to each so they could take a bloom. Fin hesitated.

"I can't see she'd want tribute from me, or accept it."

"You'll show her respect, and give her the tribute. She must understand you've fought and bled with us, and we can't defeat Cabhan without you. We have to try, Fin. Can you offer forgiveness to her for the mark you carry, with the tribute?"

"I have to try," was all he said.

Together, all six approached Sorcha's grave.

"We place upon your grave these pure white blooms to mark the anniversary of your doom. Bring wine and honey and bread, a tribute of life given to the dead."

It grew colder. Branna swore she could all but feel the rise of Cabhan's excitement, his greed. But she found no name in the undulating fog.

"These herbs we scatter on the ground to release your spirit from its bounds. With respect we kneel and make to you this appeal. Sealed with our blood, three and three, fire burn in through the night and meet our need most dire, grant us what we ask of thee."

One by one they scored their palms, let the blood drip onto the ground by the stone.

"In this place, at this hour, through your love and by our power, send to us your children three so all may meet their destiny."

A howl came through the fog, a sound of wild fury. Fin dropped the cloak as he drew his sword, leaped to his feet beside Branna and the others.

"Send them here and send them now," Branna shouted, and Fin and Connor moved to block her from any attack. Iona, Boyle, and Meara worked quickly to cast a circle while she finished the ritual.

"Those with your powers you did endow. Three by three by three we fight." She shot out fire of her own to block Cabhan from pivoting into an attack as her friends hurried to cast the circle, and open a portal for the first three.

"Three by three by three we take the night. Mother, grant this boon, let them fly across the moon and set your spirit free. As we will, so mote it be."

The ground shook. She nearly lost her footing as she spun around to race toward the circle, glanced back quickly to see Cabhan hurl what looked like a wall of black fire toward Fin and Connor. Even as she reached for Iona's hand, to join what they had, the wind picked her up like a cold hand, threw her across the clearing.

Though she landed hard enough to rattle bones, she saw Fin battling back with flaming sword and heaving ground, Connor lashing the air like a whip. Light and dark clashed, and the sound was huge, like worlds toppling.

Meara charged forward, sword slashing, and Boyle released a volley of small fireballs that slashed and burned the snaking fog. With no choice but to attack, defend, it left Iona alone to complete the circle.

He's stronger, Branna realized, somehow stronger than he'd been on Samhain. Whatever was inside him had drawn on more, drawn out more. The last battle, she thought; they knew it, and so did Cabhan.

He called the rats so they vomited out of the ground. He called the bats, so they spilled like vengeance from the sky. And Iona, cut off, fought to hold them back as hawk, hound, horse trampled and tore.

Duty, loyalty. Love. Branna sprang to her feet, rushed through the boiling rats to leap onto Aine's back. And with a ball of fire in one hand, a shining wand in the other, flew toward her cousin and the incomplete circle.

She lashed out with fire, with light, carving a path. She called on her gift, brought down a hot rain to drown Cabhan's feral weapons. When she reached Iona, she released a torrent that drove all away from Sorcha's cabin.

"Finish it!" she shouted. "You can finish it."

Then came the snakes, boiling along the ground. She heard — felt — Kathel's pain as fangs tore at him. The fury that burst through her turned them to ash.

Branna wheeled her horse to guard Iona, but her cousin shouted, "I've got this! I've got it. Go help the others."

Fearing the worst, Branna charged through the wall of black fire.

It choked her, the stench of sulfur. She pulled rain, warm and pure, out of the air to wash it away. The fire snapped and sizzled as she fought her way through it.

They bled, her family, as they battled.

Once more she wheeled the horse, pulled her power up, up, up.

Now the rain, and the wind, now the quake and the fire. Now all at once in a maelstrom that crashed against Cabhan's wrath. Smoke swirled, a sting to the eyes, a burn in the throat, but she saw fear, just one wild flicker of it, in the sorcerer's eyes before he hunched and became the wolf.

"It's done!" Iona called out. "It's done. The light. It's growing."

"I see them," Meara, her face wet with sweat and blood, shouted. "I can see them, the shadows of them. Go," she said to Connor. "Go."

"We'll hold him." Boyle punched out, fire and fist.

"By God we will. Go." Fin met Branna's eyes. "Or it's for nothing."

No choice, she thought, holding out a hand for Connor so he could grip it, swing onto Aine with her.

"She's hurt. Meara's hurt."

"We have to pull them through, Connor. It's the three who bring the three. Without them, we may not be able to heal her."

Kathel, she thought, bleeding from the muzzle, from the flank, Alastar slashing hooves in the air, hawks screaming as they dived with flashing talons.

And for nothing if they couldn't bring Sorcha's three fully into the now.

She rode straight into the circle, slid off the horse with her brother. She took Iona's hand, Connor's, and felt the power rise, felt the light burn.

"Three by three by three," she shouted. "This is magick's prophecy. Join with us no matter the cost, come through now or all is lost. Stand with us on this night and by our blood we finish this fight."

They came, Sorcha's three. Brannaugh with bow, Eamon with sword, Teagan with wand and great with child. Without a word they joined hands, so three became six.

Light exploded, all white, all brilliance. The heat of power poured into her, staggering, breathless, beyond any she'd known.

"Draw him away from them!" Branna heard her voice echo over the shaking air. "We have what will take him down, but they're too close."

"For me." Sorcha's Brannaugh held out the hand joined with her brother's. Arrows flew from her quill, flame white, to strike the ground between the wolf and the remaining three.

Crazed, the wolf turned, charged.

Branna broke the link; Connor closed it behind her.

"Hurry," he told her.

"A bit closer yet, just a bit." But she

reached in the pouch, drew out the poison. The bottle throbbed in her hand, like a living thing. As the wolf leaped toward the circle, she sent the bottle flying.

Its screams rent the air, slammed her so she staggered back. All he'd called from the bowels of the dark flamed, and their screams joined the wolf's.

"It's not done." Iona gripped Teagan's hand. "Until we kill what lives in him, it can't be done."

"The name." Branna staggered, but Eamon caught her before she fell. "The demon's name. Do you know it?"

"No. We'll burn what's left of him, salt the ground."

"It's not enough. We must have its name. Fin!"

Even as she started forward, he waved her off, dropped to the ground with the bloody body of the wolf. "Start the ritual."

"You're bleeding — and Meara, Boyle. You'll be stronger if we take time to heal you."

"Start the ritual," he said between his teeth as he closed his hands around the wolf's throat. "That's for you. This is for me."

"Start it." Meara sprawled to the ground with Boyle. "And finish it."

So they rang the bell, opened the book, lit the candle.

And began the words.

Blood in the cauldron, of the light, of the dark. Shadows shifting like dancers.

On the ground, Fin dug his fingers into the torn ruff of the wolf.

"I know you," he murmured, staring into the red eyes. "You're mine, but I'm not yours." He tore the stone away, held it high. "And will never be. I am of Daithi." The brooch fell out of Fin's shirt, and the wolf's eyes wheeled in terror. "And I am your death. I know you. I have stood at your altar, and heard the damned call your name. I know you."

What was in the wolf pushed its dark until Fin's hands burned, until his own blood ran.

"In Sorcha's name I rebuke you. In Daithi's name, I rebuke you. In my name, I rebuke you, for I am Finbar Burke, and I know you."

When it came into him, it all but shattered his soul. The dark pulled, so strong, tore so deep. But he held on, held on, and looked toward Branna. Looked to her light.

"Its name is Cernunnos." He heaved the stone to Connor. "Cernunnos. Destroy it. Now. I can't hold much longer, much more. Get her clear." His breath heaved as he called to Boyle, "Get Meara clear."

"You have to let it go!" Tears streaming, Branna shouted, "Fin, let it go, come to us."

"I can't. He'll go into the earth, into the belly of it, and be lost to us again. I can hold him here, but not much longer. Do what must be done for all, for me. As you love me, Branna, free me. By all we are, free me."

To be sure of it, he threw out what he had so the stone ripped out of Connor's hand and into the cauldron. And as the light, blinding white, towered up, he called out the name himself.

"End it!"

"He suffers," Teagan murmured. "No more. Give him peace."

Sobbing, Branna called out the demon's name, and heaved the poison.

Blacker than black, thicker than tar. Through the whip of it rose wild, ululant cries; deep, throaty screams. And with it thousands of voices shrieking in tongues never heard.

She felt it, an instant before the light bloomed again, before the cauldron itself burned a pure white. The clearing, the sky, she thought the entire world flamed white.

She felt the stone crack, heard the destruction of it like great trees snapped by a giant's hand so the ground rocked like a stormy sea.

She felt the demon's death, and swore she felt her own.

It all drained out of her, breath, power, light, as she fell to her knees.

Blood and death follow, she thought. Blood and death.

Then she was up and running as she saw Fin, still, white, bloody, facedown on the blackened ash of what had been Cabhan, of what had birthed him.

"Hecate, Brighid, Morrigan, all the goddesses, show mercy. Don't take him." She pulled Fin's head into her lap. "Take what I am, take what I have, but don't take his life. I beg you, don't take his life."

She lifted her face to the sky still lit by white fire, threw her power to any who could hear. "Take what you will, what you must, but not his life."

Her tears ran warm, dropped onto his burned skin. "Sorcha," she prayed. "Mother. Right your wrong. Spare his life."

"Shh." Fin's fingers curled in hers. "I'm not gone. I'm here."

"You survived."

And the world righted again, the ground settled, the flames softened in the sky.

"How did you — I don't care. You survived." She pressed her lips to his face, to his hair. "Ah, God, you're bleeding, everywhere. Rest easy, easy, my love. Help me." She looked to Sorcha's Brannaugh. "Please."

"I will, of course. You're all she told me." She knelt down, laid hands on Fin's side where his shirt and flesh were rent and scorched. "He is my own Eoghan to the life."

"What?"

She squeezed Branna's hand. "His face is my own love's face, his heart, my own love's heart. He was never Cabhan's, not where it mattered." She looked down at Fin, and touched her lips to his brow. "You are mine as you are hers. Healing will hurt a bit."

"A bit," Fin said through gritted teeth as pain seared him.

"Look at me. Look into me," Branna crooned.

"I won't. You won't take this. It's mine. The others?"

"Being tended right now. Damn you to bloody hell, Finbar, for making me think I'd killed you. It's too much blood, and your shirt's still smoldering." She whipped it away with a flash of her hand. "Ah, God, some of these are deep. Connor!"

"I'm coming." Limping a little, Connor

swiped bloodied sweat from his face. "Meara and Boyle are healing well, though Christ, she took a blow or two. Still . . . Well, Jesus, Fin, look at the mess you've made of yourself."

To solve things, he gripped Fin's head in his hands, and pushed his way into Fin's mind, and the pain.

"Ah fuck me," Connor hissed.

Minutes dragged on for centuries, even when the others joined them. Before it was done, both Connor and Fin were covered in sweat, breathless, quivering.

"He'll do." Teagan brushed a hand down Branna's arm. "You and my sister are very skilled healers. Some rest, some tonic, and he'll be fine."

"Yes, thank you. Thank you." Branna pressed her face into Connor's shoulder. "Thank you."

"He's mine as well."

"Ours," Eamon corrected. "We came home, and we had a part in destroying Cabhan. But he played the larger role in it. So you're ours, Finbar Burke, though you bear Cabhan's mark."

"No longer," Teagan murmured. "I put the mark on Cabhan, and our mother put it on his blood, all who followed. And I think now that she and the light have taken it.

For this is not Cabhan's mark."

"What do you mean? It's —" Fin twisted to look, and on his shoulder, where he'd worn the mark of Cabhan since his eighteenth year, he now wore a Celtic trinity knot, the triquetra.

A sign of three.

It stunned him, more than the fire of the poison, more than the blinding flames of the white.

"It's gone." He touched his fingers to it, felt no pain, no dark, no stealthy pull. "I'm free of it. Free."

"You would have given your life. Your blood," Branna realized, as her eyes stung with pure joy. "Its death from your willing sacrifice. You broke the curse, Fin."

She laid her hand over his, over the sign of three. "You saved yourself and, I think, Sorcha's spirit. You saved us all."

"Some of us did a bit as well," Connor reminded her. But grinned at Fin. "It's a fine mark. I'm thinking the rest of us should get tattoos for matching."

"I like it," Meara declared, and swiped at tears.

"We've more than tattoos to think of." Boyle held down a hand. "On your feet now." He gripped Fin's arms hard, then embraced him. "Welcome back."

"It's good to be here," he said as Iona just wrapped around him and wept a little. "But Christ, I'd like to be home. We need to finish altogether." He kissed the top of Iona's head. "We need to be done, and live."

"So we will." Eamon held out a hand, took Fin's in a strong grip. "When I get a son, he will carry your name, cousin."

They set the ashes on fire, more white flame, turned the earth, scattered them, salted all.

Then stood in the clearing, in peace.

"It's done. We're done with it." Sorcha's Brannaugh walked to her mother's grave. "And she's free. I'm sure of it."

"We honored her sacrifice, fulfilled our destiny. And I feel home calling." Eamon reached for Teagan's hand. "But I think we'll see you again, cousins."

Connor took the white stone out of his pocket, watched it glow. "I believe it."

"We're the three," Branna said, "as you are, and as they are." She gestured to Fin, Boyle, Meara. "We'll meet again. Bright blessings to you, cousins."

"And to you." Teagan looked over at their mother's grave as she started to fade. "She favored bluebells. Thank you."

"It's finished." Meara looked around the clearing. "I want to dance, and yet I'm shaky inside. What do we do now that it's finished?"

"Have a full fry. Dawn's breaking." Connor pointed east, and to a ribbon of soft pink light.

"We go home," Iona agreed, laughed when Boyle swung her around. "And we stay together for a while. Just together."

"We'll be along. I want a moment more. A moment more," Fin said to Branna.

"If you're much longer, I'll be making the eggs, and she'll be complaining." But Connor kissed Meara's hand, then mounted.

Iona cast one glance back, laid a hand to her heart, then swung it out toward Fin and Branna, forming a pretty little rainbow.

"She has the sweetest heart," Fin said quietly. "And now." He turned Branna toward him. "Here, where you first gave yourself to me. Here, where it all began, and where we've finally ended it, I have a question to ask."

"Haven't I answered them all?"

"Not this one. Will you, Branna, have the life with me we once dreamed? The life, the family, the all of it, we once imagined?"

"Oh, I will, Fin. I'll have all of it, and more. I'll have all the new dreams we make. And the new promises."

She stepped into his arms. "I love you. I

have always, I will always. I'll live with you in your fine house, and we'll have all the children we want, and none of them to bear a mark. I'll travel with you, have you show me some of the world."

"We'll make magick."

"Today and always."

She kissed him by Sorcha's cabin where the wall of vines had fallen away, where bluebells bloomed and a little rainbow lingered on the air.

Then they flew, with horse, hound, hawk, into tomorrow.

ABOUT THE AUTHOR

Nora Roberts is the #1 *New York Times* bestselling author of more than 200 novels under her own name. She is also the author of the bestselling futuristic suspense series written under the pen name J. D. Robb. There are more than 400 million copies of her books in print.

The employees of Thorndike Press hope you have enjoyed this Large Print book. All our Thorndike, Wheeler, and Kennebec Large Print titles are designed for easy reading, and all our books are made to last. Other Thorndike Press Large Print books are available at your library, through selected bookstores, or directly from us.

For information about titles, please call:
  (800) 223-1244

or visit our Web site at:
  http://gale.cengage.com/thorndike

To share your comments, please write:
Publisher
Thorndike Press
10 Water St., Suite 310
Waterville, ME 04901